MARTHA GRIMES

THE KNOWLEDGE

A RICHARD JURY MYSTERY

Grove Press UK

To my awesome grandson, Scott Holland
(who could pass this test with one hand on the wheel)

First published in the United States of America in 2018 by Grove/Atlantic Inc.

First published in Great Britain in 2018 by Grove Press UK, an imprint of Grove/Atlantic Inc.

1 3 5 7 9 8 6 4 2

A CIP record for this book is available from the British Library.

Trade Paperback ISBN 978 1 61185 502 9
E-book ISBN 978 1 61185 936 2

Printed and bound by MBM Print SCS Ltd, Glasgow

Grove Press, UK
Ormond House
26–27 Boswell Street
London
WC1N 3JZ

www.groveatlantic.com

BLACK CABS

1

H e was a dead man and he knew it.
As soon as he ceased to be of any use to this bastard, the guy would shoot him.

So Robbie Parsons had to keep on being of use.

He was glad he'd earned his green badge; he was grateful for all of those months of routing and rerouting himself around London that had qualified him to drive a black cab.

Robbie had maps in his mind. He would entertain himself, while cruising around looking for a fare, by setting destinations involving landmarks he would have to either pass or not pass in the course of getting to a certain location. Maps in his mind, so no matter where this black guy told him to go (and he'd told him nothing thus far), Robbie knew how to take the longest way round without raising suspicions. The guy behind him wasn't a Londoner, but then most Londoners knew sod all about London, anyway. He was a South African, or Nigerian, or Kenyan—from Africa, not from one of the islands.

Robbie knew this because he'd been driving every sort of person around for thirty-five years. Still, he wasn't clever enough to sift through all of the countries in Africa to pin down which one this guy came from. Ordinarily, bits of small talk in the back would float up—a passenger mentioning Cape Town or Nairobi or Victoria Falls, something like that—but his passenger tonight was not interested in small talk. The silence loomed. Robbie had never known silence so heavy.

But then he'd never known silence with a gun in it.

It had been less than an hour ago that he'd been driving down Ebury Street, poking around in Belgravia and turning into Beeston Place where sat the Goring Hotel. He'd seen the doorman looking for a taxi, and past the doorman, the couple he was apparently getting one for, while trying to shield them with a huge umbrella. Not easy in this rain.

They were a very handsome pair. Robbie pulled up in front of the Goring and the doorman yanked open the door and ushered in the woman, who was truly beautiful, hair as pale as moonlight, face like a pearl enhanced by her whitish-pink dress. The man was tall and dark and wore a dinner jacket beneath a black cashmere coat. He shoved himself into the cab, shaking the lapels of his coat to get the rain off, but careful not to get it on the woman.

Robbie slid the glass panel open, said over his shoulder, "Your destination, sir?"

"It's a club in the City. I was told it's on a hard-to-find street."

Isn't it all to the uninitiated?

"The name of the club, sir?"

"The Artemis. A casino?"

"Very exclusive club, sir, one of the best in London. You're lucky to be getting into it. The waiting list is a year long."

She said, "Why would anyone wait a whole year to get into a casino?" and then laughed.

"I see your point, madam."

The man said, "They have all kinds of rules. You have to arrive at an appointed time and you really have to dress for it. Rather strange just to do a spot of gambling."

Robbie melted into the traffic heading toward Knightsbridge. "I think the Artemis considers itself as more than a casino. I've heard about those rules. They don't want too many people there at any one time and don't want a lot of cars crowding the driveway."

"I hope there's no secret handshake involved," she said, "because we don't know it."

Robbie laughed as he lifted his hand to the panel, thinking it would've been easier for Eurydice to find her way back from the Underworld if she'd just flagged down a black cab instead of waiting around for Orpheus. Strange to think of this couple in those terms. Orpheus, right down into the Underworld to bring her back. Robbie just had the feeling this man would do it, for her.

The man tapped on the panel and Robbie opened it again.

"You can find this place with just the name?"

"I can, sir, yes."

"You don't have a GPS, though."

Robbie rolled his eyes. "No, sir. We don't need those."

"That's astonishing. Cab drivers in Manhattan—you've got to be able to tell them the nearest cross street to your destination. Once I asked the driver to take me to the Waldorf and he'd said, in that grumpy way New York drivers talk, 'Whatsa cross street?' Can you beat that?"

The woman said, "I've always been amazed at how you drivers know this city."

Robbie was amazed at her amazement. Her accent said she was a Brit, but his was American, definitely. What kind of service were Americans used to? New York. How could you drive around a city and know it so little? What fun was that, to be a stranger in your own hometown?

Now, having driven away from the Artemis Club, the black cab was in Old Broad Street in the City. The bloke in the back with a gun in his hand.

Robbie tried to be cool. It wasn't easy. "If you could tell me your destination—?"

"When I need to tell you, I will. Drive."

All right, then. He'd drive to some congested area in the West End—Charing Cross or Piccadilly—hoping that might give him an opportunity.

The quickest route would be to go around Bank and head down Walbrook to Upper Thames Street. Then to the Embankment. A route he had no intention of taking. This guy wouldn't know the difference. Wherever Robbie was going, he wasn't going in a hurry.

At this hour on a Friday night the closest most congested area would be Piccadilly—from Green Park past the Ritz to Piccadilly Circus and Shaftesbury Avenue with its theaters—so he decided to head in that direction. But first he snaked around and came out on the A40, which he drove along to Holborn Viaduct. In another few minutes he made a right into Snow Hill.

There he slowed down a bit as he looked around for police cars, but all he saw of police presence was a couple of uniforms coming out of the Snow Hill station. All of the police in the City should have been alerted by now. Carefully, he switched his bright lights on and off, on and off, and saw the coppers stop and turn and recede into the distance. The radio was out of commission, of course. The man had seen to that.

"That was a police station back there."

"Yes, sir, there's three thousand of them in London. Hard not to come on one."

The guy moved to one of the jump seats just behind Robbie, stuck the gun through the open panel again and said, "Try."

Robbie said nothing. He heard the weight shift back to the passenger seat.

"Where are you headed?" the man asked.

"West End."

"Why?"

"As you haven't given me an address, I'm just driving. As you said."

The man merely grunted.

Jesus, thought Robbie.

Twenty minutes before, Robbie had pulled into the half-moon driveway of the Artemis Club and up to the front door, quite free of other vehicles. You'd have thought the Artemis never had customers, from the lack of cars. That was undoubtedly because patrons were told when they could come and also because attendants took the cars and drove them to whatever car park the club paid for.

Robbie had braked and was sliding open the glass panel when he was surprised to see an overweight woman in orange coming up the drive, her car possibly having been commandeered by one of the attendants. She was huffing up to the front door.

"Is this it?" said the beautiful wife.

"Yes, it is. You'd never know, would you?"

"Very sedate," she said, as her husband got out and went round to open the door for her. He paid Robbie with a little "keep the change" wave, and it was some change—it was a huge tip. The two of them, looking rich and handsome, stood for a moment as the lady in orange was about to go in the door.

"Oh, I'm freez—" the wife started to say.

But it was the moment that froze. Robbie heard an unfamiliar crack and the husband stumbled before he fell straight down, right on his face. A few seconds later, another crack, and the woman fell beside him. At first perfectly still, she then slowly stretched her arm toward her fallen husband. And then, dead still. Those beautiful people; that beautiful woman: her pale skin and Grace Kelly hair, all blending in with the diaphanous dress—Robbie thought, when he'd seen her in the Goring's driveway, she was so white and lightweight, so insubstantial that she could have been blown away by the wind and the rain, transparent and spectral.

A ghost, that's what she'd looked like.

Now fallen, a ghost was what she was.

Robbie was completely befuddled; he shoved open his door, started to get out, when a large shadow fell across his path and he was pushed back behind the wheel, as, simultaneously, the intruder's other hand put the radio out of commission by bringing the gun down on it like a hammer.

The man yanked open the passenger door and piled in.

"Drive," said a deep voice.

That, mate, thought Robbie, as if the words were a broadax breaking through a frozen lake of fear, *could be your first mistake.*

From Snow Hill he drove to the Embankment, followed that into West End, took Grosvenor Road, turned into Chelsea Bridge Road and up to Sloane Square. On this side of the square there was a taxi rank.

When he saw a police car pulled up at the corner of the King's Road he considered speeding up or even broadsiding it or running up on the curb. But then not only would he likely be dead, so would the driver of the other car.

Sloane Street was wide and handsome and undisturbed, not a glutted part of London. From where the police car was stopped, he skirted the square to the side that held the rank.

"This Mayfair?"

"Sloane Square. Chelsea, one side; Belgravia, the other. That's the King's Road up there."

His passenger said nothing.

There were half a dozen taxis lined up at the rank, which surprised him as it was a wet Friday night, one of those times when people fought over cabs.

He drove past the line as slowly as he could without giving rise to suspicion. As he passed the taxis, Robbie switched on the FOR HIRE part of his sign, then switched it off again. He did this twice more as he looked out of the passenger's window to see if he knew any of the drivers. He recognized Brendan Small, if not an actual friend, a good acquaintance; he also thought he knew another driver—James somebody, couldn't think of his last name. But he didn't think they'd spotted him. He knew he couldn't go round the square again, so he had to depend on this single try.

He glanced in his side-view mirror and saw that Brendan was out of his cab, standing by the driver's door and apparently staring in the direction of the King's Road, which Robbie had just entered. Past Peter Jones, past a bus stop where several people, clearly tired of waiting for the number 22 or number 19, were trying to flag down a cab.

He killed the FOR HIRE sign, but that didn't seem to deter them. One or two watched the back of his retreating cab with a "How dare you?" look. Taking umbrage, Londoners were so good at that.

Something caught Robbie's attention in the mirror. There was a light winking two cars behind him. It was a black cab and the FOR HIRE sign was going on and off. *Brendan! You old bugger, you, you're answering my signal.* Then he saw that behind Brendan another cab was turning his sign on and off. And behind that, there was yet *another* cab. No wonder the people at the bus stop were going crazy: it wasn't just Robbie, but also three other cabs with their signs lit up refusing to stop when people tried flagging them down.

How long would they follow? All he could do was consider his next move—getting from the King's Road to South Ken, then Mayfair around the Green Park Tube station and the Ritz. When the fellow behind him suddenly said, "All right, all right!"—as if Robbie had been arguing with him all along—Robbie jumped.

"We've been long enough driving that nobody could be following—"

Not unless you consider three black cabs nobody.

"Greenwich."

Greenwich, bloody hell. With its long lonely stretches of cavernous parkland, its scattering of terraced houses and empty playgrounds. "An address, sir?"

"You'll get that when we get to Greenwich."

Bugger all.

He wondered if London cabbies were as good as he thought they were, which was the best in Europe. Best in the world, even. Forget America; we're clearly beyond that. Ask the passenger for a cross street? Don't make me larf.

Robbie thought about all of the thousands of miles he and the other knowledge boys had to drive around London on their mopeds learning not just every street within a six-mile radius, but all of the theaters, like the ones on Shaftesbury Avenue, and *in proper order*, no, let's not forget that; every bloody point of interest, every memorial, every monument—all of it etched on the mind. He could have crosshatched a sheet of paper with streets, monuments, restaurants and sports venues without referring to an outside source.

Many years before, he had done this test for sixteen months before he'd sat in a cab with an examiner. He'd had a bad moment when the examiner had directed him to go from Marylebone to St. Pancras without taking Euston Road or even going round Euston Station. The area they were in was a web of one-way streets and public works. There literally wasn't any way through all of this without using Euston Road.

"Can't be done," Robbie had said.

"Really? So what do you do, lad, if you've a fare that has to catch the two o'clock Eurostar?"

"I wouldn't be in this part of Marylebone in the first place."

The examiner liked that; it was by way of being a right answer. Then he had posed a series of, if not actually trick questions, questions that took a lot of thinking outside the box.

He thought of all of this driving along the King's Road. He turned into the Fulham Road toward the Old Brompton Road. What he was doing was going back, running a course parallel to the way they had come. His passenger must have been paying some sort of attention, for he said, as they passed the South Ken Tube station, "Thought South Kensington was where we came from."

"Right. It's a very large area. This is the section that borders Mayfair."

"Mayfair? I just told you to take me to Greenwich, didn't I?"

Robbie said smoothly, "Yes, but to get there, we have to go through part of Mayfair. And you need to give me an address. Greenwich is an even bigger area. I have to cross the river and need to know which bridge to take."

"Take the nearest one."

The first cab, which was probably Brendan, was right on his tail, and the driver had switched off the FOR HIRE sign. The others, if they were back there, had too, but Robbie couldn't tell which were in his entourage and which were regular cabs with passengers.

As he approached the crowded pavements of Green Park Tube station and the Ritz Hotel, Robbie turned on the FOR HIRE sign, looked in his side-view mirror to see the cab behind do the same, and beyond that two other cabs between cars in busy Piccadilly were also alight.

At least a dozen hands shot up in the air, couples from the Ritz, black ties and velvet, and before their astonished eyes, Robbie, then Brendan plowed on by. As did the two other FOR HIRE cabs. This was unthinkable: a whole crowd of people were now yelling; some were running. A small mob of Londoners, incensed that here were cabbies violating a cardinal rule.

Robbie's passenger—kidnapper, more to the point—twisted round and stared out of the back window at the fracas, which was now becoming a police fracas. There were uniforms around the Ritz and at least one police car had joined in.

"What the hell's going on?"

"Don't know." Robbie was delighted with the now stalled traffic.

"For God's sake, get moving!"

"We're stuck in traffic, aren't we?" A couple of well-dressed middle-aged men had caught up with their cab and were banging on a window. Unfortunately, space opened and he had to drive forward. All the way down Piccadilly to the Circus, cars moved out of the way, right and left, as if every driver in front of him felt cold steel plugged against his neck.

Any other time, he thought glumly, nobody would have given an inch. You'd think he had the bloody Queen in his cab. He rounded Piccadilly Circus as far as Shaftesbury Avenue, where a hundred theatergoers should be wanting cabs if he weren't too late.

"So how far's Greenwich?"

A week away, he wanted to say. "Half hour, depending on traffic."

Covent Garden, to Aldwych and the Strand. From here he could see Waterloo Bridge, but then so could the SOB behind him. Robbie guessed he'd better take it. There were plenty of places to get lost in in Southwark and Greenwich or wherever Wyatt Earp back there wanted to go.

Robbie was really mad at himself for missing his chance with the Met at the Ritz. If only he'd wedged his cab in a little between curb and cars, or if only . . . if only, if only. Moreover, he'd now lost his pals, who had probably got jammed up with the cops.

"This is Waterloo Bridge," he said. Might as well point out the landmarks.

"Let's get the hell across it."

Southwark at the other end was heavily populated. They'd be passing Waterloo Station, the Old Vic. Robbie idled at a light directly behind a new dove-gray Mercedes. What about a little accident? Just a rearender, maybe? That would bring the cops. It would also bring a furious owner, barreling out of the driver's seat, back to the cab. And the gun. No, Robbie couldn't involve anyone else.

The light changed. The pristine Merc moved on. Robbie moved too.

The traffic fanned out near Waterloo Station and Robbie was about to take a left when the voice from the rear seat said, "Here."

Sharply, Robbie turned. "What?"

"Here. Drive into Waterloo."

"Waterloo Station? But you said Greenwich."

"No. Here."

Robbie shook his head and pulled into the station.

Was this it, then? Robbie swallowed hard. The chips he'd eaten two hours ago threatened to make a return visit. They were hard in his stomach, like fear.

He was stopped in the line of cabs under the station's long arch.

A hand thrust money through the open panel. It was not holding the gun. Two fifty-quid notes fluttered onto the seat. "Keep the change. You're a helluva good driver." The rear door opened and his passenger was gone.

Robbie sat frozen as the guy moved through the glass doors, faded fast into the crowd. For such a big man he was agile.

Not death, but a compliment.

Robbie was so dazed by the fact of being alive, he forgot for a moment that he'd just dropped off a killer. *Do something, arsehole, don't just sit here!* he ordered himself. Ignoring the protests of the taxi rank chief, Robbie left his cab and ran inside, searching for the police. Had all the bloody cops in Waterloo taken a hike? He ran back outside and along the line of cabs, looking for drivers he knew. He found Brendan Small.

"He's gone into the station. We've got to do something."

"What the hell's going on, Rob?"

"Who else was following?"

"Don't know. They just took it up."

"My radio's out," said Robbie. "We've got to find him. He's over six feet, black guy. Gray overcoat, red scarf. He killed two people in front of the Artemis Club."

"What?" Brendan's eyes grew wide. "He kills two people, then takes a train?"

2

Detective Chief Inspector Dennis Jenkins looked down at the bodies of the victims as a small crowd of people stood back, two City Police uniforms in front of them in case the little crowd decided to surge forward. But they seemed content to remain on the low stone step in front of the door of the Artemis Club.

The man, the shooter, "just came out of nowhere." This was the observation of the middle-aged woman he was questioning, a woman wearing too vivid an orange for her age and girth.

Jenkins asked, "Could you think back to that moment? There's not much of a 'nowhere' to come out of here." He nodded to the left and right. The Georgian property that housed the Artemis Club was flanked on the right by a redbrick building with a brass plaque that read "Peterman Insurance"; on the left was an undistinguished gray stone structure, unsigned, unidentified. "No cross street, no alleyways, only a few trees and low bushes." On the other sides of the three buildings here on this little rise of ground were rows of terraced houses that could have been private dwellings, but were also businesses, small ones. Jenkins had dispatched two of his men, right and left, to knock on doors.

The woman in orange was impatient at having her story called into question. "All I know is I had just stepped out of my car down there—"

She pointed toward the street. "I was walking up the drive and was about to go into the club when this man just *appeared*."

"What about the victims? Where were they?"

The word "victims" gave her a chill; she was not looking their way. "Well, they had got out of their cab—"

"You didn't have an attendant park your car?"

"No. It's a brand-new Lamborghini and you know how these people who park cars love to ride around in them."

Jenkins didn't know. "Did this man appear at the same time the couple got out?"

She put her beringed hand to her forehead, thinking it over. "I was here," she said, pointing down. "The cab was there, the man with the gun there, walking toward them."

"So you didn't see him before that?"

"No, he was just *there*. As I said before."

"Yes, you did. Sorry to make you say it again. We appreciate your cooperation. Now, if you could just describe him."

She shook her head. "I didn't get a good look at his face. He was tall. He was a black man, I think. Well, you must see how traumatic it all was. A person doesn't take in everything—"

"Boss."

This came from his detective sergeant, Nora Greene.

Jenkins looked up from his notebook. "What?"

"Do I get to question him?" She was looking toward the knot of spectators on the wide step.

Jenkins followed her line of direction. "Who?"

"That's Leonard Zane," she whispered excitedly.

Leonard Zane was neither film star nor sports icon. He was the owner of the Artemis Club and a well-known art dealer. The combination of art gallery and exclusive casino had fascinated the press.

"He wasn't outside when it happened, Nora," said Jenkins.

"That's all you can say?"

"No, I can also say 'no.'"

"Come on, boss, let me—"

"Burns talked to him, Nora. You go and talk to the parking guy."

"Guv—" She was whining and standing first on one foot, then another, as if she had to pee.

"Nora." Jenkins's tone and eyes put a stop to her pleading.

Jenkins left it to the medic to shift the two bodies from the drive to the mortuary van. He made his way through the knot of bystanders to the front door. All had been briefly questioned by Jenkins's men. The couple had been shot when the gamblers and diners were all inside, in either the casino or the restaurant. No one had been standing before the high windows looking out on the drive.

The Artemis Club was one of London's hot spots; some would say, the hottest. The casino gave the gallery juice; the gallery lent the casino gravitas. It had been Leonard Zane's idea, this one-two punch.

Inside, Jenkins had run his eyes over the restaurant on the right and over what looked like a library on the left, walls studded with books, upholstered chairs and library lamps. There was a beautiful wide staircase with a velvet rope drawn across it. Jenkins was about to unhook the rope when he heard a voice behind him.

"The gallery is closed."

The man who spoke was the one that Nora had been so eager to interview: Leonard Zane.

"Mr. Zane? I'm Detective Chief Inspector Jenkins, City Police." Jenkins held up his ID.

"I'm not sure what art has to do with this shooting, Inspector."

Leonard Zane was in his forties. He was unmarried, rich, handsome. Jenkins knew this because Zane was so often in the paper. He hated having his photo taken, yet photographs kept appearing. He hated interviews, yet interviews were always turning up in newspapers or magazines such as *Time Out*. Zane put out his arm by way of invitation. "Could we sit down in my office and talk?"

"Of course," said Jenkins as he followed Zane into a very snug room off the library. It was small and elegant: a lot of zebrawood and mahogany, oriental carpeting, paintings and a safe built into one wall. They sat down, Zane in his desk chair, Jenkins in a club chair on the other side of the desk.

Jenkins said, "I'm not sure what art has to do with it either. Only it's part of the crime scene."

"The crime scene is outside, surely."

Instead of commenting on that, Jenkins said, "You didn't know this couple?" Jenkins looked at his notebook "David Moffit and his wife, Rebecca?"

"They'd never been to the casino. I'd have said so, if they had."

"Everyone who visits the establishment is vetted. That's my understanding. No cold callers come here."

"That's true, Inspector. Only I don't do the vetting. My assistant does that."

"He is—?"

"She. Maggie Benn. You'll want to talk to her, I expect."

"I will, yes. Tell me, what's the maximum number of customers you allow on any given night?"

"Fifty. That pretty much fills the room. Of course, people leave the casino floor for the restaurant. If the crowd in the casino thins out enough, we let others come in."

Jenkins was mystified by this. "You make it sound as if people are queuing at the door."

"There's no queue, though that might be fun—thanks for the idea."

Thanks for the idea?

"City Police are full of them, Mr. Zane. But as there isn't a queue, then how do these people know they're welcome?"

"They get a call. They're told that if they come right away they'll be admitted."

"And people go for that?"

Zane nodded. "I'm not sure why; I think it's quite amusing."

Dennis Jenkins thought it was quite outlandish. "Is there really that much cachet attached to your club?"

"Apparently." Zane made it sound as if he didn't figure in this transaction. "You're City Police, is that right, Inspector?"

Jenkins nodded. "Chief Inspector, actually." He thought he'd work a little of his own cachet into this.

"Oh. Sorry. I ask only because if these people were Americans, why isn't the American embassy getting involved?"

"Who said they were Americans, Mr. Zane?"

Leonard Zane lobbed that ball back handily. "The fact that I don't do the vetting doesn't mean I don't know who's coming. I get the list of each night's guests by around six P.M."

"So this list told you the Moffits were from the States?"

"It told me more than that. It told me David Moffit was known in gambling circles—I leave it to you to sort out what percentage of the population that might cover—known for winning with some sort of system."

The door was open and Jenkins heard steps approaching across the soft carpet.

"Leo!" A distraught, youngish woman appeared in the doorway. "My God, Leo—"

He stood. "It's all right, Maggie. This is Detective Chief Inspector Jenkins. Maggie Benn, Chief Inspector."

He stood, but she barely glanced at Jenkins; her attention was all for Leonard Zane. "Two people shot right in front of the club, in front of the *Artemis* Club!"

As if a shooting in front of any other club would have been acceptable, thought Jenkins. He found Maggie Benn to be an oddly dressed-down version of a casino manager. The place was glamorous; she was not. Jenkins had seen the chandeliers, the shadowed wall sconces, the crystal, the sweeping staircase. Maggie Benn hadn't a touch of glamour. Her hair was pulled straight back in a bun; she wore no makeup except for a faint wash of lipstick, no jewelry except for a blue gemstone ring.

Jenkins said to her, "So you knew the Moffits were coming."

"The Moffits? Of course I knew."

"They were Americans."

She shook her head. "He was; she wasn't. She was British. Dual citizenship."

"Did they live in London?"

"No. In the States. New York . . . at least he taught there."

"I don't get it," said Jenkins. "It's my understanding you have a waiting list a year long. How did he get in at such short notice?"

"Well, it wasn't that short. He wrote from the States. And because of who he is."

"And who's that?"

"He's a well-known professor of physics at Columbia University. He's also a gambler."

"You know a lot about him."

"Ten minutes on the Web."

Leonard Zane said, "Mr. Moffit had been asked to leave a casino in Atlantic City after something like seven or eight consecutive wins at the blackjack table. That's improbable. He must have been cheating." Zane shrugged. "If he wasn't, I'd love to know what his system was."

"Leo, the *Mail* has already called. They want an interview."

"You know I hate that, Maggie. How in hell did they hear about this, anyway?"

Jenkins studied Leonard Zane. There was some inherent contradiction in him: he ostensibly hated publicity—photos, interviews—yet he was always being photographed and interviewed. But he managed never to say anything of substance about himself.

Smoke and mirrors, thought Dennis Jenkins.

Waterloo Station, London
Nov. 1, Friday night

3

———

"Where are the kids?"

"I'm gettin' 'em," said Brendan Small, tapping a number in on his mobile. "Jimmy—we need you to eyeball a guy and follow him. Tall, black, gray overcoat, red scarf. Get the word out. We want to stop him but don't want you kids doin' anything foolish . . . Yeah, very funny. Just see if you can keep this bloke in your sight. Henry can see through brick. He's good . . . Oh, don't be so touchy, kid. We know you're all good or you wouldn't be workin' for us. Now get on with it."

Henry could indeed see through brick, so to speak. His eyes were lasers and they were currently trained on a little drama taking place near the Portsmouth departure barrier: a guy in suit and tie who looked like a businessman but was really a dip had his hand in a big sequined bag casually slung over the shoulder of a woman dressed in splendid clothes and gabbing nonstop on her mobile, all unaware of the hand removing something. What? Henry's eyes narrowed to slits—Wallet? Too thin. Passport? Likely. The thief then slicked off through the queue waiting for the Bournemouth train and the others just waiting. Henry would have done something about this theft, followed the guy and slipped a hand into his pocket and retrieved the passport or whatever it was. Henry being a dip himself, for there was nothing quite as satisfying to his trade as dipping a dip.

Only he got this call from Jimmy. "Okay. Sure. Right on it." He hung up and punched in a number for Martin.

"Henry," said Martin. "I'm right in the middle of something . . ."

"Drop it."

"I just did."

"I mean you're to watch out for somebody." Henry described the shooter. Martin stored the fake gold bracelet in his rear pocket, smiled at the sucker he'd been about to fleece, then knifed through the crowd to a place that served as a great vantage point for the station.

Almost immediately, before he could punch in Suki's number, he saw him: big guy, hard square face, gray topcoat and still with the red scarf round his neck. Why not? Maybe he was meeting someone and the poppy-colored scarf was the sign. Fuck's sake, did he have to choose a color that would tell the world?

He had Suki now. "Where are you?"

"Same place as always, at the caff."

Suki would stand near the door of this café, her big brown eyes and her puppy looking starved. Martin had never known anyone who could look more in need of a meal than Suki. How she managed to suck herself in, he didn't know, because she wasn't thin. It never took Suki more than five or ten minutes before the mark—usually a woman—had her at a table, ordering food. Sometimes, the woman would ask Suki to watch her belongings whilst she went to the loo. The pockets of Suki's little cargo pants would soon be stuffed with whatever was lying around—money, jewelry, lipstick.

Hearing Martin's voice, Suki immediately lost her lost look, secured Reno's thin rope leash and looked puzzled. "Why's he still got the red scarf?"

"He's meeting someone's my guess."

"But he must be catching a train. Why else Waterloo?"

"To get lost in. Move around in."

"Wait. I think I see him . . . Near WH Smith . . . over there. Hold on, he's talking to someone—Jesus, it's the Filth."

Martin said, "They got him?"

"He doesn't look got."

"This guy shot two people outside the Artemis Club."

"Artemis Club? Oh, cool." The Artemis Club was Suki's notion of heaven. She'd never been inside, of course, being nine years old, but dreamed of it. "So this idiot's wandering around Waterloo with a scarf like a flag . . . Unless . . ." she said to Martin, "the second guy isn't really a cop."

He wasn't really a cop.

Suki, with Reno on his lead, followed the big man (now divested of his red scarf) through an exit to Station Approach Road. "Shit, they're heading for a car. God, it's a Porsche."

"Get the reg and call Robbie."

"Now they're just standing there and talking."

Suki let Reno off his lead and motioned for him to go. Reno trotted off toward the two men.

"That your dog, kid?" asked the one dressed as station security.

"Yeah. Did he bother you?"

"No. But he should be on a lead."

The black man said nothing, only looked at her indifferently, as if he found the incident monumentally boring.

That annoyed Suki. She should garner more interest than that. "He's always getting off his lead. I'm sorry."

"Come on," said the big man. "Let's get going." He had the passenger door open and a foot in the car.

But the other man was now focused on the dog. Then he put his foot in on the driver's side. Suki heard him make a shuttered comment about Heathrow and the terminal and Emirates as he slammed his door.

"Heathrow, Terminal Three. Em—what's that airline?" Suki said into her mobile when she called Martin back. "Who do we have?"

Martin groaned. "Emirates, maybe. Terminal Three's a zoo. It's its own fucking city. We've got Aero and Patty."

"This guy is getting out of the country, so he comes to Waterloo to make the cops think he's just getting out of the city, or what?"

"He has to get by passport control," Martin said.

"Control to where? What country? How do they ID him? The guy shot somebody only—what?—a couple of hours ago? There wouldn't be any pictures yet."

Martin didn't like it when Suki started reasoning. "Call Aero and tell him there'll be two guys pulling into Terminal Three and that our guy is really big. And black."

"There are a lot of big black guys."

"This one'll be getting out of a Porsche. He'll know."

4

A ero could canvass the entire arrivals section outside Terminal 3 in ten seconds flat. When Suki told him the big guy would be getting out of a Porsche, Aero said spotting him would be a piece of cake.

Twenty minutes after the call, Aero saw him—hell, the guy must have been six feet three or four. Hard to lose yourself in a crowd when you're that big. And black.

Aero was spectacular on a skateboard. (Indeed he was good at anything that required balance.) But skateboards were not allowed at Heathrow, so he had outfitted himself with a pair of specially made skates that were so low to the ground all anyone could see was a kid moving very quickly along the pavement.

The skates themselves drew up into the shoes' thick soles like the wheels-up of a plane. Aero could both fly and walk. The shoes were invented by his friend Jules, a man who made his living as a cobbler. He made custom shoes and had his shop on the ground floor of his little house in Notting Hill. Aero's aunt and uncle lived in Notting Hill, an area of London that Aero couldn't stand since that old film with Julia Roberts in it. Seeing Julia Roberts's tits, apparently, was supposed to be the event of a filmgoer's lifetime. Endless stretches of sand in *Lawrence of Arabia* were far more exciting than anything Julia Roberts had to offer.

He saw the guy. Damn! But that was some car! He took out his mobile and tapped in Patty's number.

"We want to know where he's traveling to," she said.

"He's flying Emirates as far as Suki could make out."

"He won't be queuing. He'll be heading for a gate." Patty flipped her phone closed and stuck it into the back pocket of her jeans.

Sometimes she was stopped by security, who wanted to know if she was okay, and who she was meeting, and other none-of-your-business questions.

"My mum's right over there," she'd say, pointing to any woman who happened to be looking in her general direction. Patty would wave, and sometimes the stranger would smile bemusedly and wave back for no reason. The guard usually would then leave her alone. If he continued to hog her air, Patty would go up to the woman and say something like, "You look just like my Aunt Mildred that's supposed to be here," and, as long as the guard was watching, continue with this vapid conversation. When he stopped, she'd say to the woman she'd just accosted, "Oh, there she is!" and skip off toward another stranger.

All this was really annoying; it pretty much ruined surveilling, having to interrupt to stage this scene. So if she was following somebody, she kept her mobile to her ear to make security think she was on it. Sometimes she'd run off into a group of strangers.

Once when a guard was being a particular prick she made her way to a young man with a bedroll sitting against a wall. The guard had actually had the nerve to approach him and ask, "Is this your little sister?"

Without blinking, he'd said, "Yeah. Y'r business? Why?"

No answer from the guard, who just walked away.

But tonight there was none of that problem; security seemed to be looking the other way. Maybe they were looking for him, the tall black guy in a gray coat. Aero had filled her in.

She had her passport (her "Smith" one; she had several more), but she needed a boarding pass and she needed it for Emirates, if that was the airline he was taking. She went toward the Emirates ticket counter and watched the line of passengers waiting to collect their documents. She took out a little notebook and a ballpoint pen and walked along checking the luggage identification, looking for a female "Smith." No one paid any attention to her, until a heavyset woman, who probably had to know everything, asked her what she was doing.

Patty said, "I have to write an essay for school about the kind of luggage people carry."

A couple heard that and thought it cute; a few others looked at her indulgently. That was when she saw the name on a bag belonging to a harassed-looking youngish woman: Alicia Smith. Alicia. That would do, although Patty would have preferred "Tricia."

After this woman collected her boarding pass and checked her luggage through and turned and walked off, Patty followed her. Alicia Smith had stuck her boarding pass into an outside pocket of her big carry-on bag (how stupid!), which she flung over her shoulder, where it pounded against her back along with her camera and binoculars. She was also pulling a bag on wheels.

That was far too much to jam around her seat and certainly too much to keep track of. As soon as Patty had the boarding pass in hand, she ran around Alicia Smith and sprinted to security. She got there way ahead of Alicia. She could hardly stand behind her, or she'd have to listen to a hysterical Alicia Smith bewailing the loss of her boarding pass. Then Patty wouldn't be able to use it.

Naturally, they would question her being by herself with a passport that read "Patricia," not "Alicia." To the baggage security guard who started in, she said breathlessly, as she jigged from one foot to the other, "My mum's just over there; we got separated." Pained look, jig, jig, jig. "Please tell me where there's a toilet, quick!" Jigjigjigjig—

The guard pointed the way.

Patty jigged off.

The man had not gotten far ahead of her. When he came to the next set of restrooms, he hurried into the men's, and Patty went into the ladies' for thirty seconds and then came out again to stand by the water fountain and wait.

When she saw him exit the restroom, she quickly turned to the fountain, drank and continued following. They were coming to the last stack of shops along this corridor. After the shops it would be gates, where it would be harder to run into him by accident. She hoped he'd stop—

He did.

There was a line in this newsagent's as it was the last place to buy reading matter, candy, refrigerated drinks before going to the lounge and waiting for the plane's departure. He wasn't in the line yet; he was looking over the newspapers. Patty went to the refrigerated unit and pulled out a bottle of water, then moved to the magazines, where she looked for something that might get his attention if he saw it. Nothing in magazines; she went to the books.

When he appeared to be moving toward the counter, she snatched up a book about cards and got there before him so that she was standing in front of him. When the woman ahead of her left with her chewing gum and lotion, Patty set her water and her book on the counter and got out her change purse.

"That'll be six pounds ten, love."

Six quid! Good grief, books were expensive. She handed over a five-pound note, a pound coin, and ten p in change. As she was picking up the water, she shoved the book onto the floor. Of course he picked it up and looked at the cover before handing it back to her and receiving her thanks.

"*Poker: Small Stakes Strategies.* This is what you do in your spare time?"

"Me? No, it's a present for my dad. He likes to gamble."

And, of course, he spoke to her as she stood in the open doorway looking left and right, puzzled.

"Looking for your family?"

"What? Oh, no, I'm just wondering which way is Gate Twelve."

He smiled. "Same way I'm going. Come on."

As they walked, he said, "Your family is going to Dubai?"

"No, just me. My aunt's meeting me there."

"You're alone? That's a very long way for someone to go alone."

He meant, of course, for a child to go alone.

"Well, I travel a lot. It's my dad. His job takes him to a lot of different countries. My mum's dead. I stay with aunts and uncles a lot." That, she thought, sounded sloppy.

"You know, you're the same age as my great-niece. I wouldn't like her to be on her own in airports and on planes."

"Neither does Pop. But what can he do?"

They were in the foyer of Emirates now. He put out his hand. "People call me B.B. Bushiri Banerjee. Father was Bengali, my mother Kenyan. How do you do?"

"I'm Patty Smith. They got my boarding pass wrong and put down Alicia instead of Patricia." She showed him the pass she'd lifted from Ms. Smith. Winsomely, she added, "It'd be nice if we could sit together."

B.B. seemed to be thinking this over. "I might be able to fix that." He had his boarding pass out and took hers too.

Patty watched him as he went up to the flight attendant, spoke to her. She nodded and turned to her computer. She turned back and said something and he took out his credit card and handed it to her. After this transaction, he returned to Patty and handed her a new boarding pass.

Her eyes widened. "This is first class!"

"Well, that's how I'm going. We won't be sitting together because we'll each have our own room, but we can visit. It's very nice on this airline."

She thanked and thanked him and wondered if this guy was such a careless killer, such a hapless hit man, that he could be conned by a kid.

Or was she just a really, really clever kid? She gazed up at B.B. with a thankful look, preferring to believe the latter.

Her mobile twittered. "Hi."

It was Aero.

"It's my aunt. Would you excuse me a minute?" Patty went out into the aisle, out of B.B.'s range. "His name . . . let me think . . . Anyway, flight's to Dubai on Emirates. Where in hell are the cops? This plane is going to leave and the gate'll close in another five minutes."

B.B. was standing now and motioning to her.

"Trouble is, this guy you're following hasn't been identified by anybody but us."

"What about Robbie? Why isn't he here with the police?"

"Don't know."

"So the Filth hasn't got it together."

Aero chuckled. "Why d'ya think they're called the Filth?"

"This is London's finest?"

"No, Robbie and them's London's finest."

"The plane's about to take off. Have I got to go to Dubai just to keep an eye on him? Where's Dubai?"

"My God, Patty, don't do that! Are you crazy?"

"Somebody's got to be. His name's B.B. Or that's what he's called. The plane's leaving! Bye."

Patty ran to the line and to where B.B. stood near the gate. "That was Aunt Monique. She was calling from Dubai; that's why I couldn't hear too well." How ridiculous.

The attendant behind the counter moved over to take the boarding passes when their flight was announced. She smiled at B.B. and looked benignly at Patty, and said, "Aren't you the lucky girl?"

Patty agreed that she certainly was.

What she wanted to say was it wasn't luck, lady.

Islington, London
Nov. 2, Saturday morning

5

———

Detective Superintendent Richard Jury was dealing with his own smoke and mirrors in the person of his upstairs neighbor, Carole-anne Palutski, not a policewoman, although at times she thought she was. She had come into his flat early on Saturday morning with a pint of milk and his *Times*.

She handed him the milk and sat down on the sofa to read the paper by opening it wide, ignoring the important news, looking for ads for whatever Christian Louboutins or Jimmy Choos might be walking her way. After a bit of this browsing, she looked up at him. "You were awfully late coming in on Thursday night. And you forgot our date to go down the Mucky Duck."

Jury had turned to take the milk into the kitchen and now turned back again. Why was she waiting until now to upbraid him? Now was Saturday morning. And this alleged "date" he had no memory of making. Which was often the case. But all he said as he continued into the kitchen to pour milk into tea was, "At the Yard." In case she'd forgotten where he worked.

"Doing what?"

He debated bringing up the Starrdust, as he didn't want to get into a discussion of her psychic powers and David Moffit's dark future. And he certainly didn't want to go into his dinner with the Moffits at the Goring. So he lied. "Working overtime." He walked the two mugs of tea back into the living room. She thanked him with a sighing insincerity when he handed hers over.

She said, "You're a superintendent. You shouldn't have to put in overtime." She was holding the paper the way no one holds a newspaper who's really reading it. Front page—citing the usual outrages—and back page visible, paper fanned out in two parts.

David's worried look came back to Jury and he said, "Someone came in who needed to talk to a detective."

"He could have seen any detective."

"I happened to be there."

"Probably, he saw you go in and followed you."

Jury frowned. "What are you talking about?"

"People know you after all the publicity." She turned a page of the paper.

"Carole-anne, that was over a year ago."

"You think people can't remember back that far? And excuse me, but don't you have reception at New Scotland Yard?"

"We do have a front desk that's manned by a couple of uniforms. We don't call it 'Reception.' We're not the Connaught."

"And they just send anyone upstairs who walks in and says they need a cop?"

"No, they do not. They get a detective to come *down* from 'upstairs.'"

"And that happened to be you. Ha." The "ha" sent this piece of information into the deductive hinterland where it belonged. "There's a new gym opened in Islington. Called the KO."

"That's in the *Times*?"

"No, it's in Essex Road." She lowered the paper and looked him up and down as he stood in the kitchen doorway with his mug refilled. "You never took my advice and joined a gym."

"That is correct." He drank his tea.

"You need exercise. You'll lose what looks are left." She went back to her paper, turned another page.

"I'm glad there's any left at all."

As she resettled herself, the front page of the paper fell away and Jury could see the inside page and nearly dropped his mug of tea. His mind shouted, *No!* His mouth went so dry he couldn't seem to move his tongue to shout it aloud. In two steps he was at the couch and grabbing at that page.

Carole-anne looked up in alarm. "What's wrong?"

Jury stared at the photo of David Moffit. Then on the other side of the printed column at his beautiful wife, Rebecca. The headline read: *Couple Shot Outside Trendy London Club.*

Jury dropped the page and fell into his easy chair. He put his head in his hands.

Carole-anne had quickly retrieved the page of the newspaper and said, "Oh, my God. He was in the Starrdust on Thursday. Did you know him?"

Jury didn't answer.

Carole-anne read the brief account aloud:

"The prestigious Artemis Club in the City of London was the scene of a double murder when Americans Rebecca and David Moffit were shot down in the courtyard as they exited a cab.

The gunman 'came out of nowhere,' to quote one of the customers, 'got into the same cab and drove off.' City of London Police, led by Detective Chief Inspector Dennis Jenkins, came to the scene when they got the emergency call. Dr. Moffit was a physics professor at Columbia University in New York, where the couple lived."

She looked over at Jury. "Super—?"

"I met him at the Starrdust."

Her frown turned to surprise. "That handsome guy! I told him his fortune!" She had the grace not to add, "*I warned him.*"

The only bit of good news in all of this was that it was Dennis Jenkins who'd got the case. Jenkins was a good friend. Jury got up and moved to the telephone.

"I've got to make a call." He dialed the Snow Hill station and asked for DCI Jenkins.

When Carole-anne saw how he looked, she walked over and put her hand on his arm, and made to leave. Jury's phone calls she ordinarily took as part of her domain, but not this time. "I'm sorry, Super. If you need anything, you know where I am."

As he waited for Jenkins to come on the line, Jury sat staring at a rubbed spot on his carpet, hardly aware that a tear had run down his face until he saw the drop fall on the worn place. He was thinking of two days before, remembering the Starrdust and David Moffit.

SPOOKY ACTION

Covent Garden, London
Oct. 31, Thursday afternoon

6

"Would you look at that, sir?" said Detective Sergeant Alfred
Wiggins.

As if Jury were blind to this shopwindow with its assortment of miniature ghosts, ghouls and graves, more than one of which had been disturbed by a skeleton or moldering body pushing its way out of the ground.
The ghosts and ghouls were equally active, some on the ground, some in
the trees, a few flying about a church spire. The lighting was key, profes-
sionally done by means of tiny LEDs that moved within the scene, spot-
lighting whichever figure was performing from one moment to another.

Wiggins went on, brave companion and guide in the country of the
blind, reporting back to his boss, Detective Superintendent Richard
Jury, New Scotland Yard CID, on the action in the window: "See there,
that zombie on the left, he's about to pour—there it goes!—that tiny
bucket of blood all over the top-hatted man strolling along the path. Got
him! Covered in it, he is."

Jury was about to punch him, when Wiggins quickly pointed out
the Frankensteinian figure coming out from behind a tree. As Wiggins
stood giggling, Jury said, "Good. Now if you'd just hand me my cane,
Wiggins, I could tap my way into the shop."

These two were not the whole of the audience for this little Hallows
Eve extravaganza, for they were surrounded by kids of varying ages. The

shop was the Starrdust, one of the most popular venues in Covent Garden. Jury was very fond of its owner, Andrew Starr.

"Cane, sir?" Wiggins then lost interest immediately, turning again to the action in the window. "I just don't see how they do it."

"They" were the shop assistants, Meg and Joy, who, with the help of Andrew Starr's electrical engineer, had been "dressing" the windows of the Starrdust for years, paying particular attention to the night sky, the constellations, the planets. Andrew Starr made as sure as Copernicus would have done that they got that part right. Andrew was a much admired and respected astrologer. He made up horoscopes for some very important Londoners who had been consulting him for years; Andrew was also canny enough to see the drawing power of Meg and Joy, who didn't take it seriously at all. Hence the unfolding drama of miniature goblins and buckets of blood. Andrew knew the value of entertainment.

The shop was a mecca for adults and children alike who'd had a bellyful of the "real world" and were only too happy to walk through the door of an unreal one where the source of music was an old phonograph that played only songs that referenced the heavens. Hoagy Carmichael's twangy rendition of "Stardust" was pretty much the theme. Dinah Shore's velvety version of "Stars Fell on Alabama," or Nat King Cole smoothing out "Moon River." The interior was only a few amps brighter than the shop windows, albeit lit well enough to see the goods for sale: books, periodicals, vintage editions of volumes on astronomy, Freemasonry, alchemy; collections of children's books and stuffed Maurice Sendak "Wild Things"; music boxes and fancily dressed dolls. Although the room was small, Andrew had installed a number of library shelves, among which several customers were currently roaming and reading. One of these was a tall, very handsome man who had propped himself against the end of a thick shelf, holding a hideously thick old book and watching the proceedings closely.

And then there were the various internal structures, such as the yellow-framed hut called the "Horrorscope" whose so-called "horrors" were far more Maurice Sendak than Wes Craven. Wiggins spent a good deal of time in this little place, which always emitted shouts of laughter.

(He was in there now, having headed for it the moment they walked into the Starrdust.) Not the least of the attractions was the silver tent that housed Madame Zostra ("famous clairvoyant"), a.k.a. Carole-anne Palutski, Jury's upstairs neighbor in Islington. Businessmen spent a lot of lunch hours getting their fortunes told by Madame Zostra. She was not in her tent at the moment.

Andrew Starr was standing with arms folded looking up at the domed ceiling. This was Jury's favorite spot. In this shop given over to heavenly effects, the biggest of all was this section of ceiling that had been turned into a small planetarium. Its constellations, its stars and planets, revolved continuously, parts lighting up, other parts receding into darkness, new parts—right now, Jupiter—lighting. It was another miracle of engineering and invention. Right now Meg (or Joy—Jury couldn't tell them apart) was up on a tall ladder having shiny things handed to her by Joy (or Meg). He called them the Starrdust twins, they looked so alike. They wore shiny things in their hair and gold or silver suspenders on their designer jeans.

"Hello, Andrew," said Jury, moving to stand beside him. "You rearranging the planets?"

"Superintendent! Didn't see you come in."

The ceiling-sky's movement had momentarily stopped and Meg or Joy appeared to be making a planetary adjustment, moving one of the tiny objects a mite to the left.

"You know how many millions of miles you just moved Uranus, don't you?"

This voice had come not from Andrew but from the tall man at the bookcase behind them. In a good-natured tone, he added, "Better shove it closer to Saturn or we might all be out of jobs by morning."

Both Meg and Joy giggled. "But it's only just a bit," said Meg, as if they had been at the Creation and were here now only to help out whatever gods needed them.

"A bit from your vantage point could be a hundred thousand light-years up there on your ceiling. And Lord knows how far you've moved it from Saturn."

"Only Saturn is way over there," said Meg, pointing to some indefinable position.

"Remember nonlocality," said the man at the bookcase. "What we could be seeing is spooky action at a distance."

Andrew laughed. "I like that." He turned and gestured to the man at the bookshelf. "David, come on over here. I want you to meet someone." When the tall stranger walked over, Andrew said, "This is Richard Jury, Scotland Yard CID." Then to Jury, "David Moffit, from America. He teaches at Columbia University, and he teaches astronomy, if you can believe that coincidence." Andrew sounded pleased as Punch, as if he'd personally arranged the teaching post.

"Wow!" said David Moffit. "A Scotland Yard detective! The Met!"

Jury's hand was shaken in the firmest grip he'd ever encountered. He felt a jolt. He had no idea why, since the fellow didn't remind him of anyone he'd ever known, yet Jury felt he knew him. David Moffit simply had *presence*. It wasn't because the man was so good-looking, or so affable. He simply was a commanding presence one rarely came across, a stranger with whom one felt an immediate bond.

"If you're an astronomer, you've come to the right place, then," said Jury. "You're a friend of Andrew?"

"I am now," said David, with a smile that Carole-anne Palutski would crawl on hands and knees to witness. "I just discovered the place by accident, walking round Covent Garden."

"Had your fortune told by Madame Zostra yet?"

He didn't see Carole-anne, but she'd never have missed a chance to get this guy into her tent.

"Where is she, incidentally?" he asked Andrew.

"Out getting cakes and things for tea."

David said, "You mean the red-haired beauty? Told me I was in extreme danger—"

"That'd be the one. And told you to come back, or it could go worse for you?"

"Right. Does she have any psychic powers?"

"Well, she knows whenever I've lined up a date for the evening."

David laughed. Andrew had moved off to help a customer at the counter. "But I wonder," David went on, "how she knew I liked to gamble."

"Because you said something. She was using cards, wasn't she? The tarot sometimes; sometimes just an ordinary deck. So you said something she picked up on. Simple."

As they walked out from under the planetarium, Meg and Joy called out good-bye and David turned to wave and smile. Then he said, more seriously, "Superintendent, I wonder if you'd have the time to go somewhere and maybe have a drink? There's something I want to talk to you about."

"If I have time to hang around the Starrdust, I expect I have the time for a drink. Something wrong?"

"Yes." David Moffit didn't embellish. He just stopped talking and looked worried.

"Let's get at least to the fringe of Covent Garden. It's a bit too fey these days. The White Lion's not far. Let me go and alert my sergeant that I'm going with you." Jury made for the Horrorscope to tell Wiggins.

The White Lion was situated on a corner, its facade black and gold, its interior dark wood and old framed mirrors. David picked out a table by a window as Jury went to the bar to get a couple of pints of Guinness.

He returned, set them down and said, "What's wrong, David?"

"I think I'm being followed. No, maybe 'watched' more accurately describes it."

Jury frowned. "Go on."

"Rebecca—my wife—and I got to London less than a week ago. For the last twenty-four hours, I've felt I'm being . . . I don't know, but when I leave the hotel, I feel something like a physical presence behind me. I turn and see no one, nothing suspicious. Today I escaped into the Starrdust. A kind of sanctuary." He shrugged and looked embarrassed. "I feel something terrible is going to happen."

"Any reason you should feel in danger? I take it you don't know anyone in London you'd regard as wanting to harm you?"

"No." David turned his pint, hardly drunk, by the handle. "Only—"

"What?"

David grew thoughtful. Then he said, as if in sudden inspiration. "Look, could we talk sometime on Saturday? I'll know more then."

Jury was completely puzzled. "What do you mean, 'more'?"

"I feel really dumb talking about this when all I can do is guess at it. We're leaving on Sunday to go back to the States."

Jury thought for a moment. "Why did you come to London, David?"

"So Rebecca could visit her mother. Rebecca's British—well, now she's both. We have a flat in Chelsea, but we're staying at a hotel so Claire, her mom, can use the flat. She likes to come to London. She lives in . . . High Wycombe, is that the name?"

"Yes. That's not far from London. It's pretty generous of you to give up your own flat to your mother-in-law."

David didn't seem to hear that. "We were going to stay another week, but I feel this danger's real. So I changed the return to Sunday. Rebecca's fine with that."

"Where do you live in the U.S.?"

"New York. My family home is in Connecticut. My mom's there. Dad's dead, worse luck."

He looked extremely unhappy when he said this.

"You're how old?"

"Thirty-eight."

Jury was surprised. He looked twenty-eight.

David noted the expression and smiled. "My mom says I haven't aged since I was twenty."

Jury was surprised to find his own guess seconded by this unknown ally, David's mother.

"Looking so young presents problems. I had to do a hell of a lot of talking to get the post at Columbia. I think looking young is the only reason my students listen to me."

Jury was sure that wasn't true. "You really teach astronomy?"

"Not exactly, although Andrew Starr likes that part of it. I'm an astrophysicist."

"How does 'astro' differ from the rest of it?"

"It's a branch of astronomy. The physics of the universe. The nature of heavenly bodies—stars, planets. The light they emit."

"Not string theory? Not the Uncertainty Principle? Not Heisenberg's equation?"

It was David Moffit's turn to look surprised. "Good Lord, Superintendent, I don't hear that question very often from strangers. You're into physics?"

"Actually, that's a good way of putting it. I have an acquaintance—" he wasn't going to call Harry Johnson a 'friend'—"who's a physicist. It's just very—intriguing, I guess. But if you're teaching this at Columbia, you must have a PhD, so it's not 'mister,' right? You're Doctor Moffit."

David shrugged. "A PhD, yes." He paused. "You know, I've always been enthralled by the stars. Seriously, I spend a lot of time looking at the night sky. When I was a kid, my dad built me a tree house with a glass roof way at the top of a huge maple behind our house. I could see the sky through the roof. A lot of nights, I'd sleep there." He looked upward as if the glass roof might be there. "It's still there, the tree house."

"And do you still sleep there?" Jury smiled.

David nodded. "I do. There are some things you never get over." He looked at Jury. "Childhood is one of them."

Jury felt his throat tighten and took a drink of beer. "You've got that right."

"From your expression, I'd guess you didn't have a tree house."

"You've got that right too." Jury told him about his own mother and father. "I was only a baby. I think it was the last bomb ever to hit London that got my mother. I grew up for some years in an orphanage."

"Christ, but I'm sorry. I honestly don't know what I'd do if anything happened to my mom. I really love her."

It was such a clear, plain declaration that Jury couldn't respond. How often did one hear a child say something like that? He thought he had never seen any face so musing, any expression so wistful. He watched David rub at his eyes. Tiredness or tears, Jury couldn't tell. He felt he should bring him back to the present and asked what courses he taught at Columbia.

"Well, the graduate course is called 'Night Sky.'"

"Simple name. Mightn't your students infer from that simplicity that the night sky itself is simple? From the Milky Way to Andromeda to—where else is there?"

David laughed. "Many elsewheres. Many. Trillions of galaxies. Think of the distances between them, think of all that space—two and a half million light-years between our own Milky Way and the nearest galaxy, Andromeda. That's what the students don't understand. That all that distance, all that space, is really terrifying, even nightmarish."

"Not beautiful, then?"

"Oh, of course it's beautiful, but it's also terrifying."

Jury said, "So should I know what the bloody hell 'spooky action'— what was the rest of it?"

"Spooky action at a distance. Scientists have been debating this for decades. It's a way of talking about nonlocality. Einstein didn't believe in nonlocality. He had a huge argument going with Niels Bohr about it."

"That clears things up. I've no idea what you're talking about except it must have to do with quantum mechanics."

"If you know that you know more than anyone else in this pub, I'd venture to say. Nonlocality is a theory that says two particles—" Here David placed the mustard pot next to the plastic bottle of ketchup. "—these two particles can know about each other no matter how far apart, no matter if they're separated by billions of light-years. This is in direct contradiction to Einstein's idea of locality, which insists that an object is influenced only by its immediate surroundings. He said it was impossible that one could influence the other no matter how far apart mustard and ketchup were. Nonlocality means the two are 'entangled'; thus, they act in concert." Here David shoved the two containers to opposite ends of the table. "That these two things would act together no matter how far apart was what Einstein called 'spooky action at a distance.'

"Listen—" He looked at his watch. "Have dinner with us—Rebecca and me." He started to get up.

Jury rose too. "You mean you walk in with a perfect stranger and it doesn't bother her?"

David was getting into his coat. "No, we're like that. We think pretty much alike." He reached down and shoved the mustard and ketchup together. "Entangled."

Jury moved the pot and bottle apart again. "Then it makes no difference, right? Isn't that entanglement?"

David laughed. "I wish you'd come and teach my course sometime."

Everyone seemed to have left Covent Garden, as if the terror of which David had spoken hung above it, and all beauty fled.

"I'm looking at Uranus. Hard to see it without binoculars and an astronomical chart. But this'll do." He reached inside his coat and swung out an instrument anchored to a leather strap over his shoulder.

Jury said, "We've got people over here who do that with Uzis."

"We've got people over there, and more of them. It's a telescope." He unclipped the brass and leather object and rolled it out. "Now, hold this to your eye and try and aim it toward Uranus. You'll see a greenish-bluish planet, or should."

Jury did so. "Wow!" His visit to the Starrdust planetarium showed him far more of the solar system than he was seeing now, but the sky through an instrument he was himself controlling seemed far more wondrous. "I see the greenish glow. What causes that?"

"Methane cloud. The ice giant, they called it. Uranus has many moons and moonlets. The Romantics had no idea, did they? 'Bright star, would I were steadfast as thou art.' Keats didn't know that behind his bright star hung hundreds just as bright, and behind them hundreds more still.

"All of that remoteness. It's a vastness I can't cope with. The rings of Saturn are over a hundred and fifty thousand miles in diameter, and yet no thicker than the Houses of Parliament. The void, the waste, the black blackness. After hours of looking I feel annihilated, obliterated, crushed. It's a kind of horror, all of that space. At the beginning of class every semester I tell my students, 'If you've come here for solace, go back. If you've come for consolation, you won't get it.'"

"Well, there I disagree."

"You think there is solace up there for those kids?"

"No. I think there might be down here for your students: you."

David looked surprised, but thanked him.

As they walked, David said, "Andromeda is around two and a half million light-years away. The bad news is it's hurtling toward the Milky Way. Which means toward us. It'll take four billion years for it to reach Earth."

"And that's a 'hurtle'?"

"In galactic terms. The good news is we'll have time for dinner with Rebecca. Come on, let's grab a cab somewhere."

They picked one up near Leicester Square, and David directed the driver to the Goring Hotel. They were driving by the Hippodrome.

"That casino. How late is it open?"

"Into the next century. I'm not sure it ever closes. You've been there?"

"No, but I want to go. I'm addicted to cards. Blackjack. You call it Twenty-one, I think."

"That can get expensive."

David shrugged. "I can afford it."

Jury laughed. "Fact you're staying at the Goring suggests that."

"I like to apply physics to cards. Heisenberg, Gödel."

"How does that work?"

David laughed. "Well, it doesn't, not seriously. I like to call it a system, though. I win most of the time. Got barred from Caesars in Atlantic City."

"What happened?"

"Won too often. That'll do it." He laughed again.

* * *

As they made it into Belgravia, it started to rain. Wind blew the small trees along the Mall. The taxi turned into Beeston Place and pulled up in front of the hotel. The cab idled in the driveway; the doorman opened the door.

"Rebecca! What's she doing standing out here?"

Jury looked past him to see an ethereal figure, backlit from the Goring's many chandeliers, standing with an umbrella, but little else to protect the wispy white dress that was blowing in the wind and rain. Her long straight hair shone in the half-light. She was so pale and blond she might have been transparent. She waved.

David thrust a fifty-pound note toward the driver and hastened to the door, yanking his coat off as he went. Jury was right behind him.

"My God, Beck, it's raining, and you without your coat—" He tossed his about her shoulders.

"I'm okay. Who's this?" Her smile was warm.

"Sorry, Richard, for dashing away like that. Superintendent Richard Jury, my wife, Rebecca."

The hand she put out to him was white and cold, but firm. "How do you do? Superintendent. That sounds like police. Are you?"

Her accent had been Americanized, but it was still strongly Brit. "All of them," said Jury. "The whole damned lot. Your husband wants you out of the cold. So let's go inside."

"He's bossy. Sounds like you are too." She laughed as the three of them went into the lobby.

"That's why we make a good pair," said David.

"No, a good three," said Rebecca. "You've got to have the bossee for it to work."

And as she laughed and all but flung David's coat back at him Jury felt the truth of it: they made a good three.

In the Goring's handsome gold-and-white dining room, Jury and David ate beef Wellington; Rebecca had the lobster omelet. They talked about Columbia; Connecticut; the tree house; Rebecca's mother, Claire

Howard. The Chelsea flat they had given over was in a little house in Clarence Mews.

Now they were talking about the proofs of dark matter.

"I thought dark matter was invisible," said Jury.

"It is. We know it's there. We know it makes up over ninety percent of the universe. We can't see it, but we know it's there because of gravitational pull; we know it through inference. The way you solve your cases."

Jury was about to drink, but instead put down his glass. "'Inference'? Not reason and rationality?"

"It's not a puzzle."

"But it is. I have to take bits and pieces from various places and sources and cement them together."

"There is no cement, Superintendent. That's an illusion. If the bits appear to be clinging, that's because they're attracted—like electrons and protons—but they could just as easily fly apart. No, you're finding answers by leaps of faith."

Jury laughed. "Tell that to Sherlock."

"Oh, he was the greatest demonstrator of the leap of faith. Wasn't that really the substance of his famous dictum: when you have eliminated the impossible, whatever remains, however improbable, must be the truth?"

"That sounds like logic. Rationality, reason. To an inevitable conclusion."

David shook his head. "I don't think it is. There's too much left out and too much left over. How many improbables might be lying around to answer as the truth? What's the 'impossible'? And unfortunately the line appears in one of the worst detective stories, 'The Sign of the Four.' Consider how Holmes figures out what Watson has been doing before appearing in Baker Street: He tells Watson that he must have gone to the post office to send a telegram. How does Sherlock work this out? On the sole of Watson's shoe is a little bit of orange earth or dirt and as they have been digging up the pavement around the post office, Watson must have stepped in it, he must have gone to the post office. Now, he knows Watson hadn't written a letter and that the drawer in his desk has an ample supply of postcards and stamps; hence, he didn't go to mail a letter. QED. Watson's mission must have been to send a telegram."

"Well," said Rebecca, her pointy chin resting on the little bridge of her clasped hands, "that's a perfectly fair piece of deduction."

David grimaced. "No, it isn't. What about the other pavements where this orange dirt might be found? If they're digging around in one place, might they not be in another? And there could have been many other reasons Watson went to the post office other than just to mail a letter. Maybe he got a notice that something had come for him. Perhaps to meet a friend. To buy stamps different from the ones he had. You could go on and on. That's what I mean by too much left out. Other probabilities. The 'deduction' simply narrows things down. What Holmes is masterly at is observation; nothing escapes him. What makes him a great detective is his imaginative grasp of a situation. Observation, imagination and intuition: from there you make a leap of faith. Didn't Sherlock really see the whole in the part? The entire dance in the position of the shoes?"

"And that's deduction," Jury insisted.

"No, no. It's *observation*. But what I'm saying is that what he saw was organic. He saw it all at once; not in bits and pieces."

"He inferred it from bits and pieces."

"No. Look at it from an artist's point of view. Did Michelangelo see the figure of David in the marble in bits and pieces? No, it was in there, an entity he was trying to carve his way around. And is that the way van Gogh worked? Bits and pieces? He painted his bedroom at Arles by first noticing his yellow bed and then adding sticks of furniture, paintings, bedclothes and so forth?"

"Those are poor examples. They were looking at something already there."

"Oh, you mean the way Monet was looking at his water lilies?"

Rebecca sighed. "Oh, do shut up, David, and get another bottle of wine."

Jury laughed. "Yes, get another bottle. And the dessert menu, while you're at it."

David signaled the waiter, who came without seeming to hurry, although it took him only five seconds to cross to their table. "Sir?"

"Another bottle—" He tapped the wine cooler. "Or perhaps something else with dessert. Whatever dessert might be."

"I can recommend the chocolate ganache or the coconut and honey gateau. And perhaps a muscat to accompany?" said the waiter.

David nodded and the waiter swanned off.

"Why are cakes over here called 'gateaux'?"

"Because it sounds better," said Jury.

"David, why don't you not talk about solving the CID's crimes and instead write a monograph on the art of murder?"

"I didn't say murder was an art. It isn't. I'm saying it's detection that's an art."

A couple of weeks before, Wiggins had dragged in a murder board and Jury had dragged it out again. Wiggins had objected: "Sir, it's a great help in getting the details all together so you can see everything at once." He had done the usual: tacked up small photos and newspaper pictures and articles; victims, "persons of interest," their habits, their histories.

"No, it's not a help; it just shows things in pieces," Jury had said to Wiggins. "But they're the same pieces I have filed in my mind, Wiggins. As do you."

"But it, like, pulls them all together."

"That's an illusion, Sergeant." And he suddenly realized he had said exactly the same thing to Wiggins that David had said to him just now. *"There is no cement, Superintendent."*

David broke into these thoughts. "Why are you smiling, Richard?"

"What you were saying about art and detection: I think you're right."

In mock horror, Rebecca threw up her hands. "Oh *please*, Superintendent, don't encourage him. He's already too . . ." She was looking for a word.

"Too what?" David said. "Arrogant?"

"You're not arrogant. You're just too—*certain.*"

He laughed. "Beck, that's the last thing I am. I was merely suggesting Richard try a perspective that's more, say, artistic. Draw some stuff."

"'Draw some stuff'? Is that what you actually said?"

"Sure. Art frees up the mind."

"What I have at my disposal in my office is a box of crayons."

"Nothing wrong with crayons. You could also get some colored pencils."

"Thanks for not suggesting I work in oils."

"Wouldn't hurt."

"I love the way you're still telling a Scotland Yard superintendent how to solve crimes," said Rebecca.

Jury, puzzled by the Saturday engagement David had mentioned in the White Lion, asked him what they were doing the next day, Friday.

"We're going to this club in the City tomorrow night—the Artemis Club. Do you know it?"

"Not being a whiz at the gambling tables, I've never been there. Read about it, though. Isn't it hard to get in? Weirdly difficult?"

Rebecca laughed. "That's why he wants to go so much. He wrote to them months ago from the States."

Jury said, "It's an art gallery, too, isn't it?"

David nodded. "A pretty good collection. I stopped in for a few minutes yesterday. Bought this." He pulled a small velvet box from his pocket, opened it. The blue stone was bezel-set in a scrollwork band of white gold.

"But that's beautiful, David."

Jury thought it interesting that she did not reach for the ring and try it on. She did not assume it was for her.

"It's for Mom," he said. "Even though she doesn't really fancy jewelry, I think she'll like this. It's tanzanite."

"She'll love it. What a beautiful blue."

They ate their gateau and drank their wine and talked more about the art of detection until they found they were the last guests and decided to leave.

The doorman outside was getting Jury a taxi when David said, "Look, just in case . . . I mean, if anything happens to me, could you give this to my mother?"

Jury cut across that. "Nothing's going to happen to you. I'm going to see you on Saturday."

"I know, but just in *case*—" He looked so young, so earnest. "Would you see my mom gets this?"

Jury frowned deeply, but took the little velvet box. "But—"

"Because if something happens, she'll come here, almost certainly, and—" David looked at the box, touched it. "This will make her feel better."

"David, that's so—" Frightening, he didn't add.

"Could you come here to the hotel around eight on Saturday evening?"

From danger back to safety. "You bet. Let me give you my number in case you need to reach me." On his card he wrote his home number, not his mobile, as it was always out of juice.

They said good night, David apologizing to the patient doorman, who looked as if he hadn't a duty in the world except to wait on David Moffit.

Maybe Jury wasn't the only one so affected.

7

———

Jury was so deep into these thoughts about his dinner with the Moffits two nights earlier that Jenkins had to say "Hello" three times before Jury answered.

"Dennis, sorry. It's Richard—"

"—Jury! How the hell are you?"

"I just read the paper."

"This Artemis Club baffler. Is that insane or what? From the information we've gathered so far, it appears the guy's a Kenyan. Lives in Nairobi. Police there contacted us only this morning. Name's . . . hold on a minute—" Dennis was roughing up some file. "Name's—pardon the pronunciation—Bushiri Banerjee. He must have flown from Dubai with a different passport as there was no Banerjee on the Emirates flight between Dubai and Nairobi."

"Why in hell would he fly to Dubai and *then* to Nairobi?"

"Because he didn't have any choice. There aren't any direct overnight flights. I don't think he'd have wanted to while away the night at a London hotel waiting for us to put out an all-points."

Jury sat like a stone by the phone table. "The victim. I met him. Them."

"What?"

"David Moffit. I met him in Covent Garden Thursday afternoon."

"You *knew* him?"

"Only that one day." Jury told him about the Starrdust, going on for drinks and dinner. "He was afraid he was being watched."

"Jesus! What can you tell me about him? He's an American, so I rang up the embassy. All I know is they were at the Goring. Must be loaded."

"His family is. Connecticut. Has the embassy contacted his mother? His father's dead, but his mother—" It pained Jury even to think about her. It pained him to think she would be finding out about her dead son from some embassy official. "Find out what they've done about his mother and let me know, will you?" Jury paused. "I can tell you the wife's mother is living in the Moffits' flat in Chelsea. Something like Clarence Mews. I'm going to call her if you don't mind. I want to talk to her, too."

"Fine."

"What about the driver? Did you get anything else from him?"

"I talked to him for over an hour. Robbie Parsons. That was one hell of a ride! I have to hand it to him: the guy's both brave and resourceful. He was astonished when the shooter finally asked to be dropped at Waterloo." Dennis paused. "He said there was something really strange about this guy—"

Jury gave a litttle snort. "Indeed. I'd say shooting two people and then climbing into their cab was decidedly strange."

"No, I don't mean that. When the shooter finally got out at Waterloo, he handed over a hundred quid, said to Parsons, 'Keep the change. You're a good driver.' Then he took off."

Jury frowned. "He *paid* the fare? Where is your information coming from?"

Dennis was silent.

"You can't tell me? Okay—"

Dennis told him. "Robbie Parsons and his friends got the information."

Jury frowned. "How?"

"A girl named Patty Haigh."

"This is like pulling teeth, Dennis. Who's Patty Haigh?"

"A kid. She's nine—no, ten, I think. There're maybe four or five kids, Waterloo and Heathrow." Dennis told him about the kids. "It's like a stash."

"A stash of kids. Kids as informants. I expect Social Services would like to hear that."

"These kids steer clear of Social." He paused. "You don't like the story so far. You certainly won't like the next installment."

"What is it?"

Dennis sighed. "She's with him."

"Who?"

"Who the hell've we been talking about, Richard? Patty Haigh."

"What do you mean, 'with him'?"

"I mean what that generally means."

"Christ! She's a hostage?"

Jenkins cleared his throat. "Not really. It's more like she decided to follow him—"

Jury was out of his chair. "A nine-year-old kid with a killer? Jesus, Dennis!"

"Ten. The kid's very resourceful. She already had a coach ticket. Someone else's, but it was in her possession. According to the Emirates attendant, Banerjee upgraded her to first."

"*Upgraded* her? So they *sat* together? Dennis, I can't believe—"

"In Emirates first class, nobody sits together. They each have a little room. Very private and posh."

"So what's the last communication from this kid?"

"From Heathrow before takeoff. She called another kid, told him the guy was named B.B. She boarded the Emirates flight with him. After that, it gets a bit fuzzy."

"Fuzzy? *Fuzzy?*" Jury laughed.

"According to the airline, there was a flight out of Dubai at eight forty-five A.M. And they were both on it. Don't ask me how that happened."

Jury didn't. "Banerjee got through Heathrow with apparent ease despite the police."

"We had no ID for him, then. First we heard was after he got out of the cab at Waterloo."

"What about Dubai police? Were they contacted?"

"Sure. But they only had, you know, a few hours to get anything together. Airport security in Dubai is good. But they couldn't find them. Her. The Dubai police force is very enlightened. Well, it can afford to be, given it's the UAE. You know what they drive? Lamborghinis, BMWs, Aston Martins and Bentleys. I mean those are the *police cars*."

"What about her?"

"They'll get her too."

"Dennis, she's ten!"

"Yeah, I know. We really should fetch her back before she gets in a fix."

"'*Before*—?'" Jury tried to proceed as if they were making sense.

"She managed to call this other kid at Heathrow before they left and give him this information and he then let one of the cabbies know, who then informed Robbie Parsons, et cetera. So that's settled."

"What's settled?"

"The shooter. We know who he is."

"But we don't know *why* he is, Dennis. Here's a Kenyan traveling all the way to London to shoot an American couple. Why did he do it? Is the guy a contract killer? Was this a hit? And we're all assuming the shooter was after David Moffit. But what about Rebecca Moffit?"

"Collateral damage?"

"Why would there have been any collateral damage? Why shoot her just because she's a witness? Robbie Parsons was a witness. Is anyone investigating Rebecca Moffit?" said Jury.

"Well, your lot, surely. They were US citizens. That wouldn't be left to City Police. Don't you guys communicate with one another?"

"Not if we can help it." Jury had his head in his free hand. "I'd like to talk to Parsons. I'd like to talk to these kids, too. Okay with you?"

"Sure. You want me to round them up? The kids, I mean?"

Jury thought for a moment. "They're at Waterloo, right?"

"Four of them. Two at Heathrow. Only one now. This Aero kid."

"Who are the four?"

Paper rustled. "There's Suki, Jimmy, Martin and Henry. That won't help you much, though. Even if I had the last names, you'd still have to go through the drivers to find out where these kids are."

"Then I will. I'll start with Parsons. What's his number?"

Jenkins gave Jury Robbie's mobile number. "If he answers it."

Jury had taken it down and now asked, "Why wouldn't he?"

"Well, I called him an hour ago and asked him the name of one of the drivers, which he told me. Then he told me if I called again, he wouldn't be answering because he'd be at that cabbies' pub."

"What pub?"

"The Knowledge. You've heard of it."

Jury frowned. "I have?"

"Oh, come on, Richard, everybody's heard of it. Only nobody knows where it is."

London
unmapped,
uncharted,
undated

8

Probably no map, no street guide, not even the *A–Z* with all of its cobweb entanglements, properly conveys the difficulty of negotiating London. There was no city easier to get lost in, stuck in, pinned down in, go missing in. Although it was not as neat as a spiderweb, if your car was lost in one of its disconnected byways, you knew well enough how a fly must feel. The city seemed to mock any attempt to move forward: traffic lights winking, stop signs rearing, street signs baring their little black-lettered teeth.

Yet with guts and patience, anything could ultimately be found.

Anything, that is, except the Knowledge.

It came to Maurice Benbow that in all of his years as a black cab driver he had seen dozens of Red Lions, King's Heads, Crowns, White Harts (and Horses) among London's over 5,000 pubs, but out of all of the silly, weird, wondrous names that had been thought up, from the Hung, Drawn and Quartered to I Am the Only Running Footman, he had never passed one called the Knowledge. And this despite the fame of London's black cabs and the belief that this city had the best drivers in the world; still, not one pub with that name. So Maurice decided to fix that.

The more he thought of what he wanted to do, the better he liked the idea. He considered himself fortunate in not having a family because he wouldn't have to convince others to go along with the plan.

It took him a year to find a place and he found it by accident. Or, he said later, fate. Fate in the form of a large white dog that sat like a statue on the broken pavement of a run-down bit of road where Maurice had never been before. He was astonished that there was any part of London he'd not been in, but this was it. He let his cab idle in the night as he watched the dog, curiously stolid and very white against the dark backdrop of a smallish, weathered building down a narrow lane. Finally he got out and crossed the nameless street and found that there was another dog, a black one, lying across the ground and surely dead.

Maurice was astonished: the living dog appeared to be watching over the dead one. He approached very cautiously, nonaggressively. He spoke gently to the white dog, who looked down at the other dog and whimpered. A dead mate. Had to be. He sat down on the curb on the other side of the dead dog, hoping to announce himself as an ally in this terrible tragedy. He assumed the black dog had been hit by a car. Slowly and carefully he laid his hand on the dead dog's head, ran it down the dog's neck and a bit along the spine as the white dog sat and watched. Definitely mates. He couldn't get over this kind of devotion. More than most humans, that was for sure.

Maurice kept a blanket in the cab, an electric blanket that he could run off the cigarette lighter. He had attached a long cord to the blanket after one time he'd been on the Heath and had wanted to just lie under the stars, but the blanket wouldn't reach. So he'd gotten this extension cord. He rose slowly, went to the cab and plugged in the cord and brought the blanket back. The white dog, still statue-still, watched him carefully but did nothing. The blanket warmed up and he spread it out, so that part lay across the dead dog and part across the ground, then patted it several times for the white dog to lie down. He sat there; the blanket lay there for a long time before the white dog moved. But he did move and he lay down and Maurice could tell the warmth was a comfort to him.

They kept to these positions, dogs lying, Maurice sitting, for a good hour before Maurice realized nothing, absolutely nothing had come along—no person, no car, nothing. And he began to wonder how the dead dog could have been injured by a car, for there were no cars. Behind them was an old house, clearly unoccupied. To the left was a row of lock-ups. To the right stood the sad remains of what had been a business, or a couple of them. The building in ruins.

Maurice pulled out his mobile and called one of his driver friends, Conrad Coover.

"Yo!" said Coover.

Maurice told him the situation and asked him if maybe they should get someone from the RSPCA out here to take care of the dogs.

"Why? Sounds like you're doin' a better job'n they would."

"Could you come and help, then?"

"Sure. Give me an address."

"There isn't one. I mean, there's no street sign, or anything."

"Well, just tell me how to get there."

Maurice thought. He'd been driving without paying attention. "I think maybe I went through Hackney or maybe Newham. I wasn't paying attention."

"Bloody unlikely, Maurice. You drive a black cab, man. You'd be paying attention even if you weren't."

"Swear to God, Coov, it's like the middle of nowhere."

Coover laughed. "There ain't no middle of nowhere, mate. This is London. It don't have 'nowheres.' Not for us, it don't. So get back in your cab and drive around for a bit and figure out where you are."

"But I don't want to leave the dog."

"Suit yourself. Call if you sort it."

Maurice turned and looked at the old house that sat far back off the road. It was, at least, shelter. He knew he'd never get the white dog into the cab. So he thought maybe he could get him into the house. He stood up and the white dog looked at him and got off the blanket. That was a good sign; the dog was accepting Maurice as a kind of friend. Maurice wrapped the blanket around the dead dog, pulled off the cord and picked up the dog. The white dog lifted first one paw and then another over and over. Questioning.

"Over there, buddy. Come along." He carried the black dog in the blanket and the white dog followed him into the house. Of course there was no electricity, but Maurice always had a torch. He flicked it on and ran it around the room, it fell on a big lantern that turned out to have a wick. He lit this with his Zippo and the flame sputtered up. Damn thing must still have a bit of fuel. It shed a good light.

When dawn came he walked outside and turned to look at the house. It was actually well built. Fixable. Paint, plaster. He knew he'd found it.

He knew nobody else would.

This was his future pub; this was the Knowledge.

Three months later, he'd finished with the paint and plaster; with getting in tables and chairs; with locating an amazing bar in Camden Passage, the "antiques" bloke said had come by hook or by crook (certainly the latter, thought Maurice) from Morocco. From Casablanca.

"Sure, from Rick's bar, right?"

"You got it, pal," said the dealer, winking broadly and counting the money Maurice handed over.

He had to rent a van to get the bar back to his new pub. But he got it there. The dog, now named Ben, after himself, calmly waited for him. Maurice had taken the place of Ben's dead friend. Maurice was now Ben's mate.

He had turned the old house into a perfectly ordinary London pub. Wooden beams and whitewashed brick, deal tables and mismatched chairs, Rick's bar along one wall, big fireplace, warm and cozy. Cozier than most because of its gaslit wall sconces, candles and a long row of gaslights over the bar. No one was sure of the source of the gas, since Maurice was not a fan of British Gas, nor a patron of any of the Big Six (Greater London's major electric companies). There were many easy ways of getting gas supplied to one's residence, but Maurice simply used propane tanks. Nor did he bother with British Telecom, not with the advent of the throwaway phone. He had once had a landline, which came about not by paying BT, but by hacking into his neighbor's line. Without electricity, there was, of course, no telly and one might have expected the pub's patrons to raise a fuss over not being able to watch Manchester United clobber Leicester City, or Chelsea do the same to Arsenal. But there was surprisingly little objection. TV would have required the assistance of the Big Six and also some newfangled wiring to speed up reception, but Maurice wanted neither speed nor reception. He wanted complete and utter autonomy. In the colder months, heat was supplied in part by a gas stove, but mostly by burning logs in the big fireplace. Logs that Maurice himself brought in. Wood was not delivered any more than was mail. Every once in a while one of the waggish taxi drivers would go out and check if the trees in the woody back garden were still there and found all of them standing. No one knew where Maurice got his wood. He told them Epping Forest, ha ha.

On that day over a year ago when Maurice had discovered there was no pub called the Knowledge, he decided to go one better. He would open a pub that only London's black cab drivers could patronize. The pub would be otherwise unlocatable: untraceable, unfindable, unmappable.

To get their green badges, these drivers had to pass an absolutely grueling test that took months, often *years*, of conveying themselves on foot, bicycle, moped, motorcycle or car through the streets, lanes, alleyways and roads of London. One had to learn not just the fastest routes from one point to another, but every monument, museum and tourist attraction along the way. The drivers were learning not just streets, but street*scapes*. It was organic.

The test was claimed to be one of the hardest in the world. It was called "the knowledge."

Robbie Parsons walked into the Knowledge that Friday night, or by that time it was more the small hours of Saturday morning. The pub didn't bother with closing times, taxi drivers' schedules being so erratic. There were still over a dozen cabbies at this offbeat hour.

Word of Robbie's wild ride had gotten round as quick as lightning and he was now by way of being a star. Nothing like that had ever happened to any of the others; he was congratulated again and again, clapped on the back and pounded on the shoulder.

"Don't give me all the credit," said Robbie. "There was Brendan Small and a couple of others following. Four cabs—it was quite a show."

"Hell, man, when I first heard that a guy had pulled a gun on you, I figured it was just another arsehole wantin' to get to the Knowledge!" That had brought a loud round of laughter.

"So I get home," says Robbie, "and a little later, up shows the Filth. Yeah. City Police wanting a word. I spent over an hour at Snow Hill talkin' to some DCI. I got the idea he thought I was in on it: the getaway car."

"Bloody hell!" said Reggie Reeves.

The others chimed in with their outrage, hard to muster at three A.M. when they were completely knackered.

If you wanted to be out of reach, you could become an astronaut, fly to the moon—or maybe not: Neil Armstrong had been reachable. My God, that was something to give a man pause. They can even get to you on the bloody *moon*! But not at the Knowledge, which was a lot less trouble, at least if you drove a black cab. As for an ordinary citizen, well, he might as well try and fly to the moon. When word got out that there was this pub that nobody could find, naturally everybody tried to find it. A lot of people took bets, offered bribes, made maps, asked "people of influence"—all to no avail. The cabbies got a little tired of simpletons who waved them down, got in and asked to be taken to the Knowledge.

Usually the drivers simply stonewalled, pleading ignorance when asked to be driven there. The driver would apologize, and tell the passenger that he'd never heard of it and that no such pub existed in

London. But sometimes cabbies would get inventive. One of their favorite stories was Reggie Reeves's. He had some American CEO in his cab, probably used to ordering people around, and Reggie said, "Yes, sir, that'd be south London, and it might take a bit of time, as that destination is across London Bridge and through Southwark and Brixton, then on from there to Dulwich." The man said, "Yeah, just get on with it," and Reggie did.

Then they were driving up to the massive school with its stone gates, green lawns, a cricket pitch, beautiful old redbrick buildings.

"Where in hell are we, driver?" demanded the man in the backseat.

"The College, sir. Dulwich College. Isn't that where you wanted to go? It's quite famous—"

His fare screamed at him, "No, you idiot! I said *knowledge*, not *college!* That pub called the *Knowledge!*"

Clive Rowbotham had driven an obnoxious French ("Ain't that redundant?") couple for miles and miles to a pretty little country pub whose front garden was a mass of blue flowers.

"What's this?"

Clive pointed to the sign swinging in the wind: "The Borage, sir. Ain't that what you wanted?" He too was charged with being an idiot and both the man and the woman babbled at him in heavily accented English that they had said, "The *Knowledge*, you fool!"

The other drivers had really liked that, several of them using the Borage to off-load their fares. But for the most part, it was stonewalling.

The cabbies at the bar had insisted Robbie go through the details of the ride with the gun at his neck. Which he had done, ending with the drop-off at Waterloo Station.

Coover said, "Then the Waterloo kids picked it up, I heard."

"True," said Robbie, but the others hadn't heard yet about Patty Haigh.

"You mean she's with *him*?" said Coover.

"According to Aero. He got the last message, as far as we know, before Patty took off to Dubai with this guy."

A brief silence followed, as they (presumably) bemoaned the fate of Patty Haigh.

"Poor little tyke," said Janet Swift, one of the few women drivers.

"You're talkin' about Patty Haigh," said Kevin O'Malley. "You think 'poor little tyke' is a good description?" He laughed, and the rest of the bar echoed his laughter.

Waterloo Station, London
Nov. 2, Saturday morning

9

In Waterloo Station, Jury met up with some of the drivers who had actually followed Robbie's cab before it stopped and the shooter made his exit. They did not, they said, get a real look at him. But of course none of them had known yet what was going on with the guy.

"How many kids are there supplying you with information?"

"There's five," said a driver named Michaelson. "All told: four at Waterloo, two at Heathrow."

"That's six," said Jury.

"Make it six, then," said Michaelson, happy to have Jury do the math.

"What about Victoria? None there?"

"No, sir."

"Gatwick?"

Heads shaking.

"Stansted?"

Another round of head shakes.

"King's Cross or St. Pancras?"

Shake. Shake.

"Why only Waterloo and Heathrow?"

Robbie said, "That's where they want to be. Been here for some time when we found them."

"Found them?"

"I mean, met up with them. One of them—Jimmy, it was—saw a fare leave Michaelson's cab without paying. Michaelson called after this bloke, but the guy just hurried off. This kid Jimmy went up to Michaelson, said they could stop him. For a quid."

"I asked, 'Who's "they"?'" Michaelson said. "'Me and me mates.' Jimmy said. So I says, 'Pound apiece,' and Jimmy says, 'You're on,' and took off like a lightning bolt. Couldn't've been more 'n four, five minutes later when security had this guy in tow and I collected my forty quid from him. A minute later, Jimmy shows up. 'How'd ya like that?' he says, wanting not only pay, but praise. He got both."

Michaelson went on: "So I ask this kid if he's at Waterloo every night. He says, 'Every night but Thursdays.' I say, 'Why not Thursdays?' and he says, 'Violin lessons.' And he takes off."

"*Violin?*" said Jury. "He's learning to play the violin?"

"Learned. He's really good. But not, he says, good enough."

"Then Jimmy has parents and they can't be poor." Jury expected a round of nods here, but got the same blank looks. "Well, *somebody's* paying for this kid's music lessons, and the violin's hardest of the lot."

Robbie said, "Maybe Jimmy."

"The boy's paying for his own lessons?"

"You don't know this kid. He really wants to be a master at it."

"What about the kids' families? Where do they live?"

"You don't think they're tellin' us?" said Michaelson, snorting around his cigarette.

"We don't know nuffin' about 'em," said Kevin O'Malley. "They're reg'lar clams, they are. You don't think we're tellin' Social Services about 'em, do you?"

"No," Jury said, but he thought: picking pockets, con games, shoplifting. These kids could grow up to be master criminals. He said so.

"No." All the drivers agreed on this, though it was Robbie who said, "They don't want to be criminals. They want to be cops."

Jury stared.

Robbie laughed. "A Scotland Yard superintendent? Man, you'd be a hero." He paused. "You and Joshua Bell."

"Are any of these kids here now?"

"Prob'ly," said Kevin. "But they're all over the place. It went from Jimmy to Henry to Martin to Suki. Easiest one to find's Suki. She's nine, ten years old. She pretty much hangs out in front of the City Café."

"Thanks," said Jury.

The cabbies nodded and lit up.

The little girl, possibly ten, but looking only seven, stood outside the café with her black-and-white mutt on a lead, looking starved—starved not in fact but in effect.

As Jury approached, he took a five-pound note from his clip, scrunched it up and put it in his coat pocket with a bill from British Tele-com. As he drew abreast of her, he pulled out the bill, feigned reading it studiously and let the banknote fall to the ground near her dog and her feet. He went a few steps before he heard, "Mister!" He turned.

She held out the crumpled banknote. "You dropped this," she said in a small, soft voice.

"I did? Why, thank you. You're very honest." When she looked demurely away, he added, "So's your dog."

She looked back and laughed. "He's *really* honest. His name's Reno."

Reno did a bit of tail-wagging and gave a yap.

"Reno? That's a city in Nevada. Lots of gambling."

"I know. I almost named him Vegas. I like gambling."

"Well, I think Reno deserves a reward." He went for change in his pocket.

She said, "Oh, no, sir. We don't need a reward, not for just picking up a bit of money and giving it back."

Her look was that of the most honest citizen who had ever trudged through Waterloo. Big eyes, melting. It was so fake Jury wanted to laugh. "Doubly honest. Well, then, would you join me for lunch? If you've time for it."

"Oh, I've got time. Can Reno come too?"

"Absolutely. He can have lunch."

Then she looked a little defeated. "But I don't think they'll let him in."

Jury smiled. "I think they will."

Just inside the door, a sharp-nosed woman, with dark hair pulled back as if for a hanging, said crisply, "We don't allow dogs in here."

"You do now." Turning his body from Suki in order to shield the ID, he pulled it from his pocket and held it out.

She jumped. "Oh! Well, I should call the manager."

"Why? Is he strangling the cook?" He turned back to Suki. "Pick a table."

Suki headed for the booths, Reno trotting by her side.

When they had settled in, the dog under the table, Suki looked at him wide-eyed. "Are you famous?"

"Not yet." He picked the menu out of the metal holder.

"Then how'd you get Reno by her?"

Looking at the menu, not at her, he said, "Same way you do, Suki. By being clever." Briefly, he looked up at her. She seemed perplexed.

A waitress came mincing over, set down two glasses of water and stared at Suki. "You again."

"Me again." Suki read the menu, thought a bit. "What are you having?"

"Hm. I don't know. But have anything you want for both of you."

The waitress, whose name tag said "Maureen," looked around for the other half of the "both."

Suki smiled broadly. "I'll have a super club, macaroni cheese, a ham sandwich—"

The waitress said, "Goin' for it, girl, aren't you?" She smirked.

Jury gave her a look like granite. "Take the order, Maureen, without the editorializing, please."

She frowned at whatever that meant.

"I'll have a double hamburger, rare, no mustard, no ketchup, no pickle, nothing on it at all. And a double order of chips."

Frown still in place, now probably at such spartan burger habits, she noted this down and started to move away.

Jury stopped her with, "And two bowls of water."

"What? You mean glasses of water. But I brought you—"

"No, I mean *bowls*." He held up two fingers. "Two."

"For what?" She was back now.

"Hasn't this place ever heard of finger bowls? Or do we have to go to Park Lane for something so simple?"

"What's it for?"

Suki said, with no small measure of contempt, "Sticky fingers."

Looking put-upon, the waitress marched away.

Jury said, "Suki, were you meeting someone outside before?"

"Me? Meeting?" As if meetings were as foreign as finger bowls.

Which were duly served, along with the waitress's curiosity. Which went unfulfilled.

Jury watched her leave. "Okay, mine first." He reached the bowl of water under the table to Reno.

Slurp slurp slurp.

"Shall I put mine down too?" Suki whispered.

"Let's try and keep one bowl on the table for Maureen's eyes. When the first is empty—" Jury looked. "It is. Now yours."

Suki laughed, clearly enjoying this conspiracy, lifted her bowl carefully and set it under the table. She picked up the empty bowl, brought it back.

Slurp slurp.

"Reno gets so thirsty. That was a good idea." And she looked at Jury, avid. "You must be the Wonder Keeper."

The Wonder Keeper was pouring water from his glass into the empty bowl, holding back the bits of ice. He very nearly blushed. "Suki, I've been called a lot of things, but never a Wonder Keeper."

Her pointed chin rested between her fists as she looked at him. "I don't know anybody who would ever have thought of finger bowls."

"The Queen, maybe?"

She laughed as Maureen tramped unobligingly back with the hamburger and chips. "Rest's not done yet." She seemed glad to impart the bad news. She left.

"More water!" Jury called after her.

Suki was clearly excited to see one of the burgers being broken into bits, then deposited on the plate of chips, and most of the chips redeposited onto the hamburger plate.

"Does Reno like chips?" Jury asked, lowering the plate.

A few soft woofs were his answer.

Maureen returned with Suki's lunch. "Here's your order." She set down the sandwiches and the macaroni cheese.

Suki gasped at this huge assortment of food. "Thanks."

Jury was breaking up the second hamburger patty when he said, "Suki, remember the man you followed on Friday night?"

Suki's cheeks were bulging, chipmunk-like. "Sure. He was really big."

"You'd be able to identify him, then, if you saw him again?"

"Uh-huh." She swallowed and nodded.

"Are you certain he was the same man that your friend Martin saw?"

She frowned. "Of course I am. We've followed people before. And the guy with him was wearing a uniform, but he wasn't really a cop. Not the way they were talking."

"In police uniform but not a policeman."

"Waterloo Station security. I mean disguised as station security." She shrugged. "I don't know, but I do know it was the same guy Robbie had in his cab."

"But how can you be absolutely sure?"

She gave him a look that might have cast doubts on his Wonder Keeper abilities. "Because it went from Jimmy to Henry to Martin to me. We don't make mistakes. If we did, we'd be useless."

Jury put the second burger on a paper napkin and reached it under the table.

"Reno, too," said Suki.

Jury glanced up. "Reno?"

"Never forgets a smell." She opened the ham sandwich and reached the ham under the table.

"Good for Reno. You know about Patty Haigh, I expect."

"She got on the plane with this man we were watching," said Suki, matter-of-factly.

"Yes. Is Patty a friend of yours?"

"She's friends with all of us." Suki tilted to look under the table, then sat back up.

"Are you worried about her?"

"Worried?" Frowning, Suki looked as if worry were foreign to her experience. She shook her head and pulled the menu out from its little aluminum holder. "I wish I was as smart as Patty. She can do anything." She scanned the bottom of the menu.

"Perhaps. But that's an incredibly chancy step to take, just getting on an airplane with a stranger, much less one who shoots people."

Suki shrugged. "By now, Patty's probably flying the plane. Can I— *we*—" She pointed down at Reno. "—have some sticky toffee cake?"

10

The plane landed at Jomo Kenyatta International Airport at around three on Saturday afternoon and again Patty wondered, as she had in Dubai, if the local police would be on their toes and nail B.B. She was getting tired of it all being down to her, although at this point she almost hoped that police wouldn't get him—she had begun to like him, given how well he'd treated her.

She had to admit, her tiredness had been offset by the comforts of Emirates. She'd had a little cabin all her own with a big TV and a table for eating, which she made a lot of use of; at one end of the first-class cabin there was even a spa where she could take a shower. Since B.B. didn't want his shower time, she took another one. Then she decided a shower would be nice before she tried to sleep and managed to get a third one by telling the flight attendant she felt faint with the heat.

When they had landed in Dubai at eight forty-five that morning, she was cleaner than she'd ever been in her life.

But then, in the lavish airport in Dubai, B.B. had dropped the little bomb on her that he was getting a connecting flight to Nairobi. Right now, he wanted to see her safely delivered into the custody of her aunt? uncle? before he left.

Now, for Patty to have a reason to go there, Aunt Monique would have to be in Nairobi. But she'd have sent *someone* to tell Patty . . . a housekeeper! Right over there, a regal-looking black woman in a bright headwrap and caftan was waving to someone. Patty appropriated the wave before whoever it was meant for could get it, saying to B.B., "She must have sent her housekeeper. Over there!" Patty waved and took off toward this uncomprehending woman whose eyes widened at Patty's rushing approach. In order to make the woman smile welcomingly, Patty said to her, "Did anyone ever tell you you look just like Lena Horne, that great singer?" And smiles and small talk followed, Patty practicing her few words of Swahili. The woman helped her with pronunciation. Then she rushed back to B.B. and told him that the housekeeper said her aunt was in Nairobi, not here anymore, and that (Oh, I don't know what to do!) Patty was to fly there.

B.B. had commented that this seemed an awfully slipshod way for Patty's family to be behaving—very careless of her welfare. Had she been his own daughter, none of this would have happened.

That she could well believe.

He told her he would get her a ticket when he picked up his own boarding pass, but that they might not be able to sit together. Then he took out a money clip, removed a number of bills from it and handed them to her; she didn't want to take his money but he insisted. "In case there's some emergency, you must have money."

She thought that for somebody who shoots people, he was pretty nice.

The plane left at ten thirty and the flight would take five hours. Patty was happy with this; there would be plenty of time for a shower. Two showers, unless B.B. wanted his. He told her he was sorry, but they would be flying in coach and there were no showers there.

Patty had picked up a guide to Nairobi and a Swahili phrase book. Once the plane was in the air, she visited the washroom just to double-check. No showers. Then she concentrated on the Swahili phrase book, remembering what the Lena Horne woman had told her about pronunciation. Her studies done, she went up a few rows to visit B.B.

*   *   *

The plane landed in Nairobi. This time it was her Aunt Monique—a too-French name, maybe? But she had had to think of something in a hurry as she hadn't expected to be making another leg of this journey with B.B. Why hadn't he been caught yet? Was she supposed to follow him to hell? Even if she'd wanted to, there was no sense her trying to notify the Kenyan police; they wouldn't pay any attention to her. So it was good-bye to B.B., whose real name she still didn't know, especially since for the Nairobi flight he'd used a second passport with a different name. She'd managed to get a glimpse of it when it had dropped from the counter. Now she was walking with him through the airport, Patty all the while searching for a likely Monique. Perhaps she shouldn't have chosen a Kenyan for an aunt-by-marriage, but they were in it now, weren't they?

She was telling B.B. for the third time how Aunt Monique was really going to appreciate his helping her, but that she was kind of shy with strangers so she might not—oh, *there* she was! Patty had nailed a nondescript woman in her forties, dressed half in European style—that plain black dress, half in African—that boldly colored turban, clasping her handbag to her breast and looking as if the terminal were peopled by dips just waiting to snatch it, her eyes squinting as if her vision were bad. The perfect Monique.

"Bye-bye, B.B.," Patty called back, dancing away. She flinched. Had she really said that? She rushed toward the woman, who looked understandably astonished by Patty's approach. Patty did her "Sorry, you look just like my cousin Mildred" routine, whereupon the woman became consoling, asking Patty the usual questions as to where she was supposed to meet her cousin, et cetera, with Patty being very imaginative in her search for answers as she glanced over her shoulder and looking satisfied as B.B. finally walked off. Free of police company, Patty noticed. *You could just do anything in London, you could walk in with a gun and shoot people, and then go to Africa or anywhere.*

But back to business, thanking Monique, now seeing her cousin Mildred and hopping off again through the crowd and disappearing.

Then there was security looking her over. Thank God it wasn't British Social Services, at least. Patty was used to attention from the police, so she expected the puzzled look from two uniforms as she walked by un-Moniqued and otherwise unattended. But she still didn't like the stares they were giving her.

Patty slipped into the women's restroom and into a stall, where she opened her backpack, pulled out her ginger wig and settled it expertly over her brown hair, shoving her hair underneath and adjusting the back of the wig. She always carried two wigs, the other being a washed-out blond. She pulled out a pair of sparkly rimmed glasses, removed her short jacket and put on a white sweater. She applied pale pink lipstick and very pale blush. She left the stall and wondered who this person was, reflected in the lake-like expanse of the restroom mirror. It was always a bit of a thrill when she didn't recognize herself. But *Ouch!* The sparkly glasses were entirely too much, begging for notice. She shoved them back down in her pack and pulled out a pair with thin, narrow horn rims. Much better.

Now she was off to the city of Nairobi and into the mystery of Africa, which Patty believed was a complete mystery in and of itself (and not just because she was lost in it).

She had jumped off the bus at a stop in the center of town, taking her leave of a mass of people, each of whom thought she belonged to one of the others—no surprise, the way she beamed and laughed and said her few words in guidebook Swahili to everyone. Patty was walking through the streets looking purposeful, looking in charge, not looking at all like a little girl who had lost her way.

Which was what she felt like, and it was one of the few times in her life she'd ever felt it. What? Where? When? Who? She didn't bother with the *Why did this happen*? There was never an answer to that. But *How will I get out of here? What is the best route to take?* Those were pragmatic questions. People looked at her with a fair amount of interest. Though she wondered where she was, she was afraid to stop and look round for too long, afraid someone would try to take her over.

It was dark, *very* dark. It was a new darkness. The lights of London had always hidden the darkness from her, and she wondered a little about that. The vast dark of Africa hung over cheetahs and lions moving stealthily through tall grass, hunting their prey. The vast darkness of London hung over dips and tarts prowling the streets.

Her white sweater seemed to glimmer as the dark hand of a man in a black cape-like garment stopped her. She looked up, surprised, fearing some public official.

"My child, allow me to assist you. You seem very determined to get where you are going, but also uncertain." He said this in perfectly articulated English. He wore a boxy black hat, fez-like.

She wondered if he was a Kenyan priest or something. She couldn't think what to say or how to pretend what her destination was.

"Let me get you a drink of lemonade, perhaps? And we can talk a bit."

Talk. She shook the African darkness from her head—the cheetah, the whispering grass—and prepared to tell her usual string of lies. "I'm meeting my uncle. I just flew in from London."

They had entered a café and walked out again to one of the little round tables where customers sat. While she said this, he was setting down two tall glasses of lemonade that looked quite delicious. As he sat himself down, looking surprised, he said, "He did not arrange to meet you at the airport?" His tone stood between astonishment and outrage.

"You must understand—" Patty had always found phrases like this put people on the defensive, which is why she used them. "—that he can't drive now, as his eyesight is so bad." *Idiot*, she thought to herself, there were always taxis that her "uncle" could have arranged for. "And his little village is so isolated, cab drivers can't find it." She sipped her lemonade through a straw.

He was frowning. "Where is this village?"

"Way way out in the bush." Oh God, that sounded like Australia. Or was there bush everywhere? Maybe there was bush along the Marylebone Road.

"What is its name?"

"Mozam—bimbe." She almost said "Mozambique" before she realized there was a country of that name.

"I don't believe—"

"It's way far into south Africa."

"But that's another country. South Africa."

What? Why wasn't there a south *of* Africa? There was a south of England, a south of France . . . Looking at the priest's doubting face, she
guessed not. "I didn't mean *South* Africa, only *in* the south. My uncle
told me to come to this street we're in." Patty looked up the street as
far as she could see, at the various signs. One looked like the outline of
a half-moon with a sprinkling of stars, but she couldn't read the name.
"He told me there's a little restaurant or café called the Moon something. His old and dear friend Édouard would meet me."

"The Starry Night, you mean?"

"Isn't that a famous painting?" Wow! She had certainly pulled that
out of her ear. Was this holy man trying to trick her? She nodded.

He nodded up the street. "It's along here. But why did this Édouard
not meet you at the airport?"

"Because . . . Oh! There . . . I see him . . ." Patty pointed toward the
neon moon sign.

"Then perhaps we should walk there."

Hell. "Absolutely," she said, with fake enthusiasm. Several doorways
and a knotted crowd of pedestrians later, she spotted the Starry Night
and was eyeballing an old man hunched over a Zimmer walker coming
out of it, heading for one of the sidewalk tables. He was awkwardly resting his mug of coffee or whatever it was against the Zimmer.

"There he is! Mr. Édouard! Thank you so much for the lemonade,
I've got to run." She broke away from the tall man of some-God-or-other
and threaded her way through the crowd. When she looked back, just
before she reached "Édouard," she saw the tall man in black still following, but not very quickly.

So here she was nearly falling over his walker, the old guy looking at her in alarm. Apologizing, she knew this must be a split-second

decision: help him sit down at the table and join him, manufacture conversation until the priest was upon them, or run before the priest knew what was happening.

In doubt, run. Run, Patty, run!

Wasn't there a movie called that? Long before her time, but another old guy camped under Waterloo Bridge had talked about it. Not with her name, of course, but some other name, some girl with ginger hair— Lola! That was it. *Run, Lola, Run!* And boy could she run! Patty had the strange feeling that Lola was standing right beside her, nudging her out of the chair.

Run!

Patty ran.

11

If one could ignore City Police—the forensics team still managing to swarm all over the semicircular drive on this cold Saturday afternoon—the exterior of the Artemis Club would have appeared unimpressive, which was probably what Leonard Zane meant it to be. Jury thought that it might be its very stolidness—its sturdy Georgian facade—was striking, considering the shifty, sharklike propensities of its business. The building's yellow stone had a Cotswold glow in the rush of slanting light where the sun broke through cloud cover.

The interior, though, was something else again. To his left was a beautiful room that probably served many purposes: sitting; waiting; reading a book from its floor-to-ceiling bookcases; enjoying the warmth of a huge fireplace surrounded by a green leather fender at one end of the room; having tea at that table beside a window, as a well-heeled couple were now doing; relaxing on down-cushioned sofas or in armchairs covered in a muted pink-and-blue silky material, all with cushions aplenty. The walls were papered in soft grayish blue. At the other end of the room was a mahogany door with a small brass plaque Jury couldn't read. It might have said *Office*.

On the right was a formal dining room, full of white linen, brown leather chairs and at the long windows brown velvet curtains, their ends puddling on the floor. The wallpaper here was ivory with thin brown stripes. Bronze wall sconces gave off a misty light through smoked glass shades. Art deco, squared and arched. He wondered why they were lit at midday, and noticed they weren't electric but gas, and turned very low. When the flames jumped higher at night he bet the effect was one of shadow and mystery.

The third room was the casino itself. It was the same size as the dining room, but made to look larger by partially mirrored walls in which crystal chandeliers reflected endlessly. Half of each wall was mirrored, including the wall against which the bar stood. The rest of the wall surface was covered in what looked like cream brocade. Sunlight coming through the long window at the rear was reflected in the chandeliers, casting tiny flakes of light across the tables.

Maggie Benn checked the time on her mobile. "We'd better go up to the gallery. Mr. Zane is waiting."

As they ascended the curved, highly polished staircase, Jury said, "I could live the rest of my life in any one of these rooms. Who was your decorator?"

"Decorator?" Maggie raised questioning eyebrows as if Jury had alluded to some arcane profession she'd never heard of. "Oh, Mr. Zane tried one but they couldn't agree on anything. When he described the decor he wanted, the decorator said, 'No, no, no, much too busy.' The decorator brought in swatches and bits and bobs of what *he* wanted and Mr. Zane said, 'No, no, no, much too boring.' Mr. Zane got rid of him and did all this busy stuff himself." She laughed. "He's got an eye."

"My word, I would say he certainly does. This place is spectacular."

She blushed a bit. "Thank you. Everyone seems to like it."

"Everyone *should*. But I have an idea 'everyone' does not get in here. Am I right?"

"We are a little bit selective, true. And we have a cap on the number of patrons we allow each evening. Also, a routine for arrival. It's pretty strict, but we don't want a glut of cars pulling up all at the same time—" But she stopped her comments on the stringent rules as they reached the top of the staircase.

"How many tables do you have in the casino?"

"Only twenty. Right now, nineteen: poker, twenty-one, roulette, craps, baccarat—the usual."

Jury was not sure what "the usual" was.

"We have two twenty-one tables, but at the moment there's only one. We're looking for a croupier. Hard to find really good dealers, you know, quick fingers. Looks matter, too."

Jury bet they did.

"No chance for me, then."

"Really, Superintendent."

He enjoyed watching her face as she spoke, not for its expressiveness, but for its total lack of it. The face was, actually, rather plain, squarish. Good bones, though. He imagined the face would be quite a canvas for a professional makeup artist. She wore no makeup other than a bit of lipstick. Her dress was equally artless. Her hair, very dark and quite glossy, was pulled away from her face so smoothly and tightly it looked as if it might hurt. What surprised him, in this extremely well-appointed, trendy, glamorous place, was her total lack of glamour.

"And of course, someone who can play by the house rules—or feel the weight of Mr. Zane's displeasure."

As they reached the top of the beautiful half-circle of staircase to the gallery, he began to feel the weight of the man's displeasure himself.

Yet Leonard Zane didn't register any displeasure at all upon seeing this detective on his doorsill. Quite the contrary: he seemed pleased.

Maggie Benn introduced him. "Leo, this is Detective Superintendent Richard Jury. New Scotland Yard CID."

Jury said, "I should carry you around instead of a card." He smiled as she blushed. Jury held out his hand. "Mr. Zane."

"Leonard, please. Although I won't call you Richard."

"Good." Jury was surprised by the sincere note of welcome in his tone and wondered if the pretense of sincerity wasn't stock-in-trade for Leonard Zane. Or part of it.

Instead of registering uncertainty, Leonard Zane simply laughed. "Superintendent Jury, please sit down. Have some coffee and a scone."

A matching silver pot and plate sat on the other side of Zane's desk, a long table of what looked like zebrawood. Jury wasn't much on woods. There were some prints lying on it, nothing else—no pens, blotter, landline phones. Jury moved along the wall of paintings, some forty or fifty uncrowded oils and watercolors, prints and pastels. It was an eclectic mix of works showing the influence of many schools. Impressionism, German expressionism, a poor reproduction of Rothko, a good Roy Lichtenstein. He was struck particularly by a naturalistic painting of a black woman seated outside before a fire of sticks and small branches, warming her hands, while behind her in the brush and half hidden by a baobab and a stunted acacia were a cheetah and a lion, their eyes fixed on her. The woman in her bright orange-and-red headdress gave no sign of awareness of their presence. As he repassed the paintings to return to the desk, he saw two long glass-topped display cases that appeared to hold jewelry.

He was about to comment, when Leonard Zane said, "I'm sorry about all this," nodding toward the window and the driveway below.

"It was hardly your fault, Mr. Zane."

Reflecting on this, frowning, Leonard Zane said, "I wonder."

"You do?"

"What I mean is, this casino-gallery combo—"

"Sounds like a sandwich."

Zane laughed. "Speaking of food, you didn't say if you wanted that coffee."

"Coffee, fine. Your place looks a bit like a restaurant. And that dining room downstairs—"

"It's my chef. He's terrific. He should be at La Gavroche or somewhere like that. I'm holding him back."

Since he was unfamiliar with La Gavroche, Jury knew he'd fare no better with the "somewheres."

Zane ran his storm-gray eyes over Jury's face as he poured the coffee and pushed the small silver tray holding cream and sugar toward him, together with the silver plate holding the scones. "You're strange for a Scotland Yard superintendent."

"You're not the first to say it." Jury added nothing to the coffee.

"Do you always engage in banter on a murder inquiry?"

"Always. So let's banter about why you're so delighted to see me." He stretched out his legs.

Zane's expression altered. But no more than it would have done over his tailor missing a stitch. "Perhaps you think I'm playing you."

Jury smiled, picked up his cup. "Are you?"

"No."

Still holding his cup, Jury rose and walked over to one of the glass cases. He was looking down at a necklace that would have bought him his Islington flat. "What are these stones?"

"You're not familiar with tanzanite?"

Jury shook his head. "Another gap in my general knowledge."

"You might not find it at a jeweler's because it's not very popular. People don't realize how rare it is, and becoming rarer. I have a mine in Tanzania, one of many of the small mines there."

"A mine? You mine tanzanite?"

Zane laughed. "The Merelani Hills, near Kilimanjaro. It's the only place in the world it's mined. There are a number of grades—their value is based on hue, tone and saturation." Zane pointed to a line of stones— and it was a line: some dozen examples of tanzanite ranging from one hardly bigger than a pinhead to the last, many-faceted, nearly the size of a ten-pence coin. "You can probably differentiate if you look more closely." He took a small ring of keys from his pocket, slid them around until he had the one he wanted and unlocked the case, taking out three rings of different cuts and set in a varying number of diamonds. "Never mind the diamonds, just look at the tanzanite. You see the difference?"

Jury pointed to one toward the middle. "This one seems to have more of a green cast."

"Which would lessen its value. But the end ones, you see the differ-ence in the depth of the blue?"

Jury shook his head. "Can't say I do. They're both bluer than any-thing I've ever seen."

"It's the saturation. That's the most important thing to measure. This one—" He plucked up the one less invested in diamonds. "—is very unusual, a really fine stone. Much deeper saturation than the other." He set the pieces down.

Jury bent over a ring with a stone that appeared to be the largest in the tanzanite display. "How many carats is this, Mr. Zane?"

"Twelve. Nice, isn't it?" He angled back the glass top and removed it. "Cushion-cut. A lot of diamond work that's hard to see unless you're up close. The designer does very refined work." He picked up the velvet box. "Eight thousand pounds, this one."

Jury whistled. "Is this the priciest piece you have?"

"No. There's a necklace in the other case—" Zane nodded toward the rear. "—with a fifty-thousand price tag. But of course one has to consider the settings: platinum and diamonds."

Jury frowned. "Aren't you afraid of theft?"

"Our security system is pretty good."

"The couple who were shot, Mr. and Mrs. Moffit. Did you know them?"

"I didn't. They were Americans."

"Right." Jury raised his cup. "This is delicious coffee. But you knew of them. Or at least of him."

Zane didn't bother denying this. "It's true you can't just walk in here and go to the casino. We have pretty strict rules."

"I can imagine."

Zane sounded more amused than annoyed when he said, "Superintendent, there's something about my operation here that you clearly don't like."

"That's true. Two people were shot in your driveway."

"Yes. Getting back to the rules, though. We have a waiting list a mile long. And we do check up on the people on it."

"So you knew who was coming Friday evening?"

Zane nodded his head. "Yes. A few were interested in art. So they came to the gallery."

"But you didn't know Dr. Moffit?"

"He was a doctor?"

"A PhD in physics. He was a well-regarded physicist. And a gambler. But I'm sure you must have known that, if you 'check up' on your guests.

Apparently he was interested in applying quantum mechanics to gambling. I think he was barred from one casino."

Zane looked away, growing thoughtful. "I'm going to ask Maggie why that didn't turn up in the check. She does the vetting. What was he doing? Card-counting?"

"Much more complicated, I expect. Do you get that here?"

"Card-counting? Only once that I know of. An OBE." Zane smiled and shook his head. "I didn't want to make a big thing of it, so I just gave him a lifelong pass to the restaurant if he'd cease going to the casino."

"Sounds like he got the best of that deal if your chef's as good as you say."

"Oh, he did, but I wanted to get him out of the casino in case it encouraged card-counting in others."

"And you, do you like to gamble?"

"I like an occasional go at twenty-one."

"Do you win?"

"Sometimes. But not much. I'm not very good at it."

Jury just bet. "What about art? Is that a gamble?"

Zane smiled. Brilliant. "No more than many other aspects of life."

"Such as?"

"Well, we're sitting in the City, aren't we? The financial district?"

"But surely finance is much more fluid and frangible."

Zane laughed again. "Like love. Another gamble."

Jury thought his look as it slid from Jury's face was one of a man who'd tried his luck once too often and lost. It was hard to believe Leonard Zane would have woman troubles.

"This couple, the Moffits, you don't really know why they were here. Perhaps for dinner."

"You think David Moffit might not have been here for the casino? Pardon me, Mr. Zane, but that's ridiculous, given his gambling penchant." Jury's gaze was drawn once more to the painting that he had decided was not primitive, but a highly sophisticated version of the primitive. "Why doesn't she know?"

Zane's tone was puzzled. "I beg your pardon?"

"Sorry, I mean the woman in that painting seems unaware she's in the sights of a cheetah and a lion." He nodded toward the painting.

"Oh." Zane studied it for a moment or two before answering. "Perhaps she does. Maybe there's an understanding between them."

Jury had risen to get closer to the painting. "I don't see any sort of mutual acceptance. Look at their eyes."

"Perhaps you see something I don't."

"I doubt it. It looks like a Gauguin. But it isn't."

Zane smiled. "Why do you say that?"

"Because it's still here."

Zane laughed and rose to go and stand by Jury. "Very good. No, it isn't a Gauguin. This is by a Kenyan painter, Masego Abasi. Very much underappreciated here."

"So you've been to Kenya. To Nairobi?"

"Of course."

"The shooter is a Kenyan and apparently lives in Nairobi."

"Yes, I read about that. You believe it's more than a coincidence, I'm sure."

Jury shrugged, still looking at the inscrutable painting.

"I'm surprised that this painting hasn't sold even if it isn't Gauguin."

Zane touched the corner of the frame as if making an adjustment. "I could have sold it several times; I guess I'm not ready to let it go. Any other questions?"

Jury looked back at the wall of paintings. "You don't have others by this Kenyan?"

"Yes, but I haven't brought them out yet. I have several others."

As he did not offer to bring them out, Jury said, "Like this?"

"Most are. One other is a scene of Nairobi, quite dark—I mean sinister. Abasi's brother is a wealthy industrialist. They have widely differing views about Kenya and Africa." Zane drew in on his cigarette, exhaled a thin stream of smoke. "Abasi is virtually unknown here."

"You discovered him?"

"Nothing so grand. He was already discovered by Africa. His paintings hang in Johannesburg and Nairobi galleries, but nowhere else."

"Not in European ones."

Zane shook his head. "I'm the exclusive distributor here."

"Sounds like a deal."

"And that sounds like cynicism."

"So it isn't a deal? You introduce his paintings in Europe if he gives you exclusivity?"

"We worked something out that's mutually beneficial."

"I can imagine."

"No, you can't," said Leonard Zane, annoyed. "You don't know the art world."

No, but I know a deal.

As he was leaving, Jury turned and said, "It just occurred to me: your assistant mentioned you're looking for a croupier."

Zane laughed. "You're applying?"

"It'd make a change. No, but I do know a dealer who retired last year."

"I'd rather have someone youngish. You know, who'd appeal more to women."

How condescending, thought Jury. "He didn't retire because of his age; he just didn't care for the venue. He'd appeal, believe me. He's an oddly esoteric gambler. The place bored him to death."

Zane laughed. "First time I've heard that."

"Your place is anything but boring."

"We don't have a murder every day, remember."

Jury looked around. "I'm thinking of the ambience."

"I've interviewed a half dozen applicants already. The ones that got past Maggie Benn."

"What was the matter with them?"

Zane paused. "Well, I hate to sound like a snob—"

You already do.

"They might do well in Brighton, but not at the Artemis. We have to maintain a certain level of . . . sangfroid . . . you know."

Jury didn't, but said helpfully, "No hotheaded rubbish, then."

"Right. And after seeing these applicants, I've half a mind to take over the table myself." He picked up a deck of cards and skimmed them out across the table, flipped them back again.

His hands, Jury thought, were quite elegant, fingers long and supple. "You've had experience, then?"

"Of course. A sharp eye and extremely quick hands are paramount, right?" He reset the cards and shuffled them deftly. "So I'd be glad to see your retired dealer. I really need someone now. Could he come in, say, Monday?"

"I'm sure his calendar could make room for that."

12

W iggins was in the middle of tacking up newspaper cuttings and writing names on a large freestanding board when Jury walked into the office and asked him, quite bluntly, why in hell he was bringing this thing back.

"We should have a murder board, sir."

"We've been through all of that, Wiggins. And it's a whiteboard. Don't talk like we're a TV cop show." At least Wiggins wasn't frothing up that damned green matcha tea he'd lately taken to. "And when you've done with that get me information on the import regulations for gemstones, specifically tanzanite. It's mined in Tanzania in a place called Merelani." Jury looked at the board. "You keep reminding me this isn't our case. That we're just assisting DCI Jenkins. So why are you so determined to have a whiteboard for it?"

"It's helpful to get everything all in one place."

"Everything is never in one place." He smiled, because that sounded like something David Moffit would have said. "You've interrupted the Tweedears project, have you?" Jury could only hope, as he looked at the heavy notebook of sketch paper and the glass filled with colored pencils.

"No, not at all. But this takes precedence, wouldn't you say?"

Anything would take precedence, Jury didn't say. "Getting me this tanzanite information does."

Wiggins scratched his head. "Call Customs?"

"Try the Fraud Squad."

Wiggins picked up the phone.

Jury heard bits of talk about smuggling and VAT while he looked at Wiggins's glass of colored pencils. He plucked out a couple of them and went to the "murder board." There was a clipping attached from a Reno paper. Reno? When the receiver went down, he turned.

Wiggins said, "According to Fraud, restrictions have been tightened a lot because of all the smuggling and illegal export. This stuff's mined in Tanzania but China and India do a lot of import-export of it because they're such experts at cutting gems. Gems worth billions have been smuggled into Kenya. So you have to have a certificate of origin to show that the stuff actually comes from Tanzania—export permit and receipt, invoice on custom clearance, and freight forwarding certificate. That's in case there's a first and then second buyer. Something like that. The VAT is twenty percent; tax is five."

Jury whistled. "That's a chunk right there. If Leonard Zane wants to import, say, a hundred thousand pounds' worth of tanzanite, he's looking at a twenty-five percent loss."

"You think he's doing something illegal there?"

"Certainly possible." Jury thought about this. "If that gemstone can be found nowhere else in the world, imagine how the value rises as the supply goes down."

"Output decreased because of the lack of new deposits discovered. And the cost of mining in the small mines gets higher because they have to dig deeper. That's probably happening in his own mine, wouldn't you say?"

"I would." Jury paused. "Did Jenkins call?"

"Yes, but there doesn't seem to be any news of David Moffit's mother. Nobody's been able to get hold of her. Jenkins said the American embassy rang up her house in Connecticut and somebody—housekeeper? cook? butler? She must have money with that kind of staff—" Wiggins stopped when he saw Jury's expression. "Anyway, this housekeeper said Mrs. Moffit had gone to Oregon to visit a friend who had a cabin in the mountains and was 'off the map,' so to speak."

"Police? Local sheriff? For God's sake, the woman's son was murdered and the American police can't find her?"

"It's apparently very difficult. Jenkins is keeping in touch."

"Keeping in *touch*? Get me the American embassy. Now, Wiggins, please."

Wiggins picked up the phone, got the embassy and nodded to Jury, who picked up his. Jury told the official what he wanted. "What about this friend whose cabin Mrs. Moffit is visiting? Can't anyone find out where the place is by contacting this other woman's home? Family? Staff?" Jury listened. "Yes . . . yes . . . yes. Thanks." He came close to slamming down the receiver. "So the owner, a woman named Shriver, has never told anybody where the cabin is located. No phone, no TV. Electric supplied by a generator." Jury frowned. Call Jenkins and ask him if he can get on this. We've got to find David's mum before she reads the *New York Times*."

"Well, they're hardly getting newspaper delivery—"

Jury got up to look at the murder board. "What's Reno got to do with this?"

"Report I got on Leonard Zane. Seems Leonard Zane had a casino in the States, in Reno, where a man was shot eight years ago."

"He was shot *in* the casino?"

"In the hotel where the casino was located. The Metropole. Since closed. Shooter never identified." Wiggins slapped the file shut. "Bit of a coincidence, wouldn't you say?"

"Stripped bare of extenuating circumstances, yes. I take it that there are a few other salient details in that report."

Wiggins turned to the whistling kettle, unplugged it and poured the steaming water over his Tips tea bag. He held up an empty cup to Jury, who shook his head. Wiggins opened the file again. "Not much, really. Man's name was Danny Morrissey, from Champaign, Illinois. He was shot in his room at the Metropole. Taken to hospital. He was there several hours, released. No vital organs had been hit, just a wound to the shoulder. The only thing he said to journalists was that, no, he hadn't seen the person who apparently walked into his room, where he was standing looking out the window at the night sky." Wiggins stopped, added milk and four sugars to his tea.

"*And?*"

"Nothing much. No witnesses, except there was a couple who overheard an argument going on in the casino office, quite heated, they said, between a man and a woman. Finally, the man walked out. It was this Morrissey. But they never saw the woman."

"This was in the casino? If Zane was running it, he must have had something to say."

Wiggins shrugged. "Not in this report. Neither did his assistant manager—" Wiggins tapped one of the newspaper clips. "—Marguerite Banado. Quite a looker. Just the type Zane would want around." He untacked the column and handed it to Jury.

Jury looked at the woman in the picture, whose face was partially obscured by a magazine that she had raised to shield it from cameras, but the other part of her face and the long dark hair and décolletage were visible. Even from the little he could see of her, he thought her exotically beautiful. "I agree."

Wiggins went on: "She was there, heard nothing, saw nothing. Of course, there's a lot of shootings in gambling meccas—Las Vegas, Atlantic City, Indian reservations—"

"Indian reservations?"

Wiggins updated Jury on Native American culture and gambling and suggested he read a Tony Hillerman mystery and went on in this vein until Jury shut him up. "Thank you. But back to Reno. Didn't the police investigation turn up anything else?"

Wiggins held up the file. "This *is* the police investigation, sir."

Jury sighed. "Another visit to Mr. Zane sounds in order."

"Funny, though. I mean that Leo would be involved in the same thing twice." Wiggins frowned.

"'Leo'?"

"That's what his best friends call him. Everybody else says 'Leonard.' I read that in an interview. The man's always being interviewed. He's what you'd call 'hot.'"

Jury remembered Maggie Benn saying "Leo." "You know what inter-
ests me is this present assistant of his. She doesn't fit, somehow."

"You think she's more than an assistant?"

"No. She's less. Very plain, very sedate, very un-Artemis." Jury
frowned. "What have you got on her?"

"Nothing. But I expect DCI Jenkins does. It's *City Police*'s case, sir."

"But it's our murder board, Wiggins." Jury snickered.

"What gets me is this shooter 'Banerjee.'" Wiggins went on. "He trav-
els to Terminal Three in as ostentatious a way as could be found except
for landing in a helicopter. Has a first-class ticket on Emirates. He's
conned by a little kid, for God's sake. They go flying off to Dubai." Wiggins stirred his tea and frowned. "It's a helluva peculiar way to follow up a
shooting. You shoot someone, get in a cab, go to a station you're not leaving from, meet up with someone else, drive to Heathrow . . . I mean . . ."
Frowning, Wiggins looked at Jury. "He's larking around, almost."

Jury smiled. "Hardly, Wiggins."

Wiggins shrugged, drank his tea. "Well, then, acting like somebody
who's in no danger." He added, thoughtfully, "I wonder—how did this
Banerjee know where the Moffits would be?"

"He followed them."

"If you were going to shoot somebody, you wouldn't *follow* him to
his destination. You'd need to be there *already*."

"You're right. I meant he appears to have followed David Moffit
before that night. So then, the question is: who told him?"

"What about the cabbie?" said Wiggins.

"Parsons?"

"Couldn't he have been involved?"

"Robbie Parsons? Working with the killer?"

"The more I think about it . . . This was the vehicle Banerjee got
into. It was like a getaway car."

"So you don't think getting into that taxi was a split-second
decision?"

"Look at it this way: he couldn't have been following the cab—the
shooter, I mean. Banerjee would have to have been in place when the

cab arrived, wouldn't he? That incredible ride Parsons described, that was *his* description; he was the only one involved. We don't really know that's what happened, do we?" Wiggins got up. "Back in a tick."

As he left, Jury dug out the number Jenkins had given him and picked up the phone.

"Mr. Parsons? Superintendent Richard Jury here. Scotland Yard CID. I rang you three times this morning. You're not an easy man to get hold of."

"I am if you want a taxi."

Jury thought for a moment. "I want one."

"Where?"

"Can you pick me up in front of New Scotland Yard? Say in about a half hour?"

"Sure. Right now I'm in Southwark. Take me a while, with this traffic. What do you want?"

"To talk to you."

"'About what? I told you all I know."

"You think you did."

Robbie grunted. "Yeah. Are you hiring this cab? Or am I supposed to show some public-spiritedness?"

Jury laughed. "I think you've shown enough of that to last for a long while, Robbie. No, I'm hiring."

"Good. Where do you want to go?"

"Nowhere. Or, rather, just to drive." Jury looked at the wall clock.

"Okay. But don't sit in the backseat, Superintendent." Parsons laughed and rang off.

From the shelf where Wiggins kept his matcha tea powder and whisk, Jury extracted several squares of sketch paper. On one sheet was Wiggins's unfinished replica of the family crest. It looked much like a paint-by-numbers composition that he had been filling in.

He was, however, serious enough about his crest to have visited a heraldic artist and the result was framed and on the wall above his desk. This whole family coat of arms thing had started during a case in Baltimore when Wiggins had mentioned to a genealogist (one of the witnesses) what he thought was a relation to a very distant forebear named "Tweedears." Owen Lamb, the genealogist, had pulled down some dusty tomes and searched it out, discovering that Wiggins must be the last Tweedears, a baron de jure, the title having been forfeited, in abeyance, dormant, attainted—blinking on and off over the centuries, Jury thought, like a faulty neon sign.

Jury took paper and pencils to his desk and spread out three squares of paper. He did not have a compass and Wiggins's tea bowl wasn't big enough for the circles. His eyes slewed round the office until they fastened on a glass bowl that might once have contained flowers. He went to the shelf where it sat, carried it back to his desk and drew a green circle round its bottom to nearly fill the sketch sheet. He then drew a blue one and an orange one on the other two squares. His hand was steady and the circles were perfect. Above each he put a heading. Then he took up his pencil and started penciling in names.

This occupation immediately caught Wiggins's eye when he came back in. "What's this lot, then? You're doing sketches—?"

"Hope you don't mind my using your art equipment. That's the professional rendering, I take it?" Jury nodded toward the framed coat of arms.

Wiggins was clearly proud of it. "Hand-painted, twenty-four-carat gold. Cost me five hundred pounds, this did. I'm thinking now about an illuminated family tree." He returned to the colored circles: "Reno? London? Nairobi?" Wiggins was reading off the legends at the tops of the circles. "What are you doing?"

"Trying to rethink this case."

Wiggins took a step back, with an almost affrighted expression. "You're filling in names?"

"Of the people connected with the case in these three cities, yes. Isn't that obvious?"

The obviousness of the task was lost on the sergeant, who went back to his desk and matters of aristocracy and heraldry, taking up (the virtually unliftable) *Burke's Peerage, Baronetage and Knightage*, which fell open to the once Wykham, later Wiggins family. "The ancestor I remembered was Fitz-Hugh Wykham, ninth baron de jure." He cleared his throat and read: "Crest comprised of burning bush proper, with supports: Dexter, a swan; sinister, a fish, scaled."

At the whiteboard, Jury was tacking up the "Nairobi" circle and left it to join Wiggins at his own wall. "It's very intricate, isn't it? Very stylized and permanent. And the language: 'Dexter, a swan; sinister, a fish, scaled.' In other words a swan on the right and a fish on the left."

And a sigh from Wiggins.

Jury plowed on: "So you look at your coat of arms and see something sane, tightly connected. The connections are based on millennia of heraldry: rock solid, hammered down."

Wiggins jumped as Jury brought Wiggins's heavy spyglass down on his desk three times.

Jury turned toward the whiteboard. "Then you look at my circles and see them as sloppy, mutable, shifty, entangled. While your bear, rampant though he might be, is pinned into place, my Danny Morrissey is wandering all around the circle, a ghost in the machine. Unconnected to anything. Your crest is what you think evidence is; my circle is what it is not."

Wiggins frowned. "I don't know what you're talking about. Evidence can change. A future bit of evidence can change the old one."

Jury waved his hand. "That's merely exchanging a sure thing for a sure thing. What we want is an unsure thing. A wild guess, a leap of faith, a 'What if?' For example, what if we're wrong about the shooter? What if there was somebody else in that drive, out of sight?"

"Couldn't have been another person who got away without being seen."

"Melted into the crowd."

"At that point there was no crowd. If you don't mind my saying, sir, you're grabbing at straws."

"Which is exactly what I want to do." Jury plucked his coat off the hook, stuffed himself into it, said, "So I leave you with your long line of barons. *Du jour.* Bye."

Wiggins rushed to the door and yelled to Jury, already moving down the hall, "It's not du jour, it's de jure."

Without turning, Jury gave Wiggins a wave. "Soup of the day, Sergeant."

Five minutes later, Jury was out of his office and outside the building, standing near the revolving sign of New Scotland Yard.

Nearly perfect timing: Robbie Parsons pulled up in another two minutes. As he pulled out into Victoria Street, he said, "What? I didn't tell you everything? You think I was lyin'?"

"Not at all. But no one ever tells us 'all he knows,' because you don't know all you know."

"What's that? The Rubik's cube of police interrogation?" Robbie had blended into the stream of traffic going up Whitehall.

Jury laughed. "I simply mean there are details people leave out because they don't think of them at the time, or don't think them important."

"Believe me, I told you everything important."

"Come on, Robbie—does Sherlock miss clues that Watson could discern?"

A brief silence. "So you're Sherlock, I'm Watson?"

"The other way round."

They were driving along the Strand when Jury said, "I'll buy you a drink. The Coal Hole's just down there."

"And where'll I be parking?"

"Just pull into the Savoy's drive. I'll take care of it."

Robbie did so. Jury got out, had a word with the doorman as he showed him his ID and pointed along the drive. Then he got back into the cab.

"We'll be all right for half an hour."

"Misusing police authority, tut-tut."

"That's why you call us the Filth."

The Coal Hole had actually been the coal cellar for the Savoy Hotel. Jury had always liked it for the leaded windows surrounding its entrance; for its dark wood and many-roomed interior; for its wide selection of ales.

Seated at one of the small tables with their drinks in front of them, Jury said, "Tell me about this little girl, Patty Haigh."

Robbie gave a brief chuckle. "Looks like a little girl, but acts like MI6."

"Now there's an observation. Meaning what?"

"Cunning. Clever. Brave."

"Where does this child live? When she's at home?"

"Brixton."

"Parents, brothers, sisters?"

"No, no, and again, no."

"Who does she live with?"

"Some cousin or other. I heard she's on the game."

"Doesn't sound good," said Jury.

"Listen, I expect any kid can get on a plane to Kenya with a killer can handle the downside of life with a slapper, don't you?"

"It's a point. But this kid is still *in* Kenya."

"Why can't you lot get the cops over there to find her?"

"We lot have been trying. Only, a little girl in the heart of Nairobi? That's not easy. Especially one so resourceful as she is."

"Very resourceful. More than the Filth." Robbie raised his mug to toast one of them.

13

———

S everal streets later in what looked like a square in a better part of town, Patty stopped and sat down on a low stone wall.

Across the street was a little restaurant that seemed to be dedicated to soup, for its sign bore the words "Supa Bora," which, according to her phrase book, meant "good/best soup." She hadn't eaten in a long time and was extremely hungry.

After consulting her book to find the simplest words to use for ordering food, she jumped down from the wall and crossed the street. Looking through the window of this soup kitchen, she was reassured, for there were few people inside and all of them women. Only one table was occupied, by two women, and behind the counter a couple of servers dressed in orange and magenta. She realized then that orange and magenta were by way of being the little restaurant's "colors," for she could now see that the sign had been painted in alternating orange and purplish red.

She took out her phrase book again and looked up what would best pass for "I'm waiting for my mother." She did not have time for little words like "for" and "my," so she just took a word that meant "waiting" and assumed "mama" would be pretty much understood in any country, any language. "Waiting for Mama" would be sufficient to answer any question, since the questions would all resemble one another. "What are you doing here?" "Why are you alone?" "Why are you here?" Et cetera. It made no difference what a person might ask—and she wouldn't understand more anyway—the one answer would suffice.

Registering confidence and command, Patty opened the door and sailed right up to the counter and greeted the two servers with "*Jambo*" (her favorite word, along with "*kwaheri*" for good-bye) The two women wore bright turbans.

The middle-aged women at the table, who had followed Patty's progress with great curiosity, finally returned to their bowls, bread and talk.

One of the servers smiled at her and asked a question, which Patty realized was probably a request for her order and wouldn't be answerable with "Waiting for Mama," so she just brazened it out by picking the first item written on the chalkboard and wondered what they were slopping into the big bowl. Fish? It looked like a biggish piece. If it turned out to be meat of some kind, she would eat around it. She did not want to take out the bills that B.B. had given her and that she'd rubber-banded into a roll, so she managed to separate a couple from the roll in the backpack, brought the notes out and raised her eyebrows as if asking, "Enough?"

She was given her bowl, bread and change. From a cutlery basket she pulled out a spoon. She carried all of this to an empty table, pleased with the transaction; it shored her up knowing she could survive in this country on her own. One of her life lessons from Charlie the dip had been, "Money talks." (He would have told her to toss away her phrase book.)

It was fish soup and it was very good. But she frowned when she began to wonder why she thought it was all right to eat fish if it wasn't all right to eat beef and chicken and pork. After all, fish were living things. Unfortunately, she had just spooned up pieces of carrot and tomato and now she was worrying about vegetables. If "living things" was the yardstick against which she should measure food, she'd starve. So she added "that can feel pain." But how did she know a carrot didn't hurt, or a tomato weep in some strange ways that humans would never understand?

It was only when she heard a screech of laughter that she realized she'd sat down at the table next to the two women. One was dark as ebony, the other pale and looking like a ghost beside the sturdy black woman. It was the ghost who'd screeched. Now they were both laughing, but quietly, as the ghost told a tale that seemed to encompass a visiting family. Patty was delighted to know that the woman was English—no, American, or maybe Canadian. It was not only the flat vowels, but the way she was handling knife and fork. She'd taken a largish piece of meat out of her bowl, cut it up, switched the fork from left hand to right, in that wasteful way of Americans, and now was talking about a family named "Nelson," with whom she had some connection Patty hadn't discerned as yet.

Promptly, Patty took one of her notebooks from the pack, along with a rollerball, wrote down "Nelson" and waited.

The American went on and Patty strained to listen; she could not catch every word, but she heard enough to make sense of it: "Says Emma—she runs the place—'You'll like this one, Betts.'" Here the timbre of the voice notched itself upward, so she must be quoting "Emma" and she herself (Patty inferred) must be "Betts." "'New York . . . three kiddies, but you'll only have to watch over the littlest one while the others are out sightseeing—'"

Here the voice trailed off, and the other woman picked up the conversation with questions. "Where are they—?"

Patty couldn't hear the end of this. But she heard the answer.

"Hemingways—" Blur of words.

Ernest Hemingway? Of course not. Something named—Patty thrust her hand into her backpack and pulled out her guidebook and looked up the name in the index. Hemingway, Ernest. Beneath that, "hotel." She flipped to that page. Wow.

The black woman didn't say "Wow," but her indrawn breath would, if breath, like money, spoke. "They rich?"

Betts, the ghost, said, "Piles of it, says Emma. They come every—"

Patty had it: Betts was some sort of caregiver, probably babysitter or nanny, registered at this agency run by Emma. She was to babysit the Nelsons' kids, the Nelsons from New York who would be staying at the luxurious Hemingways Hotel. And from the pictures in the guidebook (just look at that mirrored bathroom!) and the number of dollar signs heading the description, the Nelsons weren't hurting for money. Patty patiently waited for their arrival day.

And got it within another two minutes. ". . . New York . . . Cape Town. Their plane . . . Tuesday morn . . . I'm to meet . . . until Sunday. Good post," said Betts, wasting effort on switching her fork again.

Patty flicked the pages back to the Hemingways description: pool, spa, restaurants, twenty-four-hour room service. There were little pictures. A white-clothed table with tea things. Check-in time, three P.M. Check-out time, eleven A.M. They always got you, didn't they? Hotels. Kicked you out early; made you wait all day to let you in. Got paid twice for the room, to boot.

No more talk about the Nelsons was forthcoming; the women appeared to be packing up to leave, getting into coats, collecting parcels. When the black woman rose, she looked at Patty, bent down and asked if she was all right. Assumed Patty spoke English, apparently.

"*Bora*," said Patty, surprising the woman.

Now they were joined by Betts. "You're not English, then? American?"

"From London," said Patty, stirring her soup a little.

"So what are you doing alone here, pet?" Betts said, practicing her nanny skills.

She did not need to say "Waiting for Mama." "I'm going to meet up with my family. We're all staying at Hemingways Hotel."

Patty had thought vaguely of finding a room for the night; she knew she had plenty of money, but hotel people would have plenty of questions. A small girl asking for a hotel room? Money might talk, but so did managers, and to police and to the Social. She was sure the Social Service stuck their noses into kids' lives here just as they did in England. Some Kenyan version of the Social.

Hemingways (according to the guide map) was a couple of miles from Nairobi's center, about a mile from the Karen Blixen Museum and the Karen Hospital. The hotel looked too far to walk to; she would have to get a cab. It was in the Karen district. Patty wondered who Karen was; she must be famous. The Karen district also looked in the guidebook to be pretty expensive. Big homes, walls, gates.

After the cab dropped her in front of the glamorous hotel, Patty walked through the vast glass door held open by a doorman who had an inquiring eyebrow and whom she ignored. Walked up the marble stair, watched herself in the mirrored lobby for two seconds and then walked over to a little desk, in front of which sat two chairs and behind which sat a well-groomed youngish woman who radiated authority.

"I'm Janice Nelson," said Patty, radiating her own authority. "My dad made a reservation for the family for Tuesday. Our plane from Cape Town was grounded at the airport—" Which one? Which one? Oh, yes. "—in Johannesburg and there weren't enough seats for all of us, including my aunt, so Aunt Monique and I got on the plane to Nairobi. My father had business in Johannesburg, he discovered, so had to stay anyway. Then Aunt Monique got sick while we were in the Karen Blixen Museum and had to go to the hospital, so she sent me on here. With money." Here Patty took out the fattest of her rolls and quietly placed it on the counter. "So if you could just give me a single room for three nights, that will be okay." The look on her face said that yes, of course they could.

The surprised expression on the hotel clerk's face suggested, Not so fast. "Why, that's just awful, dear . . ."

Ho-hum, thought Patty.

But she did check her slim computer monitor, saying, "Ah, yes, the Nelsons. Arriving on Tuesday. If you'll just wait here, I'll get our manager to have a little talk with you."

Patty thought it safe to assume she wasn't going to call the police. Patty had a history; she had a family; she had money. No, the clerk really was going to get the manager, or someone managerial.

And here he came, reminding her of a black swan in his sleek black clothes and dark hair. Tall, long-necked, and rake-thin, he bent down to have a parley with her. Hands on knees, his elbows out like wings, he said, "Now, Meees Jan-ees. What seems the problem?"

Nicely, Patty shrugged. "There *is* no problem, sir. I explained to this lady—" The desk clerk still hovered. "—about getting separated." Bad word to use. "About my dad's business in Johannesburg and me coming on to Nairobi with my aunt. The family's coming on Tuesday, as you know. If you're sus*picious* about me, all I can say is I can pay for a room in advance." She thumbed up the roll of shillings, which she retrieved from the counter.

"Not at all, not at all, no suspicion, Meees Jan-ees. Just I think maybe I call your father? Your mother? To let them know you're here—"

"Go ahead, but I don't see how you can since right now they're probably up in the air."

"But then your auntie?—"

Patty shut her eyes, blocking out thickheadedness. "Like I said, poor Aunt Monique is in the Karen Hospital. She got violently ill from something, probably plane food. Look, I'm really tired; all I want is to go to bed." She recalled the description of Hemingways. "—And maybe a little room service. So please—?" Patty smiled quite brilliantly.

The manager became all business, signaling to one of the bellhops (or whatever they were called in Kenya), a small, rather elderly man who quickstepped to their party of three. "Take this young lady's bag—"

The young lady was quite happy to be relieved of what was becoming a very heavy weight, so she unslung it from her shoulder and held it out to the little man.

"To room—"

Here he looked rather helplessly at the clerk, who quickly held out a key card.

She said, "This one I think best." She smiled at Patty as the manager directed the bellhop.

"I'm quite sure you will be comfortable, Meees Jan-ees," said the manager, almost clicking his polished heels together. "If you need anything—"

"There's room service," said Patty, as she walked off with the little man, who seemed nearly collapsed around her simple backpack. "Good night."

The porter led her through the long sitting room and outside to a white corridor, up a few steps, down a few, and past rooms (or suites) that had been named after famous Africa-connected people. He stopped at one and unlocked the door for her.

The room was wonderful, with its crisp white window curtains, creamy bedspread and pillows and private bath. Immediately, she checked all of the little bottles and soaps and asked the porter if the shower was easy to work. He assured her it was by turning it on himself. Simple, see?

Patty peeled off a bill and was truly delighted by his gratitude, his shocked look, and wondered how much she'd given him. She didn't care.

First she called room service and ordered its version of hot chocolate and Triple Decadence Chocolate Cake. Then she undressed and took a shower. She reckoned it was her fourth in twenty-four hours.

In the morning she could have breakfast in bed and then another shower.

She would not have to abide by the check-out time. The Nelsons wouldn't be checking in until Tuesday. That meant she could spend two whole days using all of the facilities of the Hemingways Hotel—the pool, the restaurants, the cream tea in the lobby, room service room service room service. On Tuesday, all she had to do was pick up her backpack and leave. After her morning shower.

14

"Safari?" said Melrose Plant, as he sat before his living-room hearth, uncluttered by embers and his aunt, thank God. Richard Jury had to be joking. "Kenya? Me? Leave on Monday?"

"Or Tuesday."

"Don't be daft. That's only two days to prepare for a trip *to Africa?*" Melrose's voice was beginning to squeak with disbelief.

"It's either a safari or a croupier. The croupier job would involve coming to London on Monday. Take your pick."

"Croupier? What the devil are you talking about, Richard?"

"Artemis Club. In the City." Jury paused. "This is a onetime offer. It won't come again. Choose."

Melrose prepared to laugh like hell, but managed only a bark. "*Onetime* offer? You mean if I don't take you up on either of these jobs here and now, you'll never ask me again?"

"That is correct."

"Is this the most ridiculous conversation we've ever had?"

"No, we've had more ridiculous."

"Richard, read my lips—"

"This is a telephone."

"I don't want to be *either* a croupier *or* a great white hunter—"

"Okay. I'm ringing Trueblood."

"Trueblood? Hold on! May I ask—"

No, he mayn't. Melrose did not so much hear the deadness of the line as feel it. He shook the receiver. It was one thing to turn down an offer from Jury to work on a case; it was quite another to turn down an offer that would then be extended to Marshall Trueblood.

As soon as he hung up, Melrose called for Ruthven, who came with all deliberate speed (for Ruthven), and asked him to tell Martha to hold dinner back as he would be going out for an hour. The butler collected Melrose's cap and coat, helped him on with them and held the door.

It was a fine evening. He should walk. No, he shouldn't. It would take too long. In another five minutes he was in the garage and in his Bentley.

In another fifteen minutes he was out of his car in front of the village's single pub, the Jack and Hammer. He saw them through the window—Vivian Rivington, Joanna Lewes, and Diane Demorney. All three women appeared to be concentrating on something in front of them, but from his position on the walk outside he couldn't see it. He took a few steps. Ah, there was Marshall Trueblood, who owned the antiques shop next door. He was bending down, looking at something. Melrose stopped peering at them from the outside and went inside.

They were looking at cards. Playing cards. There were chips. There was a card shoe.

Melrose checked his watch. Twenty minutes since he had hung up the phone. Twenty minutes and Marshall Trueblood was sharpening his dealer skills.

"Ah, Melrose," said Trueblood. "Just in time! Care to sit in?"

"Absolutely not. I just talked to Richard Jury."

"Did you? So did I. He needs a croupier."

"How did you get all of this together in twenty minutes?"

"Well, it's just a deck of cards and some poker chips."

"And a shoe. Where'd you get a shoe? And isn't that thing Mrs. Withersby appears to be polishing a roulette wheel? Where'd you get all of this stuff?"

"My shop. Have you forgotten it's right next door?"

"But who in hell had a sale? The Hippodrome?"

"One finds the odd lot here and there—"

"In Monte Carlo, maybe."

"Good grief, Melrose, why so agitated? I just gathered the few things I'd picked up here and there and came here to get my hand in. Place your bets, please!"

Melrose squeezed his eyes shut. It was absolutely infuriating to hear Trueblood already in dealer mode.

Joanna and Diane shoved several white and green chips out. Vivian appeared to be considering.

Diane asked for one card; Joanna asked for two. Vivian scratched her head.

"What in hell are you playing?" asked Melrose.

"Twenty-one. Join us."

"No."

Trueblood slapped two cards down for Joanna, a nine of hearts and a two of clubs; one card for Diane, a king of hearts.

Diane smiled. "Twenty-one," she said, turning over an ace.

Trueblood also smiled. "Good, but no better than mine." Trueblood turned over another ace.

"Hell," said Diane.

"Not to worry. At least you didn't lose." He shoved back her chips, then scooped up Joanna's and Vivian's. "How about a hand, Melrose? Come on."

"I'm no good at cards."

"Don't be daft. This is the simplest game in the world. You're not playing against one another, only against the house." He went on to establish the rules and the value of the chips: "White, one pound; red, five; green, twenty-five; black, a hundred."

"I'd be playing against you, you mean?"

"Correct. I'm the house."

"No, thanks. What did he tell you?"

Trueblood frowned. "Who?"

"Richard Jury, of course. The job shop manager."

"Offered me a job. Two jobs, actually: this one—" He held up some chips. "—as croupier at a London casino, or another, which was a safari in Africa: Kenya, to be exact. Possibly even Botswana, Mozambique, South Africa."

"You don't have to list them all," said Melrose irritably. "Where is this casino?"

"In the City. The owner's been interviewing prospects." Trueblood dealt one card to each of the three players.

They looked at their cards.

"Place your bets, please."

"But you have no experience as a croupier."

"Well, good Lord, I've been to enough casinos in my time to know what they do."

"That's all? I think you'd need a lot of practice for the kind of sleight of hand dealers need."

"Oh, for heaven's sake. It's not sleight of hand. It's just quickness." Trueblood picked up a fresh deck of cards and butterflied the entire pack from one hand to another without dropping a single card. It was all a blur, a flutter of cards.

"Where'd you learn to do that?"

Trueblood laughed, but said nothing. "Bets? Viv?"

Vivian shoved two green chips forward. Diane pushed in a black one.

"Wow!" said Melrose. "A hundred quid?"

Diane gave him a look

"Anyway," said Trueblood, "there'll be a trial period before the post is definite. Cards?"

"One," said Diane.

"One," said Vivian.

"Two," said Joanna.

Trueblood slapped down their cards. Joanna's showed a king and an ace.

"Too much!" said Trueblood, raking her chips across the table into the plastic holder.

"Bloody hell," said Joanna, turning over her third card, a six.

"What about the safari job?" said Melrose. "Didn't you like the sound of it?"

Trueblood was sifting a pile of chips in his hand. "I did, rather. But I thought the casino job would be less taxing."

"What did he tell you about the safari?"

"That he wanted someone in Nairobi. The safari would begin in a luxury tented camp on the outskirts of the city."

Scoffingly, Melrose said, "That's not much of a safari! Hemingway would laugh himself sick."

"You talked to Jury. Why are you asking me all of this?"

"Because he didn't give *me* any information. Not a scrap."

"Did you evince any interest in his plan?"

"No."

"Then why should he?"

"You two just kill me," said Diane.

They both looked at her.

She went on: "You're talking about casinos and safaris and neither one of you knows why, do you?"

"Why what?" said Trueblood.

"Why he wants you to *do* these things."

Trueblood neatened his cards. "He has his reasons."

"It's all a game to you, isn't it?" said Vivian.

"You got that right. Bets, please!"

15

Although Jury usually found that these little mews enclaves tried much too hard to hold on to their barn door origins while at the same time being cloyingly cute, he thought the Moffits' first-floor flat pleasantly old-style British: three-bar firelit, with cretonne-covered furniture, breezy draperies, solid tables, and general no-nonsense livability.

Or he supposed it was now Claire Howard's flat and felt unaccountably annoyed that it should be. He wanted to be met at the door, not by the mother-in-law, but by David Moffit himself; he wanted to talk to him about the stars; wanted to go over that huge volume on the planets he saw was now unshelved and lying on the floor; wanted to position that telescope on the little balcony that Jury was sure was its rightful place, not hobbled in a corner by an umbrella stand.

This went through his mind in the few seconds after he'd stepped inside the living room. He looked into the cobalt-blue eyes of Rebecca's mother, a woman whose beauty he didn't give a damn about. "Mrs. Howard? I'm Richard Jury. Scotland Yard CID. I'm sorry about your daughter and son-in-law."

"It's inexpressible." She seemed to gulp in air. "So I won't say anything."

"I understand that. But I expect you have questions—"

Eyes closed, she held out her hand, a restraining palm warding off "questions." Eyes open, she said, "Please come in." She held the door wide and it was then that he saw the signs of clearing-out. Inside the door were boxes packed with clothes and crockery. Immediately his eye had fallen on the forlorn telescope, left to rove not the sky but a dark corner. He felt ridiculous, being so saddened by this sight.

Inviting him to take one of the cretonne-covered easy chairs, she offered him a drink. Interesting: not tea, not coffee, but whisky. Nevertheless, he took it.

While she went to get the drinks, he noticed on the desk near his chair a group of silver-framed photographs, family, he supposed: Claire Howard and her daughter, Claire alone, the two of them with a good-looking man Jury thought might be the father. A shot of what looked like a gallery event, people milling and drinking champagne (if the flutes were evidence). He got up and looked more closely to see if it could be the Zane Gallery, but it clearly wasn't, not with that configuration of other rooms visible through the doors. In the first room there appeared to be an ice sculpture on a table holding bottles and glasses. So this was, apparently, an event, a show. Claire Howard was talking to a dark-haired woman whose back was to the camera, face partially turned to Claire. One stunning photo of Rebecca and David (but how could it be other than stunning with those two?), another with what must have been family members round a Christmas tree in an old house. High Wycombe, perhaps? Two more of Claire with different women friends. Claire Howard missed no opportunity to get her face in front of a camera, it seemed.

On the walls, Jury saw more signs of the denuding: lighter squares where pictures had been removed, one small vaguely familiar-looking painting resting against the floor molding below the nail on the wall where it had apparently hung. The bookshelves were half empty, many of the books stacked on the rug that ran the length of the shelf, one very large one opened to a brilliant photo of the constellations. There were small items stacked in one corner, all of these things being readied for packing, he supposed, given the several brown boxes already closed up and standing in the kitchen.

On the lower shelf of the bookcase several photograph albums were heaped. Jury asked whose collections they were.

"Oh, those are mine," she said, pressing a glass of whisky into his hand. "I expect I'm overly sentimental."

No, he thought, you're not sentimental, certainly not overly. He sipped the whisky. Why hadn't she peppered him with questions about the shooting of her daughter? Painful, yes. But not knowing, surely more so. Yet some response to her remark was apparently required, some sort of nice assessment of her sentimentality.

"Either that or you prefer representations of objects rather than the real thing." He didn't add to that, letting her process it herself.

"I'm sorry?" she said, not comprehending.

"Oh, nothing. Just thinking aloud and not very well. I wonder, could I see those?" He nodded toward the albums.

A little stiffly, she rose, went to the bookcase and brought back one.

He took it and turned pages. Most of the snapshots were of Claire herself or her and one friend or another. There were a few of Rebecca, but only one he noticed of David. When he turned another page he found what must have been the occasion of their wedding in Connecticut, so it must have been on the Moffit estate. The album was largely of the wedding. And David was largely cut out of it. There were many shots of Rebecca looking ethereally beautiful. Yet only two of these showed her with David, who didn't look too much of this world himself. Had Jury been the parent of either, he would have wanted the two of them plastered poster-size all over his walls.

There were as many pictures of Claire Howard as of the bride. Most of them with her arm slung about the shoulders of one or another of the wedding guests. One where she posed between a good-looking couple, another of her with her arm round the female half of that couple, who seemed to bear a resemblance to David.

"Could this be David Moffit's mother?" He turned the album, tapped the picture.

"Oh, that. No. They were friends of the Moffits. Exceptionally nice people. I met them sometime later in the Caymans."

"Where is his mother in all of these pictures? His father is dead, I know. We're having a hard time locating his mother."

"Well . . ." She had taken the album and was looking. "You know, I don't see her . . . Somehow, this particular photographer must have missed her."

Jury laughed shortly. "But this was *her* particular photographer, wasn't it? Isn't this her estate? Be a bad PR stroke to miss her." It would be unthinkable.

"You seem to know a good deal about them." Claire Howard's tone was quizzical. When Jury made no comment she went on: "I agree. Or perhaps I just wasn't given those pictures." She seemed to want to keep the album, so Jury held out his hand. "Mind?"

She turned a couple of pages, telling him there was a beautiful photograph of Rebecca here. Then she handed it back.

Indeed there was, and Jury went back to the pages she'd skipped. Two pages of random, unrelated pictures, unposed, just people caught. Yet Claire managed a pose even if caught, as here on some beach, there on some dance floor: it was as if she noticed a split second before the shutter came down that the camera was aimed at her and adjusted herself—time to throw out a hip, to arrange a hand. Just in time, he could tell. There were a few loose pictures of the Christmas tree and a family round a dinner table—ten or twelve—Claire and Rebecca both there. Children, dogs, cats, presents. A smaller shot of Claire in the same gallery, with the same paintings through open doors. There were two very posed shots of Rebecca and Claire on a settee, the same handsome man as appeared in one of the silver frames on the desk leaning over them, his arms crossed on the back of the settee. Another of him with Rebecca alone. There were several at what could have been any racing venue, this one looking to Jury like Cheltenham, as he thought he recognized the track. Rarely did he have a chance to go to the races, but a case had taken him to this one.

"You seem truly fascinated by those pictures, Superintendent."

He was looking now at one of Claire Howard in which she was wearing a necklace the color of her eyes, further enhancing the blue.

"This necklace is something." He turned the album toward her. "Is it tanzanite, by any chance?"

She looked surprised. "You must know gemstones."

"No. I've just been to the Zane Gallery. It's his thing."

"Really? I got this at a jeweler's."

"Where? I'm rather surprised an actual jeweler would be selling tanzanite."

That was disconcerting.

"Oh. Well, this one was. Somebody in Bond Street. I can't recall the name."

He was tempted to ask her to get the necklace, but that wouldn't have helped him and would merely have put her on her guard.

She was adding another drop of whisky to his etched-glass tumbler, more than another drop to her own.

He picked his up and looked again round the room. "You're clearing things," he said.

"Clearing—"

"Packing up everything." And it was only Sunday, he didn't add.

She sighed. "Yes, but I can hardly bear to pack things up."

"Then why do it?"

"What—?" She seemed surprised. "I've been packing some of Rebecca's things. Hard to live here with all of these signs . . . you know what I mean."

He didn't help her. "But you don't actually 'live' here, do you, Mrs. Howard? Haven't you a house in High Wycombe?"

"Well, yes. How did—?"

Since she didn't finish the question, he supposed she had worked out that the police had ways of knowing such details in investigations.

She went on: "The family house, of course. Some of those Christmas shots were taken there. Drafty old place. I can't afford to keep it up, never could. Now I'll be spending much more time in London." She sighed. "Look, I know you need to ask questions. So go right ahead. It won't be any easier for me to answer them tomorrow or next week or even next year." She set down her drink and put her hand to her face.

The gesture was so poignant that Jury couldn't help but empathize.

"How can I help you, Superintendent?"

Jury said, "Well, perhaps you can speculate as to why anyone would want to kill your daughter."

Shocked, she flinched. "But—surely it was David who was the target? He was a gambler, and I assumed he'd made enemies—"

"He was a physicist." Jury felt he should defend the man's reputation since she seemed willing to impugn it.

She accepted this correction with grace. "He was, yes. David was a highly intellectual, talented man with a very original mind. I just wish he hadn't dragged Rebecca along with him."

"You mean here?"

"I mean everywhere."

"She could have refused, Mrs. Howard."

"Not easily. He was also a very domineering man."

That didn't at all fit the man Jury had met. Certainly not the implied attitude toward his wife, whom he clearly adored. "You daughter came to London often?"

"Many times. That's why they bought this flat."

"Has she friends here?"

Again, Claire Howard looked perplexed. "You do seem to want to make this about *her*, Superintendent."

"It's not that I want to, I just want to avoid assuming anything about a case. The point is—" Jury shoved his glass aside to lean toward her. "Why would this man shoot *her* if he was the target?"

"She was a witness."

Jury shook his head. "He didn't shoot the cab driver."

"Then you're saying he really meant to murder both David and my daughter. But why?"

Jury pulled his glass back. "Was Rebecca familiar with her husband's business affairs?"

"He was a teacher, that's all his business was." She sipped her whisky.

Claire Howard didn't like David Moffit, thought Jury. And he found this very strange, unless there was a particular reason for it. "A full professor at Columbia. I expect—" He'd been about to say *a very good one.*

"Yes. Well." Dismissing the professorship, she picked up her glass and this time didn't sip, but drank most of the contents in two gulps.

"Is there anything they might have done, the two of them, that would make both of them targets?"

She did not take umbrage at the suggestion that her daughter was being linked to her gambling son-in-law in something despicable. Instead, she said, "If it had happened in the States, why in heaven's name would someone shoot them down in London?"

"True. But it's surprising the lengths a person might go to for revenge, or to keep himself out of it. I don't mean to make too much of this. It's just that the killer, the shooter, wanted to kill them both. One of them, either David or Rebecca, was *not* a decision made at the moment. He wouldn't need to kill the other one. I think this man was hired—or otherwise enlisted—by someone who told him to kill both of the Moffits."

She was thinking deeply, judging from her frown. "Look, David was a gambler who spent a lot of money doing it, and, as I said, probably making enemies. He won a lot."

"Are you suggesting some connection to organized crime?"

She laughed. "David? You've seen *Ocean's Eleven* too many times. I don't think David was in debt to a casino. He was too clever for that."

Jury smiled. "Cleverness and gambling generally don't go hand in hand."

"You don't understand. David was rich. His family has a fortune. We're talking about a lot of money, very old money. And why are you ignoring the obvious?"

"Am—"

She didn't wait for his answer. "Superintendent, David, for all of his faults, was a brilliant man. He didn't have debts; he had a system. He literally broke the bank in an Atlantic City casino and was barred. So he learned to use his system to make modest winnings and even lose at times. I guess he was one of those rare gamblers who could actually control the arena, as it were; I mean walk away."

Glancing at the small painting leaning against the wall, he said, "You've been to the Artemis Club gallery, have you?"

Quickly, she looked around. "That? That's something Rebecca must have picked up."

"Then she'd been there before?" Jury found that strange, since no one there remembered her.

"I expect she got it at some gallery or other."

Jury rose and moved over to the picture, bent down to study it. "It's a Masego Abasi." This painting too showed a woman by a lagoon. It might have been a smaller study for the one in the Zane Gallery. Only in this one, there was a lion but no other animal. "Abasi is a Kenyan artist. Had your daughter been to Nairobi?"

"Not that I know of."

"Well, the owner of the Artemis Club has exclusive rights to show his paintings. So perhaps she or David might have been there."

"I don't know. She never mentioned it. I've never been to the Artemis Club, myself."

"Since this is apparently going to be packed away, I wonder if you'd be willing to loan it to me for a short while. I'll write you a receipt. The police take good care of things. I'll return it to you in a day or two." He had taken out his notebook and was already making out a receipt for the picture.

She frowned. "But why would you want it?"

"Just to show it to the owner of the Zane Gallery, find out its provenance."

"Well . . . I expect that's all right. I'll get some wrapping paper." She was soon in the kitchen, securing it.

He thanked her, placing the painting on the coffee table. He wrapped it and asked if she had some tape or string.

Again, she went into the kitchen, returned with a roll of Sellotape.

He said, "I have another request." He nodded toward the album. "Could I have some of those loose snapshots? It would help in the investigation."

"I can't think why." She shrugged and moved to the table on which it lay. She turned the pages and finally stopped, pulling out the picture of Rebecca and two or three others. "I can't stand to be without this one." She held up the one of Rebecca. "Here. Take what you want."

Having finished taping up the painting, he took the album. He went to the center of the album, scooped out a number of the snapshots. "Thanks so much for this."

She breathed more easily, glanced at her watch and said, "I'm so sorry, I've a theater date with an old friend that's been planned for weeks and I don't want to disappoint."

"Of course not. On a Sunday, though? I didn't know the West End was open for business." He had pocketed the small pictures and now picked up the wrapped painting.

"A few are. This one's in Piccadilly. *Jersey Boys*."

Jury blinked. "I'll help you get a cab."

"I expect in the circumstances you must think my going to the theater is rather crass. But my friend has had a very hard time of it too, and I—" She shrugged.

"No explanation necessary." He helped her on with her coat, his never having come off, and they left the house, he with the painting under his arm. Plenty of cabs on Upper Sloane Street, but he saw one and hailed it before they got there.

She smiled as he held the door for her. "Thank you so much. If you've any more questions, I'll be glad to help out."

He slammed the door, then looked at the cab as it drove away, and remembered: *In the circumstances you must think my going to the theater is rather crass.*

Maybe not if she'd been going to see *Hamlet* or even Harold Pinter. But *Jersey Boys*?

RAZORBITE

16

"Have a look at these, Wiggins." Jury dropped the pictures he'd taken from the album on Wiggins's desk. "See if you can get forensics to blow up the one of the gallery. I want to see the paintings on the walls if possible. I want to find out where it is."

Which ones hadn't she wanted him to see again? Was it the one of mother and daughter on a settee with the man leaning over the back of it? The one in the unidentified gallery? The one of Claire arm in arm with the couple in the Caymans?

At the time appointed for Marshall Trueblood's "interview" on Monday, Jury met him in front of the Artemis Club, Jury having come by Ford, Trueblood by Porsche—one he had acquired at an auto auction. He parked it in the driveway, not quite beside and yet not unbeside Zane's Lotus Elan.

When Jury walked up to him, Trueblood said, "Hope that's okay, sport."

"And I hope this new job isn't going to have you talking like Gatsby."

"What? Did you get hold of Melrose? Is he going to do the Kenya gig?"

"Why is every job a gig these days?" said Jury, as they walked through the front door.

Trueblood whistled. "Quite a setup." He looked around at the warm furnishings of the library and the brown velvet cushions of the dining-room chairs, the oil-rubbed mahogany staircase, the mirror-sparkle of the casino.

"It's quite exclusive," said Jury.

"I hope so. Who wants to work in a rubbishy place?"

Jury smiled. "You two should get on."

When it came to pure presentation, Marshall Trueblood was a match for any man, including Leonard Zane.

Marshall wore a navy-blue merino wool with a navy shadow pin-stripe from a tailor in Venice ("The same as runs up your Count Dracula's capes," he had later said to Vivian); he had kept the shirt and tie out of competition (off-white and subdued blue) as if even here he was practicing his gambling skills.

Jury hoped his performance would match his presentation.

He introduced Trueblood to Zane, and when they moved from the office out to the tables, he said to Trueblood, sotto voce, "Are you really skilled at this sort of thing? Or were your abilities merely honed sitting around the Jack and Hammer playing poker?"

"I'm very good at it. I was taught by a master."

"Really? Who?"

"Me."

Zane emptied a large bag of chips on the felt and said, "Let's see how fast you can count."

Count? Trueblood smiled as his two companions watched the chips fairly vaporize before coming to stand in neat stacks of five, ten, twenty, fifty and a hundred pounds.

Marshall Trueblood had grown up in a seaside town on the south coast where boardwalk slot machines were not supposed to be used by little boys, but somehow the boys managed to use them. Surveillance was not that good at the Dolphin Arcade and the Seahorse and the Brass Horseshoe.

Still, it wasn't the slot machines when he was six or the flight simulators when he was eight but a game of his own which he invented when he was ten, then took to his public school and made so popular that he had a waiting list to play a year long. The game was popular not just because the winnings were so high but because it was so dangerous, and Marshall was a master at it. Every kid wanted to be him.

The game consisted of dumping a large pile of single-edged razor blades on a table, much as Leonard Zane had dumped the poker chips, and seeing who could collect the most without getting nicked. If you drew blood (yours or a classmate's) you were out of the game.

He called it Razorbite.

Trueblood was the "house" and everyone else played against him. The celebrity, the honor, the glory that attached to a boy who could beat Trueblood was enticement only the most sensible twelve-year-olds could resist. And how many of those were there?

Cricket, football, tennis—St. Eglantine having excellent teams in all of those—couldn't come close to Razorbite in attracting St. Eglantine's students.

All of the chemists in the area sold out of razor blades, as did the local Sainsbury's. Medicine cabinets at home were denuded of blades, fathers unable to understand where the ones recently purchased had gone.

To play the game took a lot of practice and a lot of nerve. There were levels of increasing difficulty, depending on the skill of the competitors. But even at its lowest level (razor blades spread on the concrete surface of the school's rear drive) it was very difficult and the boys were always getting cut. Thus one of the unfortunate results was that the masters began to notice a lot of sticking plasters in their classes.

Boys from every form participated. There was an entrance fee of fifty pence for every game played, and the boys were eliminated one by one until there were six left, then four, then two. The entry fee climbed as the number of players decreased. If a player couldn't come up with the three- or five-pound fee when it got down to six and four contestants, Trueblood extended credit. He was at the end carrying chits around amounting to over two hundred pounds, but every debt was settled. There was a lot of honor riding on this game, far more than on the school code regarding cheating.

The second-best player was Conleith Murdock, which came as a surprise to the others, as Murdock was a thin, introspective lower-sixth-former, uninterested in sports and completely uncompetitive in any other area—girls, grades, grub—and was almost apologetic about his mastery of Razorbite, but, at the same time, obviously gratified to be the next best to Marshall Trueblood. Connie's family was relatively poor, his parents using every penny they could scrape together to keep their son at St. Eg's. Conleith wound up with a debt to Trueblood of over a hundred pounds. He paid this off by winning at poker in the back room of a local pub. He was as adept at poker as he was at Razorbite.

The game was played in odd venues at odd hours and with odd excuses (in case a chairwoman or a master got suspicious). When fewer than eight boys were battling it out, they took over the infirmary and played on the "cadaver table" (as they called the metal examination table). The surface was a killer because it was so smooth. Hoskins and Stewart (fifth-formers and inseparable friends) were especially good on the metal table, but not as good as Murdock.

Even tougher than the cadaver table was glass. Since they couldn't find a mirror big enough, Hoskins and Stewart, who were very friendly with the school nurse, would feign some sort of illness just as she was leaving the infirmary and get permission to go in and administer to themselves, an absolutely unheard-of rule breaker, but Hoskins and Stewart were, separately, extremely charming and, together, magnetic, irresistible. The room had a mirrored door, which they unhinged with screwdrivers and carted off to one of the boys' rooms and laid on the floor. It made the game especially difficult, not just because of the smooth surface, but because the blades were doubled in the mirror, which made grabbing them even harder.

Then there were the tennis courts, three of them a distance from the main building, for St. Eg's had extensive grounds. They were also in a lightly forested area, and the far one was almost invisible because of the surrounding trees and shrubs.

The courts had a nice hard clay surface.

Saint Eglantine's tennis team had never come up to any sort of snuff that would compete with other schools because few of the lads were any good or even interested in becoming so. Consequently, the sports master, Mr. Atkins, was pleased when Trueblood came to him idly swinging a racket and telling him there were a number of boys, eight to be exact, who were interested in getting themselves up to par and maybe reinstituting competition with Broadsniffer, a school Trueblood knew Mr. Adkins hated. "Only, as none of us are very good—" A lie, since Hoskins and Carruthers were *very* good. "—we wonder if we could just get out there and hit the ball around without people watching, since we'd be kind of, you know, embarrassed. In our spare time, of course. At no expense to your precious time, coach." Of which the master had precious little. He was delighted by this student-resourcefulness.

So two of them, or even four, would play their inexpert game on the first and second courts while the others, four or six, played Razorbite on the third and almost invisible court.

This went on for two months before Mr. Adkins asked Trueblood if any of them showed any promise, whereupon Hoskins and Carruthers were trotted out and slammed the ball to hell and gone for three sets.

The coach marveled. But as for the "team" itself, well, that never came into play.

The game had one detractor: a boy named Rupert Thorne, a lower-sixth, two years older and two inches shorter than the others, a pudgy unpopular lad whose chubby fingers could make no headway at all with razors. He couldn't even manage to pick up a single blade on the first, second or even fifth try, and was doomed to either watch or leave.

Trueblood, a decent chap even as a boy, had tried to improve Rupert's skills by getting him to practice with marbles and matches. But Rupert could not pick up *anything* in a single swift motion.

During one of these training sessions, Rupert told Trueblood of a dream he'd had: "It was all about Razorbite. Hoskins came equipped with a huge razor that he used like a hatchet to threaten the rest of us. Then we rounded up all of the masters and made them compete against each other . . ."

The dream rambled on as Rupert Thorne failed to pick up marbles and matches, not only because of his awful clumsiness, but because he couldn't concentrate.

"You can't focus, Thorne, that's your main problem."

Rupert, realizing he was a total failure at Razorbite, naturally came to hate the game and especially to hate its inventor, and he grassed on him to the headmaster. Mr. Nigby, although he found the whole idea of such a game complete nonsense, was always a fair man, and felt he had at least to call Trueblood in and hear his side of this story.

Trueblood sat in the headmaster's study, shaking his head sadly, looking at Rupert. He said, not unkindly, "Rupert, remember the dream you told me about? The one involving this razor-blade game?"

"That dream? Yeah. *Your* game. Razorbite." Rupert's narrowed eyes were mere slits in his pudgy face.

"You said," and here Trueblood repeated the dream in detail. "So what seems to be happening here is that you're failing to separate the real from the imaginary. You had this dream and now you think—"

"Wait a bloody minute!" yelled Rupert.

Mr. Nigby told the boy to watch his language.

"I only had that dream because you'd been playing this game. You and all the others!"

Trueblood shrugged. "No, Rupert. That didn't happen. And remember you told me how, when you were little, you'd taken your father's razor blades and—"

Rupert shot out of his chair and was yelling again that Trueblood was turning everything around and using it against him. The shouts were accompanied now by tears of frustration. Trueblood sat there, reflecting on the stupidity of Rupert Thorne: how did this most unpopular of boys at St. Eg's think he could possibly put it over on the Master of Razorbite, one of the *most* popular, most inventive students at St. Eglantine's, and easily the most manipulative?

Mr. Nigby had heard enough and led Rupert out of the room. He then called the school nurse and told her to see to the boy. After he walked Marshall Trueblood out, an arm flung about the boy's shoulders, and with apologies that they all had to undergo this, the headmaster called Rupert's parents and told them that their son was given to nightmares that were leading to a state of nervous collapse and that they should come to the school as soon as they could manage it.

Trueblood suspended Razorbite for the remainder of the school year, which wasn't a terrible sacrifice as the year had only three weeks to go. But it was just as well Rupert Thorne's parents were going to remove him from St. Eg's, judging by the outraged reactions of those for whom Razorbite had become nearly their lifeblood.

Literally, in some instances.

When Mr. Nigby was made aware of the gauze-bound wrists of two students, he did not connect this with Rupert Thorne's ridiculous story. Instead, the parents were called into his office, where he made the sad announcement that their sons had attempted suicide and something must be done. It was. They were sent down.

But even with all of this hectic sting of masters, mums and dads, neither boy ratted out Razorbite or its inventor. They gave very weak reasons for their wrist wounds, the same reasons all of the boys had been giving all along for nicks and cuts: accidents with broken bottles, falls on rough stone paths. The bottles were produced, the stones pointed out. Marshall Trueblood had one hard-and-fast rule for any boy who wanted to play the game: if he got hurt in the process, he would have to do something to account for his wounds. The best plan was a fistfight between any two so wounded, and a serious fistfight that would draw blood. For some time this served to explain the bloodletting, although several boys got sent down for fighting in the process.

It was astonishing how much punishment the boys would endure for the sake of this game. All of them wanted to be Master of Razorbite. It was a cult; it was a religion; nothing could vie with it.

Except time.

Eventually, when he finished at St. Eglantine's, Marshall Trueblood, who was never discovered as the inventor of Razorbite, packed two bags and went off to a Church of England high school.

The larger bag held clothes and books; the smaller one held razor blades.

"Good God, you're fast," said Leonard Zane, lighting one of his thin cigars. "We can forgo the week's trial period. If you want the job, it's yours."

This decision was no surprise to Marshall Trueblood, although he pretended a pleased befuddlement: "Why . . . good. Well . . . thank you, Mr. Zane."

"Call me Leo." Leonard Zane smiled.

17

In preparation for his trip, Melrose had visited the Long Piddleton library and given Miss Twinney, the librarian, the task of hunting up the best books on Kenya.

This she did, loading him with travel guides (*Lonely Planet, Fodor, Eyewitness*), collections of photographs (*National Geographic, Heritage*), essays (Peter Matthiessen, Paul Theroux) and history that leaned heavily on the rape of the Congo.

"And one or two on Botswana, Tanzania and South Africa," said Miss Twinney. "For good measure. In case you take a side trip." Miss Twinney smiled broadly.

Side trip. Melrose loved that.

He liked the photographs, hated the guides, had mixed feelings about the essays, was appalled by the history. What a battleground! What a bloodbath! Africans and British, Africans and Germans, British and Germans. German guerrilla fighting, dragging the Second World War through the length and breadth of East Africa. What a disgusting takeover was British colonialism.

Melrose had always had a lingering sense of guilt over jettisoning his titles. His father, the seventh earl of Caverness, had been a decent man who had worn his aristocratic heritage well. But now, having read this bloody chapter of British history, Melrose was happy to be joined no longer to the British peerage. Although that was a shallow estimate of individual responsibility, wasn't it?

That evening, after his second glass of Talisker, he had just about decided to reverse his decision (no matter that this would bring Trueblood in for even greater stardom) and instruct Ruthven to cancel the car to Heathrow. But then he realized he'd been reading the wrong stuff, went to his bookshelves and pulled down Hemingway.

With his fresh whisky, he started in on "The Snows of Kilimanjaro." Finished that with annoyance (what a pack of lies!) and opened up *Green Hills of Africa*. Better, but still Hemingway swaggering all over the veldt and Melrose wondering how someone who could write like that could, at the same time, posture like that.

Once again, he thought of calling Jury and begging off. Africa and he had nothing in common.

But then the image of Marshall Trueblood, who had just been to London that morning, floated before his eyes: Trueblood shooting his cuffs, flicking down cards; Trueblood in his tux and crisp white shirt, calling out, "Bets, please" in that smug tone; Trueblood in that luxury casino.

He went to the bookshelves again and pulled down Joseph Conrad.

Another hour and yet another whisky later, and with Martha delaying dinner yet again, Melrose thought he had it. For this whole question of individual responsibility was what lay between Marlow and Kurtz, wasn't it?

He was thinking about this when the phone rang. He did not wait for Ruthven to answer, as the extension was at his elbow. He picked it up.

It was Richard Jury. "You packed?"

Instead of answering that idle question, Melrose launched into his attempt to assess responsibility for the corruption of Africa by Europeans. He put it to Jury in this hypothetical way: If a fraction of Group A mistreats Group B—read: slave trade, government, British colonialism, the East India Company, et cetera et cetera—then does each individual in Group A bear responsibility? Even though not directly connected to it? Even after all of this time?

"So what this boils down to," said Jury, "is: do you have any personal responsibility for, say, Kenya?"

"Exactly."

Jury paused, then said, "You packed?"

Melrose snapped shut *Heart of Darkness*, sure he was the man for the job. Although he hardly considered himself a Marlow (well, actually, that's pretty much who he did consider himself), he would do what little he could (actually thinking he could do a lot) to wipe out the bloody footprint Britain had planted if not all over Africa, at least over a little part of Kenya, thereby restoring some of Britain's good name.

He wondered if perhaps he wasn't exaggerating this notion of personal responsibility. He would get another opinion and decided to call the person who was least likely to question personal responsibility: Diane Demorney. Diane was never a font of knowledge, but she always knew one arcane fact about virtually any subject, such as the least strenuous path to Lourdes, so that the one bit of knowledge was the subject's black hole, with a gravitational pull that sucked all of the other bits into it.

Everyone outside the Jack and Hammer's circle thought Diane was devastatingly smart—that is, everyone who hadn't twigged that Diane knew only this single fact, but nothing else, about her subject.

She was home. So was her cocktail shaker. Melrose briefly summarized what he'd been reading about British colonialism and asked, "Have you ever heard of anything more degenerate?"

There was a brief pause as she (Melrose pictured this) plugged her long cigarette holder with a cigarette. "Scorpion vodka?" she said.

He didn't think he wanted to know what the hell that was and said good-bye.

He sat staring into the fire's embers, picturing the Congo and reassessing his position. Oh, go ahead: let Marshall Trueblood shoot his cuffs and fan his cards and look like he'd schooled every croupier from here to Monte Carlo. What was far more important was for some Briton to reestablish a sense of decency, some kind of British refinement. Into this landscape of self-satisfaction, self-delusion and self-promotion (formerly peopled only by Hemingway), Ruthven came to ask him if he was ready for dinner yet, and Melrose said not quite.

Ruthven cleared his throat. "The pheasant is drying up, m'lord."

Melrose squinched his eyes shut. His imagination had him plowing down the Congo, accompanied by a native entourage, a school of lungfish and extreme moral rectitude, when the truth was that his real life was the pheasant drying up. "Just give me another fifteen minutes, Ruthven, to ponder the British Empire, will you?"

"That should be ample time, m'lord." Ruthven left.

Melrose winced. He lived in a world of dried-up pheasant and one-liners. "You packed?" "Scorpion vodka?" "Ample time."

In the dark polish of a dining room that made Melrose think of the dark continent, Ruthven poured a dry chardonnay and served a chilled cucumber soup.

Melrose asked him if he'd finished the packing.

"Certainly, sir. But not much, as I imagine you'll want only the essentials."

Melrose was not sure what the essentials were. "Do I have any khaki stuff? Isn't that what everyone wears?"

"You do, and I have packed it. You wouldn't want to be burdened with too many bags and trunks on such a long journey."

Soup tureen in hand, Ruthven was heading toward the swinging door into the kitchen, when he added, "A long journey, my lord, but I'm sure a worthwhile one, and one which you will enjoy enormously. Well, let's say, except for . . ." Here, the door that had swung open at the start of this assessment now swung shut and cut off the end of it.

Except for . . . ?

Too late, Melrose called out, "Except for what?"

HEART OF DIMNESS

18

———

E xcept for the Attaboys.
    This was the family that Melrose was herded together with the following evening in the Jomo Kenyatta International Airport by the driver for Mbosi Luxury Tented Camp. The Attaboy family consisted of Mitchell (father), Mildred (mother), Mona (fourteen-year-old daughter), Little Mitchell (eight-year-old son) and eighty-one-year-old Etta. Melrose thought that if "Attaboy" wasn't a name for the ages, "Etta Attaboy" should do it.

As they made their way through the airport, Melrose had to listen to Mildred Attaboy listing the virtues and accomplishments of Little Mitchell, the "little" always appended to the name, perhaps to distinguish him from the father.

Little Mitchell was doing nothing but making the lives of those he passed miserable: he wrestled a frozen yogurt cone away from a four-year-old, whereupon Mildred called out, "Little Mitchell! Now behave!" in such a singsong voice that no child would have considered behaving. Then, as he passed the Nairobi version of a newsagent, he swept several candy bars and peanut packets off the shelf. "Little Mitchell! Come away from there!" Which he did, Mars bars and Smarties sprouting from his pockets.

Melrose had to hand it to Etta, the only one who appeared to think the ruin left in the wake of her grandson's passing should be rebuilt.

Immediately, Etta went to the little girl and gave her money for another cone; she did the same thing to the newsagent's cashier, who was wearing a look of fixed horror.

Etta Attaboy seemed to have a few behavior markers the other Attaboys absolutely lacked. Except for Etta, the Attaboys, who were from Hampshire, struck Melrose as models for the notion of the corrupt European, minus the erudition and cunning of, say, Gilbert Osmond. Little Mitchell was the embryonic corrupt European. Attaboyism in embryo. Melrose did not want to sic the Nairobi police on Little Mitchell; he did not want to sic the first hungry cheetah flinging itself across their path on Little Mitchell; no, the one he wanted to sic on Little Mitchell was Henry James. Henry James would make mincemeat of Little Mitchell quicker than a lion could bring down an exhausted impala.

They had all been plucked from the Nairobi airport by a gangly young Kenyan in a khaki outfit and a red cap emblazoned with the name of their luxury tented accommodation. He was the driver of the vehicle that was to transport Melrose and the Attaboys to the Mbosi Camp on the outskirts of Nairobi.

As they'd strolled through the airport or squeezed together in the car, Melrose had addressed the mother and father as Attaboy. After he'd pronounced it this way three times, Mildred Attaboy corrected him, "At-ta-*bois*, as if spelled 'b-o-i-s'—you know, French—and pronounced 'Atta-bwa.'" She repeated this twice more in case he hadn't got it.

Melrose got it, but he wasn't keeping it. (He especially liked the plural, Attaboys.) He decided if Mildred was going to go the "Attabois" route, he would go the Lord Ardry one. They were terribly impressed.

"We go to national park," said the driver, who introduced himself as Badru. "About twenty-five kilometers."

"Are there animals?" said Mildred Attaboy.

"It is national park, madam," said Badru. "Of course. Except for elephant, you can see the Big Five."

"No elephants? Why aren't there elephants?" demanded Little Mitchell, in a tone that said seeing an elephant was his God-given right.

"Transplanted," said Badru cryptically.

"You mean," said Mildred, again in a worrisome way, "there will be big animals right around us?"

Melrose noticed a little smile that suggested Badru would have liked to tell her the Big Four would surround the vehicle and pose a problem to them getting out that night.

But he merely told them that Nairobi was the only capital city in the world that had a national park as one of its borders. They could see, if they looked behind them, the tall buildings of the city.

Melrose did not know what he had expected in a luxury safari camp, but he had not expected a Trust House Forte. Mbosi Lodge, the main building, appeared to have been built to this busy motorway-stop's specifications. It was much that size and shape and had masses of lit-up windows the weary traveler could spot from the M1 to the M40.

Except that the car park at Mbosi Lodge was considerably smaller than those cresting the motorway rises, nor did Forte Welcome Break caterers have zebras gnawing their grass. A family of zebras were uprooting what they could at the edge of the little car park.

The new guests were greeted the moment they walked through the door by the Van der Moots, whose name didn't sound English but whose accent did. These were Trish and Ernest, she a bit overdressed in gray silk and sequined jacket; he in khakis and a leopard-printed neckerchief. Polished mahogany-bright boots, of course. Melrose pegged Ernest as one who wanted to live up to his given name.

The room on the left of the front door was comfortably furnished with wicker and wood and easy chairs and another dozen guests. There was a large drinks table supporting a small forest of bottles, and the guests who sat and stood around in uncertain configurations were making the most of it.

The room on the right was the dining room, and Melrose saw, with dread, one long table in the middle of it, a table that looked as if it stretched all the way to Nairobi's center.

Trish Van der Moot told them that dinner had been delayed to await their arrival, and as it was now eight thirty they would have just enough time to have a drink or go to their tents and freshen up.

Melrose noted the slight emphasis on the "or."

"I expect I'll do both," said Etta, to be contrary.

Melrose applauded this attitude, for weren't they all paying an arm and a leg for the right to be contrary?

Trish, not wanting to comply, but having to, said, "Well, of course you may do that."

Standing near the dining-room table and by another long table on which were a suite of serving dishes and tureens were several attendants—waiters?—dressed like Maasai warriors, or what Melrose remembered of the Maasai from the *National Geographic* photos he'd seen. Large red scarves were passed over their shoulders and under the opposite arms and tied off. They wore white balloon-sleeved shirts and small red hats that resembled fezzes. They were tall and arrow-straight, their expressions noncommittal.

Another one of these warriors stood by Melrose's group, prepared to quickstep the Attaboys (or at least Etta) to their tent.

"Lumbai," said Trish, "will go with you and wait."

The two of them left, Etta looking like a small gray mutt beside her towering escort.

Ernest said, "There is one rule—"

Melrose bet there were many.

"You must be accompanied to your tents after dark. Animals, you know." He smiled as if he'd just yanked his shotgun to his shoulder and fired.

Mildred gasped. "You mean they come here to the *camp*?"

Before Ernest could start walking back the cat, Melrose put in, "But isn't it rather *we* who have come here, Mrs. Attaboy?" At her uncomprehending look, he plowed on. "It *is* their country."

"What? Africa?"

"If Africa were a country, the answer would be yes."

More and more inscrutable, the Attaboys' eyes were telling him.

Said Ernest, "I believe Lord Ardry is speaking of the continent and colonization."

Oh, thank you, Ernest. Had I known rudimentary history and geography were not on the menu I'd have shut up. No, he wouldn't. "Actually, I mean Joseph Conrad."

Ernest's too-well-plucked eyebrow rose. "Joseph Conrad?"

Melrose didn't enlighten him. The others were bothered that not even Ernest had managed to penetrate this opaque British peer-talk.

Trish, finding that the new arrivals were neither tenting nor drinking yet, started to shepherd them toward the living room, before stopping and saying, "Oh, just a moment." She then went to a small table near the front door, picked up little squares of plastic and came back.

To his horror, Melrose saw that these were name tags she was now pinning to the Attaboys' clothing and that the other guests were wearing them.

To his double horror, he saw her hand closing on his lapel. He shoved it away.

Her smile-mask cracked. "But everyone's wearing them just to make it easier."

"I'd much rather make it harder." He walked off toward the drinks.

He saw as he passed others that each tag was plastered not only with a name, but also with the Mbosi Camp logo, a crouching lion, clearly unfamiliar with a drinks party. Melrose wondered if the man-eating lions of Tsavo had scheduled themselves for an appearance and would soon send the whole lot of them into the sweet hereafter.

Trish Van der Moot had taken herself off toward the innards of the building, probably to deal with a chef who was going mad and tossing the chicken tikka out the door to the zebras.

Melrose himself made his way toward the drinks-laden table, edging past strangers and the inevitable, "How was your flight?"—a question put to him by a thin reed of a woman with sharp features and a tiny mouth.

"Awful."

That was not the right answer. Melrose should have known that to jump the ordinary stream of small talk only made him wade straight into a sea of conversational shallows. As she looked as if she'd been mugged, the gentleman behind her took up the oars of convention and cliché and plowed them through the water. Comments about the flight from Cape Town, the beastly conditions of the Nairobi airport, and so forth. The woman was searching Melrose's jacket for an identifying tag. Her own read Sally Sly.

Pouring himself a stiff whisky, he said, "Ms. Sly, are you—"

"*Slay,*" she corrected him. "Pronounced like s-l-e-i-g-h." She looked down at a child beside her. "And this is my daughter, Savannah. She's eight."

Eight? Savannah should have been in bed a week ago, not embedding herself in a roomful of boozing adults. And talking. Talking as if she were a windup doll and they were at a birthday party, all holding balloons instead of whisky glasses.

"I kn-kn-know all about wild an-animals," she stuttered. And clearly meant to impart her fund of knowledge. "I kn-kn-know about l-lions and tigers—"

And bears, tra-la. "There are no tigers in Africa," Melrose remarked, satisfied that this had stopped her talk dead. But how could an eight-year-old with a pointy little face and a stutter like a buzz saw possibly be named Savannah?

Behind them, a bellicose man was laughing and interspersing his talk with "damns" and "hells."

"Mommy, that man back there is saying bad words."

"Savannah is very sensitive to language," said Sally Sly.

No, she isn't, or she'd shut up. "Hell's bells," said Melrose, taking a sausage from a passing plate.

Savannah plastered her small hand across her mouth. Sally looked uncertain.

Melrose ate his sausage, and then saw Etta Attaboy carving her way through the crowd, unresponsive to whatever smiles and greetings were aimed at her.

"Hello," she said to Melrose, as if he were the only person in the room worthy of a shout. "What's to drink?" She was eyeing Sally's white wine with suspicion. Every woman in the room was holding a glass of some white nonsense.

"Everything," said Melrose. "What'll you have? I'll be barman."

"Double whisky," said Etta.

He tried to be more affable when the next guest approached him, introducing herself as Mrs. Rose Campanelli, a name with a vaguely Roman air, though there was nothing Italianate about Mrs. Campanelli, who hailed, she told him, from Cumbria. She was a very large woman with a shelf of bosom and bright green earrings, not emerald.

"Ah, the Lake District!" said Melrose, with more enthusiasm than he really felt, recalling his sojourn there. "Near Windermere? Buttermere?"

"No, no. We're quite tucked away in Outer Otter. Quite all to ourselves."

"Utter Outer?"

"No. Outer Otter."

Melrose was sorry the Attaboys didn't live there. What fun: *I'd like you to meet the Attaboys from Outer Otter.* Better still: *This is Etta Attaboy from Outer Otter.*

Melrose asked, "In the shadow of Scafell Pike perhaps? Skiddaw? Grasmoor?"

"Oh, no."

Melrose was resolute. He needed to place Outer Otter in some Cumbrian scene. He did not want to revise his mental map of the Lake District—those gleaming and sanguine waters and those majestic fells—as having "tuckings."

He found it odd that Mrs. Campanelli, a woman who did not strike him as enjoying solitude, would come by herself into the vast nowhere of Africa. She answered this unasked question by telling him that at the last minute Mr. Campanelli had decided to stay in Outer Otter.

Was this it, then?

Was this, then, it?

Was it, then, just this?

Here he was in the wilds of Kenya, on Conrad's unimaginably dark continent, and he might as well have been in the Long Pidd post office buying stamps.

At dinner, he had at least the good fortune to be sitting next to Etta Atta-boy, who immediately held her hand to the corner of her mouth in one of those stage-whispery gestures and said to him, "Only thing worse than this layout is sharing a table with my family." She sipped from a goblet of some lemony fizzy stuff after removing the miniature skewer stabbed through bits of fruit. Etta made a face. "This could be improved with a couple of shots of gin."

As a fancily garbed waiter ladled out an ambiguous soup, Melrose and Etta exchanged comments about the setups that had brought them (perhaps unwisely) to this safari and to where they sat.

"It was either Kenya or staying with my nincompoop grandchildren. Ha! Leopards I'd sooner."

Melrose waited for her to complete the sentence, but she was done with it.

Leopards I'd sooner—what? It was apparently a comment with the blood expunged.

"Your grandson Mitchell does strike me as a handful."

"How polite of you. He's a holy terror." She shuddered. "Neither of the children wanted to come. Certainly not Mona, who is profession-ally bored. Never have I seen a child from whom the sense of wonder is so absolutely missing. Even as a baby, she was bored. So when I said to Mitchell and Mildred that I intended to go along on this trip, they were utterly astonished."

A blond-beyond-reason American woman named Bobbi North with a perhaps ruby on a chain around her throat and ruby blots on her ears leaned across the candlelight and said to Etta, "I think you're very brave." She smiled. Her surly teenage son sat beside her. His name was Jefferson and he didn't smile.

"Brave?" said Etta. "About what?"

"Why, coming to Kenya."

Etta looked around the table. "You regard all of these people, all of us here, as somehow heroic?"

Melrose ate his salad (that had come from the local Sainsbury's) and wondered when this ruby-throated blonde was going to twig it.

"Oh, of course not; I meant *you*."

"Why?"

No use, Bobbi, thought Melrose. *She's going to force you to say it.*

The blonde clutched at the red stone at her throat, as if strangling were the only way out of this. "Oh, you know—"

"No, I don't. That's why I'm asking." Etta plunged her little bread knife into a knob of butter.

"It's just," Bobbi whispered, "not many women your age—"

"Oh. I get it. It's because I'm an old woman." Etta had raised her voice at this so that the comment sailed up and down the table, earning Bobbi North looks that implied she had just disemboweled a baby monkey on her dinner plate. She quickly turned to the old geezer on her right, realized that was not the best choice and that she was pretty much stuck with the monkey on the plate. She asked the waiter for wine.

The menu appeared to be much like, but inferior to, one Melrose's own cook, Martha, would have served: the soup was replaced with a steak fancily garbed in bits of parsley and thyme resting on a bed of greens. He assumed it was beef, but how did he know it wasn't zebra?

Two servers were passing round plates of vegetables. Melrose was hoping for something exotic—rootlike sprigs from a baobab tree, perhaps, or something bulbous and orange yanked up from a Okavango puddle.

What he got were roast potatoes and—could he believe it?—green peas. *Peas!* If he went into the kitchen would he find empty Libby's cans? The peas were greener than the Campanelli woman's earrings, suspiciously green. He remembered Martha's comment, "Add a pinch o' bakin' soda, y'r lordship, though of course a body's not supposed to . . ." And she had been called away by Ruthven before he got an explanation of this.

"Tell me, Mrs. Van der Moot—"

"Trish, please."

"These are the greenest peas I've ever seen. Does your chef add baking soda?"

If Etta snickered, it would confirm Martha's "a body's not supposed to." Etta snickered.

"Why, I don't believe so." She pinked up.

Apparently, she did believe so, given that she hadn't even questioned his reference to baking soda.

"I hope not," said Etta. "It's illegal, adding baking soda to green vegetables to keep them from turning pale."

Melrose smiled and ate his peas.

The other people sitting around the table stared at him. Here he was, their single peer of the realm, the one who might have offered up a bit of gossip from the House of Lords or about the PM and all he came up with was peas and baking soda.

A heavy, gloved silence fell until a voice broke it with, "We've always loved Botswana, Donald and I," from a middle-aged woman Melrose hadn't met who was sitting down toward the end of the table.

Recognizing this as condescending—"I've been here before, unlike you lot"—Melrose said, "I myself prefer the Comoros."

"Where?"

Melrose raised an eyebrow. "You know: they're islands. Where else can you see a baby mongoose lemur?" He'd picked up this bit of arcana from Diane Demorney, who'd also offered the nugget, "Except in Mauritania." He smiled. "And then there's the grizzled okapi. There is nowhere else to see that." That bit was not Diane's, but Melrose's invention. Surely, Ernest would question it.

He did, but Little Mitchell got there first. "What's that?" he asked, looking dumb.

"A ruminant." Melrose drank his wine.

"A which?" Mitchell looked dumber.

"A kind of antelope."

"You'd go all the way to some African island just to see a stupid antelope?" said Jefferson North, pulling himself out of the slough of boredom.

"I came all the way to Kenya just to see you, didn't I?"

There were looks exchanged, some laughter broken like china, an Etta snicker.

Ernest said, "Grizzled okapi? First time I've heard of that, Lord Ardry."

"They're quite rare." He wondered how well the Internet worked out here in the wild, because he bet there'd be fingers hitting iPhones.

Ernest gazed round the table. "Any of you ever heard of this antelope?"

Oh, for God's sake, the need to be right! And why didn't he ask the Masai warriors this question, instead of a tableful of white-faced whelps? Melrose, prepared to be generous, reopened the Botswana subject. "How often have you been to Botswana?" he asked Donald's wife.

It was Donald who answered. "Once. We were in Gaborone for two days."

Two days in Gaborone didn't quite do it, since most of them had never heard of it. Botswana was dropped.

So it was just as well they were on their dessert, some sort of currant-infused pudding with (God help them) a custard sauce.

"This here's Spotted Dick!" announced Little Mitchell.

Looking a bit pink, her default position, Trish said, "Oh, no, no. It's a Chablis flan with raisins. An old European recipe."

Etta said, "Isn't there a Kenyan cuisine, then?"

Little Mitchell was not to be stopped. "Call it what you want, it's still Spotted Dick."

"Shut up, Mitchell," said Etta.

He sank into a small fury, but he shut up.

Round-eyed, still blushing, Trish said, "To answer your question about cuisine, Mrs. Attaboy—" coward that she was, pronouncing it *bois.* "—since our guests come from so many different places, we attempt to keep our menu international."

Melrose threw another look round the table to see if he'd missed some Argentine, some Roman, Latvian, Czech, or Inuit. No, British and American faces beamed back, unexotic and barely international.

Coffee was served. He wondered if that, at least, was Kenyan.

Nairobi, Kenya
Nov. 5, Tuesday night

19

Patty had no idea where she was or how to get out of it. It was one of the few times she had doubted the wisdom of what she'd done; she should have lifted another boarding pass at the airport in Nairobi to get back to London. Or anywhere but where she had wound up after leaving Hemingways, after her final breakfast in bed and shower. She felt she had walked the entire length of Nairobi.

London was never dead dark. She had heard people speak of the darkness when there were lights showing everywhere: in windows of terraced houses, in tall office buildings, lampposts, pubs, cafés—everywhere. The best London could boast was a watery dark, a dark you could see through.

She kept walking away from Kibera. She was familiar with London slums, but Kibera was a world of slums, a slum universe. Little brown shacks of wood and metal siding stretched for what appeared to be miles away from the spot where she had been standing just off the road leading out of Nairobi. Walking and walking, stopping now and again to eat or drink something, she had finally stood on a dirt road on the city's outskirts.

Patty had left the dirt road and wandered into Kibera, wondering how a slum so vast could exist side by side with Kenya's biggest city.

* * *

She had brushed aside washing drying on a line—there were endless lines of clothes hung out to dry. She was walking through an alley-like opening between the backs of wood and corrugated-iron shacks. Beside her, a sluggish rush of creek-like water passed through low banks. She bet it wasn't mineral water.

"*Jambo.*" This came from a little girl backed up against a shack on the other side of the foul creek. It hadn't much purchase on the banks. Patty hadn't seen her because the child's clothes were so dark against her dark body.

"*Jambo,*" said Patty. Then she added as clearly as she could, "*Ninaitwa Patty.*" She'd no idea if she was pronouncing that correctly.

The little girl answered, "*Pat-ti. Ninaitwa Alala.*"

Patty nodded and held out her hand, motioning for Alala to jump over the water to her side. The girl hesitated.

"*Alala,*" said Patty, not knowing how to say, "Come on."

The girl didn't move, so Patty unhitched her backpack and set it on the ground. Leaving her backpack was never a smart move, but it would weigh her down in any attempt to bridge the little waterway.

Which she did, in one well-placed step. On the other side, she said again, "*Jambo.*"

The girl giggled. "*Jambo, Pat-ti.*"

Patty nodded. "Now, we go back." Patty pointed her finger first at the girl, then at herself, saying, "You? Me? First?"

But Alala only laughed, bewildered.

Patty pointed again to the other side of the stream. "Back."

The girl nodded. Patty pointed to her own chest, then to Alala's. Then she jumped over the water. She turned, held out her hand and this time Alala jumped. The two of them laughed again and set out, continuing through the backs of shacks, Alala in the lead, as she seemed to know where she was going. They passed a dozen or more random people before they came out on a clearing, not clear at all but littered with debris, strewn with broken bits of unidentifiable objects: dishes or dolls. Kibera's dwellers, and there were many of them, walked in groups or sat idly in doorways, unoccupied, mournful or angry, Patty thought,

and why not, considering this place? A white girl in this black place—
she wondered how long it would have been before she was accosted,
mugged or kidnapped had she not been in the company of Alala.

Alala stopped before her and waved to someone across the clearing.
In a semicircle around this empty space sat another row of shacks, more
tents than shacks, their canvas roofs shaking in a wind that had come
up across the vast field. Patty craned her neck up and back. What had
been blackness was now a moonlit, starlit sky. A windblown African sky.
Even the moon seemed to scud along, voyaging behind the clouds, and
that was as much travel as Patty felt she needed.

Alala ran ahead toward a row of shacks and motioned for Patty to
follow. Alala chugged up to the front of one where a chubby, pretty-faced
woman stirred a black kettle set above sticks on fire. Patty wondered at
the wisdom of anything being set alight here, but on the other hand, was
this woman to jump up and tend her Aga? The woman, probably Alala's
mother, was wearing a dark garment and a length of multi-flowered cot-
ton wound turban-style round her head. She looked at Alala and Alala's
new friend and said, "*Karibu.*"

Patty knew that meant "Come in," and said, "*Asanti.*"

Alala said, "*Ninaitwa Pat-ti.*"

"*Ah, Pat-ti. Unatoka wapi?*"

Patty had no idea what this meant, and the woman obligingly trans-
lated her own words into English: "Where you from?"

"England. *Mimi Mwingercza.*"

The woman laughed good-naturedly. "Ah, Pat-ti, good for you, you
are British. Where in British?"

"London."

"You are long way home."

Long way home. Patty thought that poetic. Long way home. It was, too.

Alala's mother stirred the pot. "You not at Mbosi Camp, Pat-ti?"

"Where's that?"

"In national park. English people. American. Europe. Rich people.
You rich?"

Patty thought of Hemingways. She liked rich. "No."

"You eat?"

Whatever was cooking smelled really good.

Soup? "*Asanti*," she said, always one to take a chance, swallowing hard.

"Taste?" The woman lifted the wooden ladle, sipped from by many mouths, Patty imagined. Why was she being so hygiene-conscious? She was plenty used to shared bowls and cutlery.

"*Asanti*," she said again, making as much use of her meager word store as possible.

"Pat-ti," said Alala. She appeared to like the sound of the name. Then she said a lot more in rapid-fire Swahili of which Patty had no understanding, but she thought it must be complimentary, for the mother's expression grew increasingly wondrous as she looked at Patty.

Alala was starting to babble again, but this must have had to do with household matters as her mother merely went about setting out plastic bowls and wooden spoons and shooing Alala off as if she were a fly.

Alala sat down on a cushion on the earthen floor and gestured for Patty to sit on the cushion beside her. The cushions looked made from the same material as the mother's turban. Patty sat down, thanked Alala's mother for the soup set before her, looked up at the top of the tent enclosure and thought she could be on safari. She thought about Africa and the animals she'd seen only in pictures and on a TV special about big cats. That program had followed the progress of a mother cheetah and her two cubs. The cubs spent a lot of time jouncing on what appeared to be nothing. Perhaps bugs. The mother would sometimes give one or the other a little swat with her paw to keep them in line. Patty didn't know in line with what. The mother took good care of her cubs.

Patty drank her soup, feeling the presence of these animals all around her—lions and their cubs, cheetahs and their cubs. Knowing that this was as close as she could get to them made her feel lonely. She thought about what Alala's mother had said. "This camp—I've heard of it, I think." No, she hadn't. But she reached around to her backpack and pulled out one of her notebooks. Turning to a blank page, she pretended to read something. "What's the name of the camp?"

"Mbosi," said Alala's mother.

"Oh! That's where my uncle is!" Patty repeated the name. "Mbosi?"

"Yes. Your uncle, he rich?"

"Very." Returning her notebook to her backpack, Patty said, "That's where I'm supposed to meet him. Mbosi Camp. So where's the national park?"

"Park huge. You go Magadi Road."

"Then I'll go and stay with my uncle."

"No, Pat-ti, too far walk. You stay here tonight."

But Patty was still thinking of Hemingways and all the advantages of richness. "My uncle might be worried about me. And the distance doesn't bother me. I walk a lot."

"Park closed now."

"If it's so big there must be some way in."

"Yes. Lots of construction. They make roads. Park not for animals no more. For people. Lots of fences, like zoo."

When Patty had finished her soup, she insisted on going to the camp. "Uncle Édouard will be wondering where I am."

Alala and her mother walked Patty back to the road and pointed her in the direction of the national park. "You watch for construction. You follow road building to old road that go through park to Mbosi Camp."

Patty crossed the wide Magadi Road and headed south. There was not a lot of traffic and there were not many dwellings. A big building that might have been offices, or flats, or government—random windows alight. Aside from that, not many lights—building, street or otherwise. She walked for an hour before she came to the park and then to some of the construction. It looked like the road Alala's mother had mentioned. It looked very dark.

Here was real darkness, where she could see nothing at all except for her feet on the rough dirt road that disappeared into the night between plane trees. She sat down by one of these trees; she had no expectations of anything happening or not happening. It would not have surprised her if something had dropped on her from the tree. At one point, something seemed to drop—not from the tree, but from the night, though it was so lightweight it might have been nothing but a breath on her neck. She brushed her hand at the invisible intruder and settled back.

Her first taste of the dark had occurred when her father died. Patty had been permitted to go into the room with the nurse who held a candlestick, the candle the only source of light. That was silly, Patty had thought, acting as if there were no electricity, but the nurse refused to turn on the lights.

"I can't see, I can't see Daddy. Are you sure he's here?" She was four years old and the bed on which her dead father lay was huge and high. It needed a little wooden ladder to reach the top, but the ladder was missing. Even when Patty was on tiptoe, her eyes came only to the top of the mattress. Had someone taken the ladder away? Had Daddy kicked it away from the bed so that no one could get to him?

Patty raised her arms to the nurse in expectation of being picked up and sat on the bed, but that did not happen. The nurse said she couldn't get up there. Patty tried to jump, but that didn't work. She went to one of the posts and tried to climb up and almost did but the nurse pulled her down. Patty ran round to the other side of the bed and pulled herself up most of the way when the nurse came round and yanked her down. Then Patty pinched and kicked the nurse so violently the woman gave up and left her there. "See how you like it here, lying on a deathbed!" The nurse left.

Patty crawled onto the mattress and up to the pillows, where lay the head of her father. She touched his hand and found it cold. She touched his face and found it even colder. She herself was hot from her exertions with bed and nurse, and she wondered if that would help him. She lay her cheek against his, wondering if her heat could become his heat and he could throw off the cold of death. She squirmed down to where his feet were and felt them. Cold, too. She took off her shoes and socks and put her feet on his feet, the way she did when he had danced with her, to move her around the dance floor. But the feet did not warm, even though hers grew no colder.

She pulled herself back to the top of the bed and lay her head on his chest where she thought his heart was. If any of her own life could get down there, perhaps the heart would start beating again.

After falling asleep and waking several times, she came to realize that her father was never going to be anything but dead anymore, that death was implacable.

And so was the darkness it inhabited.

She had brought with her an excellent torch, given to her by a friendly thief. He always used one like it when robbing houses because it had a narrow beam and it was almost impossible for someone else to see the light when it was directed downward.

That was where Patty was aiming it as she left the cover of the tree and walked through the night, still brushing at her shoulder and whatever kept wanting to land there. Were there bats in Kenya?

20

Comfortably far from the others in his group, Melrose Plant sat after dinner in the lounge in a chair so deep he could sink back into invisibility. It gave him a view of the wide back porch, where Lumbai was escorting two of the guests back to their tent. He had a gallon of whisky at his elbow, together with a decanter of water, and what with the seven-hour flight and meeting the Mbosi Camp guests, he was sure he'd be drunk inside of ten minutes.

He sat reading a book called *Instant Africa*. He had picked it off the lodge's library shelf because of a title he considered not just absurd but slanderous. *Instant U.K.*, all right; *Instant Canada,* definitely; possibly *Instant France, Instant New York, Instant London*; but if ever a place struck him as non-instantaneous it was Africa. Or he could simply sink into cliché and call the continent timeless.

Given he felt that his eyes had deceived him ever since he'd been here, he assumed they must be deceiving him now as he looked out upon the broad porch and the wide wooden steps leading up to it. It appeared someone—someone small—was advancing up those steps.

A waif. Through the screen doors she came. He was astonished to see a genuine waif in this rich people's hangout and wondered how in God's name she'd got there. Had the Kenyan night simply belched her out into

Mbosi Lodge? Moreover, how could anyone, even a grown person, be out walking on his own over this dark terrain, much less a waif?

But here she stood solidly before him as if she were Godot and he, waiting. "Hello," she said; "will you do me a favor?"

"Hello," he answered. "No."

"Oh, *come* on." Here she swept her large eyes round to take in the other part of the room, but didn't move her head. It was a remarkable exercise in non-turning. "You're not like them."

"That I know," said Melrose, flipping a page of *Instant Africa*.

"You look okay."

"I am okay."

"Just pretend you know me, that's all."

"Since I'm speaking to you, it would appear that the pretense is already established."

She laughed. It was a merry sound.

"What in God's name are you doing here all alone?" He gave in to that question.

Removing her backpack and setting it on the floor, she said, "It's a long story. Could I have some of that water?"

"Certainly." He picked up the decanter and offered it. "Whisky?"

"No, just water. I'm Patty Haigh."

Melrose poured out a glass for her and handed it over. "And I'm Melrose Plant."

"Thanks. I've walked a long way." She drank the whole glassful and handed the glass back for more.

He poured again and returned it to her. "I'd be afraid to walk even a *short* way out there." He nodded toward the night.

"Why?"

"Why? Have you come from the moon? Africa has long been known for its wild animals."

She chewed her lip thoughtfully. "Probably if you don't bother them, they won't bother you."

He sighed. "That sounds like an admirable setup for disaster."

"And what have we *here*?" Mildred Attaboy pulled up before them like a schooner with wind full in her sails.

Melrose had a real aversion to the "what have we" kind of question. "We have my niece, Patricia Haigh."

"Patty."

He gave her a dark look.

"Your niece? Well, my, how did she get here?"

"A car just dropped her off."

"I didn't hear a car!"

"It was a Bentley. One doesn't hear them," said Melrose.

"A Bentley! Way out here?"

"A Bentley jeep."

"Does Bentley make jeeps?"

Talk about missing the point. The woman was a waterfall of questions. Every answer would be turned into a new question.

"Yes," said Patty, "It was driven by Prince Ramakudu. He's my uncle's friend who lives in Nairobi."

"He's a prince?"

Melrose pulled Patty up by the hand. "You must excuse us, Mrs. Attaboy. I have to speak to Mrs. Van der Moot." And he walked Patty over to where Trish was pouring coffee.

"Mrs. Van der Moot, this is my niece, Patricia—"

"Patty."

Melrose shoved her behind him. "—who has just arrived from Nairobi."

"Oh? We knew nothing about this." She smiled uncertainly.

"I know you didn't." He pulled Trish gently off to one side and said in low tones, "It's a bit of an emergency—" He pushed Patty, who was trying to get in on the emergency, farther behind him. "Her parents were caught up in a coup at their hotel in the city."

"Oh!" Trish's hands went to her cheeks.

"Nothing big and kept very quiet. I understand they're quite all right, but Patricia—"

"Patty."

Melrose kicked her foot. "—managed to get away."

"Good Lord! You poor child!"

Melrose kept the poor child behind him. "She was quite brave." That was indeed true. Melrose thought of her walking in the dark across the savanna. That took more grit than any little armed insurrection could muster. "So do you think you could arrange for her to have a bit of dinner?"

"Of course. I'm not sure we have any of the beef left, but there are plenty of vegetables. Would you like to sit with her, then?"

"Fine."

Before leaving to see to the food, Trish added, "I will bring you a little surprise."

"That was brilliant!" said Patty. "I'm really starved."

"You look it." Melrose pulled out a chair at the overly long table and she sat down. Before he took the chair beside her, he went to replenish his whisky.

Trish appeared at the table with a small box displaying a happy sailor, hand held to his white cap, saluting. "Cracker Jack," it said. "You can't get this in Africa or even in England," said Trish.

Patty was looking it over when Melrose returned to the table.

"What's this?" He picked up the Cracker Jack box as Trish said, "It's caramel corn. A nice American guest sent us a crate from the States when she returned. And look, each box has a prize inside. You'll find it down at the bottom."

Pleased, Patty shook the box.

Melrose took the rattling box from her and waited until Trish walked off before saying, "Now, tell me this long story of yours. How did you get to Nairobi? I assume you didn't walk; you flew."

"Following a killer."

Melrose slowly set down his glass. "I beg your pardon?"

"I was trailing a man who shot some people." Patty was looking toward the door she assumed her food would be coming through.

Melrose took a drink. "Tell me another."

"What's the matter with the first one I told you?"

"It struck me as being short on truth. Now, again, how did you wind up in Nairobi?"

Patty sighed, thinking she might as well bypass the Emirates spa and Dubai, but her taste for drama could not have her flying any old airline, such as British Airways, so she said. "We flew on Etihad and landed at Alibaba."

"Indeed? Are you sure that's pronounced 'Alibaba'? And then you continued on to—where?—Treasure Island?"

"Nairobi. That's where we got separated."

"You were with your family? Mum and Dad, I suppose."

She nodded.

"Brothers and sisters?"

"Two of each."

"Sounds like an assortment of sherbets."

"Then there's my Aunt Monique . . . and Uncle B.B., and some cousins."

"Good Lord, how many of them are here?"

"Twelve."

"*Twelve* people? And they couldn't keep hold of you?"

The waiter set a plate of vegetables before Patty. She forked up the potatoes and chewed and thought. "What happened was, Dad and my brothers—um, Conrad and Randy—and my Uncle B.B., yes, and Aunt Monique, they went to get a car or cab. Two cabs we'd need to go to the hotel. Then Mum and Inez and—er—Clara, they waited for me while I went into the toilet. When I came out—I guess I took a long time—they were gone." Patty stopped to put butter on her potatoes and then resumed her tale. "Well, I guessed they just went after Dad and the others so I waited a few minutes, then I went outside to where the cars were and didn't see anybody." She stopped, thinking. "Here's what I think happened: there were two cars, and the ones in the first car thought I was with the ones in the *other* and didn't discover I wasn't with them until they got to the hotel." When Melrose opened his mouth to interrupt, she said, "I forgot the name of the hotel." Her forehead pleated in thought. "I think it was the Excelsior." She had passed that hotel at some point in her progress through Nairobi.

"The Excelsior?"

"You know. Where the coup happened."

"There wasn't any coup. And when was all this, this morning?"

She shook her head and ate some more. "Three days ago." She counted on her fingers. "Or four."

Melrose nearly choked on his whisky. "*What?*" Surely the police would have been notified of a missing child. He pulled out his mobile. "I'm calling the police right now." He looked around for someone who could supply him with an emergency number. He was stupid about phone calls in foreign countries.

She shrugged. "Okay, but it won't do you any good. I went to the police station twice to see if anyone had reported me missing. Nobody had." Quickly, she added, "And the name isn't Haigh, it's Umbijawa. Freddie and Marie Umbijawa. I'm an orphan. I mean, they're my foster parents. So are Randy and Conrad and Inez. They're foster children. Don't look so worried. I'm not."

One of the waiters removed her plate and set down a dish of chocolate ice cream. She started in on that immediately.

He leaned toward her. "Patty, of course I'm worried. So should you be. My God, you're stuck in Kenya, in Africa, without anybody, no way home, no money—"

"That's where you're wrong. I've got lots!" She put down her spoon and shoved her hand into a pocket of her backpack and pulled out the dwindling roll. It was still ample. "See, Mr. Umbijawa is pretty rich and makes sure all of us kids have money. Just in case—"

"He loses you in Nairobi?" Melrose took another drink, a long one.

She mounded her spoon with ice cream, licked it and said, "I've just been with them two years, and I think maybe they haven't tried too hard to find me because they're just tired of the whole foster thing."

Melrose pushed back. "Okay, that's it. I'm ringing the police station." He rose.

"Well, if that Van der Moot woman hears you she's really going to wonder how come I'm missing. You know, me being your niece and all."

Melrose turned and walked over to the waiter, who was clearing up dishes from the buffet. He got his message across and in return received a number, which he dialed as he went back to the table.

"Ah, yes, may I speak with someone who deals with—you. Of course. I want to report a lost child." He looked at Patty, who clearly resented the description. "The family, name of—" He stumbled over it. "Umbijawa. What? Well, I guess it's U, m, b, i or e, j, a w, a, h. Something like that. Umbijawah. Fred is the first name. The child is Patricia. What? The station?—" Melrose was beginning not to care for the suspicion that had come into the tone of whoever was at the other end. "Look, never mind. I'll see she gets to the station. Thank—" The voice was raised, wanting to know his name, where he was calling from; it was a woman speaking very quickly. He raised his own voice, said, "Thank you." He thought he continued to hear babble even after he rang off.

He just looked at Patty Haigh. "Tomorrow, we—Wait a minute! I know exactly who to call!" Jury. He'd know what to do. "What time is it in—Are we two hours ahead? Or behind the UK?"

"No!" She yanked down the hand that held the mobile. "Oh, please. Not the London police." Her face started to crumple.

He frowned. "Why not? For heaven's sake, your father, or rather Mr. Umbijawa, could very well have contacted—"

"You don't understand. Freddie's in trouble with the police. They're looking for him." Now she was crying. "I don't want to get him in trouble."

"For God's sake, Patty, he appears to have abandoned you—"

Furiously, she shook her head. "I know there's some reason. And they've really been good to me for the three, I mean two, years I've lived with them. I was in awful shape when they found me. Please don't!" She wiped her eyes with her linen napkin. "I really like it here with you. Just for a couple of days, maybe? I've never been to Africa or ever seen wild animals. We might see a cheetah. Please." She picked up the money roll again. "I'll pay you back."

He had to smile. "Patty, if there's one thing I don't need, it's your money."

"Oh, good." Completely calm now, she stashed her money in her backpack. "Can I have some more ice cream?"

A child of such mercurial moods Melrose had never known. Holding up her empty dish, he signaled the porter.

"Finished!" Patty announced ten minutes later, wiping her mouth with her napkin. "Can we sit on the porch?" She picked up the Cracker Jack box and shook it.

"Hmph. I expect so. Why did thirteen of you decide to come to Kenya all at once?" They walked through the wide screen doors and took seats on two rocking chairs.

"For different reasons. Like my Aunt Monique—"

"You don't have to detail the reasons. Where were you before you pulled up here?"

"Kibera."

He recalled that name from having read a description of it just before she turned up. "But that's the huge slum in Nairobi, isn't it?"

"Uh-huh. I just got lost at one point and wound up there."

"It sounds like you got lost at every point. That place is extremely dangerous." From the continent's worst slum to the wild savanna. My God, her hair should be white.

Melrose stood. "Come on, you'll have to share my tent." They started down the steps to the path, where the guide, Lumbai, waited in case any of the guests tried going it on their own.

"I will have to accompany you, suh," said Lumbai.

"Thank you." Melrose turned to Patty. "See, that's how dangerous it is. We can't even walk to that tent alone. Then he said to Lumbai, "Tell me, how far is this from Kibera?" He was curious.

"That place? Well, as you know, it's enormous."

"Yes. But let's say, as the crow flies. I mean, in a straight line. If we were to turn and walk to it from here. How far?"

The guide laughed. "One would have to be crazy to do that . . . but, I'd say, perhaps four kilometers."

"God," said Melrose under his breath. He was afraid to think about it.

Her Cracker Jack box tight under her arm, Patty was walking hard to keep up with them, they both being tall and with long legs. "I didn't—"

"That's right. You didn't. Be quiet."

But now he was really interested in the phenomenon of this little girl's walking through lion-cheetah-leopard-infested territory unscathed. "Lumbai, tell me—" He stopped on the path. "You know a lot more about these animals than we do. Is it possible they would not attack if they felt absolutely no threat?"

Lumbai looked around. "Do they ever feel no threat? And are you forgetting hunger? That is a powerful reason to attack us. Between here and Kibera, walking? No, I cannot imagine any chance of not being attacked by something in all that distance. Impossible." He shook his head. "Let us go on."

They walked. But since it was not impossible—clearly she had come from somewhere on foot, even if she was lying about Kibera (and he didn't see why she would be). "Surely not impossible, Lumbai. There must be some circumstance where it's possible."

"Well, there are always the spirits. Perhaps a person might be in the company of a *malaiki*."

"What's that?"

"One of the good spirits. Angels will sometimes be sent to help those in distress."

Did he believe that? wondered Melrose. They were at the tent now. At the doorway—if one could call it that. Lumbai opened it and Melrose could see that the sofa on the left had been pulled away from the wall and made up as a bed.

"The partition has not been pulled down," said the guide, who then put his fingers round a handle protruding from the ceiling and pulled. What had been a white pine ceiling—or rather a second ceiling—became a wall, splitting the room in two lengthwise.

"Oooohh," said Patty.

Lumbai said, "Both sections have access to the bathroom facilities."

"This is fine," said Melrose. And it was; he still had more than ample space is his half of the huge room.

"I will say good night, suh. And miss." He smiled at Patty and left.

"I need to unpack."

That seemed almost euphemistic. What could she possibly have in that backpack?

He soon found out as she kept pulling clothes from it and smoothing them carefully over the chair and the bed. The jumpers and jeans were followed by a myriad of things like torch, combs, tissues, wigs—

Wigs?

Patty would have gone down a treat with Diane Demorney, who seemed to carry the whole of Fortnum & Mason in her big purse. He recalled one day in the Jack and Hammer when Scroggs had run out of vodka. Rooting around in this leather bag, Diane had dragged out combs and compacts, cigarettes and silver lighter, item after item until she came to the vodka miniatures. She lacked only vermouth, but that scarcely mattered.

He wondered if Patty would yank out a half-pint of Talisker. No, the next things she brought out were notebooks in several different sizes. She plucked up the largest of these, a wire-bound one, and sat on the edge of her bed with a pen.

"What are you doing?" He thought he detected a crunching sound.

"Eating Cracker Jacks. It's really good." She offered him none. "And writing. I always travel with notebooks since I never know when I'll need to make notes. Right now, I'm keeping a record for the police and so forth."

The police and so forth. Should he ask?

21

They had been sent off like kids to summer camp by the Van der Moots with nothing but a cup of tea and the promise of a big breakfast at the end of it. That had been at five A.M. There were only four Attaboys, but that was still a swarm. Etta Attaboy had escaped this early morning ambush, claiming she was too old for a five A.M. safari drive.

Melrose felt too old for a five A.M. anything. He was seated in the back of the Range Rover between Patty (and her journal) and Rose Campanelli, finding it rather remarkable that this woman from Outer Otter would brave the dawn when the supposedly sturdier American couple and Mrs. North and her son Jefferson had avoided it. So there were nine of them, besides the driver Montre and the tracker Dan-glo. They had been riding for two hours through the bush, across half-washed-out bridges and muddy streams, past gargantuan baobab trees and spiky sage, acacia trees so flat-topped he could have danced across them. They glimpsed brilliant things on the wing and fleet things on four feet; sleek cats of several species with spots; scores of impala; a leopard draped on a black branch like a window display for Liberty's fur department; the dark shadow of a herd of wildebeest thundering across the land like the Birmingham-Leeds express—

What were these inane analogies to Britain? What on earth had he ever seen in his daily jaunts to the Jack and Hammer or his bimonthly ones to Boring's in Mayfair that could possibly compare to this Kenyan savanna?

He sat next to Patty and was surrounded by Attaboys.

Melrose was aware that he was self-centered and self-absorbed (he didn't need to be reminded of it by Patty, who at the moment was writing furiously in that damned notebook she hauled everywhere), but he really couldn't get his mind round this five A.M. ride out to watch a pride of lions run down a warthog. How unsporting. The whole country struck him as an uneven playing field. The warthog escaped the lions, Melrose was relieved to see, but his fellow travelers did not appear to share his relief. He inferred they were expecting that one of the safari perks was at least one good bloodbath. Patty still wrote while some sort of lizard crept across the path of the stopped vehicle. It was quickly routed by a small wildcat appearing out of nowhere. My God, things moved fast out here. There's your carnage, Little Mitchell, but the boy had missed it because he was fooling around with his camera.

Higher the sun rose, throwing bronze and orange shadows across the land, and they were into the vast emptiness of what Melrose had always supposed to be Africa. But the color, on a short-term loan from Hollywood, faded and left behind the daily sweep of drab shrubs and grass bleached by the sun to near-transparency, where it wasn't the color of straw, and the veldt in general rose only to variations in neutral tones—tan, ochre, ivory.

Yet despite all of this color neutrality, the land was still oddly vibrant. It was more vivid than his own gardens surrounding Ardry End, spurting their intense reds, purples, yellows and blues. His garden struck him now as unalive, as if, rather than growing, the flowers had been painted there.

Bursts of light happened somewhere out there, lightning it must have been.

He stood and stuck his head above the rolled-back top of the Range Rover. Danglo was already leaning on the canvas, arms crossed.

"Very dry, need rain, that rain thirty miles away. Too dry."

"But it's the season for all that, isn't it?"

"Yeah." Danglo nodded. "But not pretty."

Not pretty. One of the strangest descriptions he had heard of Kenya. He stood there looking at the same scene as the guide, at the stubble, the dry ash-colored shrubs, grass stiff as straw, the distant line of black flat-topped acacia trees, the same scene and yet it was different to him. The difference was that they were present, seen or unseen. The veldt wasn't empty. It was full of blood.

The vehicle's radio crackled, and a scratchy voice came through, emitting another flood of information that no one could understand until Montre turned and said, "Lions with kill. Buffalo." He turned to the tracker, pointed and said a lot in Swahili as he bumped off-road, heading for a stand of acacia trees a hundred meters away.

"Vultures!" yelled Little Mitchell. "Vultures!" He barely missed Melrose's chin as he whipped his binoculars up to his eyes. "And a couple of storks."

Danglo said, "Marabou storks. And buzzards, many buzzards."

The Range Rover found what the birds were waiting for: their turn at the table, the carcass of an animal—according to Montre's source, a buffalo—that had clearly been killed many hours ago by the three lions that were feeding on it. The feeding seemed almost casual, the male lion yanking at a piece of hide, the two females drifting off and lying down.

Theirs wasn't the only vehicle. On the other side of the lions sat another filled with people from the camp, one of them, Sally Sly's husband, grinning ferociously as if he'd been in on the kill and was waiting, like the buzzards, for his turn.

It was one of Patty's opportunities to object. She managed to stand up, as if facing an audience of reprobates. "Who do we think we are?" Patty barreled on. "Who are we to come into the animals' space and watch them eat as we grin, grin, grin—" Here she pointed to the other vehicle, where Mr. Sly sat straight as a statue, the grin carved on his face. "What do we think this is? A fucking zoo?"

Little Mitchell yelled, "She said the f-word!" As if he objected.

Interest in language dissipated in the wake of the Attaboys' camera-maneuvering: they broke out every kind of photographic enhancement imaginable, as if the ghost of David Lean were beckoning across the veldt.

The morning ride ended with a fancy breakfast cooked up by one of the lodge chefs, who had followed their little party in a large van. Was this what safari-goers, Europeans and Americans, expected? That they be followed in a van with bacon and eggs? Not even Henry James could have thought that up.

The breakfast was elaborate, featuring a half dozen different sausages that neither Melrose nor Patty partook of (Patty because she wouldn't eat sausages, Melrose because he wouldn't eat sausages he couldn't identify); eggs in various combinations; pancakes of corn, buckwheat and other grains; muffins the size of parasols; quiche, toast, biscuits; and a dozen different beverages, including mango juice and passion fruit, several fizzy things and, of course, coffee and tea. The spread made Melrose sigh for the lions trying to make a meal of one warthog. And not succeeding even at that.

No wonder they ate everything they could lay their paws on. How had Patty made it all the way to Mbosi Lodge on foot for four kilometers?

She sat beside him, eating an egg sandwich she'd constructed and writing with her free hand.

"Why are you always writing?"

"To keep the Attaboys from talking to me."

"There's so much going on out here, I don't think they'd bother you."

Patty did not answer, only closed her notebook and stuffed her pencil down her sock, then continued eating her egg sandwich.

"Did you enjoy the lions, dear?" Mrs. Attaboy had sprung from nowhere.

"More than the warthog did," said Patty.

Mildred Attaboy laughed uncertainly, as she was joined by a bored-looking Mona.

Mona, meaning to discredit Patty, asked, "What are you always journaling about?"

"Is that a word?" said Melrose.

"I'm not 'journaling.' I'm making notes."

"Yeah?" said Little Mitchell, springing up between them. "What'sa difference?"

"You don't know?"

Mouth full, he shook his head. Mouth still full, he said, "Looks the same."

"A journal is for itself."

Mr. Attaboy had now moved into the circle around Patty, whom they all seemed to regard as Delphic.

The oracle continued, "A notebook is for something else."

"What else?" said Mr. Attaboy, his wide forehead creased in a deep frown.

Patty looked at Melrose, opened her notebook, pulled the stub from her sock and started writing.

One by one the Attaboys drifted away.

Patty Haigh could read a room.

Nairobi, Kenya
Nov. 6, Wednesday afternoon

22

A couple of hours later and without further incident, they were back at the camp and walking into the lodge.

There, Trish Van der Moot presented Melrose with a written and verbal message. The verbal was full of excitement prompted by the written, which stated that a Scotland Yard superintendent, Richard Jury, wished him to call. "By all means, use the lodge phone. I know your mobile might not get a decent connection." She led him to the phone.

"What artist?" said Melrose, trying to balance phone and the small paper pad he was writing on.

"Masego Abasi." Jury spelled it out and explained. "I wired photos to Nairobi police and told a chief inspector named Kione you'd pick them up. Don't forget you're Lord Ardry. Kione liked that. British colonialism is apparently still viable. When you show them to Abasi, show him the one of the painting first; see if he remembers who bought it. Then show him the photo of Rebecca Moffit. She's also in the one of the gallery. See if he can identify her; it could be she's been to his studio."

"Okay."

A pause. "Just okay?"

"Why?"

"Thanks for not asking why I'm not having Nairobi police take the photos to Abasi."

"I would have thought that's obvious."

"Only to you." Jury started to hang up, came back. "Listen, ask this Kione if they've been able to locate the missing girl."

"What missing girl?"

"A kid who wound up in Nairobi. Kione will know."

Melrose was uncomfortable. "He will, but I don't."

"A kid who was on the flight with Banerjee."

"Jesus. Kidnapped?"

"No, apparently she attached herself to him. She's the one person who can identify him, so we are, naturally, worried."

"Worried? *Worried*? Surely that's the understatement of the year. And she's in Kenya?"

"Nairobi, far as we know."

Melrose took a deep breath. "Her name wouldn't be Patty Haigh, would it?"

It was Jury's turn to draw in breath. "You've come across her?"

"You could say that."

Melrose couldn't believe it. Not knowing where to begin, he said, "Not taking notes? Presumably, that says you don't mind my talking to you."

"About what?"

Nothing. Astonishment had blotted out perfectly sensible questions. He looked at her and thought for a few moments and finally said, "Okay, tell me the real story. No, don't give me that 'Huh?' look. You know what I'm talking about: what are you doing in Nairobi?"

She shrugged. "I already told you."

"No, you didn't. You told me about your thirteen relations—"

"Twelve. I was number thirteen."

"—and about your foster parents, and the two cabs you needed, and so forth. That was all an elaborate lie. And will you just stop messing with those wigs and *sit down!*"

She'd picked a washed-out blond wig from her backpack and was trying it on. She sat down.

"Please take that thing off. You look absurd."

"The police never seem to think so." But she removed it and tossed it on the bed.

"Back to this elaborate lie—"

"What was I supposed to do if you wouldn't believe the truth?" With gestures terribly adult and composed, she crossed her small legs and locked her hands around her knees. And stared.

Melrose stared back until that Tuesday night episode rearranged itself in his mind. When they'd been sitting at the table, she having her dinner and talking, he'd got so caught up in the details of her story about her lost family that he'd forgotten the first thing she'd said. About following a killer.

"All right. So tell me again."

She told him, in greater detail than he certainly needed. After the essential details about her following B.B., she went into the nonessential. "He said he really liked this airline, but wouldn't have picked it himself because it was so pricey and someone else bought him his ticket, but of course he bought mine. He said the food was really good for airline food and that he didn't like to cook and how he liked cafés and restaurants to eat in. He gave me his shower time, too."

Melrose said nothing for a few moments. He knew what he should do was stuff this child onto a flight for London straightaway, but he simply hadn't the energy at this point to argue with her, and argue she would. So he said, "We're going into Nairobi."

"What about a car? You don't have one."

"No, but I'm sure Nairobi has car-hire firms."

"How do we get to Nairobi, then?"

"I expect they'll bring it to us; if not, the lodge personnel can give us a lift. Someone's always going into the city."

*   *   *

Trish Van der Moot said that certainly they could arrange for a car. "There's a car-hire firm that we do business with quite often. I'll call for you. Have you a preference?"

Melrose was confused. "For the firm?"

She laughed. "For the car."

Melrose shrugged. "You?" he said to Patty.

"Porsche," she said.

The Porsche showed up less than an hour later and ferried them to the car-hire firm in Nairobi. Melrose picked up a map in the office and headed for the police station.

The streets of Nairobi were full of plugged-up traffic, and every once in a while somebody pulled the plug and a small flood of cars rushed forward. The central police station was, as Trish had told him, near the university.

Chief Inspector Kato Kione extended his hand to Melrose, and did not seem to think Melrose's appearing with a small girl was at all surprising, as if the police were used to ten-year-olds taking over their wing chairs. The chair Patty had claimed had such a tall back, wide seat, and high arms that she was lost in it.

On the corner of the desk in an untidy heap sat a collection of books. Melrose's attention was called to it by Patty's leaning toward it and pulling one of the books from the pile. It was a collection of *Beano* comic strips.

Melrose reprimanded her: "Patty! You don't take things from the chief inspector's desk."

She turned her head, her mouth slightly open in a leftover *Beano* smile.

Kione laughed. "Quite all right, Lord Ardry. I keep books here for my grandson, who enjoys sitting at my desk, pretending to be the police commissioner. But that gets boring quickly, and he wants a book to read."

Kione nodded at Melrose, who was sitting in the other, plainer office chair. "You are a friend of this Scotland Yard detective. Superintendent Jury?" When Melrose nodded, he went on: "I fear we were not much help to him in his investigation of a homicide. That was a most peculiar incident. Brazen. Although I must say brazen crimes are quite common in this city."

Although Melrose thought he probably shouldn't be wedging himself into the case, he said, "This man Banerjee, the name suggests he's at least partly Indian? That doesn't make him easier to find?"

Kione laughed. "Lord Ardry, Nairobi has a very large Indian population—"

"Not all named Banerjee, though. And the subject is Kenyan."

"Bushiri," said Patty, more to her comic book than to the room. When Melrose gave her foot a little shut-up kick, she turned *Beano* around for them to see—not much, for her finger was over the space she was indicating. "I mean Bushy, Gnasher's friend."

Neither being familiar with Gnasher or his friend, the two men returned to the business at hand. Or Kione did, supplying more information: "This Bushiri Banerjee was the person we went to. He's a wealthy industrialist living in the Riverside district. Really above suspicion—"

"Ha!" said Patty, and coughed loudly when Melrose kicked her dangling foot again, making it appear as if the "Ha!" had been part of the cough. Still, this earned her a suspicious look from Kione, who went on: "Mr. Banerjee's passport seemed in order, his movements accounted for."

"He had an alibi for the time in question? The Friday night and Saturday?"

"He did, yes. He was at home with Mrs. Banerjee."

"For the entire time?"

Kione pursed his lips. "He did go to his office, where he stayed for several hours. But aside from that . . ." Kione shrugged, dismissing suspicion. "There were two other men who shared that name, but they were completely in the clear as one was in jail and the other at an all-night casino where a number of players vouched for his presence for the entire evening. He plays there often. And that's about all I can tell you, Lord Ardry. I'm sorry I could not be of more help to the superintendent."

"He appreciates whatever you have been able to do. And I expect you have plenty to contend with here in your own city without taking on London."

"That is certainly true. The crime rate in Nairobi keeps rising every year. It is the highest of any city on the continent, and we do not have enough police to cover all of the sections of the city." He sighed and went on: "This Mr. Jury. It was about photos he wired." He reached into a desk drawer and pulled out a manila envelope. "These were sent here to the station." Kione thrust the envelope toward Melrose.

"Thank you." Melrose pulled three pictures from the envelope. He had seen a similar photo in the *Times*, but he bet the picture was not a patch on the person herself. You could just tell. A camera couldn't replicate the fineness of the skin, the silkiness of the light hair. Rebecca Moffit was beautiful. The second photo was of the Abasi painting. A woman by a lagoon; behind her crouched a lion. The third was the gallery photo.

Melrose pulled the book from Patty's hands and shoved it back in among the others, one of which, he was surprised to see, was *City of Glass*. "You're a fan of Paul Auster?" he said to Kione.

"Ah! Mr. Auster! A great writer. His mysterious depictions of New York fascinate me. I love New York, though I've never been, alas." He was leafing through *City of Glass* as if he intended to settle down and read it. "What a wondrous city it must be. It's strange, but despite its size and all of those boroughs, it has always struck me as all of a piece, organic."

"Not everyone would—" Melrose started to say, but was interrupted.

Just then the door behind them opened, after a brief knock that wouldn't have given anyone time to put away the gin, and someone entered, not approaching the desk but stopping at the back of the room. Melrose turned to see a tall, uniformed man who looked to outrank Kione, given all of the insignia and gold braid on shoulders and chest.

"Ah, Inspector." Kione did not introduce him to Melrose.

"Chief Inspector Kione, I will need two more men for Longido, if you can spare them. Only for a few days."

He had a very pleasant voice, undemanding, which lent him even more authority, to judge from the reaction of Kione.

"Certainly. Right away."

The policeman left.

Said Kione, "Tanzanian police sometimes enlist our aid." This pronouncement sounded rather smug.

Melrose said, "Chief Inspector Kione, I wonder if you're familiar with a painter here named Masego Abasi? This is one of his paintings." Melrose held up the photo.

Kione looked at the photo, shook his head. "No, I don't believe I am."

"If you could perhaps provide me with an address? He has a studio in Nairobi."

Kione clicked the button on his intercom and gave the address request to whoever was on the other end. In another minute he had the answer and hung up. Then he tore a map from a pad of them sitting on his desk. He turned it to face Melrose and unhesitatingly trailed a ballpoint pen through the thicket of streets in the center and out of it. He did this without once lifting his pen or his eyes from the map, as if he'd been giving exactly the same directions to people who asked for them continuously.

"Have you questions?" he said, finally looking at Melrose and Patty.

"Nary a one. Thank you."

"This is a very difficult city to find your way about in. If you like I can have someone escort you, or drive you to this man's house. Nairobi's quite a shambles, really. I call it 'city of broken glass.'"

Outside in the car, Melrose studied the map. Patty, he noticed, was un-Patty-like silent.

"What's up, kiddo?"

She was chewing her lip. "We should go to this Riverside section."

"You want to check the industrialist's passport?"

"Well, that police inspector said he was gone for hours."

"He'd have to have been gone for longer than that, for God's sake. Come on, will you? Our charge is to go to this artist's studio, and that's where we're going."

23

Were there no narrow streets in Nairobi? No cobbled twisty little lanes with houses all cramped together? If this was what Kione thought of as a hard-to-find street, the city must be full of more boulevards than Paris.

The street was another quarter-mile-wide one with space on either side for flourishing open-air businesses. Most of them seemed to have to do with furniture—making it, restoring it, selling it, exporting it, leaving it out by the curb for passersby to sit on it.

Masego Abasi's studio was located behind one of these furniture purveyors in a little two-room cottage. Abasi himself was a small, compact man who looked as if he might have been carved from mahogany. The large front room was heated by a wood-burning fireplace and had a huge skylight. The artist's studio was so vivid with color Melrose thought it might have erupted in flames and the pictures done the heating.

Even Patty seemed fascinated by the paintings. After the introductions had been made, she stood in front of one and said, "These are really good. I really like them."

"Well, thank you, Patricia—"

She didn't correct him.

"And why do you like them?"

"Because they're real. The people in them—like her—" She pointed to a woman kneeling by a river, scrubbing clothes. "She's using a washboard and you can tell she's really scrubbing. I used to have a washboard."

Abasi was enthralled. "And you feel like you're her?"

"No, I feel like she's me."

Abasi and, certainly, Melrose were taken aback not just by the distinction but by the person making it.

Patty plowed on. "Look at her face." As if the artist hadn't. "She's not happy. She has to scrub clothes all the time. There's nothing happy in this. You see it, don't you?"

Abasi braced his hands on his knees and squatted down to Patty's eye level and looked intently at his painting, which depicted the washer-woman against a backdrop of hot sun and dry grass and burned-looking trees. "Yes, you are right. She does not look happy. But consider that what she is doing may be necessary. Her husband or father or brothers might not be able to go to work without the clean clothes. And if they do not work, there will be no money for food. The family might fall apart completely if the clothes are not washed."

Patty stood there with her arms crossed, scratching her elbows and looking doubtful.

Abasi started to say something, but Melrose stepped in: "I really need to conduct the business I came on."

For a moment they both gave him a look that said *interloper*.

And then Abasi's brow cleared as he apparently remembered why Melrose had come. "Ah, yes. You wanted to show me some photographs."

From the manila envelope, Melrose pulled the photo of the painting. "Is this one of your paintings, Mr. Abasi?"

Abasi took it and nodded. "Yes, this one I called *Woman and Moon*. An early one. Why?"

"Do you remember the person to whom you sold it?"

"You understand, I'm under contract to the Zane Gallery in London."

"I know that. But that doesn't prevent your selling works from your studio here, does it?"

"That's true. And you think that might be the case with this painting?" He tapped the photo.

"I don't think anything, Mr. Abasi. That's why I'm asking." Perhaps the man was protecting himself; maybe he thought Leonard Zane had sent Melrose to check up on him. Melrose then took out the photo of Rebecca Moffit. "Does this woman look familiar to you?"

The artist moved with the photo over to a brightly lit lamp. "She does . . . yes . . . .and yet . . . no. I don't know." He shook his head as he handed back the photo.

Melrose had the feeling Abasi was telling the truth; he might have seen Rebecca Moffit, but he couldn't be certain. "But you can't say if she was here? It could have been before you signed a contract with the Zane Gallery." He thought that was smooth, in case Abasi was still worried about Leonard Zane. "Have a look at this, will you?" Melrose showed him the other picture, the one of the gallery. "It's not the two women here I'm interested in, but the gallery itself. Do you recognize it?"

At first Abasi shook his head, but after further study of the photo he smiled. "Little Rita," he said.

Melrose frowned. "Rita?"

Here Abasi put his finger on the dark-haired woman. "Reminds me of Little Rita."

"Who's that?"

"A little girl who would come here with her nanny. It was the nanny who was my friend. She said Little Rita—"

My God, thought Melrose, as long as it wasn't Little Mitchell.

"—loved to come here. Her nursemaid said she loved the paints and brushes. She was a sweet child." Abasi turned to Patty Haigh. "You remind me of her, too."

When he reached out his hand, Melrose was afraid the artist was about to make the unforgivable mistake of putting it on Patty Haigh's head.

But Abasi didn't. He had closed his eyes and was thinking. "Wait a moment. I do remember someone came here to my studio and I did sell this painting perhaps two years ago. But . . ." He shrugged.

"The important thing is that it did not go to the Zane Gallery."

"It did not, no. Someone definitely purchased it here, in the studio." He closed his eyes, frowning. "Yes, it was a woman. But I do not know if it was this woman." He tapped the photo of Rebecca Moffit. "Why is this important?"

"Because she got murdered," said Patty helpfully.

After she slammed herself into the car, Patty said, "Okay, this Riverside district."

Melrose sighed. "Patty, the police checked Banerjee's alibi."

"It sounded pretty iffy to me." She clicked her seat belt and drew it tight. "'Iffy?'"

"Like, if he was on a business trip, there are plenty of ways he could've ducked out of sight and people would think he was still around."

Melrose stepped on the gas. "Not for twenty-four hours, and his absence would more likely have been two days. From Nairobi to London, kill two people, then a wild cab ride, then back to Nairobi. He would have to have been gone longer than just a few hours."

"Aero was gone for a whole weekend once and we thought he was still there."

Melrose did not want to visit the subject of Aero as the steering wheel jumped in his hands and he nearly ran down a goat. What was a goat doing on a street in one of Nairobi's most urban districts? "From what you've said about Aero, that doesn't surprise me. But we're not all Aero."

They drove through ever less crowded urban streets to a neighborhood saturated with flats to one that was clearly quite different from the area that Masego Abasi lived in.

Riverside Drive was hilly and winding and guarded. Rich-looking houses were nestled in lush gardens, each property walled and gated. Add to that a security guard and there wouldn't be much casual hanging about in the street.

"So how do we get to see him?" The question appeared rhetorical, for she answered it herself. "I could climb over that wall, maybe."

"And maybe get shot by the guard." Melrose thought for a moment. "He doesn't live here."

"Why? He had a lot of money. He's probably rich."

"Possibly, but you told me he liked cafés and restaurants and was always eating out. If you lived there—" Melrose nodded toward the long, low house. "—you'd have a cook."

"We can just sit here a while, can't we?"

"That guard will get suspicious. I think we should drive on by, maybe come round again." Melrose turned the key, told Patty to make herself invisible and drove by the house. "We'll haul up here, wait a minute, then drive back the other way. Now you can sit up."

"But if he's giving a fake address, why this one? Why not a flat or a little house in a crowded street? Harder to find."

"He's not giving the address. It's a matter of record." Melrose paused. "But why are we assuming it's a fake address? Why not a fake name?"

As they drew near the house, Melrose saw the gate cranking open and a Mercedes edging past gate and guard.

Patty watched it for a few seconds, then opened the passenger door and jumped out.

He yelled, "Patty, wait!"

She didn't wait. She darted across the road, unnoticed because the Mercedes had paused and the driver beckoned to the guard. He went round to the driver's side to say something. The guard just missed seeing Patty, who, as the car slowly proceeded from gate to road, flung up her arms and scissored them back and forth.

Now of course the guard did see this little tableau and hurried toward the car as it stopped. But Patty had got to the driver's side first and said something. The car idled as this brief conversation took place, and the driver apparently reassured the guard, when he appeared, and the guard backed off. Melrose could see that the driver looked a little worried as Patty backed away and waved the car on, smiling.

As it drove by, Melrose slid down in his seat.

Patty returned to sit beside him. "You were right. That's not him."

"B.B., damn it, could be anyone, then." Melrose put the car into gear. "Let's go back and see Kione."

"He's not anyone. He's a policeman."

"*What?*" Melrose stomped on the brake.

"He's *that* policeman. At the station."

Melrose gasped. "You can't be talking about Chief Inspector Kione! He'd have recognized you."

"The one who came in the room."

"The one who came in? But, Patty, for God's sake, why didn't you say something to me before now?"

"Well, because I wanted to see who *this* Banerjee was. To make sure."

"Patty, you didn't see the policeman who came into the room." And nor had the policeman seen her. The chair hid her.

"I heard him."

Melrose frowned. "But his voice wasn't—"

"You never heard him before."

He had never known anyone to sound so certain.

"If you don't believe me, let's go back to the police station and find him. If I see him, I'll know him."

Melrose pulled away from the curb. "That doesn't sound like a good idea."

"Why not? He'll remember me. He liked me."

"Not that much, kiddo."

"You're telling me he's a cop?" said Jury when Melrose called him at home. Jury added. "This killer is a policeman?"

"And one high up the ladder, given Kione's attitude toward him."

"What did Kione say?"

"I didn't tell Kione, did I? The only evidence we have is Patty Haigh's. Do you really want to put her in between Kenyan and Tanzanian police?"

"From what I've heard, they'd be the worse for it. What about Masego Abasi?"

"The only thing he's sure of is that the painting didn't go to the Zane Gallery—unless whoever bought it from Abasi later sold it, but that seems unlikely. He couldn't identify Rebecca Moffit. At first he said no; then he looked again and said maybe."

"That's odd, in a way. I'd think a face would be almost engraved in an artist's mind. Especially that face."

"I agree."

Jury sighed. "So all we know is that she didn't get the painting from the Zane Gallery and, consequently, there's no necessary connection."

Melrose was standing at one of the lodge windows holding the phone and now he looked into the black night. "There's one other thing—"

"What?"

"If she *did* go to Abasi's studio, why?"

There was a silence while Jury thought this over. "You mean why was she looking for an Abasi painting?"

"I mean both: what would have taken her to the studio? This is not exactly a street lined with shops, boutiques, antiquarian bookshops and shoes, that someone might be strolling along. What took her there? For that, she'd have to have been a real admirer of his work," said Melrose.

"And obviously seen it before. His stuff does hang in some galleries. Johannesburg has one, Dubai, too, I think Zane said."

"You don't go to Nairobi by way of Johannesburg. Or Dar es Salaam. Dubai, possibly. But consider this: you're a tourist on her way to Nairobi. You'd go direct from London. Even assuming you had a layover in Dubai, would you start hitting the art galleries, and even if you did would you hit the right one with Masego Abasi's work?"

"It doesn't sound very likely. What is far more likely is that she saw his work—"

"In London. In the only place that has it: the Zane Gallery."

"Good job," said Jury.

"Yes, wasn't it? So how's the croupier doing?"

"A good job." Jury rang off.

24

A night drive, for God's sake?

There had already been a five A.M. drive followed by Nairobi police, guards, and gates. Surely that was enough activity for any person? "No thank you."

Enough for any person wasn't enough for Patty Haigh. "Oh, come on." Her tone was a near-wheedle "The Attaboys aren't going. Just us and Lumbai and Montre."

"No."

"Well, I'm going anyway."

"No, you are not."

Hands on hips. "You can't tell me what to do. You're not my da."

"No, but I *am* your unc, remember? You don't want me to tell the Van der Moots I'm not, do you?"

Patty moved closer to his chair and looked straight into his eyes. "You wouldn't rat me out!"

"Oh, yes, I would."

"No, you wouldn't. You're not a rat."

Melrose didn't know whether to be complimented or just plain irritated. "They would not let you go on your own." Considering how Patty had fetched up here, that was a pretty ridiculous concept.

"We'll see." She ran off toward Trish Van der Moot, and Melrose watched the transaction going on between them. A flurry of hands and words before she came trudging back.

"I can only go if you agree."

"I don't."

Patty fell down into the other wing chair like a rag doll.

Melrose looked at her sulky little face and thought it over, the story that he had, of course, disbelieved because it was so outlandish: Patty following a killer. Patty boarding a plane to Dubai and then to Nairobi. Patty befriending perfect strangers because they would serve her purpose and then dismissing them when they no longer did. Patty inveigling her way into the Hemingways Hotel. Patty in the dangerous zone of Kibera. Patty walking alone from that slum to the Mbosi Camp.

That this same Patty would not be permitted to go out with two adults on a safari drive without him or at least his say-so seemed unbelievably absurd.

"Okay," he said.

Her quick look was all gratitude. She jumped up. "You'll go?" Her voice was a childish squeal.

He wondered how often Patty got to act like an ordinary child. He nodded.

She danced around his chair.

They had been driving for an hour over every rock in Kenya when Lumbai spotted the leopard. His binoculars raised, his torch lowered, he directed the eyes to the left. "Leopard cub. It's very near. We must be quiet."

Patty stood up ramrod straight beside him. "A cub!"

In a flash, before anyone knew what she was doing, she had flung open the door, jumped out and started toward the cub.

"Patty!" Lumbai whispered fiercely. "Stop!"

But she paid no attention, lurching across the space in a stumbling run toward the leopard cub that seemed more fascinated than afraid of this sudden onslaught of unfamiliar creatures. For Melrose was out of the car and running after her. He wanted to yell but that would only worsen a situation that really seemed as bad as it could be. The cub. Patty. Patty who hadn't seen the mother leopard in the tree above her.

The leopard draped across an overhanging branch now rising scyth-like from the black branch above them. Melrose felt even his breath violated a necessary stillness. While he plowed through the knee-high grass he saw in the next two seconds the leopard on the branch connect with Patty's presence. It was as if an electric current had swarmed down the tree and parted the grass.

The branch was empty; the grass was full of black shadow. Melrose was only a few feet from Patty. He flew toward her. It was hard to believe he and the leopard were moving at nearly the same moment.

Melrose sprang.

Patty fell.

The leopard leapt.

Far from being grateful to Melrose for saving her life, or to Lumbai for his aim with the rifle, or that her life had been saved at all, Patty wailed and complained all the way back to Mbosi Camp. Her principal complaint, though, was aimed at herself: "It was all my fault!" she kept yelling. Its being her fault did not keep her from yelling at the others, at Lumbai for shooting, at Melrose in general as she pelted him with her fists. "Its mother's dead!" A fist clubbed Melrose's biceps. "The cub's an orphan! The cub's an orphan! You've got to go back! You can't leave that cub on his own. He's an orphan!"

In an evenness of tone that Melrose attributed to child-mastery, he said, "No, Patty, the cub is not an orphan. He has Kenya. He has Africa." Melrose found this a beautiful sentiment, that the continent could parent the orphaned cub.

"Like I have *Brixton*?" she shouted.

*   *   *

Melrose was personally so relieved to find himself still alive that he didn't resent that no one had told him how brave he'd been. Except for a splintering crack, he had heard not a sound, felt not a twitch from the animal that lay in silence beside them. The leopard had dropped with the weight of the night. In those few moments of pulling Patty away from danger, he understood what someone had said about Africa: "It doesn't matter whether you're a lion or a gazelle. When the sun comes up you'd better be running."

He looked out at the black night, with its spillage of oddly lightless stars, and felt for a moment that he too had Africa.

Nor did she stop once back in the tent. She was at least aware enough of Melrose's having saved her life to thank him, grudgingly. But then she returned to her wail (at decreased volume) about the leopard's death.

"Where was the father," said Melrose, "in this family tableau?"

"So you're going to blame it on *them*, the leopards? We're the ones with guns."

"And they're the ones with cunning and claws. I would take your side, Patty, if we were back in the days of Hemingway and the white hunters, but in this case the rifle is merely a defensive weapon. We would both be dead if Lumbai hadn't fired."

"So instead of us being dead, the leopard's dead."

"Right."

"But who gets to decide?"

"Who, indeed?"

25

When Jury walked through the door of the Artemis Club the next morning, the first person he saw was Marshall Trueblood, who asked him what the brown-paper-wrapped thing under his arm was.

"A painting. A Masego Abasi."

"What—?"

"Never mind. What've you been doing?"

"I had a bit of a rummage in the gallery," said Trueblood.

"Rummage?" said Jury. "How in hell did you manage that? Zane watches the place like a hawk."

"Not during dinner. He's quite serious about dinner, which he has in the dining room. So he has one or the other of us take over."

"'One or the other'? Surely he doesn't put any trust in you? You've been here less than a week."

"You give me too little credit, Superintendent. I have an antiques shop, remember. You've never actually seen me sell the stuff. I'm a great salesman. You also forget that Leo Zane is a snob and a seeker of prestige. I expect he'd kill for a title. Melrose Plant would have wowed him."

"What has that to do with you, then? I mean, you don't have a title to wow him with."

"No, but a great-uncle was a well-regarded painter named Abu Kabiga. He was a Kenyan."

"*What?* Are you telling me you're part Kenyan?"

"Of course not. The relationship—if there were such a person—would be by marriage. It's what I told Leo Zane, sitting in the gallery. I told him I was fortunate enough to own a couple of my uncle's paintings. Abu had been a great tribal leader."

"What tribe?"

"Maasai, of course.'"

"Why of course?"

"The Maasai are the haute couture of tribes. May I continue? Zane said he'd like to see them. 'I'm extremely fond of Kenyan art,' he claimed. I made some insightful remarks about the Abasi paintings and Postimpressionism which quite startled him. He asked if my uncle painted in that school. Abasi's vivid strokes and colors."

"I told him no, my uncle was more in the Tingatinga line."

"What the hell's that?" asked Jury.

"Hold on," said Trueblood; "just wait. Zane's hope of finding new Kenyan art dwindled. He said, 'Tingatinga artists are thick on the ground. That art's a bloody factory of art.'

"'Oh, but my uncle was early Tingantinga, which is quite rare.' His interest piqued again. 'I expect it would be,' he said, and asked if I'd had the paintings valued.

"'Last year. A hundred thousand for one of them, two hundred thousand for the other.' Leo whistled at that, but said, 'I've never heard of this Kabiga.'

"'Why would you have? He rarely sold a work and when he did it was only to kings and presidents. Remember President Nyerere?' Of course he didn't. I went on: 'When Tanganyika and Zanzibar joined and became Tanzania, it was Nyerere who was the first president. My great-uncle knew him.' Well, Zane was fascinated. He said he had to see the paintings; said he wanted to have one in the gallery.

"I told him I didn't know that I'd want them on public display. Abu Kabiga wouldn't. He was an extremely modest man. So, one evening he asked me to keep an eye on the gallery when he had dinner. I know his schedule. He always eats at seven and takes half an hour doing it. While he's gone he has somebody sit by the door of the gallery to make sure no one gets in. I said of course I'd be glad to.

"After he went down to dinner I went in. He keeps his desk drawer locked. Naturally, I wanted to see what was in it, so I picked the lock."

"How?"

"With a paper clip. There was money, but not more than a few hundred. There were photos: pictures of three paintings that are hanging on various sections of the wall, none of them good. I'm wondering, why the snapshots?"

"Perhaps he wanted to show them to prospective buyers, I mean send the snaps to see if the buyers were interested."

"A picture of the picture wouldn't tell you anything."

"There are postcards that show Mark Rothko."

"There are postcards that show squares of color, not Mark Rothko."

"Well, you'd know, wouldn't you, your great-uncle being the famous Abu Kabiga."

Trueblood ignored this, saying, "I think the snapshots are there to identify them for some reason. And what if the reason is that what you see is not what you get?"

Jury frowned. "Meaning—"

"The bad art is covering up something good. Wouldn't be the first time."

"Valuable paintings that have been painted over?"

Trueblood nodded. "And that's not all. Unlocking the center drawer at the top of the desk also unlocks the side drawers."

"And you found—?"

"What was even more interesting: the drawer that looks like a file drawer is filled with broken glass and double-edged razor blades." Trueblood smiled.

Jury registered surprise. "For God's sake. To what end?"

"To secrete something."

"But what?"

"Well, I didn't have time to investigate, did I? Furthermore, who would do it? There are like shavings of glass, like broken lightbulbs. Rip your fingers right up, wouldn't it? If he's got something valuable—"

"But why do something so elaborate as that? Keep the stuff in the wall safe in his office."

"Why? Because he's Leo Zane. He likes games. And I'm not sure that a drawerful of broken glass wouldn't be more of a deterrent than a safe. Get a safe open and there you are. Get this drawer open and there you aren't. Besides, who would think it?" Trueblood lit up a pink Sobranie with his gold lighter. "I'd like to get Diane here."

Jury was so used to Trueblood's shifting conversational gears that he barely blinked. "Diane Demorney?"

"How many Dianes do we know? I need a distraction."

"You have too many as it is."

"Not a distraction for me. A distraction for Leo Zane. I want to get into that drawer. You think he's smuggling tanzanite, didn't you say?"

"And you think that's where the stash is? Or do you just want to practice your pilfering skills?"

"Very funny. You know, I wonder what Dr. Moffit's system was. Maybe it wasn't how to beat the house. Maybe it was for something else," said Trueblood.

"Physics. What kind of application would that have to Leonard Zane's world?"

"That's rather begging the question, as we don't know what Zane's world is."

"Art, gambling. David Moffit."

"But you don't know there was a connection to Moffit."

"Sure, I do."

"How?"

"Because he died on Zane's doorstep."

"And the shooter?"

"Mr. Banerjee appears to have melted into the Nairobi night."

26

Leonard Zane held the painting up to the sunlit window. "Where did you get it?"

"From the Moffits' London flat."

"Moffits? You're talking about the couple who were shot?"

"Rebecca Moffit, yes. According to her mother, it was Rebecca's. But you had never met her."

"That's right, I hadn't."

"Yet she must have been in your gallery in order to acquire this Abasi painting."

Leonard Zane frowned, looking at it. "I don't recognize it, and I think I would." He pulled over the leather "sales" book; started leafing backward through the pages, over which he first ran his eyes and index finger; and finally shook his head. "I see no record of the sale. You're welcome to look." He started to turn the book round for Jury.

"No, thanks. I'm sure there'd be no record."

Zane closed the book and shoved it aside. "You want to establish a connection between me and the Moffits."

"It's not that I *want* to. It appears it's already there, unless Mr. Abasi has broken his contract and is allowing other dealers to sell his works here. Although I would find it a hell of a coincidence that Rebeca Moffit would have found one of his paintings elsewhere."

Leonard Zane offered Jury a little smile. "My contract with Masego Abasi does not extend to his studio in Nairobi. He was perfectly free to sell a painting to anyone who happened to stop in there. So Mrs. Moffit or her husband must have been in Kenya."

"Wouldn't that also be too much of a coincidence," said Jury, "that Rebecca Moffit would happen by this obscure artist's studio in Nairobi?"

"In Kenya he's not obscure. Or couldn't someone else have given it to her as a gift? There must be a dozen possibilities."

"I don't think so. I see only four: The one you just mentioned—a gift. The Zane Gallery—that's the most likely. The artist himself, if she was in Kenya. Another dealer who shouldn't be selling Abasi's work. That's unlikely."

"There's a fifth possibility: accident. That the painting passed through other hands before it got to hers. Estate sales, a relation handing it along—you know."

"All right, that is possible. However—"

Without a prior knock, the door to the gallery opened.

It was Maggie Benn. "Oh . . . sorry, Leo. But there's a bit of a fracas downstairs. I mean out there—" She pointed toward the window they had left. Jury went back to it. She continued: "The woman in the black suit. She's trying to get to the place that's roped off and the police are trying to stop her."

Jury looked out and down at the drive. From this angle he couldn't be sure, but—suddenly, he started to move. "I'll see to it," he flung over his shoulder. Once out of the room, he was down the staircase at a run.

Outside the front door he stopped. A DS from City Police had walked over to him and said, "She's making a bit of a fuss, sir. I pointed out the crime scene tape was still up, but she insisted on the flowers, sir. Got a bunch of chrysanthemums—she's his mother, or so she says."

Jury froze. He was looking at a dark-haired woman in a black suit in the center of one of the most desolate scenes he could imagine for her: murder scene, empty day, mum, dead son. A handful of already spent chrysanthemums she had probably picked up on the fly. In front of her stretched the "Do Not Cross" crime scene tape that she clearly had crossed in order to place the flowers on the gray stone of the drive. And then obediently returned to stand behind the blue tape. That detail Jury found infinitely mournful.

Quickly, he crossed the drive. He put out one hand to raise the tape, the other to take her arm. "Please forgive us—you're David's mum."

"Mum" was too much for her fragile shell of composure and she started to cry.

Jury put his arm round her shoulders and led her to the front door and then inside, to where Maggie Benn was now standing. He apologized again, saying, "We didn't know you were coming today, Mrs. Moffit. We've been trying to get in touch since last Friday night. We'd have met you at Heathrow. I'm so terribly sorry."

She shook her head as she tried to find a handkerchief or tissue or something to wipe the tears away and finally settled on the sleeve of her black suit. "I was in—I was out of touch, didn't know about—David and . . . Oh, hell. Hell." Crying again, she gasped, "Is there a restroom?"

Jury asked Maggie to show Mrs. Moffit and Maggie led her away. He watched her cross the deep-piled dark blue rug. Although nowhere near being the stunner that Claire Howard was, Paula Moffit was attractive, but then she'd have to have been: David's looks couldn't have come wholly from his father.

Her clothes were low key, but structurally elegant. She wore a perfectly cut suit. Beneath the jacket was a gray cashmere sweater. No jewelry, not a piece. And no makeup, unless it had been washed away by tears.

She was back in five minutes. They were seated in the library; she seemed a quiet person, restful, almost, even in these circumstances. She said, "David was our only child. My husband died some years ago. I feel alone."

"Yes. I've never had children. The death of one strikes me as the worst loss imaginable, one you don't recover from. Ever."

"Thank you for not saying it will get easier. I've heard enough clichés to last me a lifetime. Why do people think that sort of remark makes you feel better?"

"Because it's easier than coming up with something meaningful. It's odd what some people think is comforting, like, 'Be happy for the time you had him,' which is astoundingly callous. How could you feel anything but despair remembering?"

"I'll never see him again, never. I can't—"

"No."

"I'm sorry you didn't know him; you'd have liked him."

"I did know him, and I did like him."

"But where? . . . How?"

"In Covent Garden in a shop we both happened to be in. The owner's an astrologist. There was something about your son that was . . . intensely compelling. You know what I mean?"

"I certainly do. People were drawn to him. When David walked into a room, you knew he was there."

"He had presence."

Paula nodded and dropped her head in her hand. "I think I'd better lie down."

"I'll take you to—where are you staying?"

"The Ritz, but I haven't been there yet."

He rose and helped her out of her chair. As he was retrieving her coat, Leonard Zane came hurrying down the stairs, putting on his jacket. "Superintendent, Maggie told me Mrs. Moffit—" He stopped and held out his hand to Paula. "I'm Leonard Zane, Mrs. Moffit. This is my place. I can't tell you how sorry I am about your son and his wife."

She took his hand and laid her other hand over it, almost as if in condolence. "Did you know him? Did you see him?"

Zane shook his head. "No, I'm sorry to say. Where are you staying in London?"

"I reserved a room at the Ritz."

"Not the Ritz. It's much too big, too ostentatious, and hasn't enough—the Park Lane would be much better."

Maggie Benn said, "They never have anything."

Zane gave a quirky smile. "Well, now they do. Get Simon Parkington for me."

Paula Moffit made to protest. "Oh, please don't trouble yourself. I'm sure the Ritz will be fine."

Zane let his ice-gray glance slide from Maggie's face, as if she'd been the author of this argument, to Paula Moffit. "Please, the very least I can do is see that you're comfortable while you're in London. It's no bother." He took the mobile phone from Maggie. "Simon, hello. Leonard Zane." A pause. "Yes, I know, but—" He walked off, out of hearing range.

Maggie asked Paula, "How long are you here for?"

"I don't know. A few days."

Leonard Zane ended his call, came up to them and said to Maggie, "Tell Jim to bring the car round."

"Oh," she said uncertainly. "To go where?"

"The Grand Residences. That is, if you're ready, Mrs. Moffit."

The car was a Bentley and Jim a full-blown chauffeur, though without a cap, which made him appear that much more official. Jury accompanied Paula to Park Lane.

It was not a room, but a small luxurious flat with a living room and a well-furnished kitchen. Paula said she'd like some tea and Jury offered to make it.

"Not on your life, Superintendent; except to pick up the phone, we neither of us will lift a finger. Get it from room service."

They did. Paula toed off her shoes and sat back in the armchair. "I love English furniture, it's so wide and deep."

"We're a lazy lot."

"Ha. I can see that. I'm tired, but I know you have questions you need to ask. So ask away."

"Do you feel like talking about this?"

"Remember, you knew David. You think I wouldn't want to talk about that? I'll sleep a little and I'll be fine."

After the tea arrived and was poured and the waiter had gone, Jury said, "Rebecca struck me as being the perfect wife for your son."

Paula Moffit registered surprise. "You met her too?"

"Had dinner with them at the Goring."

"For heaven's sake," Paula said after a moment. "You know, I was always surprised that any girl could take a backseat to the cosmos."

"But to hear him talk about her, I don't think she was taking a backseat to anything. He really loved her."

"Yes. He did."

"Strange for one so addicted to the night sky that he could tell his students what he told me he did."

Paula looked puzzled. "What was that?"

"'If you've come here for solace, go back. If you've come for consolation, you won't get it.'"

"What do you think he meant?"

Jury slipped down farther into his chair, looked up at the ornamental molding. "I think he was pointing out how superficial our experience of the cosmos is. We gaze at the stars and remark on their beauty. He looks up there, at infinite space, and feels—felt—the terror." He wished he hadn't changed the tense when he saw her expression. "I'm sorry."

"I'm astonished. You met him once and you know as much about him after only a few hours as I do after years."

"No, I don't, Paula. Not at all."

"I wish only that you'd known him longer."

Jury returned his look to the ceiling. "I feel I did."

There was silence for a few moments, after which Jury shifted ground. "Given that you live in the United States and she lives here, I expect you didn't see much of Rebecca's mother after the wedding."

"As much as I ever wanted to," said Paula Moffit.

It was the evenness of the tone as much as the words that surprised Jury. As if anyone who knew the woman would feel the same way.

"You don't care for Claire Howard?"

"No, I don't." The same matter-of-factness. She had unclasped her bag and pulled out an interesting Victorian-looking cigarette case, offered it to him.

"No, thanks. No more. I stopped."

"Don't you miss it?"

"As much as a perennially absent lover."

"Oh, dear. I hope you don't have to suffer both of those at the same time. One would be enough to flatten you. Though you don't look easily flattened."

"I am, though. Why don't you like Claire Howard?"

She eyed him through the smoke of her cigarette. "You met her."

"Yes, I did."

"You found her beautiful and charming."

Jury nodded.

Paula Moffit added, "And sincere."

Jury smiled slightly. "That's questionable, perhaps."

"Highly. She isn't. Have we an ashtray? Smokers are such a nuisance."

He got up and found a blue-green glass ashtray on a small side table. He put it down before her. She went on: "I didn't trust Claire Howard." She drew on her cigarette as if she didn't trust air, either.

"Why not?"

"Well, for one thing, she's an opportunist."

Jury frowned, puzzled.

"You know, the sort of person you wouldn't introduce to your lover because she might . . . No, that's too obvious. Say instead, the sort you wouldn't introduce to your jeweler."

Jury laughed. "Why not?"

"She'd insinuate herself into his good graces and walk away with the best deal on a gem you yourself were supposed to get. A more literal example: after the wedding, when she returned to England, she got in touch with two or three of my friends and I found out later from one who regularly took a vacation in the Caymans that Claire Howard had been invited to join them. I had no idea about this until long after it had happened. That's what I mean by opportunist. She's extremely manipulative, which of course goes along with the opportunism."

"And Rebecca, did you think she was like her mother? A gold digger, maybe?"

"Oh, gold-digging." Paula dismissed that with a little snort. "Gold digging is much more honest. No, Rebecca wasn't at all like Claire.

Rebecca was a genuinely honest and gracious girl. David met her on a trip to London. Some convention of physicists." She smiled. "Doesn't that sound enchanting?"

"Indeed." Jury returned the smile. "And a romance followed?"

"Yes. Rebecca is—was—quite unusual. Complex for a beauty. Beautiful women generally don't bother being much else. Well, she would have to be complex to snag David."

They drank their tea in silence for a moment.

Jury said, "I understand he'd devised a gambling system that somehow involved physics."

"Not the best use of his discipline."

"Nor, I'm sure, the only. He did have a professorship at Columbia."

"Yes, he did."

"He didn't tell you about this system?"

"Me? Heavens, no. I know he was especially interested in—the uncertainty principle, is it?"

"That you can't know the velocity and the position of anything simultaneously?"

Paula stared. "Well, good Lord, Superintendent! You know quantum physics?"

"No. I just know a physicist." Who's also a pathological liar, but Jury didn't bother with that detail. "Your son was applying the uncertainty principle to cards?"

"Blackjack. But I'm not sure that's what it was. Some theorem about completeness? Oh, I don't know what he was doing." She was silent for a few moments and then said, "The thing is that even though David was addicted to gambling, it couldn't compete with his work; it couldn't begin to compete with the night sky. He saw in it unimaginable depths and brilliance. Everything else was the color of ice." She sighed. "I think I'd probably better get some sleep. I never sleep on these long flights."

"Of course. If you can think of anything at all, later on, that might have some connection with what happened, please ring me." He took out a card. "I'm adding my home and mobile numbers. Or ring me if you just want to talk." He handed the card to her.

Looking at it, she said, "If you need to talk to me again, please don't hesitate. I'll be here. I'm afraid I've been of little help so far."

"On the contrary, you've given me a lot of information about your son and his wife, and a new perspective on Claire Howard. That's a lot of help, and I appreciate it. Call me."

And with that Jury left.

27

"It's only a little after seven A.M. and you nearly got killed by a leopard last night," said a groggy Melrose Plant, thumped roughly awake by Patty Haigh. "No, I will not go on a walking safari with Ernest."

"He'll carry his Winchester."

"That's in *favor* of going? I don't think so."

"But he said we'd see rhinos, maybe even a white one."

"A further bit of bad press. Go eat your breakfast." The last few words were barely decipherable since Melrose had buried his face in his pillow.

"But we can see animals we haven't seen before."

Melrose thought that was another bad PR move. "I've seen enough to last a lifetime. The only animals I want to see in the future are my horse and my goat."

"*You* have a goat?"

She seemed to think this almost as good as a rhino. "I do. His name is Aghast."

Patty clamped her hands over her mouth as if to restrain impolite laughter.

"Would you kindly get off my bed?"

She did, and just stood there.

"And out of my room?"

"Are you getting up?"

"It's only seven, as I said before."

"Come on. If there's a safari walk at eight—"

Melrose planned on taking his time dressing; he intended to miss that lot.

She stood there like a cement figure in a garden.

"You're still in my half of the room."

"I know. I'm talking to you."

"Well, go into your half and talk through the partition. Go on, go." He waved her away.

They passed the Attaboys leaving the lodge as he and Patty were walking toward it.

Mildred Attaboy had to stop them to grip Patty's shoulder. "You poor dear child! We heard about your *appalling* encounter with the lion!"

"Leopard," said Patty. "It wasn't so appalling."

"But of course it was!" insisted Mrs. Attaboy, who hadn't witnessed it and therefore could judge. "A big cat pouncing on you!"

"It wasn't me it pounced on, it was him it did." Patty nodded toward Melrose.

Melrose could have done with fewer pronouns, but the Attaboys apparently caught the drift, and without a consoling nod or word to Melrose simply moved on.

They served themselves breakfast from a selection of dishes: eggs—scrambled, fried, poached and omeleted in ways Melrose didn't investigate—and sausages that he also skipped, choosing instead a few rashers of bacon and some toast.

Patty's plate bulged with pancakes that she took to the table and then went back for a pitcher of syrup and a few pats of butter. She shoved the butter between the pancakes in strategic positions and poured a cross of syrup over the stack. She dug in.

"A leopard encounter really does wonders for the appetite, doesn't it?"

She took the question as rhetorical and didn't bother with it.

Trish Van der Moot interrupted their breakfast to inform Melrose there was another call from Scotland Yard.

Melrose was delighted that, whatever the nature of this call, he could turn it into an ironclad excuse for avoiding the walking safari.

"He's an Inspector Buhari—Benjamin Buhari. Tanzanian police. And according to Kione, he's the brother of this Banerjee."

"Right. The *brother*?"

"Yes. The Banerjees have been acting as foster parents to Buhari's daughter since her mother walked out. The mother was a European. Swedish, Danish—Kione wasn't sure. She left him when the girl was very small. Buhari's an inspector in a district called—" A silence as papers were being shuffled in New Scotland Yard. "Longido."

Melrose set down the phone to inspect his map, picked it up again. "I don't see the name."

Another paper shuffle. "Near Arusha. That's near the Merelani Hills."

"Am I supposed to know these hills?"

"Where tanzanite is mined. The only place where tanzanite is mined. It's about a five-square-mile area."

"Arusha's in Tanzania."

"No kidding. But I do wonder, why would a Tanzanian police inspector be asking Kione for men?"

"I think Kione was simply being helpful. Why don't you just have this shooter arrested?" said Melrose. "Have Kione take him in. Or you lot. Let Scotland Yard arrest him. He certainly faces extradition."

"We have no more evidence than we had four days ago." Jury sighed. "What we have is a trail of near-sightings—"

"What? You're not calling Patty Haigh's a 'near-sighting,' for God's sake!"

"You keep thinking she's an eyewitness. She isn't. Her ID depends on what came down the line. First from Parsons, then the three kids at Waterloo, then this boy Aero, who then told Patty Haigh. Look, a tall black man gets out of a cab at Waterloo, his progress is then noted by one kid after another until his car gets to Heathrow and two other kids take it up. Think about that. A half dozen kids are keeping visual tabs on a tall black guy in a gray overcoat making his way through Waterloo and then to Heathrow's Terminal Three. Now we may be convinced these kids have eyes as sharp as knives and minds to go along with them, but any half-decent defense team could tear that story to shreds."

"Richard, we know he did it. Parsons saw the whole thing—"

"Half-saw. Not even Robbie Parsons is one hundred percent certain he could identify Banerjee. Remember, he shattered the mirror and shot out the cab's radio. Only when he paid his fare—which is something I can't get over—did Robbie get a glance at his face.

"No," Jury went on, "I don't think Banerjee should be approached until we've got more than we have now. And I also want to know his connection to Leonard Zane. But that's not the only reason." Jury was silent for a few moments. "I'm not so sure this fellow is the main . . . Well, let's just say, there's more going on here and in more complex relationships than we thought. I know it all looks completely transparent, as open-and-shut as any murder could be, but . . ." He paused again. "You there?"

"Of course. Sorry." Melrose was trying to hold the map with his free hand. Arusha wasn't actually that far. He saw a road that connected with the main Nairobi road. "Ye gods, Tanzania? That means passports."

"You didn't bring one?"

Ha-ha. "Patty Haigh has been agitating to go to Zanzibar—"

Jury said emphatically, "Patty Haigh will *not* be going with you. You're going to put her on a plane back to London."

Melrose looked at the phone receiver as if it were speaking in tongues before putting it back to his ear. Dream on, Richard. "You do not know Patty Haigh, Superintendent."

"For God's sake. You're flummoxed by a ten-year-old?"

Melrose refused to comment on the flummoxing. He said, "Arusha, huh? It's not far from the border. I'll take a drive there. Thank the Lord I've got my Porsche."

Jury was silent for a moment. "In the middle of Kenya, in the middle of lions, leopards, tigers and cheetahs—"

"There are no tigers."

"Well, you'd know, wouldn't you? You've got your Porsche."

"I really don't think that's a good idea, Lord Ardry," said Trish Van der Moot, anxiously. "You should take one of our vehicles, the Range Rover. Lumbai or Montre could drive you."

"You're probably right about the car, Mrs. Van der Moot. The Range Rover would be far better, but the distance is not remarkable and I'd prefer to drive myself."

"Do you shoot?"

"Do I shoot what? You mean a rifle? Yes, quite a lot."

Quite a little. He heard Patty make a sound in her throat.

"There are wild animals out there."

Good Lord, she could say that after the previous night? Patty made another sound in her throat and Melrose stepped on her foot.

He told her she would not be going and waited.

Patty looked at him for a few moments and turned and stomped out of the lodge.

When he got to their tent, she was tossing stuff into her backpack, including rhinestone-framed glasses, notebook, pen and money roll, which she first counted.

Reclining on his bed, Melrose watched this for two minutes and said, "What are you doing?"

"Packing." She shoved in a pair of jeans.

"Just for overnight? Or the rest of your life?"

"A couple days. In case." She picked her passport from the top of the dresser.

"You're not going with me. Superintendent Jury gave strict orders you were—"

She cocked her head. "Who said with you? Zanzibar."

Melrose shot up. "Now you just listen, Patty—"

She stood quite still, wig in hand, listening.

Was he supposed to say more? The "just listen" carried with it under-stood commands.

Hearing only silence, Patty dropped in the wig and zipped up the backpack.

"And just how are you—?" Was he really going to ask something as stupid as *How are you going to get there*? No. "Do you take bribes?"

"Depends."

"Say, could I get you to go to London for maybe two thousand quid?"

She looked off, thinking or not, he couldn't tell.

He raised it: "Five?"

"It's not the money. I'll just never get another chance to go to Zanzibar."

Another chance? "I don't see your chance right now."

"It's only like an hour and a half to fly." It was, to her, mere logistics. "There are a lot of flights."

"What would keep you from taking off for Zanzibar? Meaning, what bribe besides money?"

She just looked at him.

He shook his head. "No. No, you cannot go with me to Tanzania."

An hour later, Patty Haigh had her binoculars, her camera, her smart-phone, two Coca-Colas and a thermos of tea, and was sitting in the Range Rover.

But to his credit, Melrose felt he had attempted to do what Jury insisted upon—by way of cajoling, threats and bribes, and stopping just short of beatings. So he had given in, first extracting a promise that she would stay within view and would not hector him about detours to Zanzi-bar. He reminded her that the purpose of the trip was to visit the Merelani Hills tanzanite mines and also to find out what they could about her great friend B.B. (Before he finds you, Melrose did not chillingly add.)

She promised.

It had all the conviction of assurance from a leopard that, yes, of course, he could play with her cub.

28

———

They had been driving along the A104 for two hours.

"Will we ever come to anything?"

Patty was studying her map. "Tanzania, maybe."

"Thank you."

"Or the Indian Ocean."

The country grew increasingly hilly. They saw road signs pointing to the Tsavo National Park. "My God, this country has a lot of national parks. Are we still on the A104?"

"Yes. I'm hungry. Can't we stop somewhere?"

"I'm sure we'll pass a Little Chef soon."

In another few miles, Patty said, "There's a town. Namanga? That's what we're looking for, isn't it?"

Namanga was a dumpy place, with a lot of what in the U.S. would be called tract houses. There were a multitude of shacks selling various drinks and snacks. They passed, or would have passed had Patty not dragged at his sleeve, Joe-Dan's Bar and Grill, a much larger wooden shack, with a porch and a number of vehicles pulled up round it.

"We might as well never have left home," said Melrose.

"Maybe they do fish and chips."

"You're vegetarian," he said, opening the car door.

"Except for fish and chips."

The restaurant was half full of customers of various ethnicities— European khakis, truck drivers' billed caps, tribal dress. There were two empty stools at the bar so they climbed onto them. Joe-Dan, if this were he, was a broad-faced, friendly-looking Kenyan who did not do fish and chips.

He said, "How about nice ostrich burger?"

Patty said, "I'm sorry. I'm a vegetarian."

He smiled even more broadly. "All right. I will make you nice veg-nut-burger." He set down Melrose's beer and went to make the nut burger.

"Tell me," said Melrose, when Joe-Dan put the burger before Patty. "I know there's a huge national park around here, but I was wondering if there was any mining going on?"

"Of course. This is the neo-belt. All kinds of mining."

As if they should know the neo-belt. "Gemstones?"

Joe-Dan nodded. "Rubies, emeralds, sapphires, tanzanite, tourma—"

Melrose interrupted the catalog. "Are these large mining companies?"

"No. Mostly very small."

"Are they all legal?"

Joe-Dan laughed. "Nothing is all legal, is it?"

"But no diamonds," said Patty knowledgeably.

"No. But there's tsavorite. Some rarer than emeralds, except it's hard to get one more than a carat or two. But there's lots of mining of it." Joe-Dan wiped the bar.

"We're looking for Longido. And then for Merelani. The hills."

"Oh, not far. Twenty-five or -six kilometers. Half hour to drive." Joe-Dan brought out a map. "Here." He pointed to a dot on the map in Tanzania, then trailed his finger past Arusha, much larger, and to Merelani. "That's only about ten kilometers from Arusha. The road is good for a few kilometers, afterward, very rough."

Finishing beer and burger, they thanked him, slipped off their stools and made for the car and the Tanzanian border.

*   *   *

"This isn't a very pretty town," observed Patty as they drove along the dusty street between stacks of low buildings that in the UK would have probably been euphemistically called "housing estates" for those in Social.

"It wouldn't be, seeing as it's a border town with all of its consequent traffic."

Melrose found it interesting that Kenya and Tanzania seemed to be sharing the same border patrol facility. The Kenyan inspector emerged from one door, the Tanzanian out of the door on the opposite side. Neither looked at Melrose or Patty with any particular interest beyond asking for documents. They were more interested in the Range Rover that, Melrose would have thought, was a fairly common vehicle over here, pricey though it was. They were waved on—or, rather, away—as if Kenya could hardly wait to be rid of them, and Tanzania didn't much want them.

In Longido, in front of the police station, several light-uniformed policeman were deep into the inspection of two automobiles, bending over the trunks. There was little activity otherwise, until Patty provided it by punching Melrose and saying, "That's him. There."

"You mean looking at the cars? Where?"

"No, no. Just came out of the door of the station." Patty hunkered down in her seat.

It was indeed the same policeman who'd walked into Kione's office. Tall, elegant, authoritative-looking, his gaze hovered over the unfamiliar Range Rover, which was not surprising as there was otherwise not much new to be seen in Longido.

Melrose grabbed the blanket from the backseat and tossed it over Patty. "On the floor."

But Banerjee—assuming this was he—did not move toward the car.

Buhari—wasn't that the name Jury had given him? It was certainly not Banerjee, or Kione would have said something. He didn't think he'd take this opportunity to find out. "Let's get out of here,' he said, as quietly as possible starting the car and slowly backing away from the station, then just as slowly driving away down the narrow street and following the first sign that said Arusha.

As it had an international airport, Arusha was a good-size, well-populated town. Certainly one advantage was that the cellular service was greatly improved. There was another call from Jury.

"This official in Dar es Salaam? I told him you had extensive holdings in gemstones and were interested in developing one or more of these boutique mines—"

"You didn't really say *boutique*, did you?" Melrose snickered.

"Yes. To differentiate it from the big operation. Of course you wouldn't be going *into* a mine; you'd be trying to gather information, in the guise of a rich peer with nothing better to do with his millions than invest in mining and in such a way that the Tanzanian government would be swell with it. Garnering taxes, et cetera."

"As to the 'et cetera,' what are you talking about? Meaning what would *I* be talking to *them* about?"

"What you'll talk to them about is your intention to mechanize things. Not on the order of the big operations like TanzaniteOne, but definitely using cutting-edge methods. Superior equipment and much-improved safety measures. My objective here is to get information about Leonard Zane's own mine output."

"But I can hardly go into his mine, can I? He wouldn't—"

Jury sighed. "Of course you won't be going into Zane's own mine. But this is Merelani, I mean all of Block D where the independent licensed mines are. They're all sort of razor-wired off, but the workers—"

"Razor wire? That's what I'm supposed to go through?"

There was dead silence on the other end. Speaking into it, Melrose said, "Sorry. Go on."

"You're very good at ferreting out information. I've observed this over the years. Why else would I use you?"

The first half of this observation had Melrose lighting up a self-congratulatory cigarette; the second half had him chucking the cigarette out the window. "'Use me'?"

"I didn't mean it that way; I meant in the sense of being 'useful.' Which you are. So, these miners and the people who run the mines probably know a lot of what's going on in the surrounding mines. Wouldn't you imagine the competition is fierce? Not to mention the corruption. I want to know what's coming out of Zane's blue seams. I think it's more than he's displaying in this gallery. He could be smuggling the stuff, and I'm wondering if this Tanzanian police inspector is in his service."

"We've—I mean I've—seen him; he was in Longido. What do you want me to do?"

Jury was silent for a few moments. He said, "I still want you to see these mines. Wait. Is Patty Haigh on her way to Heathrow?"

"Eventually. Bye."

Melrose threw the car into gear. The road, as Joe-Dan had said, was quite good beginning at a sign that announced they were entering an area maintained by the Tanzanite Foundation. For several kilometers it was graded, but then it simply stopped. As if the Foundation had suddenly run out of money and left the driver to take his chances. It was a horrible road. He would have thought that the Foundation, which must have been rolling in money, could have forked over a little more for the benefit of the poor souls who had to travel its dust-clouded surface daily.

Nor was the landscape anything to praise: hard, dry, suffocatingly hot, thirsty and monochromatic. Melrose had never seen a colorlessness to match it except at his tailor's, when the old man, in the hope of educating him in the difference between superior and inferior cloths, brought out a cheap tan tweed and set it against a fawn merino wool. Somehow the neutral color of the wool had glowed next to the turgid tweed.

But then he saw Kilimanjaro.

"Does all Tanzania look like this?" said Patty. "It's all one colorless color."

"Of course not. If you'd just raise your eyes you can see that mountain in the distance. That's Kilimanjaro."

"Wow." Even Patty could be wowed. A mile or so along, Patty said, having erupted from her funk, "Maybe that's it, the town."

The map told them it was. Signless, directionless, and utterly lacking in horses, grocers, saloons and gunplay. It was vacant. It was dust.

He found the office in a narrow building where he got a permit.

"Yes," said the official in charge, "a Scotland Yard policeman spoke with the minister. You understand, of course, that Block C, which is mined by TanzaniteOne, is out of bounds."

"Would it be possible—"

The man didn't even let him finish the sentence before the perfunctory "No."

"May I ask why? It would almost seem they're hiding something."

He did not even bristle. "The problem is safety."

"But TanzaniteOne is the best of them, isn't it? The most modern. Safety would be far less of a problem."

The official kept shaking his head almost laboriously, as if sheer effort might overcome the stubbornness of this rich, sniffy Englishman. As he handed Melrose the permit, he said, "You have permission to go to the mines in Block D. The manager of Blue Vein mine, Mr. Adisa, will take care of you."

What care was taken? Mainly it was getting through the barbed wire that surrounded each of the small mines. The manager, Sayko Adisa, was a pleasant, round-faced youngish man. He was the one who opened the barbed-wired gate for them.

There looked to be some thirty or more miners aboveground, crowded round the step to the rough-framed one-room office where they were headed.

Others were standing round the opening to the tunnel, which looked exactly as he'd pictured it: a hole growing blacker the farther the wooden ladder descended. The top of it was outlined by splintered, broken boards.

Patty burst out, "Oh, can I go down there?"

Adisa's "No!" was more kindly spoken than Melrose's "Don't be ridiculous!"

"But we want to see them hack it out of the walls!"

"Believe me, Miss Patty, you would not think it worth the trouble when you got down there and had to crawl on your belly like snake."

"But, see—" And here she pointed to a row of children sitting on a bench against the fence, eating something. "—you've got kids here who're doing it, from the looks of them."

Adisa was about to answer when a miner coming up the ladder poked his head over the rim, followed by his thick shoulders. At first Melrose thought the gray he was seeing was just the hard hat and shirt. But as the figure completed his rise from the pit, Melrose saw that the whole man was the color of graphite—head to toe, hard hat to boots.

Melrose felt a chill. These teams of men were down there for hours at a time every day. How long would the lungs collect this stuff before raging emphysema or something worse set in? And the children, my God.

Yet this miner was smiling, probably at the sun, the light of which touched his lashes coated with slivers of silver. In his hand he held a thumb-size stone that the others gathered round to see.

"Is that a piece of rough tanzanite?" Melrose said.

Adisa laughed. "Wish it were! You can see small strip of tanzanite. But mostly graphite around laumontite, maybe two carats tanzanite."

Patty, of course, headed in her own direction, toward the kids on the bench. Melrose asked Adisa if that was all right: "I mean, is it safe for her to go wandering around?"

Adisa smiled. "No. But as you see she's not wandering. The children are limited to one little area when they're aboveground."

Melrose stopped. "You don't mean those kiddies go down the mine, do you?"

"They do, yes. Sad, but their families need the money."

Sad, but was it legal? Melrose didn't voice this question. "It's so dangerous, though, in this kind of small operation, isn't it?"

"Oh, yes. The expense of safety measures like big mines use, well, we just don't have the money, do we? Please, sit." They were in the small office now, a desk and several chairs the main furnishings. There was one cot. "So many of our small mines are closing. Too expensive to run because we have to go deeper and deeper to find a vein. The big operations have the equipment for that; we don't."

"So business, I take it, has not been good?"

"How could it be, with all the smuggling? Millions from Arusha to the Masai Mara—"

"Kenya?"

Adisa nodded. "From Kenya, then to India and China. Most of the cutting is done in Jaipur. It is terrible, what is lost to Tanzania. Eighty percent of receipts, I hear. They tighten the inspection, maybe in Nagamba, but there are all of the private cars moving between Arusha and the Masai. It is impossible to control the smuggling."

Melrose thought for a moment, then said, "We saw some vehicle inspections taking place in Longido. Police station. Incidentally, do you know these policemen? There's one who looks pretty high-ranking. Tall man, I think an inspector, or a commissioner of some kind?"

"Probably Inspector Buhari."

"And do you know him?"

"He inspects this mine. To that extent, I do."

"Has he ever warned you about any, ah, irregularity?" Melrose had no idea how to ask exactly what this inspector did.

"No more than in all the mines. He complains about the children. Employing anyone under age eighteen is illegal." Adisa shrugged and looked toward the yard. "But we all use them. This police inspector has tried for years to bring charges against any mine that does this, but he's only one policeman and how much time do they have to spend on this issue? There are many government bills on the books about child labor, but what good does that do? There are too many of our little mines and not enough labor inspectors. I have never seen one here."

"But he's fair? Honest?"

"Yes. But, like I say, his biggest worry is the children. When he comes, he often talks to them."

Melrose rolled a mental ball around, like a cue ball on a snooker table. Then, click, he hit it with a cue. "What I'm really interested in doing is buying into an existing mine. Rather than opening one on my own. I've seen several, and am considering two or three. Yours is one."

Adasi's eyes opened wider. "And who are the others?"

"The Zane mine. Do you know it?"

"Ah, yes. It is very successful, more than any other I know." He looked downcast.

"Why would that be?"

"More lucrative seams, I guess."

When they were back on the A104, Patty reached into her backpack and drew out a small rough stone.

"And where did that come from?"

"Abi. At the mine."

"Who's Abi when she's at home?"

"One of those kids. This is tanzanite. She took it from the mine. It's so small nobody noticed."

Melrose was shocked. "Patty! You've just smuggled something out, for God's sake."

"Oh, don't be so stuffy. Anyway, I didn't smuggle it, Abi did."

"Sophistry, that is." Melrose had pulled over to the side of the road and was now inspecting the stone. It looked like a smaller version of what the miner had brought up. Tanzanite embedded in graphite. The graphite made up most of it, he imagined. The whole was probably not more than two centimeters, less than an inch. "There's probably not even a carat of the gem in there. Well, you'll have to leave it behind, nonetheless."

"Oh, of course."

He started up the car again, giving her a sideways glance. He didn't care for the easy acquiescence.

*   *   *

Back at Mbosi Camp once more, he called Jury and reported on his trip
to the Merelani Hills.

"Sorry, Richard. I found out nothing about Leonard Zane's mine or
possible smuggling. And I learned nothing useful about Banerjee. Or,
rather, Buhari."

"But you did. He loves children."

29

Although Jury was not a gambler, he was drawn to this room at the Artemis Club with its mirrored walls and high ceilings, its bronze light fixtures, its French doors leading onto a terrace with a wrought-iron balustrade that overlooked a surprisingly large garden. Where had this space come from in the City, otherwise occupied by skyscrapers of high finance? He liked the half-moon bar at which sat well-tailored men and women fashionably dressed in sequined and otherwise embellished gowns. For a room packed with gamblers and dealers, it was not only rich but genteel.

What really drew him was Marshall Trueblood's table. Trueblood could make what Jury assumed was plodding luck look like a hurricane of skill. Jury took a seat between a trim, mustached, gray-haired man and a woman awash in a sea of emerald: at her neck, her ears, her wrists, her fingers. She looked as if she'd sink under the weight, but she didn't; she simply placed her bet when Trueblood asked for them. "Bets, please."

There were three other players to the lady's left, but Jury hadn't time to note anything other than their existence because he was trading twenty-five for a short stack of five chips. He noted the sign on the table that advised the minimum bet was five, which was probably why True-blood had shoved those chips toward him. The maximum bet was two hundred. He was glad of that.

Jury didn't know where the skill came into this game. You weren't playing against the other players, but against the dealer. So there were only two hands to watch: yours and his. You had cards; he had cards. He had rules; you didn't. He had to take a hit if he had under seventeen; you didn't. Jury shoved in another green chip and then said, "Double," in what he hoped was a carelessly knowledgeable tone. Trueblood just gave him a nod. Jury held a ten and a queen. The card showing in front of Trueblood's was a ten. He turned over his hold card: a seven. They were the only players left. Trueblood treated Jury to a thin smile and took another card from the shoe and turned it over—it struck Jury as a deliberately slow-motion turn—it was a four.

"Twenty-one," said Trueblood, with a look at Jury in case he couldn't count, and he raked in all the chips. There was something so pitiless in Trueblood's look that Jury wanted to snatch his chips back, but Trueblood was too fast for him

This time Jury took out a fifty and asked for the ten-quid chips. He got five in return for his money. Trueblood looked at the green chips: Jury could almost see them getting up on little chip legs and strolling away.

The emerald-bedecked woman next to him slipped some fifty-pound notes toward Trueblood, who then shoved back five black chips. Since she already had a small mountain of green chips—at least three hundred pounds' worth—Jury thought it rather a showy thing to do; but, then, look at that ring, that bracelet.

The other players sat with their current stash. Jury's current stash was his five blue chips; perhaps he should have put another fifty with it and asked for one black chip. One chip. That would have been a real showstopper.

Trueblood dealt and asked for bets. Jury folded. He had a three and a five. Even with an ace, he'd have only nineteen and the dealer already had a ten showing. Jury would have bet all his chips the hold card was a face card.

More bets. Trueblood fulfilled requests for hits. All four players to his left busted. The gentleman to Jury's right doubled down with a king and a jack.

Too bad. The dealer had a king and a *queen*. The house won again. Surprise.

Jury decided his luck, or whatever Trueblood was making of his luck—wasn't about to change, so he took his chips and went looking for something he knew how to play. Which was nothing. He considered roulette, since that seemed to demand even less skill than twenty-one, though he was probably dead wrong about that, too.

"Trying to decide where to lose your money, Superintendent?"

Leonard Zane stood at his elbow. That was a break, the only one in the evening's play: Jury wouldn't have to go looking for him.

"Where else to lose it, you mean? I just tried out your new croupier."

"How was he?"

"Ahead."

"Good."

"Way ahead."

"Better."

"I think he cheats."

Zane burst out laughing. "I doubt that."

"Don't they ever?"

"Yes, but not here."

"Can't a truly practiced roulette croupier tell where the ball will land?"

"No."

"So there's no cheating?"

"Of course there is, but by the players."

"Such as?"

"You want a short course in cheating?"

"Definitely." Jury was watching Trueblood, who had been replaced by another dealer and was now talking on his mobile while walking across the room toward the bar. His moving to the bar, ordering a whisky and lighting up a cigarette was the signal to tell Jury that Diane Demorney was on her way to the club.

Zane picked up a couple of chips from the roulette table, nodding to the dealer. "This trick is old; it's hiding chips. Take a thousand-quid chip—"

"Is there such a thing?"

"Yes." Zane held up a dark blue chip between index and third fingers. He put a black chip on the felt and slid the dark blue chip beneath it.

Trueblood was at the bar now, drinking a whisky. That meant five minutes.

"So instead of betting two hundred," said Jury, "you're betting a thousand plus a hundred, but the dealer thinks it's just two black chips?"

"You catch on quickly."

"What happens if you lose? The dealer takes your chips."

"You have to pick them up before he does that."

"But that's against the rules."

"Of course it is. You bumble around, apologize, then set down two black chips."

Jury frowned. "That strikes me as an awfully sloppy operation and one that would cause a lot of suspicion."

"It does, but a lot of players have made a lot of money doing it."

"Well, enough of your games," said Jury, with a smile, "and now back to mine. Would you mind having another look at the crime scene, Mr. Zane?"

Zane frowned. "You mean outside? Why?"

"Because it's the crime scene and it's yours." Jury's smile broadened. "And I'm asking."

Leonard Zane smiled himself and shrugged. "All right."

They stepped through the front door of the club and across the driveway to the spot where Robbie Parsons had stopped his cab.

"Where were you standing when the cab stopped?"

"Standing? I wasn't. I mean I was still inside, as I told you."

"You were in the library, the room on the left, I think you said."

"That's right. I didn't go outside until I heard the commotion, the shouting. Look, Mr. Jury, you've heard all of this before, what's the point of hearing—"

Just then a limousine was pulling up in front of the Artemis Club. The chauffeur got out and walked round the car to the passenger door.

"What's this?" said Leo Zane thoughtfully, as they recrossed the drive.

The chauffeur was assisting a woman gowned in black and white, who, when standing on the pavement in very high heels, proved to be Diane Demorney. She looked sensational. She had gone all-out, no problem for Diane, who was very much an all-out person. The gown struck Jury as an architectural wonder much like the Sydney Opera House, with its sharp angles and shadows, its curves and points around her shoulders. She stood there waiting for somebody to light the cigarette pushed into a white holder as long as her heel was high.

Leonard Zane stepped forward immediately with his silver lighter. He did not seem to question that here was a guest who was appearing out of nowhere, unless he'd misread the invitation list.

"Thank you," said Diane, looking upward at the classic facade of the club. "Very unpretentious. Which can only mean, very successful. You are Mr. Zane, aren't you? I've heard about you."

"But I haven't heard about you. Enlighten me," he added, drawing her arm through his.

"Oh, I intend to do exactly that once I get to your blackjack table."

And she apparently was, if Jury could go by the increase in chips before her.

Jury sat on a bar stool surveying the room. He became aware for the first time that there was no color. Everyone was dressed in black and white. All of the dealers were wearing evening dress, and perhaps it was expected that the men in attendance would also wear evening dress, which they did. But the women? It surely wasn't a prerequisite that they too must dress in black or white, and yet that was the way they were dressed. Black chiffon, white satin, a bold black-and-white stripe. Diane Demorney had melted into the small gathering of players at the blackjack table. A bit of color was furnished by a flash of emerald or a wink of tanzanite. But all of this arrangement in black and white struck Jury with a sense of hazard.

And in the doorway smoking a cigarette stood Leonard Zane himself.

Jury was now alone at the bar. Everyone else was at the tables. He could see Diane's back and Marshall Trueblood's face, saying something to her. Diane had before her one stack of chips that Jury could see, and probably others he could not. He wondered how much she was betting and if Zane had removed the limit. Jury would have enjoyed watching this little sparring match between Trueblood and Diane (for he had no doubt that Diane knew her way round a card table), but he did not want to drag Zane's attention from Diane to himself. He stayed planted at the bar.

She was sitting with a nest of chips in front of her, most of them black. There must have been several hundred pounds showing there. Would Trueblood take the chance of letting her win? Zane would know every trick in the book.

Five minutes later, Diane raked in another high-stakes pot.

It was 10:30, time for Trueblood's break and Zane's late supper. The same dealer who'd taken Trueblood's place before stepped up to the table. So did Leo Zane, who said something to Diane, and she smiled and rose, accepting a wire basket from Trueblood and shoving all of the chips into it. There were a lot, most green and black.

As Zane walked Diane forward toward the door and the dining room, Marshall Trueblood moved to the bar and ignored Jury, who thought it interesting to watch the two paths cross and veer in different directions.

He was sitting half facing the room, his back to the bar stool beside him. Trueblood ordered a whisky. When Zane was well away, he said, "She just picked up nine hundred and change. Let's call it a thousand. He's stopping in his office to exchange the chips for the money. Then the dining room for supper. Frankly, I think he wants to pick her brain. I'm going to down this and then mosey along to the gallery."

Jury said, "I'll be here."

Trueblood left the bar.

*   *   *

Trueblood paused to look into the dining room, where he saw Leo Zane and Diane at a table in the big bay window. He knew that Diane could be depended upon to keep Zane unoperational, as she would put it, for a half hour or so.

He would have to be quick. Never tempt luck; it would almost always be the bad kind.

At this latish hour, Zane didn't guard the gallery door, merely kept it locked. But the lock was barely a nod to security. It was so simple, he could have nudged it open. Why bother at all? But Zane probably reasoned that any serious safecracker would hardly be put off by a locked door. The lock was there just to keep the curious out.

The desk was slightly more problematic. But dealing in antiques had acquainted him with lockable desks. Of course, locks had improved since the eighteenth century, so he had already reacquainted himself with locking drawers by visiting a number of locksmiths and office furniture shops. He did not expect to get a match with Zane's desk, but he found several desks of various vintages that showed him what he'd need.

He drew on a pair of skin-thin Italian leather gloves and unlocked the center drawer. If the side drawers were locked at all, it was inside the center drawer that the device could be found to unlock them. No one wanted to go to the trouble of unlocking every drawer, which was, Trueblood thought, why security didn't work: no one wanted to go to the trouble.

He pulled open the bottom drawer, ordinarily a file drawer, and observed the obstruction of fragmented glass. Very funny, Mr. Zane.

He worked his way into the middle from the four sides. All of his movements were very slow, very deliberate. As he ran his hands down the left and right sides of the drawer, bits of glass snagged on the gloves, but didn't cut. Any stone as large as this one would soon be discernible in a space this small. He had got all of the information he needed about tanzanite from the Geological Museum, which was now part of the Natural History Museum.

He checked his watch. Less than ten minutes all told. He'd allow another ten. And in another two he touched a hard substance. This was it. He moved his thumb around toward his index finger so that he could grasp the stone. He pulled it to the side and allowed it to shear its way upward through the glass fragments. He realized of course that having excavated the tanzanite he would have to bury it again, but it would not have to be returned to exactly the same place, since he doubted Zane's fingers went exploring in here very often.

He had the stone out and positioned on the desk. It was a cushion-cut of the most highly saturated blue he'd ever seen. He had read in some arcane tome on wildlife that deer, although they had poor color vision in general, could see blue better than humans could. That, he'd thought, was an odd fact. How could one see color "better than" any-thing? But the blue deer saw was far bluer.

Trueblood pulled the miniature camera from his jacket pocket, snapped several pictures, then pushed the tanzanite back into the drawer. Much easier to get it in than out. He untaped his sleeves, locked the desk and made for the door.

In the promised ten minutes he was back at the bar and ordering another whisky. As he took a sip, he dropped the camera into Jury's pocket. "The screen is too small to show you. You can download this onto your PC. It's quite a stone."

"I'm betting the supply will be exhausted in another couple of decades or even sooner. So I think Zane is getting his hands on all that he can and will sell it at a big profit." Jury glanced at Trueblood. "It's a deep blue, isn't it?"

"It's the blue deer see." Trueblood checked his watch. "I'm on."

Jury watched him go back to his table. *The blue deer see?* Puzzled, he felt for the camera and left the club.

30

"Patty Haigh!" called Little Mitchell.

Patty regarded him with distaste.

"Somebody looking for you. Uniform. I'd say police. Whatcha been up to?"

"Minding my own business."

As she walked off, Little Mitchell called after her, "You better watch out. This guy looked mean. Big, black and mean."

Patty hesitated but refused to stop. She wouldn't give him the satisfaction of letting him know she'd heard and was scared by it.

She went looking for Melrose.

"He didn't see you," said Melrose, when she'd tracked him down in his favorite place on the veranda. "You were lost in that huge chair in Kione's office. That police inspector didn't know anyone was there with Kione except for me, and he didn't even look at me. And he certainly didn't see you in Longido." Reassuring words that Melrose believed to be true; nevertheless, he was worried. What if Banerjee had later on asked Kione about the stranger in his office and Kione had told him there'd been *two* strangers in his office, and hadn't Banerjee seen the little girl? Or what if he'd been looking before they had seen him standing in the door of the Longido station?

A description would have been asked for. And a description would have been furnished.

And how many little girls of that description might be concerned with police business?

Only one: Patty Haigh.

It would be simple for a Tanzanian inspector to discover where Patty Haigh might be staying.

Melrose went into the living room, where Trish Van der Moot was plumping up cushions. "I've only just found out my aunt is extremely ill. We'll have to be leaving. Can you get me information about flights to London?"

"Oh, I'm terribly sorry, Lord Ardry. Yes, of course. When you say 'we' do you mean Patty will be leaving too? But what about her parents?"

He'd forgotten Patty didn't belong to him. Or to his sick aunt. "We'll be meeting them at the airport. They've finally managed to sort things with the embassy."

"My goodness. What a trial. I'll find out about flights."

A few minutes later, Melrose returned to the porch and said to Patty, "Pack. There's an Emirates flight in three hours."

For once she took the direction without argument or even comment.

Back in the tent, soundlessly, she went to her part of the room and dragged out her backpack.

In another half hour, the Range Rover was taking them to Jomo Kenyatta Airport.

The airport was jittery with people. And police, Melrose noticed. But there was probably always a large police presence here given the spiraling crime rate in this city. Wallets nicked, passports stolen left and right.

When he had phoned earlier he had purchased two first-class seats, but of course they still had to pick the tickets up.

There was a restroom nearby. "Go in there," Melrose said, "while I get the tickets." She had already handed over her passport to him.

Patty went into the ladies' room with her backpack and he strolled to the Emirates counter. He stood in the "Premium"-class line that held only himself, and then went to the resplendently uniformed lady behind the counter. He supplied her with the two passports and his credit card.

With a smile that more than matched his own, she looked from him to his passport, then from Patty's passport to nothing. She looked over the counter, saw no small person.

Melrose said, "Oh, sorry, she had to go to the ladies' room. Poor little thing, not feeling tiptop, absolutely hating to leave Kenya."

The Emirates attendant smiled understandingly

Melrose drummed his fingers, shrugging Patty's absence away.

The Emirates lady said not to worry and returned both passports and boarding passes.

"Thank you." It was wonderful the unquestioning faith people had in those who spent great wads of cash.

But if the police were looking for Patty Haigh, Melrose was surprised they didn't have a cop stationed at both ends of the ticket counters.

He did not know until she'd walked right past him who she was: flaming red curls, beaded glasses, polka-dot jacket.

"You didn't recognize me. Neither will they." She nodded toward a policeman.

"Neither will Emirates. What are you doing in that getup? Come on."

She hurried to keep up. "It's one of my disguises. How do you think I ever got all the way here, following B.B. and stealing boarding passes and not being caught? Slow down."

"We're in a hurry, remember? And since I forgot my beard and mustache, somebody might recognize me."

"Oh, you look like everybody else."

Melrose contested this, stopping to sweep an arm round. A lot of beads and turbans, coffee-colored and honey-colored faces.

The backpack rode confidently along the black belt in security, sailed beneath the microscopic lens of the equipment and out the other side. Attention was diverted by Patty doing jumping jacks inside the security pod, explaining, when a guard yanked her out, that she was only going by the diagram inside.

They all thought Patty Haigh was a hoot.

"How much do you think it's worth?"

"Your life, Patty Haigh. But given you have nine of them, not to worry. Come on."

Melrose had to admit the first-class accommodation on Emirates was the best he'd ever seen. From the private room to the assortment of spirits to the spa, it was quite an experience. And would have been more of one had Patty Haigh not knocked on his door every ten minutes to ask him what he was going to order for the meal, or how he liked the shower, or what they were going to do when they got to London.

But the latest interruption was different. He took off his headphones when she said, "I think we're being followed."

"Don't be dramatic. In the little bit of time between when you came to the tent and when we left in the car, no one could have found us out."

"Little Mitchell could. He was there when B.B. came to the camp."

"That disgusting child? How did he know it was B.B.?"

"Well, he didn't. He just said it looked like police and he was black."

"This is Kenya. There are many black people, in case you haven't noticed. Anyway, how would Little Mitchell know enough to have you thinking somebody's following us?"

"He's always hanging around the lodge. He listens in on phone conversations. He could have heard Mrs. Van der Moot telling you about the flight to London and getting the car to drive us."

Melrose was doubtful. "Surely, though, he wouldn't have called the police."

"Surelyhewould." She said this onewordwise.

Melrose was suspicious. "Incidentally, what did you do with that lump of uncut tanzanite? You'd better not have it stuffed in your backpack."

"What?" Her expression and voice changed utterly. "Oh, you mean my Cracker Jack ring?" She held up her hand, displaying the now smaller piece of uncut tanzanite, glued to the little pronged opening of the cheap metal band that had once held the fake gem of the "prize" ring.

"Good Lord, where'd you get that? I mean how did you get that into the ring in the box?"

"Lumbai did it. He managed to file away some of the graphite or whatever. And glued this into the metal ring."

"Do you really think you could make that story stick?"

"Yes. I brought the Cracker Jack box too, just to show where I got the ring."

He snorted.

"What are we arguing about? And we're not being followed because of my ring!"

"We're not being followed, period."

"He was trying to get to the business-class bar. But they beat him back."

"You just saw some drunk. You're fantasizing, Patty."

"Am not!" she declared with childish insistence.

"You are too," he said, irritated that she had him doubling down on childishness, as he replaced the headphones.

THE BLUE DEER SEE

31

Jury had visited several small galleries by way of determining if Masego Abasi's contract was being honored by the artist and by dealers.

One was in Bond Street, one in Regent Street; two were in South Ken. Three of the dealers were familiar with the name, one was with the paintings, all were with the Zane Gallery, of which they had a high opinion, although some questioned the taste of combining it with a casino. Rather tawdry, said the Bond Street dealer.

For some reason, Jury felt moved to defend Leonard Zane. "But what a marketing idea!"

It was clear the dealers who found the casino of questionable taste were jealous, because of their own lack of custom. In Bond and Regent Streets, no one at all came in while Jury was speaking to the dealers; in South Kensington, one or two people stepped in every so often, but it was hardly a steady flow. Given their proximity to the Victoria and Albert Museum, Jury would have expected that the V&A's own collection might have inspired at least a trickle of people to stop into the nearby galleries.

The marketability of Zane's gallery was clearly not lost on the South Kensington dealers, who certainly had no high rollers stopping by, indeed no rollers at all. Their rooms were largely empty except for the presence of New Scotland Yard.

In the last gallery in South Ken, where the manager, Mr. Gibbons, was acquainted with Abasi's work, Jury spent more time talking— or, rather, listening. There were intermittent interruptions, caused by potential customers, and the manager quite naturally attended to them *tout de suite.*

During these little breaks, Jury studied a few of the paintings, sculptures and other artifacts. He saw an object hanging on one of the walls that at first confounded him, then intrigued him, then enthralled him. It was a circular piece of glass that contained something that looked like blue sand, hanging between a Jackson Pollock–type piece of art and a sentimental rendering of farm animals in a meadow. When, he wondered, would a pig be chomping grass? The price of this pig was seven thousand pounds. The price of the fake Pollock (a painter he kept trying to connect with and not doing so) was one hundred and fifty thousand. My God. Since the price of the blue sand was a mere two and a half, he thought it a bargain.

He was so fascinated by this blue sand that he hadn't noticed Mr. Gibbons come up to him until the man said, "Unusual, isn't it?"

Jury nodded. "Tell me, do you ever give discounts to Scotland Yard?"

Mr. Gibbons laughed. "The subject has never arisen, as Scotland Yard pretty much steers clear of the place."

Jury liked that turn of phrase and laughed himself. "Okay. This is a first, then, and the question still stands."

Holding an arm across his front, Mr. Gibbons buried his small chin in his small hand and looked thoughtfully at the objet d'art. "Hmm. Let me just ring the owner. Back in a tick." He took himself off toward a landline on the desk at the opposite side of the room.

Jury kept telling himself that his savings were earmarked for a place in the sun following his retirement from the Met. This internal harangue continued for another few minutes as he stood there, hypnotized by the circle.

"Superintendent," said Mr. Gibbons, breaking into Jury's mental picture of the Côte d'Azur, "Mr. Tallow—he's the owner—has agreed that a discount is in order, saying we should support the Metropolitan Police." Mr. Gibbons smiled broadly, or as broadly as his narrow face permitted.

"Great!" said Jury.

"Would a reduction of, say, five hundred pounds be of interest?"

Since Jury hadn't expected nearly that much, he also smiled broadly. "It certainly would, Mr. Gibbons. I'll take it."

While Mr. Gibbons had been having his chin-wag with the owner, Jury had kept looking at the circle of sand. Of course he could not afford it, even discounted. He had the money, as he had for years had virtually no expenses: dirt-cheap rent for his flat, considering what was going up now; he spent little on clothes, cars or pricey electronics. Most of his expenses involved taking Carole-anne to the Mucky Duck, or taking Phyllis Nancy to dinner in more expensive venues, but this was a rarer experience than he would have liked, anyway. Consequently, he spent a mere fraction of his Met check. *And for God's sake*, he chided himself, *when were you ever interested in a place in the sun? You loathe places in the sun.*

Thus he could afford it, or at least rationalize its purchase. He could indulge himself and, as an added bonus, probably drive Sergeant Wiggins—already half crazy from Jury's colored circle drawings—into full-time craziness.

New Scotland Yard, London
Nov. 8, Friday afternoon

32

Sergeant Wiggins walked into the office after one of his cleansing lunches—farro and alkaline water—and stopped dead.

His "murder board" had been appropriated: photos taken down, pictures of the Artemis Club driveway gone. In their stead were his boss's highly questionable colored circles, headed by the names of the places to which they referred—or, rather, to which the string of names written inside each referred.

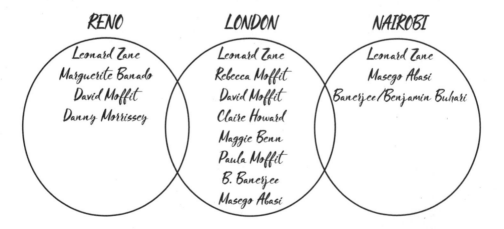

RENO	LONDON	NAIROBI
Leonard Zane	Leonard Zane	Leonard Zane
Marguerite Banado	Rebecca Moffit	Masego Abasi
David Moffit	David Moffit	Banerjee/Benjamin Buhari
Danny Morrissey	Claire Howard	
	Maggie Benn	
	Paula Moffit	
	B. Banerjee	
	Masego Abasi	

Only now there was something *else* hanging on the other wall. His boss had obviously hung this up—him, that had never so much as tacked a family picture to a bulletin board—the superintendent had actually got a hammer and nail and hung up this circle of glass. It was filled with something like sand. Blue sand. Moving sand. Wiggins quickly took a step back. Then he squinted and stepped closer to the circle. The container itself—that is, the glass—was *moving*, but the movement was so incremental that it was almost impossible to see; it had to be, since the sand was dispersing itself into little hills and hollows, especially around the perimeter. It was shifting spookily, falling away in tiny drifts, beginning at the top, moving, stopping, as if micro-movements of ghostly hands were rotating the glass. Well, at least it was another circle, thought Wiggins, aiming for consistency of purpose in Jury's new approach to crime.

It was, in some strange way, hypnotic, so that Wiggins hadn't noticed the door open until the cat Cyril walked in and jumped up on Jury's desk, sitting motionless to stare at the sand.

"Interesting, right?"

Wiggins was almost afraid it was Cyril who'd spoken, until Jury hooked his coat on the wooden tree at his back. "Cyril certainly likes it. Fiona helped me hang it up." DCS Racer's long-suffering secretary.

As if that explained things. Wiggins tried to pretend non-involvement by moving around his desk and plugging in the kettle. "It's another circle."

"But isn't everything circular?" Jury came to lean against the sergeant's desk. "Is that all you see in it?"

"It's blue sand."

"Right. It helps me think."

"*Think?* I assume you're talking about this case, and I don't see how blue sand is connected."

"I'm trying to connect in different ways."

"With what? Dodgem cars and Ferris wheels?" Wiggins swept his arm out in a gesture meant to take in the new office. "It's all like a fair, isn't it? Kids' games. Why don't we set up a little bowling alley and name each pin and see how they fall?" Wiggins sniffed and set out the tea mugs.

"Not a bad idea at all. What I meant was I'm trying to make connections in different ways. The point is, once you get your mind running along the same old lines and your thoughts in the same old trenches, it's hard to shake them loose. Think of the word 'left.' If asked to name an opposing word, practically everyone would say 'right.' How many would say 'taken'?"

"That's hardly got anything to do with this case," said Wiggins, dismissively, and ignoring the point. "It just seems logical to me that as we know who the shooter is, and where it happened, and—" (here Wiggins took himself over to the murder board) "and that the same person, Leonard Zane, was in charge of both casinos, here—" (he put a finger on Reno) "and here—" (another finger inside the London circle) "that there's every likelihood he's behind these shootings. Remembering, too, that he's probably personally involved with the shooter." Wiggins threw up his hands. "What more evidence do you need?"

"A lot. You're making the same old connections, Wiggins." Jury nodded toward the whiteboard. "But how about this? The people inside those circles are all connected. All of them."

Wiggins frowned. "I don't see any connection between, say, Danny Morrissey and David Moffit."

"I do. Leonard Zane, for one."

"We went all through that, sir. Gamblers. Crime. Shootings. Coincidence that Zane was connected with both casinos in Reno and London."

"That's what Leonard Zane said. Uh-uh."

"You say they're all connected. May I remind you you're the one who filled in the names yourself. They didn't just pop up inside those circles."

"They're the principals."

"But you don't *know* they're the principals! There were probably a hundred other people in that casino in Reno. You're just *selecting* these names; it's completely arbitrary." He pointed to the Reno circle. "Marguerite Banado, for instance."

"It's not arbitrary. She was the assistant to Leonard Zane."

"Well, he had other people working for him."

"Not people who would have known as much as she did."

Wiggins opened his mouth as if trying to draw in air or perhaps reason. "What about the witnesses? The couple who saw Morrissey come out of the office? They're not in the bloody circle." He slapped Reno.

"They're not suspects. They're not connected. They don't turn up in either of the other two places."

"Neither does Danny Morrissey." Wiggins thumped his fist on Danny. "Neither does Claire Howard." She got a good thumping, too.

Jury stood silently staring at the whiteboard. He muttered, "Masego Abasi . . ." Another silence, then, "Wiggins!"

Wiggins jerked, nearly spilling his tea. "What?"

Now Jury was at his desk, searching the top drawer. Then he remembered he'd given the snapshot of the unidentified gallery to Wiggins. "Hasn't forensics done that blowup of the gallery yet? I want a copy to go to Chief Inspector Kione. Tell him to take it to Abasi for an ID."

Wiggins looked doubly mystified. "But Mr. Plant has already—"

"Abasi looked more at the women than at the gallery itself. I want him to see the photo again."

"Check with them. It's important." Jury was at the whiteboard, his thin-line marker poised in the NAIROBI circle. He wrote in *Claire Howard*.

"You mean it was her that went to his studio?"

"It's certainly possible. Abasi almost recognized Rebecca Moffit. You know how much alike they look."

"But . . . why?"

"Haven't worked that out yet."

Wiggins's look was dismissive. "That's a hell of a leap, just on the look-alike basis."

"Hell of a leap, you're right. And I'm especially interested in that gallery."

"Could it be the Zane Gallery, then?"

"No. That's clear from the two other rooms you can see through the two doors. I'd like to know where it is and whose work it's showing."

Cyril's tail twitched. Jury watched as a hillock of sand fell gently. He said, "Read that report again from the Reno newspaper. I mean the bit about the shooting in Reno. Morrissey had his back turned—read that." Jury leaned against his desk, next to Cyril.

Wiggins gave a put-upon sigh. "He was in his room—number 2042, twentieth floor—at the Metropole. He said, 'I was just standing at the window, looking at the night sky, when I heard this crack and felt the blow to my shoulder. It knocked me over. No, I have no idea who it was. The door wasn't locked; someone had just opened it and walked in. But no harm done, thank God.'"

"Danny Morrissey," said Jury softly. Cyril's tail twitched again. Another hill of sand shifted. "The night sky . . ." He got up, went to Wiggins's jar of colored pencils, took one to the whiteboard, drew a blue line through the name.

"What? Why'd you cross him out?"

Jury turned. "I'll bet my next check there is no Danny Morrissey." Jury turned back again and drew another blue line in an arc up to David Moffit.

Wiggins looked only a shade short of scandalized by this sudden leap of unreason. "Pardon me, but that's preposterous—"

"But it isn't. Wiggins, why does all of this—" Jury gestured from the whiteboard to the blue sand. "—make you so angry?"

"Angry? It doesn't! It's just that it's all a massive waste of time. Because cases proceed along lines of evidence, straightforwardly, as we discover more and more evidence."

"Oh, come on. We've never had a case that was straightforward."

"That's not true at all."

"Name one."

Wiggins dropped a fresh tea bag into his mug and pursed his lips in thought. He brightened. "Yorkshire. The Old Silent. That case strikes me very much like this one—where Nell Healey shot her husband in the chest right there in the pub. Right out in public. Just took a twenty-two out of her bag and—wham!" Wiggins made a sign with index finger and thumb.

"Straightforward? Chain of evidence? That case was a miasma of misinterpretations and misconceptions, and mostly because our thought patterns were so ingrained. Take the Lincolnshire murder. Do you remember the Red Last? How Pete Apted cracked that case in Lincolnshire by pointing out that 'last' had more than one meaning. That 'listen' could mean two different things?"

"Well, it's a long way from the Red Last to circles on a murder board and blue sand that keeps shifting around." Wiggins was miffed.

"No, it isn't." Jury faced the wall against which his desk stood and studied the shifting sand. "I'm just trying to see the blue deer see."

"*Wot?*" Wiggins was on the fringe of outrage that seemed to heighten his northern accent.

"Deer can see a blue we can't." After Trueblood's opaque remark, Jury had searched the Internet for an explanation. "It has something to do with their having more rods in their eyes and short-wavelength vision." He plunked Cyril from his desk to the floor and was rewarded with a look of outrage that exceeded even Wiggins's.

Wiggins looked from the murder board to the circle of sand on the wall. "Well, pardon me, but it's my opinion that people just don't think like this!" Miffed beyond measure, he dumped himself back in his chair.

"Oh, but they do. I can name several: Sherlock Holmes, Sigmund Freud, Kierkegaard—"

Unmiffed, but astonished, Wiggins shot up again. "Sherlock Holmes! You can't be serious!"

"—and David Moffit."

33

"Where're we going?"

"Oh, it's still *we*, is it?" said Melrose. "I thought *we* was an African experience."

"It is. We're still having it." She looked behind them and then adjusted her backpack. "You know what I think?"

"No, but I'm sure you'll tell me." They were headed with the other passengers toward baggage claim.

"You shouldn't pick up your suitcase. We should avoid baggage because he'll be looking for us there."

Melrose sighed. "Patty, no one's following us. And even if they were, the person wouldn't know I have baggage to collect."

"Unless he's stupid. Sure he does. You're not carrying anything, so unless you went to Kenya in the clothes you're standing up in, you must have baggage. And you definitely are not a clothes-you-stand-up-in person."

Melrose stopped. "No? How do you know that apart from the fact you saw my suitcase?"

"Because look at your suit. I bet it's bespoke and cost a thousand quid. You're rich. Let's just get out of here and go to the Dorchester."

They resumed walking. "Why not the Ritz?"

"Too flashy."

"Oh, dear. Well, you in your rhinestone glasses would know."

She had donned another disguise in her first-class cabin: a chromium-blond pixie wig and a bright pink top.

"But tell me, Mistress of Illusion, how does your disguise help if you're still with me? And if he's tailing us, he can do it to the Dorchester."

"A good cab driver could lose him in a minute and I know a lot of good cab drivers."

They were nearing the exit. Melrose had jettisoned his suitcase for the time being. She was probably right. "But then a good cab driver could *follow* another good cab driver," he said smugly, as he fished out his mobile. "What we need is a police escort."

"Don't be daft. That would only call attention to us."

"How much more attention could be called?" Melrose pulled up his screen of six names. "Nor do I want to be at the mercy of Kenyan police."

"Tanzanian."

"Oh, well, that's all right, then. No place in London is safe—Damn." Jury wasn't answering his mobile. The call didn't even go to voicemail. Melrose tried New Scotland Yard, his sixth address. "May I speak to Superintendent Richard Jury, please . . . No? Well, then Sergeant Alfred Wiggins, is he there?" Long pause. "No? Thank you." He switched off the mobile.

"Who're they?"

"New Scotland Yard."

"That friend of yours? Wait!" Patty grabbed his arm.

"Do I look like I'm going anywhere?"

"I know!" She took out her own mobile, tapped a number. "It's Patty. I'm back. Yes. Listen, who's at Heathrow? We need a cab, and a really good one, and . . ."

She had turned away and Melrose couldn't hear what else they'd need.

She turned back. "Come on."

"To where?"

"Taxi."

He looked at the line for the black taxi rank. "We're not waiting in that!"

She was looking across the road. Melrose saw headlights winking. She grabbed his arm. "Come on!"

They crossed the road at a run; she yanked open the door of a taxi, clearly not in the rank, and pulled him in. The driver opened the glass divider between front and back. "Hey, Patty."

She returned the "Hey" and he closed the window and drove off, not "Heying" Melrose.

The cab took the M4 into Hammersmith, and then on to South Kensington and the Brompton Road, where it stopped in front of the Victoria and Albert Museum in a line of waiting black cabs.

Here, Patty threw open the door on her side, turned and said, "Get out!"

"What—?" But Melrose, noting the urgency in her voice, climbed out and followed her lead into one of the standing cabs.

Melrose was about to question this maneuver when, as before, the glass partition slid open and the driver turned.

"Okay, Patty?"

"Yes, thanks, Jonah."

"I think maybe Victoria."

"Good as any," said Patty.

What, wondered Melrose, was this coded conversation?

The driver looked in various mirrors, slid out of the line and into the flow of traffic on the Brompton Road. After passing Harrod's, he turned into Sloane Street. When they got to Victoria, he joined the fleet of black cabs inching along under the arch, then stopped.

Again, Patty got out, pulling on Melrose's sleeve, and again they piled into a cab two ahead of the one they'd just exited.

"Hi, Billy," she said when the panel slid open.

"Patty."

Melrose said, "What are we *doing*?" The tone demanded an answer.

He didn't get one. There was a Billy–Patty exchange, and they pulled out of Victoria.

This cab-switching maneuver was repeated twice more: in Lambeth and Southwark. It was while they were going through Southwark that Patty said to Melrose, "Close your eyes for a minute."

Fool that he was, he did, and in a flash a black cloth was pulled over his eyes and tied behind his head.

A blindfold! "I'm being kidnapped! Believe me, you won't get any ransom! Nobody will pay it!"

The blindfold remained there for some time before Patty removed it. Melrose blinked his eyes, looked out of the window upon a complex of wretched little streets that could have been London or could have been Mars. There were no street signs.

"Why are they going to so much trouble for us?"

"It's not us they care about, it's the Knowledge."

"The what?"

The cab had stopped in front of some mean little buildings, the middle one of which had a light showing, and a sign unreadable.

"The Knowledge. It's the only place in London guaranteed we won't be found."

34

"Don't be so cagey—What's all that noise? I can barely hear you," said Jury. "You? *You're* at the Knowledge? *You?* Don't make me larf; nobody knows . . . Okay, where is it, then?" Jury looked up at Wiggins, who was standing by the door, mouth agape. He had just handed Jury the snapshot from Claire's album and the forensic blowup of the snapshot.

Jury was half-studying it as he continued to talk to Melrose. "Sworn to secrecy? Oh, for God's sake, Plant . . . What? Following . . . who? . . . Jury pulled over a piece of paper, wrote, *Look up anything the Yard has on the Knowledge,* and held it out to Wiggins.

Wiggins turned the paper over and wrote.

Jury said to the phone, "I've got to talk to you about Kenya. Have you forgotten I've a double murder—" He looked up to see Wiggins displaying the bit of paper: *Nothing.* Jury would have slammed down the phone, except it was a mobile. "Good-bye!" Shoving the mobile into his pocket and bringing the forensic result up closer, he said, "This is certainly an Abasi painting, I'd say."

"More than that, sir. Didn't you notice?"

"Notice what?"

Wiggins brought the tip of his pen down on one part of the picture. "This blowup shows the paintings in the other rooms, see? Through the doors. They're not absolutely clear but Sammy over in forensic photography says they look to be by the same artist."

Jury scrutinized the picture even more keenly. "And that would mean—"

"It's an Abasi show, right?"

"That couldn't possibly be taking place anywhere but in Africa and probably nowhere but Nairobi." Jury pocketed the snapshot and got up. "Come on!"

"Where to, sir?"

"We're going to find this goddamned pub." He was up and yanking his coat from the coat tree.

"Wouldn't surprise me if it's underground."

Wiggins, staunch, said, "No, it isn't. We've had men walking Tube lines, men down the public toilets—nothing."

"We've got twelve thousand miles of sewers under this city. What about that?"

"That's where you want us to go?"

Jury charged out of the office.

"Sir!" Wiggins called after him, down the corridor. "Wait while I get a car!"

"We don't need a car. We're taking a cab."

Outside St. James's Park Tube station Jury flagged one down as Wiggins caught up with him, saying, "People have been trying this for years, boss. It never works."

"Well, they didn't have this, did they?" Jury mashed his ID against the driver's window. The window lowered and the astonished driver said, "Yes, sir? Some emergency?"

"The Knowledge. And don't mess us about." Jury jerked open the rear door and piled in, with Wiggins following.

The taxi driver slid open the partition. "Sorry, sir, I didn't get that . . ."

"The Knowledge. You know what I'm talking about."

Both the engine and the driver idled. "No, sir, I don't."

Jury said grimly, "What's your name, driver?"

"Ray Rich. It's right there with my license, sir. Now, perhaps you can give me some idea as to what part of London this place you want is."

"If I knew that, I'd drive myself."

Still the driver hesitated. Then he said, brightly, "Ah, yes. I know."

"Thought you did," said Jury as the cab took off.

The driver asked cheerily, "Do you want to go by way of Covent Garden or cross the Thames—?"

"You're asking *us*, driver? *We* don't know where you're going, do we?"

"Right, sir. I'd say Covent Garden, then, and along the Mall toward—"

"Just do it," said Jury wearily.

"Sir," said Ray Rich.

They ended up in Whitechapel.

"This doesn't surprise me."

The cab pulled up in front of a pub . . . No, a strip club. The building was run-down, grotty, but then so was Whitechapel High Street, in which it stood.

"What the hell is this, driver?"

"Nag's Head. Isn't that what you said?"

Jury gritted his teeth. "No, it is *not* what I said, and I think you know that." When there was no response, Jury said, "I said *Knowledge*!"

The driver looked apologetic, touched his ear. "Oh, sorry. My hearing's not what it used to be."

That little hearing aid Jury could have sworn hadn't been there before. He and Wiggins piled out of the cab.

Wiggins told the driver to wait and slammed the passenger door. "What do you want to do, boss?"

"Well, I don't want to go to a strip joint. Bloody hell. Thinks he's being clever, does he?"

"That's what these drivers do. When all of that stuff was in the papers years ago about this pub, I personally know half a dozen people who got in cabs and asked to be taken to the Knowledge and all of them wound up at places that sounded a little like it. One person got driven into the Home Counties, Essex or Surrey or one of them, to a pub called the Cow at the Hedge. Took two hours to get there, two to get back. But what's the connection, sir?"

"Connection? To what?"

"To the Moffits' killing?"

"None. Come on, let's go back to the Yard." Defeated, Jury got back into the cab, told the driver to take them to New Scotland Yard, and did he think he could find the place, or did he need directions?

The driver assured him he knew where it was and in the rearview mirror regarded Jury with what the Superintendent could only call merry eyes. He pulled out his mobile and hit Plant's number. When Melrose answered, with what sounded like a merry voice, Jury said, "I want you to get out of there and go somewhere we can meet. Go to Boring's. Nobody knows where that is, either."

Melrose protested that he wouldn't be safe anywhere else in London.

"Don't be absurd. Even if you are being followed, which I doubt, nobody saw you arrive there, since nobody knows where it is, so nobody's going to see you leave, right?" When this was met with silence, Jury went on: "Look, I'm a CID superintendent and I'm working on a case that involves these drivers. Wouldn't they make an exception in my case?" Why hadn't he thought of that before? "Ask."

Melrose turned from his mobile and, for a couple of moments, Jury heard various noises. Melrose's voice returned. "I asked. They said no. Unanimous."

"This is ridiculous. I want to talk to you. This case—there are bits and pieces starting to fit together and I want to run them by you. All that time you spent in Kenya and Tanzania, and you're the one who talked to Masego Abasi. You and Patty Haigh."

"Who you just want to worm the address of this place out of."

"I do not. Look, you don't think that guy at the airport—you're not really in danger, are you?"

"No, but she does. I'm humoring her."

Jury heard cheering, whistling, feet stomping. "Sounds more like they're humoring you. What's going on there?"

"It's one of their musical nights. Clive Rowbotham is singing something from *Gypsy* and taking off his clothes."

"*That's* the sort of thing London's finest get up to?"

"You're London's finest."

"No, we're the Filth. Come on, Melrose. Get the hell out of there. I'll send you a police escort."

"Oh, I can hardly wait to tell them. Hold on."

Jury heard a brief mumble and then a bray of laughter.

"Still unanimous. This place is a lot of fun and I'm really popular. We're all taking turns buying rounds."

"I'll bet you're popular! Every round you buy for a dozen cabbies, they buy you one."

Melrose was indeed popular. He had upward of five million pounds (not on him), and a Black Card (on him).

"You're not going to give me one lousy clue, then?"

"You're never good with clues."

"Bloody hell!"

Wiggins jumped in his seat. They drove for another fifteen minutes, then, as they pulled up in front of New Scotland Yard, he watched Jury yank out his wallet and count his money. He paid the driver and they got out.

Jury stood there, saying, "I've got over two hundred quid. Here. You take a hundred, I'll take a hundred. You take that side of the road, I'll take this."

"For what, sir?"

"We'll start hailing cabs. Don't tell me there isn't a bent driver in London. There's a bent everything else."

"Oh, come on, sir!"

"It's worth a try."

No, it wasn't.

For twenty minutes, Jury and Wiggins managed between them to stop ten cabs and offer the driver of each a hundred quid to take him to the Knowledge. There was the usual "misunderstanding," the usual "Beg your pardon?" and the usual "Hard of hearing."

"Look, I'm a detective superintendent at Scotland Yard!"

"Sir, you could be the commissioner, and I still wouldn't know this place."

So in the end it was always, "Sorry, mate." Unanimous.

The City and Islington, London
Nov. 8, Friday night

35

Jury made one last attempt to buy off the black cab system, getting into the one that pulled up before St. James's Park Tube station and offering the driver fifty quid to be taken to the Knowledge. Before the cabbie could respond, Jury leaned toward the open glass panel and said, "And I don't mean the Borage or the Cow at the Hedge."

The driver laughed. "Cow at the Hedge, sir? Never heard that one."

Jury gave him his Islington address and added, "But I'm sure you've heard others." To his surprise, the driver didn't automatically deny it.

"Dozens, sir. Fares are always asking to go to that damned pub. Demanding, that is. Prince William got into Clive Rowbotham's cab— he's a friend of mine, Clive, not William—with two security guards and commanded old Clive take him to the Knowledge. Of course Clive denied knowing anything about it. William asked him if he'd consider an OBE. Joking, everybody assumed, except Clive. Clive knew a serious offer when he heard one."

Jury's laugh was freer than it had been in days. "Would the Queen have complied?"

"Rumor is she tried it on herself a few years back. In disguise, of course."

"That I don't believe."

"Me neither. God, the stories you hear about people trying to con cabbies into taking them to that pub. Especially tourists. My favorite story is the one about Brad Pitt. He and that wife of his—what's her name? Angela something?—got into a cab and Pitt offered the driver a thousand quid to take them to the Knowledge. So when Roy, the driver, says, 'Sorry, sir, I don't know it,' Brad Pitt tells him that he's making a new movie and he's got a contract in his pocket and he'll sign the cabbie for a speaking part then and there if only he'll take them to the Knowledge. Then Roy, he says, 'All due respect, Mr. Pitt, and I do admire your acting, but that last film of yours didn't gross much.'"

Both Jury and the driver laughed. "Pretty rich, eh?"

"Would you have refused Pitt?"

Brilliant pause, simulating thinking, and the driver said, "Not if I'd known where the place was, that's for sure."

They had left the Embankment and were driving through the City of London, when the driver spoke again, "I'll say this, though. There *ought* to be a pub by that name, considering all of us have to go through that god-awful test and considering what we know about London."

"I couldn't agree more." As they came into Clerkenwell, Jury thought about Joey and that dark doorway where he'd found the starving dog, and the cabbie who'd known where an animal hospital was. "Saved my dog's life, you did, a little while ago."

"Is that right, sir? Well, I'm glad to hear it."

"As far as I'm concerned, you should all get OBEs."

The City was known as London's "Square Mile." As they drove through Clerkenwell, Jury thought it was his own square mile, considering the time he'd passed through and into it. Up there, along the Farringdon Road, the big red "Z" atop the Zetter Hotel, where he'd first encountered Lu Aguilar. The murder of Billy Maples. The bar called Dust.

"Isn't Barts Hospital near here?"

"In Smithfield, yes, not far back."

"Is it in the City?"

"Barts? Not quite."

Not quite was near enough. Barts was where Lu had lain for weeks in a coma.

"You know where Tower 42 is?" An absurd question; of course the driver knew.

"Yes, sir. Right near the Gherkin, that'd be."

The Gherkin. How wonderfully silly Londoners could be. An architectural wonder of dark green glass and they called it a pickle. "There's a bar on top of Tower 42—" said Jury.

"That'd be Vertigo. Always did like that film. Never been to the bar. A bit pricey for me."

"Are we near Snow Hill?"

"We are, sir. Snow Hill police station's right up there."

City Police. Inspector Mickey Haggerty. Jury would never get over that.

"You like the City, do you, sir?"

"No, I don't like the City. It's too—unprotected." The Artemis Club. Even Kenya had walked into the City of London and shot it.

"You think so? You don't feel the City of London Police do as good a job as the Met?"

Jury laughed. "Better, I'm sure."

"Oh, no police is better than the Metropolitan."

Jury smiled at that and then said, "Did you know there are still dragons marking the places where the gates in the wall of London once stood? I'll bet you know them all."

"The dragons?"

"No. The gates."

"Well, let's see . . . There's Ludgate, Newgate, Aldersgate. Then there's Aldgate, Moorgate . . . Bishopsgate . . ."

They were through Clerkenwell now and into Islington. "One more," said Jury, who then realized he was being allowed a leftover gate to name.

"We're in Islington, sir. Ain't that a dragon?"

Off to the right, a winged dragon near the Angel Tube station. Jury had actually not made the connection before. "Cripplegate. I'll be damned. So this would have been outside the wall."

"Only just barely."

They drove along Upper Street toward Camden Passage, where he'd first seen Jane Holdsworth. Now he saw her ghost.

The past was weighing on him like cement. This trip had been a ride along the Boulevard of Broken Dreams.

They were passing a little fish stall that advertised mussels and Jury was reminded of that dinner in Fells Point he had shared with Plant and Wiggins and Ellen Taylor. That trip had been the occasion of a three-part murder, one of the victims a homeless man who shoved his goods around in a supermarket cart, muttering to passersby, "I got the doin's, I got the doin's."

Jury smiled. His smile grew broader as they left Upper Street and drew close to his own street. He took the little notebook from his inside coat pocket, found a blank page and wrote a message. He tore out the page, folded it, and as he wrote Plant's name on the outside, he said to the driver, "Tell me, do you consider yourself a good driver?"

"The best, sir," said the cabbie without hesitation.

"Good enough to lose a car following you?"

"Done it more than once, I have."

Jury wrote "Lord Ardry" beneath Melrose's name and got some money out of his wallet. "Okay, now, if there was a pub called the Knowledge and you happened—"

"As I said, I'm not—"

"I know. For the sake of argument, of supposition, hypothetical and theoretical: if you happened by chance to find this pub tonight, I'd very much appreciate your finding this person, a friend of mine—" Jury turned the scrap of paper, behind which a fifty-pound note was perfectly evident, "and giving him this message. The money is yours. See if you can convince him you can get him to where he wants to go without incident."

The driver read the bit of paper. "Lord Ardry? He's a peer, is he?"

"Indeed. If you can convince Lord Ardry that you could get him to Mayfair without his being set upon by men with guns, he'll be very grateful and I know will pay you well. The note is for him. The fifty is for you, no matter what happens. And here's my card, too." Jury included one of his CID cards, writing his home number on it.

"Well, I'd certainly be glad to do this for you, sir, but I strongly doubt he'd be—"

"—at this pub? Why's that? I'm willing to bet fifty quid you might just stumble on it and him."

"And where in Mayfair will I be transporting him?"

Jury noticed the driver's slip of the tongue: "*will* I be," not "*would* I be."

"A club called Boring's."

"I'll consider that. We can be glad of one thing, sir."

Jury was happy there was one thing.

"We're neither of us the bloody Lord Mayor."

"Right." They'd pulled up in front of his building. "But there's also an official called the remembrancer. Do you ever feel like him?" Jury was out of the cab and handing the fare in through the passenger's window.

"Wasn't aware of that, sir."

Oh, sure you were. "Thanks, driver."

The cabbie was reaching his hand toward the open window. "Here's my card, sir. Name's Ben Churchill. Now, if you ever find out a bit more about that place they'd never take Brad Pitt, you just ring me. I'd be glad to take you there."

"The Knowledge?"

"That pub. Just ring me. 'Night."

"'Night." As the black cab pulled away, Jury stood looking down at Ben Churchill's card and felt, for a moment, happy. It had sounded almost like an invitation.

It had sounded as if he'd put one over on Brad Pitt.

If one were to take the hot pink top as position and the orange skirt as velocity, Carole-anne's outfit sent the uncertainty principle south. One could certainly measure them simultaneously. The two were one and the one was standing in the doorway of his flat.

But, then, he was not looking at a microcosm when he looked at Carole-anne Palutski. "What I can't understand," he said, deep in medias res, "is how anything on a microscopic level could influence our day-to-day existence."

"Huh?" said Carole-anne, unprepared to discuss quantum mechanics. "Saw you get out of a cab."

"Come in," he said, despite Carole-anne's already being in. She had got from Jury's doorsill to his living-room sofa without his having been aware of it. That must have something to do with quantum theory. Superposition, that was Carole-anne in a nutshell.

"It's early yet. Let's go have a meal. Did you hear about that new restaurant in Upper Street you can't get into for a month? Bruschetti, or something like that."

"No good trying there, then, is it?"

"We could go to the Mucky Duck."

"Can't tonight. Sorry."

Disappointed, she sighed and inspected a hot pink–polished fingernail that must have been defective.

"Tea?" He was holding his old earthenware pot.

"You mean leaves?"

"That's generally where tea comes from."

"As long as it ain't Earl Grey."

"It ain't." He carried the pot into the kitchen, added a few teaspoonsful of Ceylon and when the kettle screamed, filled it with boiling water.

"Steeping." He sat down again in his worn easy chair and watched her apply Hotsie Totsie polish to the fingernail. The hand that wielded the tiny brush was wearing a ring he hadn't seen before. It was a deep blue. "Is that a sapphire?"

"This? Fat chance. My mum gave it to me. It's some piece of junk jewelry she picked up in the Portobello Road or some other flea market."

"It's not tanzanite, is it?"

"What?"

"Tanzanite. A blue gemstone from Tanzania. I've just got it on the mind. May I see it?"

She shifted the brush and held out her hand.

"Your mother gave it to you?"

"About the only thing she ever did." Carole-anne took back her hand and ring.

"You never talk about her."

"If you knew my mum." Any knowing of her would, apparently, have decided things.

"I take it you didn't get along. Why?"

Carole-anne shrugged. "I think maybe she didn't like having a daughter around prettier than her and the older I got the more she didn't like it. Made her look less good, I expect, by comparison."

"You'd make anyone look less good by comparison."

She didn't take the compliment, apparently made unhappy by memories. "Times I think she really hated me, wanted me gone. So I went." She shrugged again.

"Oh, surely—" Jury stopped himself before he said, "Surely not." He despised that sort of easy attempt at consolation. He thought of Paula Moffit, and that he hadn't called her.

Who was he to say, after all, whether her mum wanted Carole-anne gone or not? Had he forgotten the love-starved mothers of Greek mythology, like Medea?

He looked at her and thought she looked, somehow, older. "Come on, Carole—" But at that moment his landline rang.

"Churchill, sir. Stroke of luck!"

"You mean you found it? Him?"

"It. Not him yet. But not to worry. I'm pretty persuasive."

"That I believe. Good man. The destination is Boring's—"

"Right. Mayfair. Well, I could hardly take fifty quid and not deliver, sir."

"A lot could have. Well done, Churchill. Thanks." Jury rang off.

He turned to Carole-anne. "Listen, love, I've got to go out right now. But word of honor, first chance I get I'm taking you to any restaurant you want to go to. How about this place with the monthlong waiting list?"

"Bruschetti? But how'd we—?"

"Get in?" He took out his warrant card. "You seem to forget where I work."

Instantly, whatever years she'd suddenly added had just as suddenly fallen away.

36

J ury walked up to the desk behind which stood an ancient porter.
But weren't they all? Only, this one was unfamiliar.

"May I help you, sir?"

"Yes. I'm meeting a friend of mine here, Lord Ardry—"

"Ah. Of course I know Lord Ardry." The man's smile was more of a
simper.

"I'll just wait for him in the Members' Room, shall I?" Jury started
away.

"Pardon me, sir! I'm awfully sorry, but we don't permit anyone in
the Members' Room unless they are, you know, members. Or unless a
member is here to vouch for them. You understand."

Jury could easily have produced his warrant card, but he didn't want
to make the elderly porter any more nervous than need be. Instead he
said, "Oh, but I am a member. I'm Tweedears."

"I *beg* your pardon? *Tweedears*, sir?"

"*Lord* Tweedears." Jury's raised eyebrow suggested that doubt was
not an option. "And you are—?"

The old porter stepped back from the desk. "Uh, Aubrey, sir. My
name is Aubrey."

Jury smiled. "Well, Aubrey. Let me augment my information.
Although the Tweedears title was forfeited in the sixteenth century,

there was a long line of barons de jure—fifth baron de jure, sixth baron de jure, up until the twelfth baron de jure." How he remembered these details of his sergeant's pedigree, he couldn't imagine. "I am the fifteenth baron de jure. Feel free to look me up in *Burke's*."

Aubrey still hesitated. "Well, I . . . I . . . it's not usually—"

Jury sighed. "I could have Lord Ardry verify this if you like, only he isn't here at the moment. That's why I'm waiting for him."

Trained to give in gracefully, if giving in at all, Aubrey said, "Certainly, sir. I'll be happy to show you to the Members' Room." He started out from around the desk.

"Don't trouble yourself. I know where it is. Thank you, Aubrey."

Jury walked into the Members' Room and sank down into a chair by one of the fireplaces. When a young porter moved to his chair, Jury ordered a whisky. He wished Colonel Neame and Major Champs would put in an appearance; at least, they could vouch for him. Aubrey, Jury noticed, was looking his way with apprehension.

Jury left the chair facing the front of the Members' Room, picked up a newspaper on the other side of the fireplace and, as if that had been his goal, sat down in the chair with its back to Aubrey.

Half an hour later, Melrose Plant rushed in. "Tweedears!" he exclaimed, and wrung Jury's hand.

Jury's cabbie had finally found him.

And after he was settled in with a drink, Melrose told the story of his four days in Kenya and Tanzania, accompanied by Patty Haigh.

"Where in hell is she?"

"At the Knowledge. Unless they've ferried her back to Heathrow, but I think that's unlikely, given their fear that something might happen to her. Which considerably outweighed their fear something might happen to me." Melrose drank his whisky.

"I still can't believe that she followed this shooter to Nairobi."

Melrose said, "And then killed a couple of days mucking about in places like Hemingways Hotel and Kibera until she wound up at the camp."

"Moreover—" Jury paused.

"Moreover?"

"You know where the Knowledge is." Jury smiled. "And I don't. You must be the only non-cabbie in London who knows."

"Well, don't get your hopes up. Because I couldn't tell you how to get there even if I wanted to." Melrose drank off his whisky. "So you've got the doin's? I hope you didn't wheel a supermarket cart in here with all of your earthly possessions. Come on, we're having dinner."

"This late? God, man, it's nearly eleven o'clock. They're still serving?"

"No, but I called ahead. After all, you're Tweedears." Melrose looked around for Young Higgins. "Higgins!"

Young Higgins, the head porter and the oldest one by far, came loping over.

"What's for dinner?"

"I believe the chef has prepared a Dover sole, my lord."

In the dining room, their Dover sole before them, Melrose went on: "So you think Banerjee—or rather Buhari—was getting tanzanite into England for Leonard Zane?"

"I don't know, but it's possible, given his position as inspector."

"But why would there be a problem exporting it?" said Melrose. "Leonard Zane has a license, so it looks legal."

"It's getting it into the UK. That too is legal, but the VAT on gemstones is twenty percent. You import, say, half a million, you're stuck with a hundred thousand in VAT. That's a lot of money lost in taxes. Zane wouldn't want to pay that. The guy needs money. We had a look at the mortgage on his property. Way overdue. Even though he's apparently doing a hell of a lot of business, he's not keeping up with his debts." Jury frowned. "And that might not be the only thing being brought in illegally. Trueblood found pictures. Shots of three paintings that were hanging in the gallery. We wondered why Zane was keeping pictures in his desk of pictures on his wall." Jury reached into an inside pocket and pulled out the snapshots Trueblood had furnished.

Melrose frowned at them. "That is odd."

"Only I can't get to them. Can't get a warrant. There could be other art behind the art we're seeing."

There was silence for a few moments, and then Melrose said, thoughtfully, "Bea Slocum."

"What about her?"

"You recall our little fracas with the Fabricant Gallery right down there?" Melrose aimed his cigarette in the direction of Albemarle Street.

"You mean the Siberian Snow scam. The white nothing that was covering up the Marc Chagall painting."

"The Chagall stolen by your notorious lady friend from the museum in St. Petersburg, yes."

"Never mind, please—"

"Sorry. I was only thinking that we might have the same thing going on. Could Zane have a bent painter who's covering something valuable with something else? It wouldn't be this Masego Abasi, would it?"

Jury shrugged. "You met him. What do you think?"

Melrose smiled. "It's probably more what Patty Haigh thinks. Patty and Abasi connected."

"Patty's ten."

Melrose blew that objection away like the smoke from his Dunhill. "That's why I'm thinking about Bea Slocum. Don't forget, she's a very good painter. You can't get probable cause, you said."

"Right."

Melrose smoked that objection away, too. "Use your imagination, Richard."

"Haven't got one. Like I don't have a cognac." He pulled back in his chair. "Lord, that was good."

Melrose raised a finger to Young Higgins, who came so smoothly he might have been on Aero's skateboard.

"Coffee and cognac out there, please, Higgins." Melrose pulled a silver money clip from his pocket, sheered off notes. "Please thank the chef for staying on and for the excellent sole." He handed Higgins two small-folded fifty-quid notes.

*   *   *

Back in the Members' Room with cognac and another cigarette, Melrose said, "But what about Leonard Zane's connection with Moffit?"

"I don't know, except that there must be one." Jury told Melrose his deduction about Danny Morrissey. "Morrissey's room was on the twentieth floor and before he was shot he said he was standing at the window, looking at the night sky. The night sky."

Melrose frowned. "Why is that significant?"

"Reno isn't Las Vegas, but it still has impressive casinos, lit up like fireballs. If you were looking out over Reno, what would you most likely be looking at? The casinos, the lights. And how many people would say 'night sky'? A person would most likely say, 'standing at the window looking out.' Period. But David Moffit was obsessed with the night sky. For him far more impressive than all of the lit-up buildings in the world. Believe me, I know. I took a walk with him. He carried a damn telescope around with him. Night was David's business."

Jury went on. "Yet Zane claims never to have heard of David Moffit. How many winning gamblers are also professors of physics? With a system? He didn't go in for huge wins, just consistent wins. Of course Zane knew the name, if not the actual person."

"This man sounds very canny. Not going in for big winnings, only for consistent ones. But none of this sounds like a reason to shoot him. And certainly not his wife."

Jury was quiet for a minute, then said, "That painting in the flat . . . Zane is the only one who has the right to sell Abasi's stuff."

"But remember, Abasi half-recognized the photo I showed him. So Rebecca Moffit might have got it directly from him."

"Her passport shows no visa for Kenya, no visa for any country in Africa."

"What about him?"

"Same thing. Of course, there's plenty of traffic in fake passports, so that doesn't actually prove anything. Only . . . it's the Moffits. I somehow can't picture them . . ."

"'The doin's,'" said Melrose. He snorted. "And where are the 'doin's'?"

Jury removed the brown envelope from his jacket pocket and pulled out the pictures he'd taken from Claire Howard's flat.

Melrose put on his glasses. "My word, but mother and daughter look alike."

"Don't they?"

"Are you saying Abasi could have seen *Mrs.* Howard?"

"But he said nothing about her when you showed him the picture taken in the gallery."

Melrose frowned. "He was more interested in the dark-haired woman Claire Howard was talking to. He said she reminded him of 'Little Rita,' a little girl who liked to come to his studio years ago with her nanny. The nanny was a friend of Abasi. He didn't seem to recognize the gallery, either."

"I'm forwarding the blowup to Kione and asking him to show it to Abasi again."

"But if Claire Howard was the woman who bought the painting, that means—"

"She's been lying all along."

37

The next morning, Melrose rang Bea Slocum and asked her if she'd meet him at the Zane Gallery in the City.

"Where that couple got murdered? That gallery?"

"That one, yes."

"God." She paused. "But I've got my job."

"It's Saturday. I thought you didn't work Saturdays."

"Yeah, I am."

Melrose had bought two of her paintings at the Fabricant Gallery and he knew she felt hugely indebted to him. He let her feel it. "Oh, come on. Surely they can manage without you for a couple of hours. And this job will interest you if you still have your criminal bent."

"Meaning?"

"I'm not sure what I mean."

"No surprise there. Okay, Fingers. The Zane Gallery."

Bea knew every gallery in London, although she had paintings in only two or three. He said, "Right. In an hour; I'll meet you at the front door. And Bea, come looking rich, will you?"

"Don't own rich."

"Doesn't matter. Just drape it or shorten it or wear it round your neck. And bring your portfolio."

"What makes you think I got—?"

Melrose rang off. He knew she'd got.

*   *   *

Why, he wondered an hour later, hadn't he allowed for the fact that Leonard Zane could easily turn up right where he himself stood outside the gallery's front door?

Zane drove up in his Lotus Elan, sunglassed, silk-suited, vicuña-coated and looking as if he owned an island off Antibes.

Good Lord, Melrose thought; this man needed money?

Zane was out of his car and walking toward Melrose, when the black cab drove up behind the Lotus. "May I help you?" said Zane.

"No, thank you. I'm just waiting for a friend."

They both watched as the door of the cab opened and a leather boot landed on the drive. This was followed by another boot, a very short and supple leather skirt, a hot pink leather-trimmed top, an angelically pretty face topped by short blond hair. Wow. Beatrice Slocum, who could look like something either the cat or the Queen dragged in, had chosen the Queen.

"If this is your friend, I envy you."

"I'd envy me too, but it isn't." Melrose checked the time on his mobile. "I don't know where he is." He took out his small silver note-book, knowing that Zane had his eyes on the advancing Bea, and wrote his own mobile number. He tore out the little page and folded it, simultaneously taking one of his peer-heavy cards out of the notebook, as if that had been his purpose.

Zane was asking another "May I help you?" as she came up to them, carrying her portfolio.

"I'm looking for Mr. Zane. Would either of you gentlemen—?"

Melrose marveled that she had the presence of mind not to say hello to him, apparently taking his own non-hello as a sign that they were strangers.

"I would be," said Leonard Zane.

Keeping the black portfolio tightly molded to her side, Bea said, "I wonder if I could have a few minutes of your time."

"You certainly could. Come along to the gallery." Zane turned. "And you, sir—?"

Melrose said he would continue to wait for his tardy friend but would do so inside, and handed Zane the card that claimed he was the seventh Earl of Caverness, fifth Viscount Ardry, and a string of other things. He had no idea how he was going to pass the note with his mobile number along to Bea, much less the information she needed. How stupid of him.

Bea and Zane walked toward the staircase and stopped. She'd said something to stop them. She turned and walked quickly to Melrose, who said, under his breath, "Sorry. Laugh at whatever I say, will you?" And he pulled the three photos out of his jacket pocket, palmed them, fanned them out. "Buy one of these. You'll be able to tell, they're not very good—bear, cheetah, roses—on a wall full of very good stuff." He handed her the number from his notebook, replaced the photos in his pocket. "Ring when you're through."

She'd started laughing at "Sorry," and kept it up, ending with, "You are a caution," in a voice loud enough to carry. She returned to where Zane was waiting and again said something Melrose couldn't hear. Zane laughed, too. They ascended the stairs.

Melrose went into the library and sank into a down-cushioned chair, thinking, "Buy one," was hardly an adequate instruction. Would Zane be *selling* them? Yet, again, why would he have the paintings on the wall if he weren't?

How would she handle it? He didn't see how she could.

"I'm terribly sorry for intruding and for not making an appointment, Mr. Zane. You must be extremely busy. But I've heard so much about this gallery—"

He smiled. "Before recently?"

She looked perplexed. "Pardon?"

"Don't you read the papers, Miss Slocum?"

She shook her head. "I haven't read one in days. I've been too busy."

"Good for you. Are you represented right now by any gallery?"

"The Fabricant has sold several of my paintings. And T. Smith's. I haven't had a show."

"Let me see what you've got."

She handed over the portfolio and the dozen photographs within it, saying, "Would you mind if I looked at your paintings?" Bea nodded toward the left wall.

"Mind? Of course not. You do that while I do this." He opened the portfolio.

A man walked in, looking like money, said, "Leo."

"Max!" said Zane, enthusiastically shaking the man's hand.

A minute later, a couple walked in, apparently gem enthusiasts, for they were hovering over the glass display cases.

While this was going on, Bea took out her mobile, looked at the bit of paper and touched in Melrose's number. "Mum?" she said when he answered. "Happy birthday!"

"Thanks. Listen, the three paintings are on different parts of the wall—" He stopped because just then Maggie Benn walked in, moving slowly, since she was reading as she walked, her face turned down to a book or magazine. She opened the office door with a key. He had no idea whether she could hear him or not. He moved out to the foyer. "Someone just walked in. Cheetah, about the middle of the wall. Near it, a bear; third is a boring bowl of roses, lower right, near end." Melrose rang off.

Bea spotted the three. How rich did she have to look to buy one of this lot? Able to afford four hundred quid, at least, which is what the roses cost. She moved her eyes back to the middle of the wall, to the Spirit Bear, or whatever bear it was, saw a twelve-hundred-pound price tag and frowned. Technically proficient, but nothing behind the technique. Next to the bear, and far better, hung a small painting of a Highland terrier that she moved closer to. A tiny brass plaque in the frame said *Charlie*. Bea smiled. Despite its clear superiority to the bear, it cost but half as much.

Bea looked round to see if she was interrupting any transaction, saw the moneyed man had gone and said, "Mr. Zane?"

He'd started toward the tanzanite case and the couple there and turned. "Miss Slocum?"

"This still life—" She gestured toward the roses. "—I think I'll buy it for my mum. She likes paintings of flowers; she likes still lifes. 'Quiet lifes' she calls them."

He smiled. "I like her description, but I'm afraid that one is sold."

Sold? Of course. She moved a few feet and stood looking at the bear. "Well, she really likes animals, too. Perhaps this one—?" When he had moved to where she stood, she went on: "This Spirit Bear—if you'll pardon me—has no spirit. Yet the price is pretty steep. Good color, good technique, but no soul. But Mum wouldn't see that."

Leonard Zane smiled. "Good assessment. This is one of Bergeron's—" He bent down and studied the corner. "Yes, Henri Bergeron. He's a Canadian and extremely popular. Ah, yes, but I'm afraid that one is also sold."

"But why do you have the sold paintings still hanging?"

"Begeron likes me to keep his paintings up until the client actually wants to take possession of them. He wants people to keep on seeing them. Does a lot of animal stuff."

"Well, he didn't do *Charlie*." Bea pointed to the little Highland terrier.

He laughed. "You're quite right. The dog is far superior. A new artist; I like her work."

This was not one of the suspect paintings. "Reason I'm asking is because my mother's birthday's here. 'Bea,' she says, 'couldn't you paint a kitty now and then?' You know, as if painting were a now-and-then pastime, done to paint fluffy things."

Again he laughed.

"But you know what? I'd like to buy that terrier for her. She'd love it and it's good. My uncle's named Charlie, too. So there's that."

"Wonderful." He looked at the price. "I'll let you have it for five hundred."

She gasped at this largesse. "That's really generous of you." Now Bea realized that she couldn't go for a purchase of the third painting, because

Leonard Zane would surely be suspicious. She was rather desperately looking for another still life and saw one of several pieces of fruit, the apple, pears and plums rather recklessly arranged. She was superb at sizing things with just a look; she looked from the fruit to the roses and saw they were almost exactly the same size. "Oh, and this one she'd really like." It was seven hundred. She could put it on her credit card. The terrier painting would go on her debit card.

"Two paintings? You must be very fond of your mother."

Bea hadn't seen her mother in years. They'd never got on. "I missed her birthday last year and feel I should make it up to her. Thanks so much for knocking a hundred quid off the terrier."

"Not at all. Tell her I said, 'Happy birthday.' I'll get my assistant to take your card details and bring something to wrap these in." He removed both paintings from the wall, laid them on his desk. He tapped on his mobile and told Maggie to come up and take care of a customer. He slipped the phone back into his pocket and said to Bea, "I've got to look after these people right now. Maggie will be up in a minute." He left her for the couple on the other side of the room.

Immediately, Bea took out her own mobile and tapped in Melrose's number. When he answered, she said, "Mum, distraction is needed here."

"I'll see to it." Melrose rang off.

In another minute, a plain-looking youngish woman who, Bea assumed, must be Maggie came in with a large brown envelope, made small talk as she put the cards into a portable machine and then shoved the fruit painting into the envelope.

As she taped it closed, Bea said, "That's very clever as a wrapping. Saves effort and time." All around, she thought.

Maggie said, "I should have brought another wrapping. I'll just go and get—"

"Please don't bother. It's a small picture and I can certainly carry it without getting it scratched or anything."

Maggie looked doubtful. "Well, if you're sure—"

Bea told her she was and retrieved her cards. "Thanks."

Maggie left. Leonard Zane was still apparently negotiating with the couple about a piece of jewelry.

Bea was standing by the window, trying to work out her next move, when she saw two City Police cars, blue lights winking, stop below near the front door. A third car appeared to have stopped at the curb. Three uniforms emerged from the cars in the driveway; a plainclothes officer came walking up the drive to the door.

"What's police doing?" she said in a voice loud enough to reach Zane's ears.

"What?" He turned from the couple at the glass display case and moved to the window to stare down at the cars. "Oh, for God's sake. Not again."

"Again?"

"I'll be right back." He plucked up his mobile, punched a number and said, "Maggie, come up here, will you, and take care of the couple viewing the tanzanite." Then he hurried out of the gallery.

Bea figured she might have two minutes, moved to the front of the desk (first assessing that no one was paying any attention to her transaction), exchanged the suspect bowl of roses on the end for the painting in the brown envelope and hung the fruit painting in the place where the roses had been. She picked up *Charlie* and, with the two paintings and her portfolio—quite a load—left the gallery.

She passed Maggie at the top of the staircase. They nodded pleasantly to each other.

Melrose saw Bea, but could say nothing; wanted to help her with this formidable load of stuff, but couldn't. But Sergeant Wiggins could: he stepped forward and said, "Let me help you, miss."

"Oh, thank you, officer." She handed over both of the paintings, moved to the spot where Leonard Zane was arguing forcibly with the two policemen. "Sorry to interrupt. Mr. Zane, thanks so much for your time and help. My mum will be delighted. And I'll be in touch." She held up the portfolio. "I'll be taking this, as I'll need it. I really appreciate your help."

He said, "Look, I'm truly sorry I didn't talk to you about your work; I liked what I saw there." He nodded toward the portfolio. "Please ring me so that we can set up a time to get together."

"I will."

Leonard Zane said good-bye to her and returned to his argument.

Wiggins walked out with her, saying loudly he'd get her a taxi, then walked her down to the curb where, out of sight, they both climbed into an unmarked Metropolitan Police car and drove away.

Melrose Plant merely gaped. After saying a few words to Leonard Zane, who was still engaged with the police, he too managed to extricate himself.

38

The woman was Barbara Porter, of the scaled-down Arts and Antiques Unit of New Scotland Yard. Scaled down to nearly nothing except for Barbara herself, because funds had been drastically cut. Art and its theft were no longer considered a top priority. Physically, she was unprepossessing—round and marshmallow soft. Everyone agreed she was an escapee from a Beatrix Potter book. But Barbara's specialty was botany and she was extremely adept at identifying dyes.

She was bent over one of the paintings, scanning the frame, when Jury walked in.

"Hi, Superintendent. You've good reason."

He waited. Nothing. "You mean 'to believe'?" She was known for her elliptical manner of speech.

"Yeah. I've done a lot of dabbling in woodsy stuff."

Jury loved that "woodsy." He stood behind her, looking over her shoulder at the painting. "What about the woodsy stuff?"

"The wood here is Madagascar ebony."

"Beautiful. Very dark."

"And wavy. The finish makes it difficult to see any joining. This frame is in two parts. Very hard to see where the parts meet because the grain is so fine and the waves are so variable. Madagascar wood has a lot of illegal trade going on. The Chinese especially like it for its imperial look. Look here: you can hardly see the matchup." She ran her finger down the side of the frame. "You see this line?"

Jury shook his head, surprised by this turn in the painting inspection.

"That's what I mean."

"Are you saying it's the *frame* you're suspicious of?"

"Of course. The two parts are glued together. It could be the framer wanted a particular thickness for aesthetic purposes—"

"Or for smuggling purposes?"

"Exactly."

"Well."

"Give me a half hour. I don't want to damage the frame."

It was a half hour well spent.

"Reasonable grounds?" Detective Chief Superintendent Racer's small mouth bunched to hide his smile. The smile came from having scotched—or being about to scotch—Jury's request for a search warrant.

"Illegal import of tanzanite," said Jury.

"That's not reasonable grounds, Jury. That's just your theory."

"No, it isn't. He's been smuggling it in picture frames."

Racer just frowned at Jury.

"And we found a beautifully cut, very large piece of tanzanite in his desk drawer."

"And how is it you were searching his desk, eh?" said Racer, ignoring the more important point in favor of the lesser one.

"I wasn't. Someone else was."

"Someone you put up to doing it, no doubt." Racer spread his arms wide. "So what? I keep a gold nugget in mine. That doesn't amount to reasonable suspicion, either."

"You keep it buried in a drawer full of broken glass?"

"What's he do that for?"

"To keep people from stealing it, I expect."

"Well, it's not illegal."

"One of this size—twenty to thirty carats—certainly is. And it's undoubtedly slipped under the VAT radar. "He's linked to this shooter. Not only did it happen at the Artemis Club, but Leonard Zane owns a mine in the Merelani Hills in east Tanzania."

"The source for the name 'tanzanite.'"

What a coup! "The shooter is a Tanzanian police officer."

"What?"

"A Tanzanian policeman." Jury would treat anything Racer said as literal. "An inspector known as Benjamin Buhari. I think he's got something to do with Zane's mine."

"So you think Leonard Zane paid him to shoot the Moffits?"

"Actually, no. I think Leonard Zane is badly in need of money. But I also think he's got some hold over this policeman Buhari—and somehow manipulated the man into doing the shooting. But I don't think Zane planned on having it happen in front of the Artemis Club."

Jury got Racer's agreement, albeit grudgingly, and took himself off to the magistrate for the warrant.

39

"Of course, you have a warrant," said Leonard Zane, who was standing in the doorway of his office when Jury walked in with four other people—two forensic techs, Barbara Porter and Sergeant Wiggins.

"Of course," said Jury, pulling the warrant out of his pocket, holding it up and letting it waterfall in front of Zane's face.

"Just what are you looking for?"

"Illegally imported goods: gemstones, works of art, and proof that you paid the VAT for same."

"Christ," said Zane, before turning back to his office. "What a waste of everybody's time."

The forensic technicians stood at the bottom of the stairs and Jury motioned for them to ascend to the gallery. Once inside, Jury walked Barbara over to Zane's desk and pulled out the bottom drawer on the left-hand side. "Look."

"What the bloody hell? That's glass shards. And razor blades? Looks like smashed lightbulbs."

"Right. This is what's in among them." He showed her the picture of the tanzanite stone.

Barbara whistled. "That could be near thirty carats, guv. That's illegal, right there. There's a limit to the size of a stone you can import."

Jury shut the drawer. "Leave that for the moment. There are two other paintings whose frames I suspect, and neither painting being really good, I suspect them even more. One is that painting of a cheetah." Jury moved toward the middle of the wall. "The other is this bear. These are two of the three Zane had shots of in his desk. Though why he couldn't remember which frames were packed with stones I can't imagine."

"Maybe it was for someone else. To identify them, I mean."

"Possibly."

Wiggins was at his elbow. "I found these, boss."

"These" were a number of import forms listing the Abasi paintings with their declared value, which seemed low, but not scandalously low; several forms detailing some of the tanzanite stones now in the display case in front; other forms citing a few of the pieces of sculpture.

Wiggins said, "Keeps good records."

"I bet he does, when he keeps them. These two—the gemstone forms —see if you can match up these stones to the ones in the display case."

"Bit of a challenge that. He's had them done in settings."

"You were always a man for a challenge, Wiggins."

When Wiggins left, looking overly challenged, Jury walked over to the left-hand wall and took a closer look at the paintings. He studied the poor Rothko reproduction, and wondered why he was so sure it was poor, never having understood Mark Rothko in the first place. His glance trailed along to the Abasi painting of the lion and woman that he really liked. After a few minutes he'd worked his way over to Barbara, who had put away the laser toy or whatever it was and was now running her fingers over the frames.

"Should we take them with us?"

Jury thought for a moment. "No. Take one of them—the bear—and also take a couple of others as a blind. We don't want him to know we know."

"But doesn't he already suspect we do? Your friend took one this morning."

"He might have thought that was because his assistant took it down."

"Which ones do I take, then, besides the bear?"

Jury looked behind him. "Take that small Matisse-like painting. And the Rothko copy. Maybe Mr. Zane will think *we* think there's art forgery going on. And that won't bother him at all." Jury motioned Wiggins over.

"Write up a receipt for this stuff we're collecting."

"The paintings? What about that stone?" Wiggins nodded toward the desk.

"We'll leave that buried for the time being."

Jury nodded to the forensic fellow named Cornelius Zimberlee. "How did the forms match up with the tanzanite pieces in the case?"

Zimberlee said, "Pretty well. Of course, they'd have been cut, some of them, to size, to make the various pieces. I'm assuming from what I've seen that all of them can be accounted for."

"Okay. Good. Then let's go."

Jury and the team restored order and went down the staircase to join the one who had finished his search of the ground-floor office.

Leonard Zane was lounging in the doorway of the dining room, smoking a thin cigar.

"Thank you, Mr. Zane. We'll be going."

"With my artwork, I see. If you're transporting those paintings, please wrap them."

"Of course. Newspaper?"

Zane asked Maggie Benn to get the brown envelopes or some wrapping paper. "How can I be sure I'll get them back in good condition?"

"Here's your receipt, Mr. Zane. Nothing will come to harm. We're always very careful."

Maggie was back with a stack of paper; they proceeded to wrap and tie the paintings. Barbara Porter took charge of them and they left.

"What do you expect to find in those paintings, sir?" asked Wiggins as they climbed into the car.

"This." Jury held out his hand, filled with a dozen small blue stones, ones that Barbara Porter had handed him in an evidence bag when he left Racer's office.

"*Tanzanite?*" Wiggins whistled, held one up to the light. "What a beautiful blue."

"Isn't it? These were inside the frame Bea Slocum got. There are two others. Now, are we going to idle here all afternoon or are you going to start the car?"

Wiggins started it, but was still surprised and still idled. "I don't get it. Why? It's not illegal to import gemstones."

"Neither is it to bring in diamonds, but a lot of smuggling goes on there, doesn't it? Move on, Wiggins."

Wiggins pressed a little too firmly on the gas and they nearly hit the low concrete wall against which Zane's car was parked. They nearly hit that too.

"Sorry." Wiggins applied his foot more gently this time and they slid out of the parking area onto the road. Wiggins continued: "But diamonds are valuable. Tanzanite isn't. You can pick up a piece of that stuff online for a song. I looked."

"Well, there's cheap everything. And I'm guessing you won't be able to do that much longer, because there's a very limited amount of tanzanite. They expect that in another decade, or two at the most, it'll be gone. The mines depleted. Zane owns one of those mines. And there are very few big ones. Value has a lot to do with scarcity—"

"You think that painting of Rebecca Moffit's was one of them?"

"No. That painting is too small to be of much use."

"But the artist must be in on it."

"The artists might have been kept in the dark. I mean there might have been one framer Zane used who of course would know."

They were nearing St. James's and Jury asked Wiggins to continue on and drop him off in Chelsea.

"Not going back to headquarters, then?"

"Not unless it's near Sloane Square. I'm going to have a talk with Claire Howard. She's still at her daughter's flat."

"Peter Jones is there."

Jury smiled. For some reason, Wiggins had a particular liking for this department store. "Peter Jones and Mrs. Howard."

40

———

"I've just come from the Zane Gallery," said Jury, after having been invited to take off his coat and sit down. He sat, but kept the coat on. "You said you'd never been there."

"That's right."

"You're sure?"

Her sigh was rueful. "Mr. Jury, you keep wanting me to have been there. I've told you before, twice, I have never seen Mr. Zane, nor been to his gallery. I've never been to the casino."

"Why not?"

"I have no interest in gambling."

"But you do have an interest in art."

"Do you know how many small private galleries there are in London?"

"Yes, and I particularly know the one where your daughter was murdered. Yet you show no interest in it. That's why I said, 'Why not?' Because I'd think a parent might want to see the place where a child died."

Claire Howard's expression didn't change. "Would you like a drink?"

"No, thank you."

"I would." She turned to the drinks table in front of the window and poured herself a half inch of whisky. Then she turned back and said, "You don't have children, do you?"

He shook his head. "Does that nullify any opinion I might have on parenthood?"

"No. But is it so impossible to believe that the scene of the crime might be the last place I'd want to see?"

"Yes."

She sat down on the arm of the sofa. "Well, then, just count me as an unnatural mother."

He said, "It was the first place Paula Moffit went. Even before her hotel."

"That was *her* response. Is it conceivable that she's less sensitive and can bear these things more stoically?"

"No."

Claire gave a short laugh. "David's mother has clearly evoked a sympathetic chord in you that I never did."

"On the contrary, the first time we met, I felt a great deal of sympathy for you."

"But not on subsequent occasions."

"You and your daughter seemed to be virtual strangers. You've said so little about her—"

"We weren't very close, that's true." Impatiently, Claire said, "What do you *want* of me?"

"Nothing at all. I'm only trying to discover why Rebecca and David were killed."

"I've told you everything I know."

"And asked nothing. Your lack of curiosity surprises me. Didn't you wonder why they were shot in front of a casino?"

"Given David's love of gambling I expect it wasn't surprising—"

Wasn't *surprising*? "And by a Kenyan. You didn't say anything about the shooter's being African. Who he is, what he was doing at that casino, why he murdered your daughter and son-in-law." Jury frowned. "It's not David's penchant for twenty-one that's the surprise. It's that he was shot in the head."

Her reaction to that blunt account was to exhale a lacy stream of smoke and smile. "Mr. Jury, you're determined that I've been to that gallery, that I know the owner because of that painting which you swear must have been acquired there, or this tanzanite ring which must have been bought there. But all I know of Leo Zane is his picture in the *Times*.

He seems to be a handsome man with an interesting mind. Anyone who would combine a casino and an art gallery certainly sounds intriguing."

Jury just watched her. She seemed not to know what this was all about and kept talking as if in an effort to hit on it, to strike the right chord, to finally sort it. He stared at the wall but no longer at the Abasi painting. His eyes traveled to the grouping of silver-framed photographs on the desk. They had been rearranged and there were fewer in the group now. The one with the three of them—mother, daughter, father—was gone. The shot of the unidentified gallery was not there. Nor was the one of Claire Howard and one of her friends. He thought again of the album and the missing snapshots.

"I remember there was a photo there—" He nodded toward the desk. "—of your husband. The three of you."

"I'm just packing them up."

"Some of them."

"Those I left out because they have some particular meaning."

No, thought Jury, it's the others that do. Or one of them. "Could I see it again, the one of your husband?"

She shrugged. "Harry? Certainly. I don't see why—"

"It's my forensic pathologist. She always wants to know as much as possible about a victim's family. Don't ask me why." Had Phyllis Nancy ever heard that, she would indeed have asked him why.

Claire rose, walked into the little study and returned with the picture in its silver frame. "Here he is."

Jury looked at the enlargement of the snapshot: Rebecca, Claire, and Harry. His wife and daughter had been positioned by the photographer together on a love seat, father behind them.

"I've always envied Rebecca's eyes, I can tell you. My own are just an ordinary blue."

"Yours aren't ordinary at all."

She laughed and again offered him a whisky, which he declined as he rose and handed the picture back to her. He had no interest in it.

Yet he thought he'd been looking at everything but the one thing he should have been. The words of David's mother: *He saw in it unimaginable depths and brilliance. Everything else was the color of ice.*

Paula Moffit may not have remembered everything her son had said, but what she did remember, she remembered with extreme precision and clarity. Jury thought of the City official he'd mentioned to his cab driver: the remembrancer.

Paula Moffit was a remembrancer. She was a mother.

Which Claire Howard honestly did not seem to be.

"One of those pictures was of some sort of gallery event, wasn't it?"

She frowned. "Oh? Oh, yes. Probably a showing. I go to quite a few of them." But she did not move toward the study.

"Could I see that again?"

"It's packed away. I'm not sure which box—"

"I'll help you look."

Having little choice, she said, "No bother. I'll get it."

She was in and out of the study again in a minute. "I think this was several years ago, perhaps in Soho, but I'm not sure. There are so many galleries in London."

He looked at it, held it at arm's length, brought it back. Certainly a much better representation than the snapshot and it would serve forensics better in blowing up the details. But in this larger picture, the painting on the wall behind Claire Howard was clearer. Without asking, Jury picked up the magnifying glass on the desk. He pulled the picture closer, frowned.

"What is it?"

When he said, "This painting—" and looked up at her, he thought she looked relieved. "It looks like a Masego Abasi."

"Does it? I wasn't that acquainted with his work . . ." Relief ran into uncertainty.

"That's not the point. This is a gallery. But outside of the Zane gallery, the only place one can see his work is in Africa. You said you hadn't been to Kenya."

"Well, I have been to Johannesburg."

"You haven't mentioned that."

"South Africa isn't Kenya, Superintendent."

"It's pretty damned close, though, isn't it?"

Boring's, London
Nov. 9, Saturday night

41

Jury had been getting looks from Aubrey if not precisely suspicious, certainly baleful, so that after a half an hour of this he was glad to see Young Higgins had taken the place of the other porter and was carrying a tray through the Members' Room to a party of three on the other side. When he was finished serving this party, Jury beckoned him over.

The elderly porter was himself happy to see Jury. "Good evening, Superintendent. Another whisky?"

"Higgins, I wish you would assure Aubrey over there that I am not a terrorist."

Higgins gave a muffled little laugh behind a gray-gloved hand.

Jury went on: "And that I am indeed a friend of Lord Ardry and that it is he for whom I am waiting to have dinner." Jury thought it better not to embroil Young Higgins in the Tweedears imposture, nor would it be necessary since Higgins himself could vouch for Jury. "And, yes, I'd like another whisky. A double. Thank you, Higgins."

Young Higgins bowed, scraped and departed.

Not even Major Champs and Colonel Neame were around. Boring's seemed bent on denying Jury citizenship this evening. It was just as well to set his back to it all and try to do this crossword puzzle that Melrose Plant could wrap up in fifteen minutes. He heard Higgins approach and happily reached up his empty glass, which was taken and placed on the tray. But no full one was set in his hand.

"I'll have that, thank you. You can fetch another for the Superintendent. Tweedears, old chap!"

Jury smiled. "Why don't you be quiet and sit down?"

"Well, don't expect me to thank you for pulling me away from the most convivial company I've had outside of the Jack and Hammer."

"What convivial company?"

"At the Knowledge, of course."

Jury gaped. "You mean you've been back there? Again?"

"You don't seem to understand. I have a pass. I saved Patty Haigh."

"What do you mean, saved?"

Melrose reflected. "Well, half-saved." He told Jury about the leopard cub experience.

Jury raised his glass, "Well done, my friend. That was courageous."

Melrose shrugged. "Just a reflex."

Jury smiled. "Funny how many people wouldn't have that knee-jerk response to a leopard. But getting back to your newfound friends—It's your Black Card that has the pass. And if that place is using credit cards, how can it stay off the map?"

Melrose shrugged. "They don't use them in the ordinary way."

"I'll just bet." Jury pulled out the snapshot and the enlargement of Claire Howard in the unknown gallery. "Look at this. You can keep the snapshot."

Melrose studied the pictures. "Where's this gallery?"

"I'm guessing it's in Nairobi, although she says she's never been there. Said that must have been in Johannesburg." Jury went on. "Claire Howard called Leonard Zane 'Leo.'" She said, 'All I know of Leo Zane is his picture in the *Times*.' A small point, but still . . . In the *Times* he was referred to as 'Leonard.' Dennis Jenkins said that was true of all the newspaper accounts. So, then, why the 'Leo' reference? I've only heard that from Maggie Benn and Trueblood."

"She was lying about knowing him, then?"

"I think so. Why lie? There's certainly nothing wrong with knowing Leonard Zane. There's nothing wrong with having an affair with him, for that matter."

"You think she is?"

"Or possibly was."

"There's nothing wrong about it except she lied. As she lied about Kenya. Where is this leading, Richard?"

"Nowhere very nice, I suspect. Did I show you this?" He handed over the account from the Reno newspaper. "Keep it; it's a copy. I'm sure this Danny Morrissey is really David Moffit."

"My God, shot in two different casinos? That beggars coincidence." Melrose frowned. "Moffit, with all of his gambling expertise, must have been the target for some reason; the wife surely must have been collateral damage."

"There was no collateral damage. I think they both had to die."

Melrose sipped his whisky. "Why?"

Jury shook his head. "I'm still thinking."

"But Zane is the one who got the shooter, right?"

Jury frowned. "I think so."

"What are you going to do?"

"I don't know. I'm short on actual evidence."

Melrose shook his head. "Patty Haigh was putting herself at horrible risk."

"When do I get to meet Patty Haigh?"

"Never, probably."

"Thanks. We really ought to do something about her situation. How she lives and so forth." Jury sipped his coffee.

Melrose frowned. "Do something—? What in hell are you talking about?"

"Find her a good home, someone to take care of her. She's a little girl, Melrose. She shouldn't be spending her days at Heathrow, scanning for villains. She should be safe."

The other members who were awake turned wide-eyed stares at Melrose, who was laughing so hard he was doubled up in his chair.

"Just what the hell is so funny?"

"Take care of her. This is *Patty Haigh* you're talking about. The same Patty Haigh who got through Heathrow security on a pinched boarding pass; who wangled her way into B.B.'s good graces and flew to Dubai;

who outwitted police in London, Dubai and Nairobi; who carries in her backpack a full selection of costumes and wigs to meet any eventuality; who requisitioned strangers to be her aunts, uncles, parents; who roamed around that godless slum, Kibera, on her own; who got into the Hemingways Hotel without paying a penny; who crossed the dark veldt between Kibera and Mbosi Camp protected only by her wits. This is the person we should keep safe!"

"I see your point." Jury smiled. "Incidentally, Vivian's here, too. They're both—I mean Vivian and Diane—at the Connaught. I'm picking them up when I leave here to go to Zane's casino."

"Viv in a casino? Can't imagine her coming all the way here just to gamble. She's no good at it, doesn't even like it."

"Well, that's not the reason she's here, is it?" Jury tuned his careless tone to even greater carelessness. "She's off on the Orient Express again."

The effect was electric. Melrose nearly strangled his whisky glass. "Orient Express? Venice? What the *hell*? We all sent Count Dracula packing years ago; he lies in his earth-filled coffin with a stake in his heart and no alarm clock."

In a quizzical tone, Jury said, "Who said Venice? The Orient Express does make other stops. You know: Shoreditch, Limehouse, Gravesend."

"Very funny. Where *is* she going?"

"Paris."

"Taking the Orient Express just to go to *Paris*? That's absurd. Meeting Franco Giopinno in *Paris*? Even more absurd."

"Who said it was Giopinno?"

"What? What? Who else could it be?"

"You've been in Kenya, remember. She met someone."

Melrose, who'd leaned down to search for his cigarette lighter, hit his head on the coffee table's edge on the way. "What is this? I'm away for a week and she's got someone new? What someone?"

"A French someone. His name is Alain—" Jury searched his mind for a name. He nearly wrecked on *Delon* until a little rudder of memory told him no, Alain Delon was the actor, one of the handsomest actors who'd ever lived. "Resnais, I think. Alain Resnais." That sounded familiar too.

But apparently not to Melrose, who just sat fuming.

"We're having a little breakfast party, a send-off in Victoria, in a couple of days. Orient Express leaves at ten A.M., I think. But you remember from last time. You're free, aren't you?"

Melrose, free or not, went on fuming.

"Care to join us tonight at the Artemis Club?"

"No, thank you. I'm going back to my friends at the Knowledge."

So there.

"How are you going to get there?"

"With a certain driver and a blindfold."

Jury rose. "Before you go back to your mates, read that Reno paper column, study the picture and think."

"'Think'?"

"Something's wrong with mine. My thinking, I mean. There's something I'm just not finding." Jury drank off his whisky. "Find it for me, will you? 'Night."

It didn't make sense. Jury was sitting in a taxi at a stoplight in Victoria, thinking about this. If she'd been in Johannesburg, why not tell Jenkins? Or him? Why give the impression she'd never been to Africa? To distance herself from the killer?

He was only a few minutes from the Yard.

So was Sergeant Wiggins. "Thought you were going to the Connaught."

"I am. Just stopped by to have a look at the murder board. And I have an enlargement of that snapshot of Claire Howard. That's definitely a Masego Abasi painting behind her. It's an Abasi show, I'm almost certain. Send this blowup to Sammy in forensics. He thought the paintings were by the same artist. He can confirm it."

"And that gallery is in Kenya, boss. Nairobi."

Jury frowned, looking at the photo he'd taken from Claire. "I thought it might be."

Studying the two women in this gallery, he thought about Plant's description of his visit to Masego Abasi's studio. *Little Rita*. He thought about the children who had to work the mine Plant visited. *He loves children*, he himself had said about Inspector Buhari. Jury plucked a colored pencil from Wiggins's cup and walked over to the whiteboard, where he wrote, under the Nairobi heading, the name of Marguerite Banado.

Wiggins was up and over at the murder board. "What? And where are you getting this inspiration from?" As if any inspiration at all were now the stuff of his boss's fevered dreams.

"'Little Rita. *Marguerite*, perhaps? Marguerite Banado, Wiggins? Certainly a possibility. Look at the Reno newspaper picture. The face is obscured here, too; so we're getting different angles, but—" Jury pressed the cutting from the paper against the whiteboard and then held the gallery shot beside it. "Of the same woman."

Wiggins squinted and then his eyes snapped open. "Wait a minute, boss. That report from Kione about the Banerjees' relation to Benjamin Buhari. Well, we knew that the Banerjees were acting more or less as foster parents for the brother's daughter. Buhari's daughter. Kione said that Elspeth is Mrs. Banerjee's name."

Jury looked puzzled. "Elspeth? Is that relevant, somehow?"

"Somehow, yes." Wiggins marched to the murder board. Under Nairobi, beside Banerjee, he wrote in the wife's name. "Her maiden name." He smiled.

Jury looked at this, hearing in his mind the somber voice of Carole-anne: *Times I think she really hated me, wanted me gone*. He felt a small shock, a tiny implosion, like one of those cartoon characters pulled up in a puff of smoke. His gaze swerved from the small Abasi painting on the wall of the gallery in the photo to the circle of sand on the wall in front of him.

He stood there in silence, looking at the blue sand.

Plop. Another tiny hillock fell.

It had nothing to do with tanzanite, had it? It had nothing to do with Africa.

42

Diane Demorney, who'd found the Connaught's famous bar even more easily than she'd found the entire hotel, was sitting with a rink-size martini when Jury entered. The low light, dark wood and walls in some kind of silver-leaf texture, with low-key dark rose and lavender birds and exotic flowers, made the place itself look drinkable.

Jury took a seat beside her. "The cocktails here, I've heard, are an experience."

"I know. I'm having it." She held up her glass.

"That's just your usual, Diane."

"My usual experience. Unbeatable."

Jury ordered a Jameson, hoping that wouldn't raise the barman's eyebrow. It didn't. "Ready to go clubbing?" he said.

"Oh, rather. I was fascinated by Marshall's game. I had no idea he was so expert."

"If he ever wanted to quit the antiques business I think he'd have a second career as a croupier. I'm sure Leonard Zane would keep him on forever." Although Zane's forever was probably about to end. "Where's Vivian?"

"Coming down in a minute."

The minute was apparently up, for Vivian entered the bar in one of the handsomest gowns Jury had ever seen. It was quite plain, almost tailored, midnight blue, a dress that would have been at home anywhere. It was certainly at home on Vivian.

"Wow," said Jury.

Vivian blushed. "Thank you."

"He didn't 'wow' me, if it makes you feel even better."

"With you, the 'wow' is understood."

Diane smiled. "Come on, Viv, fortify yourself before we lose all of our earthly belongings to the blackjack table."

Vivian sat on Jury's other side, asked for a martini.

Jury immediately started in: "Melrose is back from Kenya." He liked their looks in the mirror, a double dose of turning and staring.

"Why isn't he with you? With us?" said Diane.

"Yes, why?" said Vivian.

"He was tied up, he said. Has a lot to do before he leaves."

"Leaves for where?" said Vivian. "You mean he's going back to Ardry End right away?"

"No. Paris. He's taking the Orient Express."

Diane poured the rest of her martini down her throat, gulped, said before Vivian could, "*Melrose?* Melrose Plant? Our unassuming, unpretentious—"

"Earl? Viscount? Baron de jure? Yes, he's taking the Orient Express to Paris."

"For God's sake, he could just swim there. Another of these, please," Diane said to the barman.

"But *why*?" said Vivian.

Jury also raised his glass for a refill before answering. "He's meeting someone in Paris."

"What?" Vivian almost slid off her stool. "What do you mean?"

"I thought it was pretty clear: 'meeting someone.'"

"Don't be smart!" said Diane. "Of course it's not clear."

Drinks replenished, Jury said, "I think it's someone he met in Kenya."

Diane said, completely exasperated, "I assume you don't mean Jane Goodall. Or one of the Leakeys."

Jury smiled. "I didn't know you were into paleontology."

Diane ignored this. "It's completely unlike him. I'm sure you're mistaken."

"I agree," said Vivian. "Melrose doesn't go round *meeting* people. He hates meeting people. He hates new people."

"Perhaps, but remember he was on safari, in close quarters with a number of people, and, like it or not, he must have met them."

Diane slugged down her fresh martini, pulled her long ebony cigarette holder from her sequined purse and said, "I can see you intend to be impossible about it, so maybe we should just go along to the casino."

It was clear that Vivian, biting her lip, was not as willing to give up on this inquiry into Melrose's mercurial behavior. "How did he meet her?"

Jury thought about this for one moment and smiled. "Patty Haigh?"

"Patty Hay?"

"Patty Hay?"

They chorused it as the three of them walked toward the door and a black cab.

"Oh, didn't I tell you her name? That's it."

"That doesn't sound like a Kenyan name," said Vivian, now having a name, wanting to walk it back.

The cab was there, and Jury opened the door and helped them into it. He himself took one of the jump seats. "I didn't say the person was Kenyan. Patty Haigh is English."

Vivian glowered. Walk it back, but not to England. Vivian had always found that the greater the distance, the looser the attachment. "But then why meet her in Paris?"

"People do go to Paris."

Said Diane, "Why else go to London?"

"We'll see in a couple of days. There's a little send-off party at Victoria. It'll just be us, Trueblood and a half dozen kids. You both are free, aren't you? You wouldn't want Melrose to go off without seeing him."

"You make it sound as if he's not coming back! Don't be ridiculous!" Vivian's face was burning. "Does she live in Paris? Is that it?"

"I don't think so. No, I think Patty Haigh lives in London."

Vivian sank in her seat and turned her face to the window. They drove for some moments in a heavy silence as the taxi maneuvered through Covent Garden to the Embankment and toward the City.

Into this silence Diane dropped another man: "How could one be as attractive as this Leonard Zane, so charming and so successful, and still be unattached?"

"I don't know," said Jury, "but unattached he won't be in a few days, so enjoy him while you can."

Diane frowned. "What on earth do you mean?"

"He'll be attached to the Metropolitan Police."

The cigarette holder nearly got Jury in the eye in her sudden swerving toward him. "What?"

Vivian said, "You mean this Leonard Zane is the—*culprit*, Richard?"

"One of them, yes."

"My God, did he murder that couple?"

"No, he didn't."

"Is your case wrapped up, then?"

"Not yet. Not quite." Not by a long shot, he thought.

"Can you tell us," said Vivian, "why that couple were murdered?"

"Not precisely; but generally speaking, money."

"How banal!" said Diane. "How pathetic. Not even for love or revenge."

The cab pulled up in front of the Artemis Club. Jury got out, held the door for Vivian and Diane and then turned to the driver and paid the fare.

"'Night, mate," said the driver.

As Jury said good night, a young fellow with fair hair and wearing a uniform jacket rushed down the stairs and seemed a little crestfallen that they had managed to exit the cab without his help. Did he realize how fortunate he was not to have been handed this task a week ago?

But he did manage to shepherd them through the front door before another car pulled up and he dashed off.

Jury stood by Vivian, who seemed uncertain of her presence here. He said, "Diane seems to like to play with black chips. That's confidence. Let's sit at the bar."

But she still stood there, unmoving.

"Something wrong, Vivian?"

"What? No. Oh, no." She followed him to the bar, where he ordered whisky for himself and a martini for her.

"Melrose's action strikes me as—inscrutable, I don't mind saying. Entirely unlike him."

"You probably know him as well as anyone does."

But her look said she did not know him at all. "One thing I do know is that he does not behave spontaneously where women are concerned."

"When have you seen him behaving unspontaneously?" said Jury unhelpfully.

As she raised an eyebrow at this conundrum, Leonard Zane walked up to the bar looking fluid in a three-piece merino wool suit, light gray with a razor-sharp darker gray stripe. "Superintendent Jury! Delighted to see you. Miss Demorney appears to be winning." He turned to look at Trueblood's table. Then back at Vivian. "I'm Leonard Zane," he said, holding out his hand.

Which she took, with a smile. "You're very busy tonight."

"I know it sounds macabre, but murder is good for business."

"Until," said Jury, "it's bad for it."

Leonard, undisconcerted by this odd comment, smiled slightly. "What eventuality might bring about that change?"

Jury shrugged. "Another murder? That might make the place seem a bit too dangerous for your everyday gambler."

"But you aren't expecting that to happen."

"No, but we didn't expect it to happen before, either."

Diane had risen from Trueblood's table and was coming toward them.

"That didn't take long," said Leonard. "Good?"

"Bad," said Diane, sliding onto a bar stool and pointing to Vivian's martini with a finger raised. "Surely by now some of your customers realize you can't beat him."

Vivian looked surprised. "But you can. You did. You won hundreds, you said, last time."

"And managed to give it right back. He let me win—oops!" She looked at Zane. "Pretend I didn't say that."

He laughed. "You're right. He does appear to be unbeatable. He's a genius at the game. I don't know how he does it. I do know he isn't cheating."

"Psychology." Diane was rooting in her sequined bag for her cigarette holder. "He can read people. I was watching him watching the play. He picks up tells immediately. There's no way you can't give yourself away."

She found her holder, planted a cigarette in it, waited for a light. Zane supplied it.

She added, "He can't control the cards, so he controls the room." She slid a look at Zane as smoothly as he had slid his lighter to her cigarette. "If you know what I mean."

"I know what you mean."

"Mr. Zane," said Diane.

"Leo, please."

"Would it be completely against the rules for us to invite that croupier to dine with us? Or is that forbidden?"

"It's forbidden, but for you I'll make an exception."

"Perhaps you'd join us?" she said.

"No, thank you. I've work to do in the gallery."

"Well, what about you, Superintendent? You'll dine with us, won't you?"

"Happily. What time?"

They would wait for Marshall Trueblood's next break.

An hour later the four of them were sitting down at a table in the gallery's dining room and being handed large menus.

"I don't know how you do it, Marshall," said Diane.

"That's good," said Trueblood, snapping his napkin awake and laying it across his lap.

"Seriously. You can look at a player and know immediately what she has in her hand."

"More 'if' she has it; if she has a winning hand."

"You knew just from looking at my face."

"Well, it was *that* look. The giveaway look."

"But I made my face perfectly blank."

Trueblood laughed. "That was the giveaway."

Diane was saying she thought she'd have the baba ghanoush as an appetizer and then the mujadara.

"My God, Diane, we might as well be at the Blue Parrot," said Trueblood, who looked at the door of the dining room and suddenly sprang from his chair. "Melrose!"

Melrose Plant was standing in the doorway. He moved to their table and said to Jury, "We need to talk." Smiling around the table, he greeted Diane and Vivian.

Trueblood had pulled a chair away from the table beside them and set it between Vivian and Jury.

Vivian looked almost lustrous, as if a light had switched on behind her eyes. Well, he had always known about Vivian; it was Melrose Plant who had been the question. She said, "What are you doing here? Not that we're not glad to see you, but—"

As Melrose sat down, Vivian said, "What's all of this about the Orient—?"

Jury said hurriedly, "Let's talk over there." He pulled Melrose out of his chair and they walked across the foyer to the library.

43

They did not sit down.

Melrose pulled the snapshot from his jacket pocket. "This shot—"

"Right. I finally worked it out. Masego Abasi told you about Little Rita. 'Rita' could be 'Marguerite.' Kione told us that Banerjee's wife's maiden name was Elspeth Banado. The question is: what in the hell is Claire Howard doing with Marguerite Banado from Reno?"

Melrose shook his head. "More than that, the question is: what is Claire Howard doing with Maggie Benn, from God knows where?"

Jury frowned. "What are you talking about?"

"Look at the two of them again."

Jury looked. "This woman Claire Howard is talking to—" Jury squinted.

"You don't see it? Even the name is a clue. People seem to like to keep initials. Like 'Danny Morrissey.'" Melrose drew a small holder from his pocket, opened it to disclose what looked like pince-nez but was actually a magnifying glass.

Jury held it up to the picture. "For God's sake! It can't be."

Melrose nodded. "Marguerite Banado, Maggie Benn. I thought: where have I seen this before? A slight attack of déjà vu." He pointed to the small picture in the Reno newspaper—Leonard Zane and Marguerite Banado coming out of the Metropole. "When I was at the gallery with Bea Slocum, Maggie Benn walked into the library. Her face was down; she was reading something. In this newspaper account, she's holding a paper that's hiding part of her face. The poses are similar. The glamorous Marguerite. Maggie's anything but glamorous, but one thing you can't change is bones. The forehead, the cheek, the chin. In both pictures, an outline of bone."

"I'll be damned. You know, I wondered about Maggie Benn's fitting in at this casino."

"The opposite of Marguerite Banado," said Melrose.

"How could Leonard Zane not have known?"

Melrose shrugged. "Maybe he did."

"Maggie Benn claims never to have been to Kenya."

"There are more people in this case who've turned up in Kenya who've never been there than I can count," said Melrose.

"So Leonard Zane—"

"May very well have no connection to Claire Howard; or he may have a connection, just not the one we've been thinking he has. Remember Reno." From his other pocket Melrose took a copy of the article from the *Reno Gazette-Journal*. "The couple in the casino heard an argument in one of the offices. The wife here said she heard the woman exclaim, '*I'll never let you*'— Leave? Go?" Melrose read from the paper: '*The shooting of Mr. Morrissey occurred an hour later. The hotel operator said she got a call from his room: She immediately got in touch with the police. The couple identified Mr. Morrissey as the man whom they'd seen come out of the office.* The shooter walked into his room and shot him in the back? Not a very good shot; the door couldn't have been that far from the window."

"Twenty feet, about," said Jury.

"Bad shot. What did he say about it later?"

Jury recalled the newspaper's follow-up: "Said he didn't see anyone; didn't hear the door open. He remembered falling and grabbing at the phone. The desk was near the window. Then he remembered nothing until he woke up in the hospital, his shoulder patched up—left shoulder is where the bullet nicked him—and hurting, but nothing more serious."

"So Marguerite Banado," said Melrose, "sounds like the obvious suspect. Didn't he tell the police who she was?"

"No. He said he was sure there was no relation between the argument and the shooting."

"Ha! I bet the Nevada police went along with that." Melrose paused. "Do you think he felt so guilty about breaking up with her that he didn't want to cause her any more pain? What about Leonard Zane? It's a bit of a coincidence, isn't it, that both times David Moffit is shot the site of the shooting is Zane's casino."

"It is indeed. Except that Marguerite Banado and Maggie Benn were also in both casinos."

"But we know she didn't shoot him in front of the Artemis Club."

"No . . ." Jury's 'no' sounded uncertain.

"Come on. You're not going to say she popped up in the bushes and fired?" Melrose added, "Only how did Moffit manage to get into this chic club with a yearlong waiting list?"

"Remember? He wrote in advance."

"And you think Zane knew she shot David Moffit?"

"I do, yes. The woman and Morrissey were in the casino office. One of the two would surely have been an employee, right?" Jury turned. "I'm going to talk to Leonard Zane," he said, moving toward the doorway. "He must have known that only someone connected to the casino would have had access to the office."

Before he could go through the door, Melrose said, "Richard. Wait."

Jury turned back.

"Suppose he didn't know."

"Who? Leonard Zane?"

"No. The shooter, Buhari. The shooting down of the Moffits in that public way was so foolhardy—why would a shooter do it? But suppose he didn't know that's what he was doing."

"You mean he was drugged or in some kind of fugue state?" Jury laughed. "Come on."

"No. He didn't know the gun was loaded."

Artemis Club, London
Nov. 9, Saturday night

44

Jury stared. "He was a policeman, for God's sake—"

"It wasn't a policeman's gun, was it?"

"But people don't die from blank rounds."

"Did he know they were dead? No blood from the first wound. It was a head shot. The second, Rebecca's, yes, but in his hurry to get in that cab, did he see blood? She didn't die immediately, either." Melrose shrugged. "And you've said things about his behavior you thought didn't make sense, given he'd just killed two people. Really, he was acting like a man following some script."

Acting like somebody who's in no danger, Wiggins had said.

"He was set up, Richard." Melrose paused. "Maybe you're headed in the right direction." Melrose nodded toward the stairs and the upper floor.

The gallery was as cool and remote as a monastery. Jury supposed this effect was a studied one.

On the long table rested a silver tray holding various dishes; a dinner plate on which sat the leavings from those dishes; a wineglass, nearly empty. The bottle of wine rested on a silver coaster.

Leonard Zane was not sitting behind the tray, but was up and holding a painting Jury did not remember seeing before. It was apparently meant for the space vacated by the Abasi painting of the woman whose remoteness shielded her from the cheetah and the lion. He thought of Patty Haigh.

"Mr. Zane," said Jury.

Leonard started, his left hand slipping from that side of the painting.

"Sorry." Jury moved quickly to help. It was a heavy picture. "That could have been a disaster." Jury lifted the left side.

"Only to my foot," said Leonard, laughing. The two of them heaved the painting to the bracketed hooks.

"You finally sold the Abasi?"

"I did. I was sorry to see it go."

"Me, too."

When the new one was straightened, Leonard said, "What do you think of this one?"

Jury stepped back and looked. "I don't know."

Zane stepped back too. He shoved his hands into his pockets, holding back his jacket. "I don't know either."

They stood for half a minute, which bothered Jury, thinking he shouldn't be sharing companionable silences with Leonard Zane.

"How was dinner?" asked Leonard.

"What? Oh, fine. Delicious." Jury hoped Zane wouldn't ask him what he'd eaten, and then he wondered why he was treating this encounter like a drinks party.

"I really like this cook. Chef, I should say. I stole him from the Dorchester."

"Shame on you."

After another long pause, Zane said, "Is something wrong, Superintendent? You look bemused." He laughed again. "You want to arrest me but you don't know how to do it?"

"No, as a matter of fact, I don't want to arrest you, and I do know how to do it. I want to talk to you. Could we sit down?"

"Of course." Zane moved behind the polished table and shoved the tray to one side. He waved Jury into one of the two chairs opposite. "Fire away, Mr. Jury."

"David Moffit. For an innocent man to be shot once is an unusual event; for him to be shot *twice* on different occasions is highly unlikely. To be shot two times in two different casinos beggars statistics, unless the same person, present at both of those events, is the shooter, or let's say someone who orchestrated the shootings."

"What possible motive could I have for killing David Moffit?"

"Probably none. But I didn't say you were the person, did I?"

Zane was clearly astonished. The relief that followed was somewhat undercut by his puzzlement. "Superintendent, you have a way of speaking in riddles."

"Sorry. I thought what I meant was perfectly clear. I don't think you did it; I don't think you planned it; I don't think you caused the shooting of David Moffit."

"But one shooting happened in Reno and the other in London. So the 'someone' connected to both events is me."

"Or Maggie Benn."

"Maggie *Benn*?" Zane spoke the last name as if Jury had made a mistake in pronunciation. He had certainly made a mistake in attribution, he seemed to be saying.

"Why was she there? I mean, in Reno?"

"She wasn't, Mr. Jury. You're confusing her with my manager there, Marguerite Banado. Marguerite said she was there to get a quick divorce from an abusive jerk. But that wasn't the real reason. She was there to shake a habit."

Jury was perplexed. "What are you talking about?"

"Marguerite was an addict."

"Gambling?" When Leonard nodded, Jury said, surprised, "She's an addict trying to get work in a casino? Why does that not strike me as a good career move?"

Leonard laughed. "Nor I. She told me about her habit one evening a couple of months after she'd started at the Metropole. I'd asked her to take over at the blackjack table because the croupier was ill. She wouldn't do it. I knew she *could*, because I'd seen her helping out a kid I'd hired who was a total loss. One night after the tables had shut down, I saw her giving him a lesson. She was good, very good. She told me she was an addict after she'd refused to take over the table. I said the same thing you did: not a good job choice. But she said she'd decided either to rise above it or drown."

"Another version of 'sink or swim'?"

Leonard nodded. "She swam."

"How could you be sure?"

"How? The same way you would. In your work you've come across hundreds of drug addicts, I expect. Me, I'm addicted to these." He raised the hand that held the thin cigar.

"Right. And every time you light up I can taste it."

"Ah. You, too. But you don't light up yourself. Why? What stops you?"

Jury considered. "A promise, I guess."

"To whom?"

"A friend." Jury shrugged it off. "But back to Maggie Benn. How much do you know about her? Who are her friends? Does she have family? Who? Where? Do you know what her name really is?"

Leonard frowned. "I didn't know there was a 'really.'"

From his pocket Jury drew out the photo of Claire Howard in the unknown gallery. Wordlessly, he shoved it across the length of the table. Leonard picked it up and studied it, also wordlessly. Finally, he said, "Should I recognize this place? It looks as if a drinks party is in progress—" He brought the picture closer to his eyes. "Those are paintings . . ."

"Masego Abasi's."

"So are you telling me that he's broken our contract? He's showing his work in another venue?"

"I'd hardly have come about that, would I? No, this gallery's in Kenya. You've probably been to it. But it's not the place, it's the people."

"What people?"

"See the two women—one in white, one in black—more or less in the center of the picture?"

Leonard nodded. "Yes, but I don't know them."

"You're sure? Here." Jury picked up a magnifying glass lying on the table and handed it to him.

Leonard held the picture up once again. "I don't recognize—wait. This blond woman looks familiar. The shooting out there—" He tilted his head toward the dark window behind them. "This looks like—" He brought the glass up to the photo once again. "No, it doesn't." He dropped the picture. "I don't know."

"It's not Rebecca Moffit; it's not the one who was shot. That's her mother, Claire Howard. You don't know her? I got the impression she knows you quite well."

"Her *mother*? No. They look very much alike." He moved to hand the picture back to Jury. "Were you trying to trick me into saying I knew her?"

"Not at all. But it's not Mrs. Howard I'm interested in at the moment. It's the woman she's talking to. Look again."

Leonard did so. He shook his head, then looked at the picture again. "Wait. She looks like Marguerite Banado."

"That *is* Marguerite, Mr. Zane. She's from Kenya. That's her real name, I believe—Maggie Benn's. They're the same person. You didn't know?"

Leonard Zane turned the cigar in his mouth and removed it in a slim stream of smoke. "I knew, Superintendent. Not immediately, but after a while, I began to suspect. Not just the physical resemblance, but . . . well, there are things you can't disguise."

When he stopped, Jury prompted. "Such as?"

"Addiction. Ever seen a recovering alcoholic around booze? You can sense a hunger there. If there's one thing I understand, it's addiction."

Jury wondered what—besides cigars—his drug of choice was. He didn't feel the need to visit that subject, however.

Leonard Zane went on: "If Maggie wanted to jettison Marguerite, I let her. She's very good at what she does here." He paused, frowned. "But . . . Kenya?"

"As Marguerite Banado, she's been there many times. Claire How-ard claims never to have been there. Yet here she is. Here they *both* are. How did you meet Maggie Benn?"

Leonard looked perplexed. "She came here when I was hiring staff. She's been working for me for a couple of years. She's very shy, with-drawn. That's why I don't simply have her take over the casino. Gam-bling bores me."

"I'm surprised by that, especially given your career in Reno."

"What do you mean?"

"The shooting at the Metropole, your hotel."

"That did happen, yes, and the shooter was never found."

"The man who was shot was really David Moffit."

Leonard Zane lurched from his chair. "What?"

"You said you'd never seen the man before who was shot in your driveway."

"I didn't know everyone who passed through the Metropole. It wasn't like this. But that fellow's name was . . . it wasn't Moffit."

"Morrissey."

Leonard stood with his hands in his pockets. "The man in Reno had very little money. That was the reason I didn't cut him off."

"He did have money. He was very rich."

"But surely this is coincidence. There's nothing to tie the Metropole to the Artemis."

"Well, there's you—and Marguerite Banado, the manager whose managing days are over."

Leonard looked ashen as he reseated himself. "So you think—or thought—Maggie and I conspired to murder David Moffit and his wife. Why?"

"That of course was the mystery—your motive, that is. Hers was quite clear. Revenge. He'd dropped her in Reno for Rebecca Howard, and Marguerite managed to keep tabs on him over the years. That wouldn't have been too hard, as he was a respected professor at Colum-bia. And of course she knew he was coming to London as he'd written some time ago to see if he could get into your club."

"For God's sake, though . . . *Maggie*? She wouldn't have waited so long to get revenge, surely."

"The thing is, now there's another motive, money, and another person comes onto the scene." Jury picked up the photo again.

Leonard frowned. "You mean this Howard woman? How did they get this Kenyan to do the shooting?"

"'They' didn't. Marguerite did. Claire Howard probably didn't know him. For Claire, the motive was strictly money. Maggie, on the other hand, knew Mr. Banerjee, who himself was not the shooter. He's a Kenyan industrialist; he's Benjamin Buhari's brother. Buhari was the shooter. The brother, Banerjee, had taken care of Marguerite since she was a child because the girl's mother had left them and Benjamin Buhari couldn't manage the little girl on his own. Marguerite Banado was his daughter."

"*What?*" Leonard looked away toward his wall of paintings, as if they'd offer some clue to all of this. "You're saying she manipulated him into—"

"Shooting the Moffits is my guess. God knows how she did it, what she said to him."

Leonard rose again and walked over to the Masego Abasi painting. He seemed to be searching for comfort. "Do you suppose they met at that gallery party?" He had turned to look again, and the look fell like a shadow across the snapshot. He picked it up, tapped his finger at the image. "She'd kill her own daughter for money?"

"We're talking about millions here, Mr. Zane."

"Nevertheless."

Leonard seemed to think that word said all that needed saying.

"Where did she come from? Marguerite?"

Zane paused. "The East Coast. New York? No, from New Jersey."

"Atlantic City, by any chance?" Where David Moffit had been refused admittance to some casino. "She met him there is my guess. Marguerite Banado was obsessed with him, and, as Maggie Benn, still was. Where is she now?"

"On the casino floor. When I leave, I have her take over."

"You give her a lot of authority, yet I thought you said she wasn't good enough to manage."

Leonard shook his head. "I didn't mean she wasn't good enough. I'd let her manage the casino were she not so diffident. Or seeming to be."

"Diffidence isn't really on the menu," said Jury, waving his arm over the silver tray before he rose. "There's one more thing, Mr. Zane." He pulled from his pocket a small bag and poured the half dozen stones into his hand and then across the table.

"That's tanzanite, isn't it?" said Zane.

"It is indeed."

Leonard Zane's face was blank. "I don't understand."

"We took two of your paintings, remember?"

He still looked blank. "Of course. I assumed you thought they were forgeries. Which they weren't."

"No, I didn't think they were." Jury braced his arms against the table. "Come on, Mr. Zane. Don't look so puzzled."

"Sorry, but I am." He ran his hand over the spilled tanzanite stones before he picked one up and inspected it.

"Not the art, the frames. I assume this Inspector Buhari was helping with the smuggling."

Leonard shook his head. "Sorry, Superintendent, but you've lost me. There was an Inspector Buhari in the Merelani district. I knew him slightly because I have a mine. And now you're saying this same Buhari was the shooter? Well, he wasn't smuggling, certainly not for me." Leonard's look was now somber. "The paintings you took weren't acquired by me, either."

"By whom, then?"

"Maggie. She asked if she could hang them with the others."

"In plain sight, you mean."

"In plain sight."

"Yet she claimed never to have been in Kenya," said Jury.

"She's lying, and it's a stupid lie, given I know she's flown to Nairobi several times." Leonard shoved the little stones about with his finger. "She told me after a while that those paintings were sold. Which is why I couldn't sell them to Miss Slocum. Is she one of yours?"

"One of my what?"

"You know what I mean. I didn't notice immediately that one painting had been switched for another. She's quite dexterous is Miss Slocum."

Jury didn't comment on this, but said, "And the extraordinary piece in your drawer, there?" He looked toward that end of the desk.

Leonard smiled slightly. "You've got me there, Mr. Jury. That was my own doing. Rather childish to keep it hidden among glass shards and razor blades, but—?" He shrugged.

Jury said, "I think that's all at the moment. I should get back to my friends."

"Of course, Superintendent." Zane rose too. "May I venture to say I'm no longer a suspect?"

"At the moment, I'd say, not in my books."

"Are there other books?"

"Indeed there are." Jury laughed and held out his hand. "Good night, Mr. Zane."

Leonard Zane shook his hand. "Call me Leo."

45

——

Once settled in Brown's Hotel, where they had gone for tea, Jury expressed dismay at Paula Moffit's leaving London. He pulled out the little velvet box. "For some reason, David gave this to me for you. In case something happened." The ring box left on his living-room table had reminded him once again to call Paula Moffit.

She opened the box, removed the tanzanite ring. "How beautiful. But what was he thinking, that he would give it to you? Did he have some sort of premonition?"

"I don't know."

"Do you know the last thing he said to me when he called?"

"You mean the night—?"

"The last night, yes." Her face clouded over and she looked as if she wished she hadn't mentioned this. And as she set down the velvet box, she looked as if she wished she hadn't picked it up. "Yes. Just before he hung up, he said, 'It's a gibbous moon again, Mom.'"

Jury frowned. "What did he mean?"

She fell silent as the waiter poured their tea after placing the triple-tiered scone and sandwich plate between them. He left the silver pot and withdrew.

"This looks wonderful," she said, looking at the tiered plate. "Why don't we have tea like this in America?"

"You do. You just don't know how to make it." Jury asked her again, "What about the gibbous moon?"

"David associated a gibbous moon with misfortune, for some reason. The moon waxes and wanes going from a full to a new moon. David could stand out there—" She inclined her head as if "out there" were actually their home in Connecticut. "—and stare upward for what seemed hours on end. When he was a little boy, one night we couldn't find him; he wasn't in his room. Finally it was our cook who found him. She'd walked around the grounds, looking up at the sky, and saw him at the top of a tree, a very tall tree. 'Looking at the sky, he was, of course.'

"When we asked her what had prompted her to look up at the sky, she said, 'Because that's what Master David would have done.'

"We called the fire department. David was very polite to them when they helped him down, but I could see that underneath it all he was absolutely seething. He was furious with us for 'treating me like I was a cat.' He wouldn't speak to his father for days and barely would he to me."

Jury smiled. "What about your cook?"

"Oh, she was all right because, he said, she used her brain; she tried to think like he would.

"Later, when he was talking to Max once more, he told him he'd been studying that tree for weeks. He'd climbed it a little at a time for two weeks, going a bit higher each night; noting all the branches, the footholds; gauging the distance from one branch to another; taking in the ones big enough to sit on if he got tired. He had calculated the time and steps necessary to go from one part of the tree to another. He had charts—Mr. Jury—*charts*, and drawings he'd made. He was nine years old.

"He said to his father, 'Do you think I'd be so foolhardy'—his word—'as to climb that tree at one go without knowing where the branches were, how long it would take, how high it was?'"

"Not only careful, but a perfectionist." He was silent for a moment.

Paula frowned. "He'd said it once before when he called me from Lake Tahoe."

"Said what?"

"'It's a gibbous moon, Mom. Bad luck.'"

"When was this?"

"Several years ago. He liked to go to Tahoe. I think because it was so near Reno."

Jury thought about the Metropole. "Are you sure he wasn't calling from Reno?"

She looked puzzled. "But why wouldn't he have said so?"

"Maybe because he didn't want you to think he was losing his shirt."

She laughed. "David never lost his shirt. He won ninety percent of the time."

"Maybe this was the other ten percent."

She moved her arm as the waiter set down another plate full of little cakes and tarts. "He knew he was addicted, but he didn't fight it. For one reason because he could afford it; for another because he rarely lost."

"Do you think he really had a system? Or was he just lucky?"

"I don't know, but I doubt he had a system. I doubt he would have bothered using his time to work one out. I expect they're very difficult to invent. He liked to tell people his gambling had to do with the uncertainty principle . . . or was it . . . what's it called? The completeness theory? But I imagine that was just a tease."

"Incompleteness." *Some tease,* thought Jury.

Harry Johnson was in the Old Wine Shades, sitting on his regular bar chair. Jury was pleased to see Mungo was also there. The dog sat up, alert, when he saw Jury. There was no other bodily action, no wriggling in delight as though Jury were the person he'd been waiting for half his life, and certainly no tail-wagging.

Jury suddenly had an idea that would not have occurred to him had he not seen Mungo, the smartest animal he had ever come across. Mungo and the kids, Tilda and Timmy; Mungo and Timmy—no, no. Of course Mungo would recognize Timmy's scent; anyway, could the behavior of a dog really count as evidence? He pictured what a barrister would do with that procedural line.

"Looks like that lightbulb just went out," said Harry. "Sorry, but your expression really did remind me of a cartoon bulb over a head."

"I look that stupid, do I?" Jury nodded to Trevor, the barman.

"No, merely expressive. Pour him a tumblerful, Trev," Harry said, inclining his head toward the bottle of Côte de Nuits resting behind the bar. "He needs it."

Jury said, "Thanks, but I want the subtle taste of struck matches." That should confound Trevor.

It didn't. Trevor nodded and moved off.

"Just to have an argument," said Harry.

"No, just to have a whisky."

Trevor set the glass before him, poured a couple of fingers of Talisker single malt into it.

"Do you know everything, Trev?" said Jury.

"Yes," Harry answered for the barman. "So don't try to be clever. Now, what was it?"

"What was what?"

Harry sighed. "Your idea du jour?"

"Nothing. It was no good, worse luck. And with Mungo here, too." Jury reached down and gave the dog's head a good rub.

Mungo bore it.

"But I do have a question."

"And I have an answer," said Harry.

"I'm sure. I'm also sure you're aware the man shot outside the Artemis Club was a physicist."

"Half of London knows that. The half that can read."

"How would you apply the uncertainty principle to the game of twenty-one?" Jury hoped the question would draw a small gasp from Harry.

Which of course it didn't. "I wouldn't."

"Poker?"

"Ditto."

"Any form of gambling?"

"Is that what this unfortunate chap is supposed to have done?" Harry raised his empty wineglass, signaling Trevor. "Ridiculous."

"You're claiming it can't be done?"

Harry grimaced. "Of course it can't."

"How can you be so sure?"

"If you recall, the 'uncertainty' in the uncertainty principle is that you can't know the position and velocity of an object simultaneously. It's not the 'uncertainty' of where things are, such as cards."

"Mathematics is applicable—"

Harry groaned slightly. "Physics is the study of the interaction of matter and energy. Not card-counting. Do you know what gambling is?"

"No."

"It's a battle of wits. It's more psychology than the way the cards fall."

"Well, what about Niels Bohr? Schrödinger?"

"What about them?"

"Other theories."

"Oh, you mean wave and particle? I can see how that would influence a poker hand. Instead of wasting your time trying to understand quantum mechanics, why don't you spend it trying to solve the problem of why a Kenyan would murder two Americans in front of a ritzy casino? Now there's an event even Niels Bohr couldn't sort out."

Trevor had come down the bar to replenish both glasses, "Don't let him get your goat, Mr. Jury," he said with a smile and a sideways glance at Harry.

"Thanks, Trev." Jury raised his glass. Then to Harry, "A man's profession might have something to do with his murder."

"Obviously. But you're trying to take this way beyond the victim's being a physicist and a gambler. You're wandering into the neverland of a straight flush depending on some theorem in physics. This professor," said Harry, with a smile, "was just winding people up."

"I guess he wound up the wrong person." Jury drank his Talisker.

"I guess he did." Harry drank his Côte de Nuits.

Jury thought about Paula Moffit's comment. "What about Gödel?"

"You mean the incompleteness theorem. That's also ridiculous. Gödel's theorems have had more harebrained interpretations attached to them than any other theory I could name." Harry stopped. "Unless . . ."

Jury was surprised that Harry seemed to be honestly considering. "Unless what?"

"That you can't prove a system from within the system. Maybe what this Moffit was doing was applying this to cards. I'm vastly oversimplifying here. What if your professor was saying that no 'system' in a systematic game of cards would work so he decided he might as well bet on nothing." Harry laughed. "And if he had enough money—he was rich, you said—"

"Very."

"So he could simply have played and waited and won. That's not exactly a betting system. Did it occur to you that he might have been reading the dealer?"

"Dealers have giveaways? Tells?"

"Not the best ones. But yes. Do you know a croupier? He could enlighten you."

Jury smiled. "I do happen to know one, yes."

"This professor. I think he might have had a hell of a sense of humor. I wish I could have met him."

It disturbed Jury that he'd like to have heard a conversation between David Moffit and Harry Johnson.

"This guy must have had both a highly original and a very quirky mind. I'm sorry he's dead."

Jury thought it was the only time he had ever heard Harry make a sincere declaration of sorrow about the life of anybody.

"That makes two of us." Jury was even more disturbed that he would make two of anything with Harry Johnson.

46

J ury called Wiggins to tell him he'd be a couple of hours late because he had something he had to do.

He'd hired a small café for two hours. The people who ran it thought he was a nutter, but since he was a Scotland Yard nutter, they went along with the crazy idea. For a price. Jury would have paid twice as much, but, again, seeing he was a Scotland Yard detective superintendent, he had to pay only half. Besides, they liked him. They thought it was wonderful that a cop was having a party for a bunch of kids and was going to the trouble and expense of keeping on the cook and a waitress and a boy to clean up afterward.

They were quite taken by his reason. He'd told them it was because the kids had done New Scotland Yard a big favor. So the café manager agreed to hang a "Private Party" sign on the door for this short period of time.

Jury told the kids to wear their best, which for most of them meant the same thing they usually wore. They asked Jury why they couldn't have this party at Waterloo as always—

Like where you always have your parties? Because the Orient Express doesn't pull out of Waterloo. It leaves Victoria Station for Paris and Venice.

Are we going to Paris, then?

No, you're not going anywhere.

But "wearing her best" was enough for Patty Haigh, who considered herself the railway costume queen. She wanted to know if Lord Ardry was coming to this party.

Jury had met Patty Haigh by having Robbie Parsons drive him to Heathrow, since he couldn't get Robbie to drive him to the Knowledge. Terminal 3. Robbie had found Patty Haigh through Aero, who was outside on his skateboard ("Pickin' pockets," said Robbie).

"My God, I'm surprised he hasn't been nicked."

"He has. Several times."

"Why didn't he wind up in care, then?"

"He knows somebody."

"Who?"

"Don't ask me. But every time cops take him in, somebody comes round and he's back 'ere again."

Jury looked down at this mite of a girl with the ebony hair and pointed chin and said, "You're Patty Haigh?"

"I'm Patty Haigh. Why?"

Jury took out his ID, hunkered down and showed it to her. "I'm Richard Jury."

Her eyes widened. "You're that friend of Lord Ardry."

"I'm that friend of Lord Ardry, right. And we're having a party tomorrow morning to which you're invited." He looked at her. "Tell me, how in the bloody hell did you do it?"

Patty looked puzzled. "Do what?"

Robbie Parsons laughed.

He was at Victoria Station at 9:30 A.M. that morning, running his eyes over the crowd—there was always a crowd—searching for the kids. He saw no one, but it was early yet. He'd told them 10:00 at the latest.

He started toward the Daybreak Café when a voice at his elbow said, "Hi." It was Martin. No wonder Jury hadn't recognized him. Martin was scrubbed, brushed and polished. He was wearing a fresh white shirt with a small red-and-white-checked cloth drawn under the collar. His brown hair was combed straight back and from the little runnels in it Jury could tell that he'd had a shower. The bright smile on his clean face was almost beatific.

"Whadya think? I look all right?" Martin took a couple of steps back and held out his arms so that Jury could get the whole picture.

"You look better than just all right," said Jury. "You look—redeemed."

"You mean like J.C.?"

"Correct."

"Yeah. Jesus wouldn't be caught dead in this lot." Martin flicked the checked scarf.

"You think you'll get a chance to use that in Victoria Station?" Jury gestured toward the skateboard.

"Sure. There's always an unpeopled platform." Aero cast about, came to the British Pullman and said, "Not that one, o' course."

"O' course," said Jury. "Let's go to the caff, shall we?"

"Where is this caff?" said Aero.

Martin pointed straight ahead toward the rising sun on the sign of the Daybreak Café. "Right there."

"Okay," said Aero. "Race you."

They took off, mauling their way through the crowd. Jury was happy to see that underneath it all, there remained a streak of normal boyhood. He lost sight of them.

Suki and Henry were waiting in front of the Daybreak. Reno sat calmly. "Jimmy's inside, tuning up," said Suki. "He gonna play something?"

"Something," said Jury, smiling. "Let's go in." They had turned to the door when a young girl with very blond hair and wearing a bright red dress came toward them. Underneath the silky skirt were what looked like reams of tulle. Definitely a party dress, thought Jury. Her bulging backpack looked as if she'd packed it with a week's wear. She was also carrying a shiny red purse on a long strap that crossed over her torso.

"Dressed up like a dog's dinner," said Suki.

Patty Haigh reached them just after Martin and Aero went into the café.

Inside, the boys pulled from their pockets and under their shirts a variety of things: wallets, passports, pound notes and a little velvet box that held diamond earrings. There it all lay on the Formica table: the swag.

The girls congratulated Martin and Aero.

Jury shook his head. "Can't we all act like ordinary citizens for one day?"

Aero said, "Yeah, maybe you can. You look ordinary enough."

"This stuff has got to be returned. Passports. Wallets. We're going straight to security with them."

"Ah, come on, guv. Wasn't easy gettin' this lot."

"Easy to take it back, though."

Jury left the cash on the table, picked up passports, wallets and the diamond earrings, which he had to bat out of Suki's hands.

Martin's and Aero's stories to security were, "Found this lyin' outside the Gents" and "This passport was in WH Smith. Someone got careless!" Similar stories accompanied the rest of the swag.

First came Vivian Rivington in a pale blue cashmere dress and matching cape—perfect for traveling, had she been going anywhere. "Seeing Melrose off?"

Next came Melrose in his beautifully tailored suit.

"Remember? I'm giving the Waterloo kids a party." Jury tilted his head in the direction of the café.

"That's nice," said Vivian, "but who are the Waterloo—"

"Sorry, I've got to go. Have a great trip," he said to them both. He clapped Melrose on the shoulder, gave him a kind of hug to give himself an opportunity to stick something in Melrose's breast pocket.

Jury went into the café and got Jimmy, brought him outside and pointed out Vivian and Melrose. "What are you going to play?"

"I thought 'Fascination,' that'd be good. It's a waltz."

Jury watched as Jimmy joined the colorful crowd on the platform. Some of them seemed caught up in an emotional turmoil as if the first step weren't Paris but the moon.

He watched this little crowd dressed in turn-of-the-century (the old century) clothes. But "costumed" was a more fitting description than mere "clothes." One woman's neck and chin were buried in a violet feathered boa; the man with her was wearing a velvet jacket and a cravat. Another couple flashed with gold and silver, some from their jewelry, some from their clothes.

Jimmy looked from Vivian and Melrose to Jury, his look a question. Jury nodded and Jimmy stuck his violin under his chin and began playing. He had a delicate silvery touch. The passengers thought this entertainment had been laid on by the Orient Express's public relations and, taking advantage of it, started dancing. Waltzing. First, it was the couple in the boa and the cravat. Then another couple joined in and another and finally Melrose held out his arms for Vivian. And that violin just kept on playing.

Jury thought it was the most beautiful thing he had ever heard.

Until Marshall Trueblood sidled up, gave his shoulder a little punch and said, "Nice try, mate."

The train was about to pull out with its pricey cargo of costumed passengers, when the kids rushed out of the café and said to Jury that they wanted to say good-bye to these grown-ups they didn't know but had a liking for because they had the nerve to wander through Victoria and board a train dressed like clowns.

"You want to say good-bye, that it?" said Jury. "That'd better be all you do."

A stagy whistle sounded and the attendants were calling for everyone to board, the train would be leaving in three minutes.

"Well, go on, Melrose. The train's going to leave."

"Me? I'm not going to Paris—"

"No? Then what's this?" Vivian flicked a polished nail at the bit of cardboard in his breast pocket.

Melrose took it out. "I never saw this before. Where'd it come from?" Vivian just looked at him. "Your pocket. You're a liar, to boot."

"To boot what? You should talk! What about your new French friend?"

"Who?"

"Don't play dumb."

Patty Haigh had shouldered her way through the passengers and was standing listening to this conversation. Again the whistle sounded and again the porters called out that the train would be leaving in one minute.

Melrose said, "Well, climb aboard, you don't want to keep Alain waiting."

"Alain?"

"Don't go, Vivian. Listen, he's a bad lot, I can tell just from the name: Alain Resnais, for God's sake! Talk about an invention!"

Just as he bent toward her, a voice called out, "Good-bye, Lord Melrose."

He changed the direction of his look. Patty Haigh! She threw her arms up in a bid for him to bend down. He couldn't believe Patty Haigh was gesturing for a hug, but he bent down and she hugged him.

He straightened as the train started a slumbrous move, as if it couldn't make up its mind which one of them was going. Vivian? Melrose?

They looked at each other as Patty Haigh melted into the thinning crowd on the platform.

"I'm not going to Paris! Who's Alain? What about your woman from Kenya?"

The British Pullman had finally woken itself up and was leaving.

"What woman? And I don't know where in hell this ticket came from!" He stuck his fingers into his pocket and felt around. "It's gone! It's—where is she?"

"Where's who?"

"The girl—" Melrose made a dash down the platform. He was back in a few moments and grabbed Vivian. "Come on."

Jury stood outside the barrier with Jimmy, who asked him, "Okay, guv?"

"Sublime," said Jury. "Absolutely sublime."

Melrose, Vivian in tow, rushed up to him. "Patty Haigh got on that train. Your ticket!"

"Patty Haigh? My ticket? I don't know what the bloody hell you're talking about."

"She's gone to Paris!"

Jury laughed. "Why am I not surprised? Well, not to worry, in a few days we'll get a phone call."

"Patty Haigh?" said Vivian, staring at Melrose. "*Your* Parry Haigh has nicked your ticket?"

Images of Kenya and Tanzania tumbled through Melrose's mind: Mbosi Camp, the long walk from Kibera, the veldt, the Merelani Hills, Nairobi, Abasi, the leopard, the cub—he smiled as he watched the last car of the Orient Express disappear into smoke. "Actually, she's nobody's Patty Haigh."

New Scotland Yard, London
Nov. 11, Monday morning

47

When Jury got to the Yard, Wiggins was there in his new gray suit, bright as a freshly minted ten-pence piece. "Fiona called just a minute ago. The guv'nor wants to talk to you."

"And for once, I want to talk to him. I'm getting two warrants, Wiggins—for Howard and Benn. I'm going to want you to go to Maggie Benn's flat in Clerkenwell when I do."

"*Another* warrant?" said Chief Superintendent Racer, in a tone that suggested Jury asked for a search warrant every time he entered Racer's office.

"Two warrants: Claire Howard and Maggie Benn."

"Evidence to suggest a warrant?" said Racer. "You know what I mean by 'evidence'?"

Jury ignored the sarcasm. "That's why I want a search warrant. To gather evidence: passports, paintings, photographs."

"God, man, you've got a killer at large and you're spending your time on two women—"

"They are."

Confused, Racer said, "This Banerjee or Buhari is the goddamned shooter!"

"I'm leaving him to the Nairobi police."

"And why aren't you leaving *this* to the City Police, Jury? It's *their* case."

"Since I knew the Moffits, DCI Jenkins was happy to get any help I could give."

As it was clear Racer was going to quash that notion, Jury went on: "We don't want to encourage the myth that City Police and the Met are rivals, do we? Or that the City Police are somehow superior?" This was illogical, of course, but Racer wouldn't attend to the logic, only to any hint of City Police being superior. "Benjamin Buhari was the actual shooter, yes. But I think there was a good deal of manipulation by these women."

"And in the shooter's case, we have rather abundant evidence, don't we? Like eyewitnesses? Like that taxi driver who carted him around London for an hour? It's with the others—your two women—we're coming up a bit short, aren't we?"

"That's the whole point. I want to see their passports and anything else I can find as evidence of their relationship. They're both lying." Jury pulled out his single piece of evidence, the picture taken in the Nairobi art gallery.

"I don't see how this proves anything."

"That they know each other; that they lied about being in Kenya; that Claire Howard had access to Masego Abasi's paintings; that she probably knows Leonard Zane, though he denies it."

"That doesn't prove she killed the Moffits or had them killed. This Rebecca Moffit was her daughter, for God's sake!"

"Of course it doesn't prove it. Proof is what I'm looking for."

Racer was too intent on showing Jury he was a great nit to notice what was going on in his drinks cupboard. Jury had to hand it to him: Racer's focus, when it came to focusing on Jury, was unshakable. Anyone else within a half mile would have heard the clatter and clink of glass.

"This other woman," Racer plowed on.

"Is even more suspicious than Claire Howard. Maggie Benn has two identities: Leo Zane's assistant and Benjamin Buhari's daughter."

"What?"

The fog thickened. "She grew up, though, with his brother—that's the Banerjee whose passport he used—a rich industrialist and his wife, Elspeth Banado. Banado is the name Marguerite used in Reno, when she worked for Leonard Zane at the Metropole. Now, surely, we can tease probable cause out of that."

Racer looked ready to chew nails. Reluctantly, he picked up his pen and signed off on the warrants. Just as reluctantly, he handed the papers to Jury.

There was a small *glug glug* sound of liquid pouring. Cyril must be mixing martinis, thought Jury.

"What's that?" said Racer, at last alerted.

When Racer looked in the direction of the bookcase, Jury had a coughing attack. "Sorry. Just me." He rose and, still coughing, went to the window near the built-in bookcase and raised it, as if he needed air. He quietly shut the cupboard door with his foot.

"For God's sake, man, it's cold in here. Shut the bloody window. Miss Clingmore!" Racer yelled.

Jury went out the door as Fiona came in. He said, in a low voice, "Cyril's trapped in the cupboard with the gin. Get him out."

Fiona nodded.

"Find that bloody cat, Miss Clingmore!"

48

At the same time that Wiggins went to Clerkenwell and Maggie Benn's, Jury went to Chelsea.

Claire was wearing her coat and clutching a bag under her arm. Not bothering to hide her impatience, she raised her eyebrows. "Again? What is it this time?"

"Sorry to bother you, but this time it's a search." He held up the warrant.

"This is ridiculous, Superintendent. And I have an engagement."

"You don't have to stay."

Still she stood there. "What on earth are you looking for?"

"Whatever might be helpful." He smiled. "It's in the warrant, if you care to read it."

She didn't. But she did stop blocking the entrance. "Very well. You won't find anything; there's nothing to find."

"Good. That will simplify things, won't it?"

She walked out.

Jury made his way to the desk and its silver-framed photos. Nothing there. He went into the room she had gone into to retrieve the photo he thought had been in the group on the desk the first time he'd been here. Only a few boxes, and one contained albums and framed photos. He pulled out photo after photo until he came to one of a dark-haired woman in a chased silver frame that looked expensive and antique. *To C., Yours, M.*

Hers, indeed, thought Jury, looking at the beautiful face of the woman he supposed to be Marguerite Banado. He wondered what someone like Pete Apted would do with this photo as evidence. Shred it, probably. Nevertheless, it was good enough for the moment. He returned to the living room and searched the desk drawers, looking for the passport, and found it stashed among some legal documents that he let alone. He wondered why people denied having done something so easily checked. But they did, all the time.

He moved over to the bookshelves, running his eyes over the spines. There were a number on physics, astro and otherwise; a half dozen on astronomy; and a couple on astrology—which surprised Jury if this collection was Moffit's. There was a book titled *Moon Phases* that turned out to be fiction. It was very artfully, perhaps showily, arranged, the different parts named for the phases of the moon. He bet that the prose was equal to the show.

"Oh, James, it's a new moon!" she exclaimed.

This banal line was followed by more dialogue of equal banality. The only two people who could get away with exclaiming over a new moon were Nelson Eddy and Jeanette MacDonald. His mum had loved them. He remembered her playing old records on a turntable over and over—

No, you do not remember your mum doing that. You were only a baby when she died. So what you remember is either the matron at the home where you grew up, or your aunt and uncle who took you in afterward. That, or a fantasy.

Thus was another memory of his mother stolen away. It had been his cousin in Newcastle, now dead, who had blasted his memory by telling him he'd been a baby when she'd died, so he couldn't possibly remember seeing her after the bomb had fallen. When Brendan, her husband, had told him he could have anything he fancied of Sarah's, Jury had asked for the photograph album.

He had searched it and searched it for even one snapshot of his mother and himself at some later age—six, seven?—and had found nothing.

Jury returned *Moon Phases* to its place on the shelf. He checked the numbers on his mobile and rang the Starrdust.

"Gibbous moon?" said Andrew Starr. "That occurs when the moon's a little more than half full. The gibbous moon waxes and wanes and then you get the crescent moon phases, which include the new moon. It takes nearly thirty days for the moon to complete an orbit."

"Is it associated with misfortune of some kind?"

"No, not to my knowledge."

"Was there a gibbous moon the night of the thirty-first?"

"Halloween? Hold on a moment." When Andrew picked up the phone again, he said, "Nope. Friday night was a full moon."

"Thanks, Andrew." As he was returning the mobile to his pocket the ring tone sounded. It was Wiggins, who had gone with a WPC to Maggie Benn's flat. He told Jury he'd turned up her passports: "One in her desk drawer. British. But the other one, the Kenyan connection, was secreted guess where?"

When Jury turned down the invitation to guess, Wiggins said "Behind an Abasi painting. The brown paper used to cover the back? One corner was Sellotaped. I found something thin tucked beneath the paper down in the corner."

"Passport-thin, you mean?"

"Right. That's basically why I'm calling. Should we take the whole painting, or just the passport?" Wiggins lowered his voice even more. "She's sitting in the living room, fuming."

"Let her fume. Take the passport and see if you can find anything of that size to put in its place. She knows we're searching her flat so she might look at the painting to see if we discovered the passport."

Wiggins said, "But what difference would it make? Like you said, she knows we have a warrant—"

"But not what we've found." Jury paused. "She knows we've reason to suspect something, but what?"

"I thought maybe the painting should be brought in because a prosecutor might think it would add to the drama."

Jury laughed. "Pete Apted would."

As he was talking to Wiggins, he was looking again at the eclectic book collection. Wouldn't David have considered astrology an aberration? Yet he spoke to his mother as if he were superstitious: *It's a gibbous moon again, Mom.*

He held on to the book and walked to the French doors. Opened them and stepped out onto the little balcony and looked up.

It's a gibbous moon again, Mom.

It hadn't been on the night the Moffits were shot.

Why had he said it? Had David known he was walking into danger? Again?

49

W iggins said, "Didn't find anything else, guv, but the passports."
He handed them to Jury.

Jury opened the one in the name of Marguerite Banado. "Well done,
Wiggins. What prompted you to look behind the painting?"

"The tanzanite. The picture frames. Do you suppose maybe it was
Maggie Benn who had that done? Who worked it out with the framer?"

"In the person of Marguerite Banado, quite probably. I did find this,"
said Jury, dropping the photo on Wiggins's desk.

Wiggins studied it for a moment, then said, "That pretty much says
it, right? What do we do now?"

"We bring them in, Wiggins. Which one do you want? Claire or
Maggie?"

"Neither, but as I have to, I think I'll take Maggie Benn. Claire Howard really bothers me."

"She does me too, Wiggins. Maybe that's why I don't mind shoving
her through our door. See if you can dig up two WPCs to go with us."

Wiggins was a little surprised. "Now, you mean, sir?"

"I can't think of a better time, can you? You're good at making
arrests. Much better than I."

Actually, this was true. Wiggins managed to wedge in a layer of
empathy when he made an arrest. It was almost soothing to suspects,

who seemed to think, given Wiggins's attitude, that if things got really rough he would step in and take their place.

Jury was accompanied by WPC Lois Watkins, who was driving the car. After a few minutes of clearly bothered silence, she said, "I hope I'm able to do this, guv. It's because I've been following this whole business and I think this woman must be some kind of monster to be compliant in the shooting of her own daughter. I've got a little girl myself, and I just feel—"

She couldn't say what she just felt. "That's okay, Lois. You'll be fine." He wondered if he should trot out a few more clichés to make her feel better.

"It's horrible, really horrible."

"Have you ever read about Medea?"

"Well, yes, but that's by Socrates, isn't it? That's Greek tragedy!"

He let Socrates go by the board. "Call this Brit tragedy, Lois."

She shook and shook her head. "What kind of world are we living in, sir, when mothers can do this kind of thing?"

Jury was looking out of the passenger's window at the flow of people along the King's Road. "It's not too late to seek a newer world," he said.

"That's beautiful, sir. To say that."

"It's Tennyson who said it, in his poem 'Ulysses.'" Jury wondered where that newer world would come from, though. From that couple holding hands and swinging along the pavement? From the baby in that perambulator? From the fellow with the classy-looking poodle? From the group of elderly women clutching at one another, thereby ensuring that if one went down, all of them would?

A few seconds after Jury's knock, Claire Howard jerked the door of the flat open, looking astonished to see not only Jury yet again, but Jury with a policewoman.

"What—?"

"May we come in?"

In mute answer, Claire stood back, pulling the door wider.

Jury was not sorry to have a relative stranger with him, to be sharing this task with a WPC who was completely unsympathetic, but completely professional; she would act as a buffer both for Claire and for Jury and could help to soak up the terrible silence and after that the terrible words.

"Is this another search?" said Claire. Then more angrily, "And what about things that've gone missing?"

"Claire Howard, I'm here to arrest you as an accessory to the murder of Rebecca and David Moffit and the kidnaping of Robert Parsons."

"What? *What?* Are you crazy? My own daughter? David? And w*ho* the bloody hell is Robert Parsons? What do you mean 'arrest' me?"

Jury nodded to Lois, who continued: "I must warn you that anything you say may be taken down in evidence and used against you in court."

Claire Howard laughed, a trifle heartbreakingly. She said, "You *know* this is ridiculous!"

"Please come with us. If you need a coat, Constable Watkins will help you." Meaning, if Claire left the room, WPC Watkins would follow her.

For the next fifteen minutes, Claire remonstrated with Jury, repeating again and again that the charge was impossible, that her solicitor would have her out in five minutes, that Jury must be mad, and ending with a strident, "And just where are you taking me?"

"New Scotland Yard."

She said nothing.

It usually shut people up.

But by the time they got to Westminster, Claire was in a rampage again. "You *know* who shot David and Rebecca. You *know* it wasn't me!" As if surely he'd see reason.

"I didn't say it was. You mentioned a solicitor. You'd better call him."

She did, and he came.

* * *

That was before Marguerite Banado was pouring out "everything" into the ear of DS Wiggins. But not the "everything" Claire Howard was spilling to Superintendent Jury.

Jury took a moment from the spillage to leave the interview room and go into the one next door, where he heard, ". . . never been to Reno. I don't know what you're talking about."

Wiggins broke in to tell the machine that Superintendent Richard Jury had just entered the room. Hearing the disavowal of Reno, Jury said, as he sat, "Don't go down that road, Ms. Banado; it's a dead end. And the police hate having their time wasted."

Her laugh was cold-blooded. "For one thing, my name is Benn, Maggie Benn. Two, forgive me for wasting Scotland Yard's time. And, three, you clearly have me confused with someone else. Light?"

She wobbled a Silk Cut in her fingers. No one lit it.

Wiggins started to rise, presumably to get matches, but Jury pulled him down. "Sorry, but there's not much smoking here these days; Sergeant Wiggins hasn't time to search for a match. Perhaps you could enlighten us as to your friendship with Claire Howard."

Maggie Benn raised an eyebrow. "Claire?"

Jury crossed his arms on the table and leaned toward her. "Let me explain something: We have a lorry-load of evidence, Ms. Banado—or Benn, if you think that helps—to tie you to attempts on the life of David Moffit; witnesses to your having been in Reno working at the Metropole Hotel under the name of Marguerite Banado—even your boss will testify that you're both Banado and Benn; strong motive for shooting David Moffit in Reno—"

"He wasn't—" That had taken her so much by surprise that she momentarily forgot why she was sitting in this room with two detectives.

"Wasn't there? It was Danny Morrissey who was shot? No. That was David Moffit, as you well know, because you were obsessed with him. That's your motive for making two attempts on his life. If you couldn't have him, nobody would."

"This is absurd! You know who the shooter was."

"I told you: do not go down that road. I'll bury you." Jury rose. "Wiggins." Jury nodded his head for Wiggins to continue, before he treated Maggie Benn to a cold, hard stare and left the room.

In a way, Jury preferred the icy temper of Maggie Benn to the weepy one of Claire Howard, who claimed she'd been overwhelmed by Marguerite Banado—her intensity, her beauty, her complete command of Claire's "situation." It was Marguerite who'd come up with the plan and Claire was (weepily) ashamed of not having blown it to bits.

Claire's solicitor was largely silent, following a few mumbled attempts to get her to desist from answering questions. There was simply no shutting her up. Why had she bothered calling him in if she wasn't going to listen to him?

"Ashamed? I should think you would be. Your daughter and her husband. Those were the victims."

It was Wiggins's turn to interrupt this time and Jury announced his entrance to the recorder.

"Mrs. Howard," said Wiggins, as he pulled the passport from his pocket, "we found this in your home in High Wycombe. You have a visa stamped for Kenya."

"I was passing through, that's all."

"To go to where?"

"Johannesburg."

Wiggins snorted quietly. "Sorry, no one 'passes through' Kenya to go to Johannesburg. Johannesburg has the largest airport in Africa and scores of direct flights from London." He pushed the passport closer to her across the table.

"Thank you, Sergeant," said Jury as Wiggins left.

An hour later, they were accusing each other so vigorously that Jury knew the accusations would meld together somewhere down the road.

*   *   *

It was after six P.M. when Jury was leaving the building. He fished out his mobile and punched in Melrose Plant's number at Ardry End.

When Melrose came on the line, Jury said, "Could you possibly delay dinner for an hour or two so that I could join you? That's about how long the drive will take to Northants."

"Good God! That would mean extending the drinks hour until eight. Well, I'll brace myself."

"Eight thirty. I'm going to need a drink, too. Drinks, I should say."

50

A t 8:00, Jury pulled up in front of Ardry End and was met by Melrose Plant, who'd heard the car approach and had come to the top of his steps.

"Still standing, I see," said Jury.

"Leaning. So tell me what happened. Which one grassed on the other first and most fulsomely?"

As they walked into Plant's marble foyer, Jury said, "Well, Claire Howard had the more convincing 'I ain't done nuffin'' story, given that Maggie Benn was also Marguerite Banado and is Benjamin Buhari's daughter. The Banerjees—the ones you saw in Riverside—had been keeping her since Marguerite's own mother did a flit and Buhari couldn't manage by himself."

"I've never understood that," said Melrose as they took their seats in the beautiful living room. "Society readily accepts that a father can't be expected to raise a child alone, without help; yet a mother is completely different. For a mother to claim she couldn't do it, well, that's unacceptable."

Ruthven came in with a tray of canapés and a bottle of Laphroaig, and poured generous measures into two cut-glass tumblers.

"Would you be able to care for a kid if your wife walked out?" said Jury.

"My wife wouldn't walk out."

"You're sure?"

"Are you kidding? Walk out on this?" Melrose swept his arm round the room. He sighed. "I'd never be sure a woman actually loved me unless she was rich."

Jury picked up a tiny shrimp on a square of buttered bread. "Oh, you poor fool."

Melrose gave him a narrow-eyed look and smiled. "That was brilliant, Richard, that little scheme in Victoria Station. Vivian thought so too, although what your point was, we couldn't work out."

Jury muttered more to himself than to the room's occupant, "Thick as two planks. God give me strength."

"Anyway, we really enjoyed it. On the way back here, we stopped in a scrofulous pub and drank and laughed ourselves sick."

"I'm glad you had a good time."

"We did." Melrose slid down in his chair. "You know, it was almost romantic."

"Did you think so?"

"Yes. That young kid who played the violin? 'Fascination'? The Orient Express? Remember? We saw Vivian off to Venice in that same spot. Franco Giopinno, God, what a fool and a cad. It doesn't surprise me Vivian didn't marry him, but it does surprise me she went with him for all of those years."

Irritated, not for the first time, by his friend's obtuseness when it came to Vivian, Jury said, "Do you think you'll ever settle down?"

"What? I am settled down. Look at me." Melrose spread his arms wide. "The fire, the whisky, the—"

Ruthven stood in the doorway, looking artfully deferential. "I'm sorry to bother you, m'lord, but Martha would like to know if you'd prefer the steak and kidney or the pheasant pie?"

"Either, Ruthven. Whichever is easier for Martha."

"Sir." Ruthven turned and withdrew.

"The choice of pies, the butler . . . How much more settled could I get?" Melrose ran the glass of Laphroaig under his nose as if he hadn't been drinking it all along.

Jury shook his head and stared at the ceiling. "Settling down ordinarily means marriage."

"It does? Why?"

Jury ignored that inane response as Ruthven came in again, this time with the telephone on a long cord. "I'm sorry, Superintendent, but it's a call from Scotland Yard. I believe the caller is a Sergeant Wiggins?"

"Thank you, Ruthven."

Ruthven whipped the cord round behind him like a lion-tamer and delivered the phone to the table by Jury's chair.

Jury loved the drama of the house phone being brought to him. He said, "Wiggins, what are you still doing at the Yard at this hour? You must be dead, man . . . He did? . . . Good, good . . . Right, now go home." Jury hung up and said to Melrose, "The Nairobi police took in Benjamin Buhari. What he told them was nothing." Jury took a long drink of whisky. "I still don't see how a man could do that—shooting without checking the ammunition first."

"You don't have children," said Melrose. "There still remains the question of the murder site. Why choose the courtyard of the Artemis Club, a public place?"

"But it really isn't 'public' in the sense of people continually coming and going. Remember, the customers are not only screened, but given a time to show up. So Buhari would have had an undisturbed few minutes, except one of the club's punters, that woman, put in her appearance earlier than she should."

"Okay, but Maggie Benn was putting the club itself in jeopardy, especially Leo Zane. Why?"

"She wanted Leo Zane to be a suspect and there was already a connection between him and her father. So he certainly became a suspect—the suspect, as far as I was concerned."

"She wanted that?"

"I think she either hated him or was afraid of him."

"Why?"

"I'd say he came across some information or evidence that Maggie Benn was the woman in his office with David Moffit."

"Where does all of this put Leo Zane?"

"At best I'd say he's innocent. He had nothing to do with the Moffits. So he was being set up."

"He's in a hell of a position," said Melrose. "I bet these two women will be implicating him all over the place. And what about Claire Howard? You said you thought she knew him because—"

"She called him 'Leo'? That's pretty easy. Maggie Benn talked about him a lot, I expect. Always referred to him as 'Leo,' and Claire simply picked up on that."

"Well, I hope he's got a good lawyer."

"He will. Pete Apted."

"Do you think he'd take the case?"

"He loves weird stuff. The more complex a case, the more he likes it."

"So where would all those millions go now?"

"Certainly not to Claire Howard, not if she's found guilty. David's money would go back to his mom. Paula Moffit."

"But Maggie Benn would be a suspect too, given the Metropole in Reno—"

"Indeed. And there she is, right now, in police custody. Many thanks to you. You should work for Scotland Yard. Wiggins and I would love having you on our team. You could be DC Melrose Plant."

"'DC'? Detective *constable*? Then Sergeant Wiggins would be over me."

"Sure. But you'd work your way up in no time."

"Snails?" said Jury.

"Escargots, please," said Melrose.

Ruthven had announced dinner twenty minutes before.

"Snails. I'm ringing Karl Mundt."

"Who's he?"

"RSPCA."

"Really. Do they do snails?"

"They do anything that walks, crawls, or flies."

"No, they don't." Melrose was excavating in a little shell pulled from an ambrosial broth.

Jury looked sadly at his plate. "Sorry, I just can't eat this."

"After Martha went to all the trouble, especially for you. Here, we'll swap our plates." Melrose picked up Jury's and put his own down in place of it. "That way she'll think you ate half, at least. I didn't know you were a snail-hater."

"A snail-lover, you mean."

"You are less fun every day."

"Thank you. As to the 'fun' quotient, have you forgotten your aborted trip on the Orient Express? I'd say whoever thought that up has a sense of fun."

"Why did you do it, anyway? You lied to both of us."

"True. So you aren't reassessing my fun potential?"

"No."

Ruthven had stepped in to replace the escargots with a smoked salmon mousse and to refill their glasses with a Pouilly-Fumé.

Jury took a bite of the salmon. "Umm. I'm eating every bit of mine and half of yours."

"No, you're not."

"But you got my helping of snails, so in all fairness—"

"Hold on: did we strike a bargain? Shake hands? Swear brotherhood forever? Sign anything?"

Having finished his mousse during this mild harangue, Jury now looked toward the kitchen, where he was sure more mousse sat.

Melrose held up his hand. "Don't even think it; no second helpings. The main course will be a knockout."

The main course was, since everything and its vegetable brother had been all but drowned in Old Peculiar. It was a steak and kidney pie.

"My God, but that smells wonderful, Ruthven," said Jury.

Ruthven was dispensing large portions, after which he placed the dish in a silver holder. It sat between a silver bowl of new potatoes and its twin of a pistachio-dusted cauliflower. A fresh bottle of wine—a cabernet sauvignon—had been decanted and was now poured into another of the three wineglasses.

"So why did you pull that stunt?"

"I thought maybe it would throw a switch."

"What kind? The nostalgia switch, perhaps?"

"No." Jury sighed.

"The travel switch?"

"As it didn't work on you or, I assume, on Vivian, who I thought was much more into reality than you—"

When Melrose appeared to be giving this matter some thought, Jury said, "You shouldn't have to think about it. Either you get it or you don't."

But Melrose insisted on getting to the bottom of this switch business and Vivian's reaction to it as well as his own. "Of course, Vivian's always been a bit of a mystery—"

Jury interrupted. "No, she hasn't. Vivian's always been utterly transparent." Jury took a bite of drenched beef. "So I was only trying to change the track by flicking a switch."

For Melrose, this seemed to make the puzzle the more puzzling. "What track?"

"Christ," breathed Jury. "You and Vivian are like two people on two trains running along side by side. You wave, you smile, you might even throw kisses, you mouth silent words."

When Melrose merely sat there staring and smoking, Jury took another gasp or two of wine, leaned closer into the table and said, "Okay, maybe this is none of my business, but given that I've known you and Vivian for so many years, and *especially* given that if it hadn't been for *you*, she would've married *me*—"

Melrose had been about to take his own drink of wine when Jury said this and was so shocked by it that the glass slipped right through his fingers. "Oh, hell!" He started mopping up the spilled drink and calling for Ruthven, who came through the door immediately to see both Melrose and Jury trying to salvage the damage.

Ruthven said, "Mr. Jury, you sit down, sir. I'll have this off in two ticks." Ruthven then called, "Pippin!"

Pippin? thought Melrose. Were they employing someone named "Pippin"?

They were, for here she came—burst, rather—from kitchen to dining room, apron strings flying almost straight out, like the hair bunches held back in ribbon.

Melrose wondered how old she was: Six? Sixty? "Ruthven, we really don't need the cloth off. Superintendent Jury and I can go into the living room—"

But Ruthven was having none of it. Pippin wasn't either, for she hardly knew what obeisance to make to his lordship: Curtsy? Fall on her knees or her face? Cross herself in the presence of one as radiant as the master? Then there was the master's *friend* . . .

"Get this vase off, girl, quick now—"

The vase of roses, Jury decided, was much too big for Pippin, so he reached for it at the same time she did, their fingers quarreling for a brittle moment before the whole lot fell right over the edge of the table, whereupon Pippin grabbed up her broom and, turning it to sweep, also knocked over Jury's glass, which splintered into shards.

It was the turn of Martha, the cook, to come rushing in and start a little snarling lecture aimed at Pippin. Jury quickly defended the poor little maid, hoping to keep her from slipping, apron strings, hair in bunches, broom, completely back into the pages of *Bleak House,* when through the breezy open window came another voice: "Trouble, oh, my!" And the gardener's face appeared. "Got me electric blower-vac right here and it'll pick up all that lot on the carpet."

For a moment, Jury was afraid Mr. Blodgett would crawl over the windowsill, but, no, he called out he'd go right round the back and . . ." The rest was lost.

So in another half minute, they were all together, Ruthven and his wife, Martha, insisting that Lord Ardry and the Superintendent sit right down and they'd have everything back together, fresh white cloth on the table, fresh glasses, fresh wine, as if nothing had ever happened.

As all of these hands were busily setting things to rights, and Mr. Blodgett was sucking up glass shards and rose petals, Melrose said over the blower noise, "You were saying it was my fault Vivian didn't marry *you*? Oh, ha ha ha. Well, we'll have to put that to a vote! Let's go to the Jack and Hammer when we're finished here. How do you do, Pippin. I don't believe we've met—" He stood.

She curtsied. Further and further into *Bleak House* went Pippin.

As Pippin's broom handle came down hard on Melrose's shoulder, Jury said, "Perhaps we should repair to the library—?"

Melrose leaned closer to Jury and whispered, "No, no. My staff would be doubly miserable if they thought they were banishing us from the dining room."

"Pippin, you clumsy girl, be careful o' that broom!" Martha's voice was strident.

"Nearly done, m'lord," said Ruthven. "I'll just pop down to the cellar for another bottle—"

"Bring up the cognac, Ruthven."

"I believe there's a fine Louis Royer, or perhaps—"

As he bowed himself out of the dining room, Martha was once again on the heels of Pippin. They had arranged everything—candlesticks, crystal bowl holding four pears, so righteously perfect they too might have been cut glass. They stood near the dining-room table looking pleased as punch at the effect of their ministrations, as if they were waiting to have their picture taken.

Ruthven returned from the cellar, bottle of Louis Royer firmly in hand, and held it out for Melrose's approval. Ruthven set down two balloon glasses.

"Well, this, Ruthven, has been a treat—to see the willingness of all hands to be on deck. Only, how did it all start?"

Ruthven had just poured cognac into Jury's glass and set the bottle on the table. "You are a caution, m'lord." He smiled broadly and took himself off with a little mumbled laughter at his master's sense of humor.

When the door swayed shut behind Ruthven, Melrose said, "But how did it?"

"We were talking about who—Vivian would rather marry, you or me." Jury's laugh was much like Ruthven's. "We were going to the Jack and Hammer to put it to a vote."

"Right," said Melrose.

"Vote?" said Jury, as they were tumbling around when the Bentley must have hit another galaxy, since the car could handle anything in this current world. "I'm not one of your nameless dogs!"

"We'll see."

When they walked into the Jack and Hammer, Dick Scroggs gave Jury a hearty hello and drew two pints, which he then came to set on the table around which were gathered Diane, Joanna, Trueblood and Vivian.

Four pairs of eyes stared at Melrose when he had the effrontery to ask the question. "So which of us would you choose, Vivian? Him—" Melrose cast a dismissive glance at Jury—"or me?"

Vivian answered, "Choose? What makes you think either one of you is such a treat?"

New Scotland Yard, London
Nov. 14, Thursday, and later

51

Chief Inspector Kato Kione called Jury to inform him that the Tanzanian police had Benjamin Buhari in custody and that he had gone with them willingly and, just as willingly, agreed to return to London and stand trial.

"The judge says no further legal proceedings are necessary regarding extradition in either Kenya or Tanzania and Inspector Buhari will be in London within the week. We can be pretty fast in these matters when we want to be."

Three days later, Jury was sitting in one of the interrogation rooms when Buhari was brought in by Wiggins and the Kenyan police officer who had accompanied the transfer to London.

Jury rose. "Inspector Buhari." He held out his hand.

Registering some surprise, Buhari shook it. There were no handcuffs. He sat down at the table and Jury nodded to Wiggins and the Kenyan policeman, who then left.

"Please sit down, Mr. Buhari. I have a few questions."

Buhari gave a crumpled smile.

It was almost childlike, that smile, almost charming.

Almost. Jury kept a tight hold on his feelings as he said, "We have your daughter here: Marguerite Banado."

"She didn't—"

"I assure you, Inspector, she did. Even if you wanted to keep her out of this, you couldn't. We know what happened, at least the versions of these two women involved in the conspiracy to murder the Moffits."

"Isn't 'conspiracy' a bit of an exaggeration?"

"No. Your daughter and her friend, this woman—" Jury shoved a picture of Claire Howard across the table. "—conspired to kill the Moffits. Marguerite Banado was obsessed with David Moffit and had been long before he came to London."

Buhari interrupted. "It was the other way around. He was stalking her; about two years ago, she found she was pregnant. This man insisted she have an abortion and said he would marry her if she complied. After she did, he dropped her."

"That's a pack of lies, Mr. Buhari."

Buhari started to protest, but soon gave it up. "Since this man and his wife are dead, I was clearly meant to kill them. I have no choice but to believe you." He paused. "What did my daughter say?"

"That she had persuaded you to do the shooting. That she had arranged with a friend of hers to drive you from Waterloo to Heathrow. She has a lot of friends in helpful positions," Jury added acidly. "What happened to the gun?"

"I left it with the driver. I assume he returned it to Marguerite." Buhari dropped his head. "Yes. It was not until I had returned to Nairobi that I discovered what had really happened." He looked up and out of the tiny window at the dusky sky. "I can't begin to express the remorse that I felt." He shook his head. "It was unthinkable."

Jury leaned into the table, trying to close the distance. "What was to me unthinkable is that it ever could have happened. You're a policeman, for God's sake. You shot this gun without examining the ammunition? Without making sure at least the cartridges were nonlethal."

"Not exactly. It was loaded with forty-five-caliber ACP Glasers when I left London. Nonlethal. And when I picked up the gun that night before I shot it, Marguerite pulled out the magazine, took one bullet out and showed me it was a nonlethal round. The other seven were obviously real."

"And the chambered one was clearly one of the lethal bullets. My God."

"You can still fault me for not looking just before I shot, but I swear to God I didn't suspect for a moment that my daughter would ask me to murder these people. Granted, she easily convinced me that he had done her a terrible wrong and she just wanted to scare him. Them. Of course I refused initially. But she also convinced me that if I didn't do it, she would. We argued for hours." Buhari paused. "Did she give you any other reasons?"

Jury had the taped interview. He did not want to play it. To discover now, after everything else, the complete contempt in which his daughter held him would simply be too much for the man to bear. It was almost too much for Jury. "Only that she felt you owed her something because you had given her up to your brother and sister-in-law. That had clearly been very painful for her." Pain had not been the predominant emotion in Marguerite's emotional repertoire. "Your daughter tricked you, Mr. Buhari. I'm sorry."

"I appreciate that, Superintendent Jury. Although I'm surprised there's room for empathy regarding my role in this. Marguerite had a powerful hold on me. I always felt guilty for abandoning her."

"But you didn't—"

"To her, it was abandonment. She was only eight years old. My work kept me away from home so much, and with her mother gone, I really felt my brother and his wife could do a better job of giving her a feeling of family than I could on my own. They had no children and had always wanted one and loved Marguerite. It seemed a perfect solution."

"Strikes me it was. And don't think the reason for her actions is that alleged abandonment by her mother and father. A psychologist might have a field day with the events in her life, but I think the effect of your having her live with your brother was minimal. It became really a club to beat you with. Marguerite is basically a manipulative, self-regarding, obsessive woman. You should face that, Mr. Buhari. But the passport; you implicated your brother by using his passport."

"Yes, that was bad of me, but I knew he was going to be in Nairobi, where there'd be witnesses to his presence, and I also knew I could get rid of the page with the visas. So his innocence would be clear. I used my own passport to go from Dubai to Nairobi."

Jury reached into his pocket and took out a card. "You'll need a good defense. This is the best." Jury pushed Pete Apted's card across the table.

"Thank you. But why are you helping me? The man I shot was a friend of yours."

Jury got up. "Because he'd want me to. You were set up, Mr. Buhari. I don't like that."

Maggie Benn and Claire Howard were indicted for the murders of David and Rebecca Moffit.

It had taken Pete Apted no more than a remarkable (even for him) twenty-four hours to get a judgment of no case to answer in the matter of Leonard Zane's role in the tanzanite smuggling.

Jury put in for a week's holiday.

"For what reason?" Racer had demanded.

"For the reason that I haven't had one in several years. Except, of course, when I was shot." Racer would have considered that time off a holiday.

But he got it. Jury received additional advice from several quarters.

Melrose said, "You know, Richard, in the 1880s they managed to produce the transatlantic cable; it was a nifty invention—"

Wiggins told him he was crazy; Carole-anne interrupted her manicure long enough to say, "Suit yourself." Phyllis Nancy said, "Good for you. It's exactly the right thing to do."

But that was Phyllis.

52

In the Knowledge Robbie Parsons held center stage with his story of Scotland Yard's arrest of two people in London and a related arrest by the Nairobi police of another, in Kenya.

"Kenya? That's him, ain't it? The bastard that shanghaied your cab?" said Ray Rich.

"Along with Rob," added Clive Rowbotham, as if that point needed to be made.

"The very one," said Robbie.

"Hold on," said Reg Keene. "What about those others you said got arrested in London? Who are they? Where do they fit in?"

"Sorry, no names, mate," said Robbie, as if he had names to divulge, which he hadn't. He picked up his pint of best bitter and took a couple of swallows.

"Who's your source, then?" said Clive.

"Well, I can hardly name him, can I?"

"Wait," said Reg Keene again. "Is this the guy you wanted to bring here to the pub?"

"That's the one."

"Wasn't he a detective inspector?"

"Nope."

"Sergeant?"

"No."

"A chief inspector, maybe?"

"Higher."

"Higher than a chief inspector? My God, must be the bloody commissioner," said Minnie Huff, who had a long-standing relationship with the Metropolitan Police, uniform branch.

Ray Rich said, "Wait. I picked up a guy in Broadway the other night. He was Scotland Yard. Really tall, seemed smart, a detective."

Robbie did not want Richard Jury claimed by somebody else. "You don't know ranks? You don't know somebody higher than a detective inspector except the commissioner? Detective superintendent, that's what."

"Yeah," said Ray, as if he knew. "That's who I picked up, a detective superintendent."

"How d'ya know he was?"

"He told me."

"Told you?"

"Well, he shoved his warrant card at me. Wanted to come here. Ha ha."

Robbie put in, "He's a good friend of that bloke that came here with Patty Haigh."

Who was now back from her Paris jaunt and was talking to Aero on her mobile, she inside and Aero outside Terminal 3.

"It's Rooster wants to know," said Aero. "This guy they want's kind of stubby, you know, squat and black, probably from Tanzania. I heard him talking on his mobile to somebody. Anyway, Rooster wants him spotted because—"

"No," said Patty Haigh. "No Kenya, no Botswana, no Nairobi, no South Africa, no Tanzania, no—"

"No shit" Aero laughed.

"I'm sticking to the EU," said Patty.

*   *   *

There were perhaps a dozen regulars and as many casuals—the haphaz-
ard clientele who poked their faces in at random and arbitrary times.
The regulars, like Robbie, were happy to have the casuals swell their
ranks, for these cabbies gave them a better idea of what London was
teeming with on any given day.

They were not snobs and they didn't treat the Knowledge like one
of those clubs up West. Most of them, naturally, had their badges, but
a badge was not a condition of belonging; the only requirement for getting into the pub was that one drove a cab or was in training to drive.
Hence, some youngsters, some of the uninitiated, were granted a kind
of "temporary membership," as long as they were on the path to taking
"the knowledge." These unproven ones were usually brought to the pub
by seasoned drivers.

Almost all of them had been asked to drive a fare to the Knowledge.
The drivers were sure that each person who asked it thought he was a
real slyboots: asking a cab driver to take you to a place meant exclusively
for cab drivers.

"Not got an address, 'ave you?"

"Of course I don't have an address! Nobody knows where it is!"

"Hmm. Well, that would include me, too."

Every so often one or another cabbie would try to get someone
—friend or relation, someone stellar, someone deserving—into the
Knowledge, but always got a thumbs-down. "Stellar" was still not
enough.

Robbie thought it had been stellar of Richard Jury to throw that
little party for the kids, but he knew better than to try to get him temporary membership in the Knowledge. Even though Robbie had a hand to
play and it was a winner. He was the one who'd driven Kenya over half
of London.

The only exception to this ironclad rule had been that Lord Melrose or Lord Ardry bloke and that of course had been because of Patty
Haigh. He had saved her life; that had got him through the door, but not
really "in." Even if he wanted to there was simply no way he could find
the place on his own; there was no route he could remember, because

there hadn't been a "route" in the first place. His drive in the black cab had been as random as Robbie's conveyance of the Kenyan bastard.

Billy Burnsides, a popular cabbie, had once come close to being ostracized because he had nearly got his ninety-year-old grandfather into the pub, and would have, too, had Cliff Nugent and Clive Rowbotham not been leaving just as Billy and Gramps appeared in the lane leading to the front door. They stopped Billy and his granddad cold.

"We don't care if it's the bleeding prime minister, Billy. You bloody well know the rules!"

Billy had argued that Grandpa Burnsides had dementia and couldn't find his own arse, much less the Knowledge, and would have forgotten the whole encounter by daybreak. Even though he suffered from dementia, somehow the fog of his brain had been lifted upon hearing about Billy's pub, and he pled to go to it.

Grandpa Burnsides had stood, short and thin and shivery, looking as if he had no idea where he was or whom he was with, and Cliff and Clive had turned both of them around and marched them back to Billy's cab, Billy pleading all the while, saying it was his grandpa's birthday treat, coming to the Knowledge, and Cliff saying that if he didn't know where the hell he was, what difference could coming here or not make?

Billy had a dozen arguments on the go, like plates in the air, and all of them as toothless as his grandfather, who was wearing his flat cap backward and yelling, "Fire!" and managing, slippery as butter, to get out of Cliff's and Clive's grip, and heading back to the lamplight of the Knowledge. Cliff and Clive herded him back to the cab.

"You see, you see! You see how much it means to him," said Billy.

"For God's sake, he don't know where the fuck he is or who we are or who *you* are."

Billy said, "If he don't know, how can he tell anybody else?"

This irrational argument had continued for another five minutes, with the old man breaking free of the others and going back down the weed-covered lane to the pub. Back and forth, pulled like toffee, until Clive and Cliff finally stowed him in the cab, shoving Billy into the driver's seat, slamming doors and yelling good night.

And there were tales of bribes, threatened boycotts (How would that work? they wondered), and more than one arrest vowed by some frustrated cop or other who'd laid a bet he could find the place.

Goddamn it! The bloody place had to be *somewhere*!

But the bloody place just went on being nowhere.

Which was why, on this particular evening around ten P.M., pints were halted halfway to mouths and cigarettes left burning fingers when a total stranger walked in and had the gall to ask, "Cab to the West End?"

Bloody effrontery! Or some form of that thought flashed into the minds of the thirty or so drivers enjoying their usual seclusion and anonymity.

The stranger was fairly tall, fairly young, and appeared to be out-fitted like a mountaineer or rock climber with his tools and ropes and many-pocketed vest. He moved to the bar as if he were already in the West End at the Salisbury. He ordered a pint of best bitter, then looked around and smiled as if he were welcome.

"Nice pub," he had the further gall to say.

The cabbies looked at one another at a total loss.

Finally, Clive Rowbotham said, "Bloody 'ell, how'd ya' find this place?"

"How? I'm a mapmaker."

"Christ, boyo," said Reed Keane, "You look like you couldn't find your own dick, much less the Knowledge."

The fellow laughed. "The name's Brian Moore. Glad to meet you."

But the hand thrust out toward Clive went unshaken. Meet who? Clive Rowbotham was quite famous for his willingness to carve places out with his fists at the slightest provocation. Or even without it.

Brian Moore was unoffended. He shoved thumb and forefinger into one of his many pockets and pulled out a card, which he handed to the man nearest him, Brendan Small, one of the drivers who'd followed Robbie on that fateful night. Moore's expression was bland and forgiving of everyone on God's green earth.

Which was to Robbie massively irritating. He did not want this arsehole's well-meaningness or approval. All he wanted was to know how he'd had found the pub, so he could slam the door before a lot of other arseholes found it and came flooding though the door. "The thing is, Brian, *nobody* finds this place."

"Sure. That's why we wanted to find it."

Robbie looked around for the rest of the 'we' and, barely glancing at the card in Brendan's hand, said, "Soho office? *Giggle*? What the fuck's that? A strip joint?"

Brian laughed again as if laughter were his calling card. "Not Giggle, for God's sake. *Google*. I'm from Google, mate. Google Earth."

He then had the cheek to raise his pint. "Cheers!"

Bloody effrontery!

OCEANA

53

"Oceana, definitely. Max was right." In the wintry dark of early evening, Jury swept his arm over the vast expanse of what could have been the grounds of a stately home in England, although the gray-gabled house itself was not that large. "You couldn't possibly call this place '417.'" Jury smiled at her. "Hello, Paula."

Paula Moffit stood frozen in the doorway, staring at him. "Superintendent Jury! What on earth . . . ?"

"May I come in?"

Saying nothing, she stepped back from the door and Jury entered. They stood in a marble foyer, a grand staircase going far up to another level, where the banister branched off to left and right to encircle the second floor. Pocket doors were open to large rooms, one painted and furnished in blue, one in brown; Jury thought sitting room and library, probably.

"How did you . . . ? Why did you . . . ?"

"I have something to tell you and I didn't want to do it over the phone. You had to get the dreadful news about David that way and I decided to deliver this news in person. It's not dreadful. Give me a double whisky, Paula, and I'll tell you a double story."

Returning to her ordinary composed self, Paula simply said, "Ice?"

"No. A thimbleful or two of water, depending on how good your whisky is."

"It won't want water," she said, starting toward the blue room and motioning for him to follow.

She had handed him a nearly half-full tumbler of whisky and it was the best he'd ever tasted.

"We can't make tea, but we can make whisky." Paula had settled down across from him with her own drink. A basket of yarn she shoved into the corner. Needles were sticking out of one of the balls.

Jury smiled. "You knit? Somehow I can't picture that."

"I'm no good at it. How's your whisky?"

"You're right: it doesn't want water."

"Good. Now, what's the story?"

"It begins in Reno. The woman was one who'd met David in Atlantic City. She worked in a casino. They had an affair. It's clear to me that she was obsessed with him—"

"But if this was just before Reno, David was engaged to Rebecca . . ." Her voice trailed off.

"The affair began before that. When he left New York for your house in Tahoe, he broke it off. Or thought he did. This woman, Marguerite, knew his gambling penchant and knew he liked Reno. So she went there looking for a job in a casino and found one—"

"But didn't she know David was at this point going to marry Rebecca?"

"Of course. But that didn't stop her. When he went to the Metropole casino, she started in on him again. Ultimately, they had a row and he *did* finally get through to her. He was going to be married at Christmas."

"So she shot him."

"So she shot him. The shooting itself is, of course, conjecture, since she still won't admit to that. But the rest of the details she was perfectly willing to talk about, although, according to her, *he* was the one obsessed. There were no witnesses except for a couple who'd overheard the argument in the casino office. But they saw only David come out—or, rather, Danny Morrissey. He'd used this alias. No one saw her. And he didn't implicate her. Felt guilty about breaking it off, I expect. Too bad. Too, too bad. You would have read about the owner of the casino if you read the paper."

She frowned. "I don't think I did. Anyway, I don't remember him."

"Leonard Zane."

"But he's the owner of the Artemis Club. What has he to do with this?"

"Nothing, strangely enough. But Marguerite Banado—"

Paula looked alarmed, as if it were not her knitting but a basket of asps that sat on the sofa beside her. "My God! Are you saying this woman shot him again?" She frowned. "But wasn't it a man who stepped up to the cab and shot them both?"

Jury nodded.

"I don't understand any of this."

"You might when I tell you the name of the woman was Maggie Benn. Real name, Marguerite Banado."

"Isn't this Maggie Benn employed at the Artemis Club?"

Again Jury nodded. "The woman in Reno, Marguerite Banado—the shooter was her father."

Disbelievingly, she shook her head. "But why would he—?"

Jury told her what Inspector Buhari had told him. A dreadful row. The threat to do it herself. The manipulation, the guilt.

"A *policeman*. Yet he didn't check the bullets?"

"She took out the magazine and handed him one. It was fake."

Paula slumped back. "But the rest were real."

"Not when he first saw the gun. Buhari was horribly misguided, but he was a cop and no fool. When she first handed him the gun, he took out all of the bullets and saw they were all dummies. 'See, Papa, it's just a joke.' You have no idea how incredibly plausible this woman is. Only then he made the mistake of returning the gun to her. He had to go through airport security that night; he wasn't about to carry a gun. When he came back—"

"The bullets were real. Oh, my God . . . but couldn't he tell?"

"David's was a head shot. There was no blood. And Rebecca actually moved toward David—when Buhari was getting into the cab. I honestly don't think he realized he'd killed them until he got back to Kenya and heard about it. And knew she'd tricked him."

"But then . . . ?"

"Then what? You turn yourself in like a good citizen, you tell the story and no one believes it, and he'd clearly have gotten no help from his daughter." Jury shrugged. "What would you have done?"

"So it was Marguerite who was really the murderer."

"It's more complicated than that."

"Good Lord, how could it be?"

"It was a conspiracy: Marguerite and Claire Howard."

When she slowly rose from the sofa, she upset her drink. The heavy glass rolled a bit, but, given its weight, it stopped. The liquid, what was left, snaked over the rosewood. Jury put a handkerchief over it.

All of the color drained from Paula Moffit's face. Jury feared she might faint. When she said the name, it came out on a whisper of breath. "*Claire?* She was Rebecca's *mother. Her mother.* It's impossible!"

"The Greeks should have written this one, Paula. I've never seen such betrayal. You're right, it does sound impossible."

He told her about the show in Nairobi of Masego Abasi's works, about Claire Howard having been the one to purchase the painting that hung in Rebecca and David's flat. He took a copy of the picture from his inner pocket and passed it to her. "Marguerite and Claire."

"They must both . . . were they insane?" The picture shook in her hand.

Jury shrugged. "They wanted the money."

She looked at him, puzzled, as if wondering how money got into this.

"David's, that is your family's, which would have gone to Rebecca since his death preceded hers. The thought being that Rebecca's money would go to her next of kin. Claire Howard. She would have to inherit, or it would all be for nothing. They would split the take."

Paula said nothing. For a good five minutes she just sat and looked into the fire. Then she rose, adjusted the silver-buckled belt at her waist and said, "I'll see if my cook's finished whatever he's making."

Jury started to get up, but she stiff-armed him. "You don't think for a moment that after you've traveled all the way from London you'll be eating at the Comfort Inn. Here—" She walked over to a sideboard, picked up a decanter and returned to the coffee table, where she set down the fancy bottle with the horse and jockey on top. "Help yourself. I'll be right back."

The dining room was huge, velvet-draped, and elegant. A dozen chairs were pulled up to the oval table on which sat a huge bowl of cyclamen and roses, light playing over it from the candlesticks and the chandelier.

"My God," said Jury, "are we going to sit top and bottom and yell at each other as in one of those BBC programs clearly aimed at Americans?"

"You're like Max," she said, her hand on the back of one of the chairs the two were clearly meant to occupy at the end of the table nearest the kitchen. Two places had been set, one at the end, one beside it.

"Like Max?" Jury held up his glass. "One more of these and I'll *be* Max."

"Max could neither ask nor answer a question without embroidering upon it, going, as we used to say over here, all the way around Robin Hood's barn. You may sit at the head; I'll sit here."

He pulled out the chair on which her hand rested and she sat down. He pulled out his own at the head. "This is wonderful. It's so damned elaborate."

"Of course it is; it's Oceana. Would you prefer trays in front of the TV?"

The door between kitchen and dining room swung open and a pretty maid appeared. Or server, he supposed.

"Penny is my maid. But she kindly agreed to put on her other hat and wait at table."

Penny's hand went to her hair as if checking on the hat. She giggled. "Oh, madam. Charlie wants to know if you'd like vichyssoisse or fruit *à la ménage.*"

Jury said, "Vichyssoisse, as it's only one word."

"For both of us," said Paula. "What had Charlie planned for the main course?"

"It's one of his famous rag-outs."

Paula smiled. "Rag-oo, Penny."

"I'll have the rag-out." Jury smiled at her.

Penny giggled again. "Oh, sir." She whisked herself off.

"My cook is Hungarian and he loves surprise guests because then he can wail that we have 'not any decent food in the house, madame.'

"'You mean no foie gras, no truffles, no pheasant? Escargots?' I say to him.

"He says, 'I don't mean I can't throw something together, of course.'"

"Well," said Jury, "he sure as hell threw together something great. What is it?"

"It's a stew. He has many versions."

As good as at Ardry End. The wine he would have liked to run by Harry Johnson. It was poured by Penny.

"I thought you said your staff had gone home."

"The cook's always here. Penny had her coat and scarf on and was nearly out the door when she happened to see you. Coat off, scarf unwound. Do you always have that effect on women?"

Jury laughed. "Not that I'm aware of."

They ate in silence for a few moments, and then Jury said, "David's alleged gambling system, that fascinates me. The incompleteness theorem, or one of them. That some truths are impossible to prove. No, that's not right. It's more that some truths are not universally provable, meaning they're true sometimes, but not at others."

"That makes no sense."

"I'm not putting it right. And we're talking about mathematics, so a context is hard to demonstrate. But say I make the statement, 'All is illusion.' You can neither prove nor disprove that, since illusion is part of the all—so illusion would be illusory."

"It sounds like a house of mirrors."

"In some crude way, it is. What I don't get is how this could evolve into a system for playing twenty-one. Unless . . ." Jury looked at her and smiled. "Unless he wasn't playing cards, he was playing people."

Paula frowned, and then she laughed. She actually clapped her hands. "I'm slightly drunk. So are you. Let's get drunker. Let's have brandy. *Penny!*"

Penny came running.

They drank tiny cups of espresso and bigger snifters of brandy out on the enclosed patio at the back of the house, where the water's dash against rock was closer.

Jury looked at the night sky, squinting. "Is that a gibbous moon, Paula?"

"Yes, I believe it is."

Silence as they sipped their coffee.

"Where's your suitcase?" asked Paula, looking around as if it had been left out here.

"At the motel. The Moonrise."

Paula gagged. "That shambles. Don't be ridiculous. I'll send Charlie to get it."

"I'm staying here?"

She sighed. "Of course you are. I'll have Penny get a room ready."

"Too much trouble."

"It is *not.*"

"Oh, yes, it is, for the room I want." Jury looked across the silvery grass to a huge oak tree and up to its top where light reflected off glass.

Paula laughed. "You can't—it's too cold. There's electricity, but— really, you can't!"

"Oh, yes, I can." He was already off the patio.

She called after him. "Turn on the heater!"

It was an easier climb now than it had been for David as a child. A wood stair circled the big tree to the platform near the top.

The first thing he did was switch on an old electric fire; he watched the fake flames flare up. An old turntable stood on a washstand, a collection of vinyl records in their faded sleeves beside it. Willie Nelson. Good grief, Willie—all the girls you and Julio ever loved before, Carole-anne's favorite. He put a record on and Willie blared out: *This land is your land* . . .

My God, thought Jury, divesting himself of his jacket, which he tossed over a rumpled chair, I could be back in my own flat in Islington.

Then, gazing at the ceiling, he thought, no I couldn't.

. . . *from the Redwood Forest to the Gulf Stream waters* . . . Yes, there were stars over London, and a moon and maybe the lapping of the Thames against the bank, but he didn't think he'd ever seen the light splinter and spill over London as it did over this glass-ceilinged tree house.

He had toed off his shoes and flopped down on the bed. He wondered if David had lain here thinking similar thoughts to the sound of Willie's guitar.

Jury felt a jolt so hard he thought the tree must have moved. But it wasn't the tree; it was more like his heart: Godammit, David, why did you have to come to effing London? Why couldn't you just have stayed in the good old USA?

This land was made for you and me.

Jury thought about those moments in Covent Garden with the telescope, looking at Uranus and the night sky. He muttered, "'Night, David," as a light faded and he looked for the gibbous moon. But it had slipped out of sight, behind a cloud, as all moons do, eventually.